By Linda Howard

By Linda Howard and Linda Jones

Prey

LINDA
HOWARD

PREY

A NOVEL

 BALLANTINE BOOKS · NEW YORK

Copyright © 2011 by Linda Howington

Published in the United States by Ballantine Books,
an imprint of The Random House Publishing Group,
a division of Random House, Inc., New York.

BALLANTINE and colophon are registered
trademarks of Random House, Inc.

ISBN 978-0-345-50691-7
eBook ISBN 978-0-345-52629-8

Printed in the United States of America on acid-free paper

www.ballantinebooks.com

9 8 7 6 5 4 3 2 1

First Edition

Prey

Chapter One

He'd won.

She'd lost.

She really, really hated losing. Losing pissed her off more than just about anything else.

The very idea made her grind her teeth, made her think twice about what she was about to do, which essentially was to throw in the towel. Okay, not exactly throw in the towel, but she was definitely retrenching, and she needed to act now. Stubbornness was one of her main faults, something she was well aware of, so before it could trip her up and make her change her mind, Angie Powell quickly scrawled her name on the contract with the only Realtor in the area, Harlan Forbes, then leaned back in her chair and tried to control her breathing.

There, it was done. Her place was officially up for sale. Her stomach was so knotted she felt as if she'd stepped off a cliff and was cartwheeling toward the ground, but there was no going back. Well, there probably was; Harlan had known her most of her life, and would probably tear up the contract right now if she asked him to. Not only that, the contract wasn't open-ended. If her home didn't sell in the allotted time, she'd either extend the contract or . . . what? What other option did she have? None, that's what. This was do or die, sink or swim, and any number of other back-against-the-wall clichés. She was damned if she'd just give up, though. Moving operations wasn't the same as giving up.

"I'll get this posted online right away," Harlan said, swiveling around to lay the contract beside his sleek, all-in-one computer and monitor combined, a surprisingly up-to-date piece of electronics in a shabby, crowded two-room office on the second floor above the hardware store. "That's how most of my contacts are being made these days." He gave her a quick glance, concern written large on his florid face. "Don't get your hopes up on having a firm offer right away, though. The listings around here are on the market for six months, average, which isn't bad in this economy."

"Thanks," she said to Harlan, who'd been one of her father's best friends. She supposed he needed to make the sale as much as she needed to sell. The downturn in the economy had hit everyone. Six months. God, could she hold on for six more months? The answer was: If she had to. She could do anything if she had to.

She got to her feet. "Believe me, I'm not hoping for anything right away."

But she was; she couldn't help it. She wished the place would sell this very minute, before she could think about it too much. At the same time, she dreaded the thought of leaving, and the two emotions pulled and fought inside her until she wanted to scream, for all the good that would do, which was none.

She shrugged into her coat and picked up her big tote bag, settled her hat on her head. She needed both the coat and the hat. November had come in cold and brisk, already dusting the valleys with a few light snows. The mountain peaks surrounding the valley were white, the wind blowing off them carrying the scent of winter, evergreen mixed with fresh snow. A warm front was coming in that should melt the snow back some, but everyone, human and animal, knew the warmth would be temporary; soon the cold would settle in for months.

She had to plan on being here through another winter. It would be nice if her place sold immediately, but if she was anything, Angie was realistic. Pie in the sky had never appealed to her, not when there was a plain old apple on the ground. Right now, however, she couldn't see either apple or pie. All she could do was try to eke out a living and stay on top of her bills enough to hold off foreclosure, until her place sold and she could relocate.

If. Now there was a word. *If* her dad hadn't borrowed a bunch of money five years ago to expand the business, buying more horses, four-wheelers, building three small guest houses, the place wouldn't even have a mortgage, and she'd be okay even with the downturn in her income. But he had, and she wasn't. Yes, she'd sold the four-wheelers and most of the horses, and used the money to pay down the principal on the loan, but even if she refinanced, the payment would be more than she could handle, and that was assuming the bank would let her refinance, as tight as credit was right now.

At least she hadn't waited until she was in real trouble. No, that big, wide streak of realism had read the writing on the wall and recognized that, within a year at the absolute most, she was going to be out of money and out of business, unless she took action. But a year was optimistic; the six months Harlan had mentioned for selling her house and property was far more like it. By then, she might not even be breaking even, and one thing she didn't want to do was dip into her savings. For one thing, she didn't have that much; for another, throwing good money after bad was a good way to lose everything.

Harlan heaved his bulk out of his squeaky office chair and walked with her to the door. "I'll be out tomorrow to take some pictures," he said.

"I'll be there. I have a guide trip day after tomorrow, so I'll be getting everything ready." Right now, that one guide trip, with a repeat client, was the only thing on her books. Three years ago, before Dare Callahan had returned home and begun carving huge holes in her business, she had gone weeks with just enough time between guide trips to replenish supplies. Even two years ago, with him set up in competition, she'd done okay, and had actually been glad to have a little time to rest between trips. Last year had been slow. This year had been disastrous.

Harlan patted her arm as he opened the door for her. "I hate to see you leave, but you know best."

"I hope so. I've done some research, and I think I've found a good location, up past Missoula." She wasn't getting her heart set on any particular place, though; she'd isolate sections where hunting guides were thin on the ground, and work from there. Moving wouldn't accomplish much if she put herself back into a situation with steep competition.

He glanced out the door, at the mountainous scenery he'd seen thousands of times, and a faintly sad expression crept over his face. "I'm thinking about leaving, too."

"What?" The unexpected confession jerked Angie out of herself and her own problems; she stared at him in shock. He'd always been here, been in these parts, and a fixture in her life from the time she and her dad had moved to the area. *She* had moved away a couple of times, once to college and then afterward to Billings, but Harlan had always been here, as reliable as the sun rising in the east. She couldn't imagine this place without him. "Why?"

There was a faraway look in his eyes, as if he'd turned inward. "Because the older I get, the closer I am to the people who've already gone on, and the harder it is to relate to the ones still here," he said softly. "Some days all I can think about are the dead ones. I catch myself talking to Glory all the time." Gloria was his dead wife; Angie had never heard him call her anything other than Glory. "And your dad . . . I still talk to him as if he were standing right here. And there are more, too many more."

He sighed. "I don't have an unlimited number of years left, you know, and I'm spending too much of my time alone. I need to move closer to Noah and the grandkids, connect more with them while I still can."

"You're talking as if you have one foot in the grave. You aren't old!" She was still too shocked to be diplomatic, but then diplomacy had never been her strong point. Afterward she could always think of what she *should* have said, but in the moment she tended to blurt out whatever she was thinking. Besides, Harlan *wasn't* old; he was probably in his mid-sixties, close to her dad in age.

But her dad was gone, and suddenly Angie thought she knew what Harlan meant. He was hearing the call of the beyond; sometimes she caught the echo of it herself, in the stillness around her that would suddenly be filled with memories. Maybe it was nature's way of transitioning from life to death, or life to another life. He knew he was probably in the last quarter of his life, and he wanted to make the most of it with the people who meant the most to him.

"Old enough," he said, and looked again at the looming mountains. "If I don't make the move now, I might run out of time."

And that was it in a nutshell. She was doing exactly the same thing, though for a different reason. She was running out of time.

"Yeah," she said gently. "I know."

Abruptly he hugged her, a one-armed, rib-crushing hug that was over before she could do more than gasp. "I'll miss you, Angie, but we won't lose touch. I promise you that."

"Back at you," she said awkwardly. The emotion of the moment left her flailing way out of her depth, as usual, but she managed a smile for him as she stepped out onto the landing. Some people instinctively knew the right thing to say, the right thing to do, but she wasn't one of them. The best she could do was, well, the best she could do, and hope she didn't screw up too much.

As soon as the door closed behind her, though, her smile

turned sad. She didn't want to leave. She'd grown up in her house, she liked the small community here even though God knows there was absolutely nothing that would qualify as a nightlife, unless you counted frogs. But so what? She'd enjoyed living in Billings, and she enjoyed living here. After a while, wherever she moved to would become home. She was who she was, no matter where she lived. Fiercely she shrugged off her sadness. She'd better get over her pity party or risk turning into what she disliked most: a *whiner.*

She took the flight of stairs down the outside of the building at a brisk pace, then strode across the cracked parking lot to her seven-year-old dark blue Ford pickup, keeping her head high with an effort. She wasn't beaten, not yet, but she'd definitely lost this battle, and the taste of defeat was bitter as gall in her mouth. The worst thing was, Dare Callahan probably didn't even know—and wouldn't care if he *had* known—that she'd been in a fight for her survival, and that as she'd been going under for the third time he had effectively put his boot on top of her head and held her underwater.

God, she hated him. No, not *hate,* not exactly, but she sure as hell didn't like him. To think that when he'd asked her out, two years ago, she'd actually been tempted to accept, that she'd even gotten butterflies in her stomach, but that was before she realized what he was doing. She knew better now. She didn't like anything about him, not the way he looked or the truck he drove, or even his damn name. *Dare.* What kind of name was that? Like he thought he was some supercool urban daredevil, able to leap small Yuppies with a single bound—except he was too cool to make the effort.

If she had to be fair about it—and she didn't feel like being fair—she supposed she had to blame his parents for his name, but that didn't mean he was completely innocent, because he could have changed his name to Jim or Charlie, something like that. But on a website, Dare Callahan, Wilderness Guide, looked a whole lot cooler than, for instance, a plain old Charlie Callahan; people probably subconsciously felt as if they were hiring Indiana Jones.

And when she compared her own website to his, Powell Guide Trips was so lackluster she had to admit she probably wouldn't hire herself, either. That was a hard thing to face, but there was no getting around it. She didn't have the extra money to hire someone to jazz-up her website, so in her spare time she'd been trying to figure out how to do it herself, though she was painfully aware that generally one got what one paid for. Her site had been set up so she could update it, but it was inspiration that failed her. She had no idea what to do to make herself sound more capable than Dare Callahan, Wilderness Guide. Change her name to Ace, maybe?

The idea struck her and she stopped in her tracks, wondering if she might have actually come up with a workable idea, something that would buy her a little more time if nothing else. Her income had been falling for the past two years. Part of it was the economy, sure, but it didn't help that she was a woman. Even though some of the big-game hunters who came to Montana every year were women, and an even larger percentage of the photographers on photo shoots were women, most people seemed to think that a male guide was a safer bet than a female one.

If there was trouble, a man was stronger, supposedly tougher, yada yada. She knew the drill. She wanted to fault it, but she couldn't, even though she knew she was good at what she did. She was five-seven, a little above average height for a woman, with a lean, rangy build that disguised how strong she was. Even given that, there was no way she came anywhere close to being as strong as most of the men around here, especially a muscle-bound jerk like Dare Callahan. But if she changed her website and, say, used her initials instead of her name so people didn't know right away that she was a woman . . . Yeah, she might lose repeat business, but that was practically nil anyway, so any new business could only be a plus.

And maybe she should concentrate more on photography trips and wilderness camping, things like that, rather than on hunting trips, which naturally leaned more toward men, as if a set of nuts was a requirement for competent guiding. From what she could tell, *not* having testicles was a big check mark on the plus side. Not only did she not have testosterone blinding her with ego and competition problems, she didn't have to worry about whether to put them on the left or right, and she didn't fall down and vomit if anyone punched her in the groin.

Talk about selling points: lifelong experience, no testicles. She could see it now, blazing from her website in brilliant red letters. She enjoyed the vision for a moment, then jerked her thoughts back to repositioning herself as more of a guide for photography trips and family outings.

Except this was something she should have done back in the spring, to pull in business during the height of the hunting season. Winter was coming fast, and with it came the end of hunting trips until next year. No, she had to face it: She was up against the wall. It galled her that she couldn't turn her situation around—at least not here, not now. Her only chance at turning this around was to move somewhere else, where she wouldn't have to deal with the competition of a jackass superstar. But she hated being a failure, at anything, anywhere, and under any circumstances. She hadn't failed just herself, but her dad and his faith in her. Why else would he have left the property and business to her if he hadn't thought she could make a go of it?

"Because there wasn't anyone else," she muttered, then, despite everything, she had to give a little laugh. Not that her dad hadn't loved her; he had. But whether or not he'd loved her hadn't factored into the decision to leave everything to her, because she was his only child and there literally hadn't been anyone else. Maybe if he'd had any inkling of having heart trouble before literally dropping dead, he'd have put the place up for sale and taken up a line of work that wasn't so physically demanding, but all in all Angie was glad that, if he had to die, at least he'd died doing what he loved. He'd been riding the range, not cooped up in a store or an office.

She'd been living and working in Billings at the time; her job had been just an ordinary one, in the administrative office of a hospital, but it had paid her rent and she'd liked it okay. The thing was, she'd never had a great ambition to do anything in particular. All she wanted at the time was to support herself. So when her dad died, the logical thing had been to move back home and take over his guide business. After all, she'd often helped him before she moved away, so it wasn't as if she was a novice and didn't know how to conduct a guide trip. She was a decent tracker, and a decent shot. At the time, she hadn't seen any reason why she couldn't make a go of it, and she was kind of ready for a change anyway, so why not?

And then she'd found something she hadn't expected to find: She loved it. She loved being out on the mountains, she loved being in charge of her own destiny. There was something special about stepping out of a tent into the pristine early morning and being overwhelmed by the solitude and beauty around her. How could she have gone so many years without realizing this was *exactly* what she wanted to do? Maybe she'd had to go away for a while in order to see how suited she was for this life. Not that she hadn't enjoyed living in a city; she had. She'd liked the variety, the people, the friends she made; she'd even taken some cooking classes and thought about maybe doing some catering on the side. But she *loved* being a guide, and enjoyed living here way more now than she had when she'd been growing up.

She did wish she'd made some different decisions, such as selling the horses and keeping the four-wheelers, instead of doing the exact opposite. Hindsight was great, except it was so damn slow in coming. She hadn't anticipated that the economy would bottom out and discretionary spending would almost disappear. She hadn't known Dare Callahan would move back home and siphon away most of her business. Why couldn't he have stayed in the military where he belonged, safely away from her little patch of Montana?

If only—

No. No *if onlies*. Never mind that she was thirty-two and he'd given her butterflies. She didn't trust butterflies, didn't let herself get carried away by emotions and hormones. Once had been enough. She'd made such a fool of herself that whenever she thought of her abbreviated marriage her stomach still curdled from an almost overwhelming sense of embarrassment. A strong desire to leave Billings, the scene of the debacle, had made her that much more eager to take over her dad's guide business when he died.

No doubt about it, if she'd been happily married at the time she'd have sold off the business and stayed in Billings, simply because she'd built a life there. When her personal life fell apart, though, she'd withdrawn so much that her friends had almost given up on her in exasperation. After moving back here and getting her feet under her again she'd mended those relationships— a woman always needed other women—but by then she'd fallen so in love with her way of life that dynamite couldn't have blown her back into an office setting.

Thinking that she needed to send some e-mails when she got home, just to keep in touch, she opened the truck door and was about to climb into the cab when she abruptly remembered that she needed some nails and staples to repair fencing, which she might as well get now while she was right here at the hardware store and save herself a trip later. She also wanted to catch up on the community gossip, such as it was, with Evelyn French, the chatty half of the husband and wife team who owned the hardware store. Their son, Patrick, had been the only other kid her age in their little community, and all during their school years the Frenches and her dad had swapped out driving them to school in the nearest real town, forty miles away. Patrick was a cop now, in Spokane, married, with two ankle-biters of his own. Evelyn was crazy about her grandchildren, two little boys ages four and two, and always had time to relate the latest tales of what they'd said and done. She seemed to relish their mischief, as if she thought Patrick deserved everything they did. Remembering some of the things Patrick had gotten up to when they were growing up, Angie had to agree.

She closed the door she'd opened and trudged across the parking lot, watching her step as she went around a deep pothole—and when she lifted her head she saw *him,* the big man, the devil, Dare Callahan himself, coming straight at her from the parking area on the other side of the store, where his big black truck loomed like a shining, sinister metal monster.

Seeing him was too much. Angie's heart gave a sudden hard thump, and the bottom dropped out of her stomach. Her reaction was completely automatic. She didn't stop to think, didn't give herself a pep talk, didn't consider how it looked; she simply turned around and headed back to her own truck, muttering under her breath. She'd pick up the nails and staples when she got back from the guide trip; she wouldn't have any time to work on the fencing until then, anyway. Running was cowardly, but at the same time she couldn't nod at him and be polite, couldn't pretend she hadn't just up-ended her world because of him. Damn it, figures she'd run into him at the hardware store immediately after putting her place up for sale, an action *he'd* forced her into taking. Sometimes coincidence really sucked.

"Hey!"

The deep bark, laden with anger, rolled across the space between them. Angie didn't look back. She didn't think he'd be talking to her—after all, for over two years she'd gone out of her way to avoid him if possible and barely grunt a hello if forced to acknowledge him—so she glanced around to see who he *was* talking to, because she hadn't noticed anyone else nearby.

With a jolt she realized there wasn't anyone else. He was talking to her.

Chapter Two

The fine gravel littering the pavement crunched under his boots as he strode toward her. Like his truck, his hat was black, and he wore it pulled low so the brim shadowed most of his face. Black hat equaled bad guy, right? She was good with that, because as far as she was concerned he was definitely the bad guy in her life—the bad guy who was coming at her like a steam locomotive. She grabbed for the door handle, then stopped, fighting her own impulses. She wasn't afraid of him. She was uneasy around men, but it was her own faulty judgment she didn't trust. Besides, just how cowardly could she let herself be before she lost all self-respect?

Evidently she'd just reached her own stopping point. Jumping in her truck and driving away was the best thing she could think of to do, especially if she flattened him on her way out of the parking lot, but, okay, she'd let him have his say about whatever had his shorts on fire. She might have lost their battle—hell, maybe even the whole damn war—but she could face him this one time, and afterward she'd never have to speak to him again, not even to be polite. Squaring her shoulders and lifting her chin, she released the handle and stepped away from the truck, her insides like Jell-O but her outside revealing nothing of that, her whole posture that of a gunfighter facing an enemy in the middle of the street.

He bulled right into her space, stopping only when he was so close that the brim of his hat knocked against hers as he glared down at her; so close that, when she looked up, she could see the white striations in his deep blue eyes. Angie took a quick, automatic breath, then wished she hadn't because the very air she drew in seemed to be filled with him, the scents of leather and coffee and denim, heated by his skin. A primitive sense of danger made the back of her neck prickle, sent chills running down her spine. Instinct screamed at her to back away, get out of touching distance, reclaim her sense of inviolate *self* that his nearness somehow threatened, but backing away now was one retreat too many on this day of all days, when her pride had already taken too much of a beating because of him.

She clenched her teeth, straightened her spine, and held her ground. "What do you want?" she asked curtly, and, by God, even if nothing else about her was steady, her voice was.

"I want to know what the hell's the matter with you," he growled, his voice so rough she had to fight to keep from flinching, as if it had actually scratched her. The words were even more guttural than she remembered. Before she could help herself she glanced at his throat, at the pale scar that slashed at a slight diagonal across the muscled column. Was his voice deteriorating, or did he sound as if he'd eaten ground glass simply because he was so pissed about something? She hoped he was pissed, hoped she'd inadvertently done something to make him so angry he could barely speak; if she could find out what it was she'd done, she'd go out of her way to do it again.

"Nothing's the matter with me," she said, her teeth clenched so tightly her jaw ached. Now that she'd looked at the scar on his throat, she found herself staring at the other scars on his face: the gouge high on his right cheekbone, another beside his mouth that actually looked like a dimple if you didn't know the scars were from shrapnel, and another sort of arrow-shaped scar on the bridge of his nose. None of the scars was disfiguring; they didn't seem to bother him and they shouldn't bother her, except seeing them made her chest hurt from something that felt inexplicably like sorrow.

She pushed that thought away; she couldn't afford to feel personal sympathy for him. So he'd been hit by shrapnel in Iraq; he was alive, he wasn't disfigured or disabled, and she could feel sympathy for him in the abstract, as a service member, without letting him elicit any other emotion from her.

She wished his breath stank, instead of smelling pleasantly like coffee . . . wished there was something, anything, about him that was physically distasteful. What kind of idiot was she that in some weak moments she'd find herself wistfully thinking about what might have happened if she'd actually gone out with him when he'd first returned to the area and asked her out, if anything would have come of it? Then doubts would set in, and she'd wonder if maybe he'd set out to deliberately destroy her business because she'd turned him down; if so, that made him a major jerk, and no good could have come from dating him. What gave her emotional whiplash was that she simply didn't know, which meant she kept worrying at the different scenarios without any way of knowing which one was true. All she knew for sure was that she wasn't good with men, and that Dare Callahan had ruined her business. She was rock solid on those two things.

With him standing so close and the truck right behind her she felt hemmed in, trapped. Damn it, enough was enough; she couldn't stand it, not for another second. She edged sideways, farther from the truck, though her damn stubborn pride wouldn't let her actually step back from him.

He adjusted his position, too, turning with her so they remained face-to-face.

"Then what makes you act as if you have a stick shoved up your ass every time I'm around?" he snapped. "Just now you turned and ran as soon as you saw me. I'm tired of it, damn it. If you have a beef with me, then tell me to my face what it is."

"I didn't *run*," she snapped right back. Instinctively she slid another few inches to the side. "Maybe I thought of somewhere else I need to go." She didn't bother even trying to put any sincerity into her tone. Instead, her good sense seemed to have taken a hike, because she sounded as if she was taunting him. She didn't want to wave a red flag at the bull, she didn't want to escalate things into an all-out argument, she just wanted to get into her truck and leave. That was what she wanted, but instead she kept standing there, and things she hadn't meant to say kept coming out of her mouth. "Maybe seeing you or speaking to you doesn't rate very high on my list of things to do."

Again he moved, keeping his position squared off with hers, and this time they both seemed to be caught in an unconscious momentum that kept them moving, slowly circling each other like angry combatants, each looking for the other's weakness. She was vaguely aware that they looked like fools dancing a hostile tango in the parking lot, and hoped no one else saw them; everyone knew everyone else's business around here, and she didn't want to field any questions about what was going on between her and Dare Callahan. Lord, please don't let Harlan look out his window right now, because he'd feel duty bound to come out and make sure everything was okay.

"Stand still," he said, still growling, though with the damage to his larynx he'd sound growly even if he was trying to sing lullabies.

"Why should I? You're the one who's crowding me, not the other way around. If you want me to stand still, then back off." She punctuated the last two words by putting the tip of one finger squarely in the middle of his chest and applying pressure; it was like pushing on a rock—a living, breathing rock, but still a rock.

She wasn't certain how easy it was to communicate with a rock, so just to make sure he understood, she repeated herself. "Back. Off."

Under the brim of his hat, his brilliant blue eyes were narrow and angry. His head cocked a little, an arrogant, combative tilt of his chin, then he put his right forefinger in the middle of her chest, on her breastbone, duplicating her movement. "Make. Me."

Furious heat surged under her skin. *Make him?* God, how she wished she could! Frustration and fury filled her chest, almost smothering her. She couldn't budge him an inch, and they both knew it. Failing that, what she would most like to do was punch him in the jaw, but she wasn't stupid. The best thing that could come of that would be that he'd have her arrested for assault, but she doubted that solution would even occur to him. No, he'd hand out the consequences himself, and even though she didn't know what form that would take she was absolutely certain she wouldn't like the result at all. Sometimes you just knew things about people, and she knew Dare Callahan was a stubborn jackass who would blow right past good manners if he had a point he wanted to make.

She also should have known he'd dig in his heels. Maybe he'd been a more even-tempered, congenial person when he was growing up, but since leaving the military and coming home he was known to be surly at best, and most times downright ill-tempered. Maybe he had reason to be a sorehead now, maybe he'd always been one. Either way, she had to deal with him as he was now, which was right in her face.

For a split second she weighed her choices as she stared up at him, torn between all those conflicting emotions, then abruptly something inside her heaved a tiny sigh and gave up. She could hold on to her pride and pretend she was leaving because she wanted to, but why try to put a good face on it? He'd won. Let him enjoy it.

She ground her teeth together, trying to get the words out.

Damn, this was hard. She took a couple of breaths, digging deep for self-control, and finally was able to say, "It isn't any of your business, but I just put my place up for sale." She kept her voice low so if it wobbled, maybe he wouldn't notice. "I'm sorry it hurts your feelings that I don't feel like dealing with you right now, but I *don't feel like dealing with you right now.* Got it?"

His expression went blank. He glanced up at Harlan's office, then back at her. "You're selling out?"

And there they went again, her back teeth locking together. Couldn't he have used any term other than *selling out*? She did some more deep breathing, blowing air out through her nose like an angry bull. "I don't have a choice. My business has gone downhill since you moved back and went into competition with me. I can either sell or go bankrupt." There, that was bald enough. She hadn't tried to protect her pride, but neither had she accused him of deliberately running her out of business. Maybe he had, maybe he hadn't. He was definitely the cause, whether deliberate or not, and that was all the credit and a lot less of the blame she was inclined to give him. At this point, it didn't matter, because the end result was the same.

His expression shifted, hardened. "And you blame me."

"I don't see anyone else around here starting up a guide business."

He stared down at her, eyes narrowed, his mouth a grim line. "For the record, I didn't go after any of your customers. If any of them were yours first, they came to me, not the other way around. And I'll be damned if I'll apologize because they preferred me."

"I don't believe I've asked you to apologize. In fact, I don't believe I've asked a damn thing of you." And she wouldn't, not one tiny thing. "You asked what my beef is, I've told you, now get your nose out of my business and leave me alone." She broke away, stepping out of their little hostile circle, and once again reached for the truck's door handle.

His hand shot out and he gripped her arm, holding her in

place. "Wait." Angie froze, her heartbeat abruptly thundering like a runaway horse as she looked down at the tanned, powerful hand that completely encircled her forearm. It was a lean, long-fingered hand, callused, and the back of it was marked by a two-inch-long white scar. His touch radiated a heat that burned through the thick double fabrics of her shirt and coat. "How much are you asking for your business?"

For a minute she couldn't believe he was actually asking her that, then she went white with anger and jerked her arm away from his grip. "I'm not selling my *business*," she snapped. "I'm selling my *place,* and getting the hell away from here, and away from you!"

She pulled the truck door open, tossed her tote bag inside, and climbed into the driver's seat. She wanted to do something violent, hit him, kick him, but contented herself with slamming the door and shoving the key into the ignition as hard as she could. The motor turned over as soon as she turned the key, and roared to life. If she'd had a clutch, she'd have popped it, but she had to be satisfied with floor-boarding the gas pedal and fishtailing out of the parking lot, though it would have been a lot more satisfying if the lot had been gravel instead of asphalt and the wheels had thrown rocks against his legs.

Immediately she pictured the scars on his face, his hand, and her imagination violently rejected the very idea of peppering him with gravel. That was too much like shrapnel, and she couldn't . . . well, she just couldn't. She'd put this part of her life in the past and move on. The future had to be better; she'd made some miscalculations, some bad decisions, but she'd learn from her mistakes and things would get better. They *would.* They had to.

Dare Callahan stood in the empty parking lot and glared after the blue Ford as Angie Powell barreled down the road as if she were escaping from Satan himself. "Fuck!" he said violently, both his fists clenching. A good, old-fashioned bar brawl would suit him right now, but the nearest bar was over thirty miles away and this time of day there likely wouldn't be anyone available to brawl with anyway. His next best choice was a punching bag, and he did have one of those hanging in the barn back at his spread, but he wanted to knock the shit out of something right now, not an hour from now. He was out of luck unless he wanted to shatter the bones in his hands beating on the weathered brick building.

That was the effect she had on him. Ten seconds in her vicinity, and he was ready to fight something, anything. She was goat-stubborn, hostile, infuriating, and made him feel like a fool. Good riddance. He'd be glad when she was gone.

Except, even though she always looked at him as if he was a pile of steaming fresh cow manure that she'd just stepped in, there was nothing he wanted more than to fuck her blind. It had been that way from the day he'd first seen her. He'd even asked her out—twice—and been slapped down twice, and her attitude made it pretty damn plain she wasn't the least bit interested in him, but his dick was too stupid to get the message. All he had to do was see that high, round ass of hers, or that dark ponytail swinging down her back, and the damn thing perked up and all but begged to be petted.

Life would be a lot calmer with her gone. Hell, it wasn't even as if she was especially pretty. Dark hair, dark eyes, the kind of strong, carved bone structure that hinted at some Native American blood a few generations back, but nothing extra. Attractive, yeah, but that was it. Except for her ass. Her ass was jaw-dropping, eye-popping, slobber-dripping *prime*.

Maybe when she was gone his dick would give up the insane hope that some day it would have a shot at having her. And maybe then he himself would get serious about looking for another woman, someone who could stand to spend a few minutes in his company, which Angie Powell obviously couldn't. He didn't spend his time crying into his beer over her; he'd been rejected before, and sometimes it sucked, but he didn't curl up in a whiny, whimpering ball because of it. Still, for some reason, having her there kind of blunted the desire to go out looking for someone else. Even though he hadn't asked her out again after the second rejection, he knew his own competitive nature well enough to realize that part of him—like his dick—had stayed focused on her and refused to give up.

With her gone, his clientele list would grow even more. He might have to start turning people down—

An idea streaked across his brain like a flash of lightning, freezing him in place. It was so obvious, yet so outlandish, that he automatically tried to discard it. She wouldn't go for it in a million years . . . would she? No. Maybe.

Maybe?

Damn. It just might work.

He looked up at Harlan's real estate office, then down the road to where the blue truck was just a dark speck.

"What the fuck," he said aloud, "why not give it a shot?" He strode across the parking lot and climbed the stairs to Harlan's office. Harlan heard him coming, of course; his boots thumped on the steps and the planks of the upstairs landing. When he opened the door, Harlan had already swiveled his chair around and was waiting with an expectant look on his florid face.

"Dare," he said in mild surprise. "I thought you might be Angie coming back. Sit down and have some coffee with me."

"Thanks," Dare said, because on principle he never turned down coffee. He never knew when he might get another cup, and he'd been deprived often enough that he never took coffee for granted. Going over to the coffeepot, he poured a cup for himself, then one for Harlan. "Black, white, sweet?"

"Black and sweet."

"How many?"

"Two."

Dare dumped in a couple spoonfuls of sugar, gave the coffee

a quick stir, then handed the cup over to Harlan. He dropped his tall frame into one of the four client chairs Harlan had optimistically put in the office. "Angie just told me she put her place up for sale," he said brusquely, in his mind the ritual of coffee having taken care of whatever social niceties there were. "What's the asking price?"

Chapter Three

Angie stared straight ahead through the windshield, her hands clamped around the steering wheel. Her eyes burned, but she refused to cry. She wasn't a crier, anyway; the only time in her life she could remember having a complete meltdown was when she'd made a fool of herself at her wedding. If she hadn't had the meltdown she wouldn't have been so embarrassed, so in her book crying was not only a waste of time but also opened the door to all sorts of bad results.

She wouldn't cry over Dare Callahan, anyway. There was nothing there to cry over. They had no history, no connection other than being in competition with each other, and that wasn't going to endear him to her. No, if she was emotional about anything, it was about selling her place. She'd grown up in that house. Her dad had loved it here in western Montana, loved the people and what he did; his grave was here. Leaving here felt as if she'd be leaving him.

No way. She was moving, she had to, but she swore to herself right then that she'd come back at least once a year, more often if she could manage it, to tend to his grave, to leave flowers, even to talk to him as if he could hear her. Love didn't go away when someone died, and she would make a point to honor him for the rest of her life. He'd been a good man, and he'd devoted himself to raising her after her mother deserted both of them for some sleazy guy when Angie was almost two.

Her dad had been enough for her. She didn't know where her mother was, if she was even still alive, and frankly didn't care. She had never done an Internet search on her mother's name, and certainly never bothered to hire a professional to search. Angie's dad had stepped up and supported her, raised her, loved her, and given her nothing but understanding and comfort when her wedding had blown up in her face. She couldn't do anything for him now except honor him in death, so for as long as she lived and was physically able, she'd take care of his grave.

"So help me God," she said aloud, and felt a little better, because saying it aloud somehow solemnized it, as if she had signed a contract. She wasn't severing all ties. She'd be living elsewhere, and eventually that new place would become home the same way her apartment in Billings had become home after she'd lived there a while. Being adaptable didn't mean she was deserting her dad's memory.

Thinking of her dad made her realize she should be concentrating on the two clients who would be coming in day after tomorrow. One of them, Chad Krugman, was a repeat client, but he almost could have been someone new because she couldn't remember a lot about him other than, as a whole, he was pretty forgettable. Thank God she had a copy of the photograph she'd taken of him and his client after the client had shot a deer, otherwise she'd have had no clue what he looked like. He was just one of those people who never made much of an impression: on the short side, but not short enough to be memorable because of it; a little balding, a little soft around the middle. Not ugly, not attractive. Just . . . kind of invisible.

Even though she'd looked at the photograph, she had a hard time holding his image in her mind. The one thing she remembered very clearly was that he wasn't an experienced outdoorsman, or a very good shot. When he'd booked her before, last year, she'd even gotten the impression he hadn't enjoyed himself very much and hadn't really wanted to be there, so she didn't have any idea why he'd rebooked for this year. Bottom line, though, she didn't care why, just that he had; she needed the income. Hunting season would soon be over, and unless a professional photographer wanted some snow shots of the mountains for a nature magazine or something, she wouldn't have anything else for the winter.

Maybe, against all odds, Harlan would get a quick offer on her place. She'd have to scramble to find somewhere else to live, but sooner rather than later. Now that the difficult first step was behind her, she was anxious to move on. It was that streak of realism again: Once she decided her course of action, she was ready to act.

For now, though, she had to take care of business, and get everything organized for the trip. She'd e-mailed Chad Krugman asking for some specifics on the client, Mitchell Davis, whom he was bringing as a guest. Had he ever hunted before, what kind of experience did he have, what was he looking for, licenses needed—that kind of thing. Mr. Davis was evidently more experienced than Chad, and he wanted to bag a black bear.

That alone raised her stress level. She didn't specialize in bear hunts, so she'd been a little surprised when Krugman had made the booking with her. Her normal MO on a hunt was to avoid bear, because she was a little afraid of them. Okay, more than a little. She worked hard to keep anyone from realizing just how uneasy she really was on a bear hunt, because no one wanted a guide who was anything other than confident. She was confident in her skill at finding bear, but that wasn't a comfort, because deep down she didn't *want* to find a bear—any bear, brown or black, big or little. Why couldn't Krugman's client want to hunt elk? An elk didn't present the same problems; it wasn't likely to chase her down and eat her. Bears, well, bears were predators, and powerful ones at that.

Angie did what she could to both mitigate her fear and keep herself and her clients as safe as possible; she employed all the bear safety rules regarding food and trash, plus she always carried two big cans of bear repellent and made certain each member of her party did the same. Still, she was well aware that pepper spray worked on bears about the same way it worked on humans, meaning sometimes the sprayed kept coming after the sprayer. She didn't intend to take any shots herself, but she'd be damn certain her ammunition was powerful enough to do the job if shooting became necessary.

She had already made certain the camp she'd leased was stocked with some basic, nonfood supplies, but there was still a lot to do; the campsite was fairly primitive, consisting of a few tents, air mattresses, and a portable toilet. The rest of their supplies would have to be packed in: food and water for three people, enough food for the horses. Krugman and Davis were bringing their own weapons and ammunition, so that was something she didn't have to handle, but a week in the mountains wasn't something that could be casually planned. She'd try her best to get her client in position to have his shot, but her main objective was to get them and herself back alive and in one piece.

Thirty-seven miles to the west, and four miles north of the campsite Angie had leased, an enormous black bear stopped his slow, shuffling pace and swung his head from side to side as the wind brought a tantalizing scent to him, unerringly identifying both the smell and the location. Satisfied with what his senses told him, he began working his way through the trees and underbrush until

he could look through a break in the brush, and he went still as
he processed what he saw. He wasn't hungry, he'd fed well that
morning, having brought down an old elk cow, but the unaware,
meandering herd of sheep on the slope below him riveted his interest, especially the half-grown lamb that had settled down for a
nap while its mother grazed farther down the slope.

Competition for food wasn't as intense as it had been; some of
the sows had already settled into dens and older bears past their
prime weren't moving around as much as the days shortened and
the cold season loomed closer and closer. But for now the weather
was still relatively mild, and the bear had continued to hunt instead of looking for his own den. He'd crossed through the territory of two other bears in the past few days, and two days ago had
fought with one, a cinnamon-colored male that hadn't survived
the battle.

The bear was three years old, big and healthy, over five hundred pounds. In the summer that was just past, he'd bred for the
first time. Also in the summer, he'd killed and eaten his first
human. It had been easy prey, unable to run as fast as goats or
sheep, without claws or fangs or antlers to defend itself, the meat
furless and sweeter than most. The man had been a transient, un-
noticed and missed by no one, something the bear had no concept of and wouldn't have cared about even if he had; all he knew,
all his ursine survival instincts had noted, was that this was easy
food. If he crossed paths with this particular prey again, he would
hunt it.

He also had no concept of fun, but he did of enjoyment, and
he enjoyed killing. Whenever he saw or smelled something that
signaled "prey" to him, he went after it, something deep inside
spurring him on and reveling in the explosion of energy, the hot
taste of fresh blood and flesh, the destruction, even the fear he
could smell as he bore down on his chosen victim. Nature had
equipped him well to be the predator he was, giving him aggres-

siveness and cunning, as well as unusual size and strength and speed.

He studied the sheep. He was downwind of the herd, the cold mountain air bringing the scent sharp and clear to his nostrils and whetting his appetite for the kill. He moved slowly through the trees, stopping whenever one of the wary sheep raised its head and surveyed its surroundings for a moment before returning to grazing. A big ram turned and looked right at the underbrush where the bear lurked; whether or not the ram had seen him move and would have given an alarm was something the bear would never know, because he didn't wait to find out. He didn't know caution; he knew only the finely honed killing instinct in him that said the moment for attack was *now*, and he exploded out of the underbrush with all the raw power he possessed, muscles bunching, claws digging.

The herd of sheep scattered; bleating in panic, the lamb scrambled to its feet and bounded for its mother. The bear swiped its huge paw at the lamb's hindquarters, claws drawing blood, but the lamb wasn't a newborn and it gave a tremendous leap that took it out of the bear's reach. Within thirty yards, the bear realized its prey was gone as the sheep bounded up the mountain into the rockiest terrain they could find.

He went into a frenzy of destruction, bellowing his rage and frustration as he took out his killing fury on the vegetation around him, tearing saplings up by the roots, shredding bushes, sending rocks as big as his head rolling down the mountain. Eventually he wore himself out and stopped where he stood, huffing and snorting. The sheep were gone. He sniffed the wind, but no other smells took his interest. He pawed through the vegetation for almost an hour, looking for some nuts or insects, but the season was late and most of the nuts were gone. After a while he lifted his head to test the wind again; his temper tantrum had left him thirsty, and this time his acute sense of smell was attuned to the fresh scent of water. He found what he was looking for, as well as something even more interesting, and he began moving purposefully down the mountain.

The hiker's name was Daniel Warnicki. He was twenty-three; last spring he had graduated from the University of California, Berkeley, but he hadn't yet found the right job, so he was making do with a drudge job during the day and at night waiting tables part-time at a popular bar. It said something that his tips almost equaled his pay at the drudge job. Sometimes the hours were tough, but he was young and the extra money meant he could occasionally afford to get away like this.

He stopped on a high curve of the narrow trail and leaned on his thick, heavy walking stick as he looked out over the breathtaking scenery that opened up before him: a huge, natural V of landscape, starting with a curling, dancing creek at the bottom, splashing white as the water flowed over jutting rocks, widening to the narrow strip of sandy gravel beside the creek, the steep rise of meadow that had lost all its autumn color but gained a different stark perspective now that the lines of the land were clearly seen, then the rugged, majestic mountains lifting up to the crystal clear blue sky.

He sucked in a deep breath of air. God, being out here like this was awesome. The air was fresher than anything he could ever inhale in the city, the scenery was amazing, and the quiet was so deep he could hear his own breathing. He loved to be lost in the trees—not *lost* lost, as in he didn't know where he was, but lost in the sense that he was the only person for miles around. There were no exhaust fumes, no cell phones ringing, no texting, no constant hum of people and machinery filling the air. There was just him, the mountains, and the sky.

This was fun. His idea of fun didn't always jibe with that of his friends—or his girlfriend—but this was pretty much perfection to him. He liked to rough it, while their idea of camping included large amounts of booze, inflatable mattresses, and they never wanted to be too far from a McDonald's. Danny liked a party as much as any of them did, but when he was camping he wanted to stay clearheaded. He even preferred a sleeping bag to an inflatable mattress. It was kind of silly, but it made him feel as if he had something in common with the settlers who, a hundred and fifty years ago, had made do with wrapping themselves in a blanket.

As for food, he was happy with trail mix and water for a couple of days. Roughing it made him appreciate the soft mattress on his own bed and a hot meal a lot more when he got home.

His girlfriend, Heather, sometimes got a little annoyed when he took off on a camping trip for two or three days at a time, but she didn't offer to come along—not anymore; once had been enough for her. If he was being honest, that once had been enough for him, too. Heather didn't appreciate quiet the way he did. She'd talked and talked and talked, scaring all the wildlife away, and most of her talking had been complaints. The going was too rough, it was too hot, or too cold, or she was thirsty, or she was hungry, or her feet hurt, or the mosquitos were eating her alive. She just wasn't an outdoorsy person—and that was the understatement of the year. They'd been living together for eight months, and while he was pretty sure he loved her, he wasn't sure he could actually marry a woman who cared more about her fingernails and her shoes than she did about . . . this.

Come to think of it, maybe she had the same reservations, but in reverse, about him. Would she want to marry someone who enjoyed something she absolutely hated? Danny shifted his backpack and moved down the trail, thinking about Heather. Okay, maybe she wasn't perfect, but she did have her good points. She didn't like the fact that a couple or three times a year he took off on his own, but she hadn't tried to get him to stay home, either. She hadn't cried, or gotten all emotional and claimed he didn't love her just because he wanted to do something without her. No, in-

stead she'd bought him a portable GPS and a canister of bear repellent pepper spray and sent him on his way.

He didn't need either, but to keep Heather happy he carried
them both. There was no personal locator on the GPS, but he'd
never gotten lost in his life. It was as if he had a built-in compass in
his head. He always knew where he'd come from, and how to get
where he was going. As for the bear repellent, it was just something extra to carry; he didn't think he'd ever need it. All the liter-
ature on bears said that they wanted to avoid humans as much as
humans wanted to avoid them. But the canister was in an easily accessible pocket of his cargo pants, just in case—to keep Heather
happy. He hadn't cheated by leaving it behind, because if she
asked him if he'd carried it, he wanted to be able to say "yes" with
a clear conscience.

Danny stopped again, peering through a clearing in the trees
that offered yet another spectacular view, but this one was framed
by some larch trees. He pulled his digital camera out of a pocket;
his hobby—well, his *other* hobby—was photography, and he'd gotten some great shots up here. They weren't good enough to sell or
anything, but they were good enough for him. When he looked
back at this picture he'd remember the solitude, the deep sense of
peace.

No wonder he was having such a hard time finding a job that
suited him. He should've lived two hundred years ago, been a
mountain man. The thought made him smile as he snapped a few
pictures, checked the quality in the review mode, then returned
the camera to his pocket.

There was a rustling noise behind him and Danny turned
around. His heart almost stopped, and for a minute he felt as if he
might pass out, as if all the blood in his head had drained to the
bottom of his stomach, which had lodged somewhere near his
throat. His mind had to work hard to process what he was seeing,
because this was just wrong. Black bear, less than thirty yards away,

lumbering straight at him. *Huge* black bear. He'd known there were bears here, but in all his trips he'd never been close to one.

For an instant he just stood there, blinking, as if somehow his eyes were playing tricks on him and all he had to do was blink fast enough to make the bear go away. No, it was still there, still coming at him. He blinked, wondering—hoping—if his eyes were playing tricks on him. For a wasted precious few seconds he was frozen, his gaze glued on the massive claws as he tried to remember all the tips he'd heard about confronting a bear in the wild.

Don't look it in the eye.

Slowly back away.

Speak in a low, calm voice.

Really? Speak to it? Like it freakin' understood English?

"Good bear." His voice shook a little but he kept it as even and soothing as he could, just as he kept his retreat slow and easy. He didn't dare look behind him, to watch where he was stepping. God, don't let him fall, not now. "Nice, big bear." His mouth was so dry he couldn't swallow; forming the words took incredible effort. "Where the hell did you come from?"

Good lord that thing was big. Slowly Danny reached down, taking care not to make any sudden, jerky movements that might alarm the monster. He fingered the canister of pepper spray in his pocket and wondered if using it would just make the bear angry, or if it would actually work. The pocket was buttoned, to prevent the canister from falling out as he climbed over rough terrain. He began fumbling with the button.

Bears were supposed to be wary of people. Everything he'd ever heard about them said that the animal should be going away from him, not steadily moving forward. Danny was careful not to make any threatening moves. He didn't challenge the animal in any way. The bear *should* be retreating.

But it wasn't. Each padding step forward meant he had to take at least two steps back to maintain the same distance between them. His instinct screamed at him to run, but he fought it down. He'd been told that was the number one rule: don't run. A human had no chance of outrunning a bear, plus fleeing triggered the response to chase.

Water. That was it. The bear was heading for the creek, and he was between it and its objective. The best thing he could do was leave the trail at a diagonal, let the bear get past him, then put as much distance between himself and it as possible.

He risked a quick look around him, because leaving the path meant the going wouldn't be as even, though in this case "even" was a relative term. He edged sideways, to his right, angling upward. To the left was the smoother way, but to the right was a rocky outcropping featuring some big boulders that would take him out of the bear's line of sight, which seemed like a good thing, if he could just get to it without triggering a charge from the bear.

He used the walking stick to brace himself as he edged across the rough, steeply sloping ground. The stick . . . would it do him any good against a bear that big? How much did that thing weigh? Four, maybe five hundred pounds? It could snap the stick with a swat of one of those massive paws.

Finally he managed to get the pocket in his cargo pants unbuttoned—too much going on, trying to think of too many things at one time—and pulled out the canister of spray. It felt terrifyingly small in his hand. He needed more than this, he needed a big can . . . several big cans. Hell, if that thing came after him, he needed a gun. That was a jarring thought, because he didn't believe in hunting. He never carried a weapon; he came up here to get closer to nature, to enjoy the solitude and beauty of the mountain.

Solitude wasn't so hot at the moment, and Danny didn't see beauty, he couldn't see anything except a mass of matted fur, and teeth and claws, and feral dark eyes. He thought of Heather, and how maybe she was right about staying close to modern conveniences. He wished he'd stayed home instead of escaping to the mountain, and if he got out of this he might not stop taking his camping trips, but he'd definitely make sure his canister of pepper spray was bigger.

He stumbled, righted himself, held on to a bush to steady himself as he navigated a particularly steep section.

The bear left the path, coming straight toward him.

Oh God. Not water, then. The bear wanted *him*.

This was wrong. This wasn't the way bears were supposed to act. He didn't have any food on him. This wasn't a female protecting its cubs, and the bear didn't seem to be wounded or sick, which were supposed to be the only reasons a black bear would attack a human. A grizzly, yeah, they were more aggressive, but a black bear was supposed to be *timid*.

Maybe it was just curious. He didn't care. All he wanted was for the thing not to get any closer to him. "Go away," Danny said, trying to sound authoritative, but his voice wavered and squeaked like a little kid's.

The bear lowered its head and swung it back and forth, a deep, coughing growl rumbling in its throat. Danny fumbled the safety off the pepper spray and held it out at arms' length. The wind . . . which way was the wind blowing? He didn't want to get a facefull of pepper spray. The left; he could feel the wind on the left side of his face, so he should spray to the left of the bear. What was the distance? The instructions on the can said it would spray thirty feet, or something like that. Not yet, then; the bear wasn't close enough.

God, he was supposed to let the thing get *closer*?

Just then the bear charged, roaring, claws digging into the ground.

It happened so fast he had almost no time to react. He began spraying as he took several quick steps back, but his aim was off, too high, and the bear was coming at him under the yellow cloud of spray. The footing was too treacherous; his feet slipped out from under him and he went down hard on his back, pulled there by the weight of his backpack, as helpless as a turtle. Then the bear was on him, hitting him like an avalanche, just as powerful and overwhelming. The sound was deafening, the smell hot and fetid, fur greasy and matted; he caught a fast glimpse of those dark feral eyes, something mean and disturbingly intelligent in them.

There was still some spray in the canister and he managed to hit the release and got the bear in the face, but it was too close, the pepper got him, too, and he lost his breath, his sight. Blindly he swung his walking stick up, frantically trying to get it between himself and the bear as if he could pry the bear away, hold those hundreds of pounds off him with what was effectively a toothpick.

The bear snorted, shook its head. Danny tried to scoot away but one massive paw flashed out and caught his scalp, peeling skin and hair down over his face. He heard agonized screaming, deep and raw, but the sound was at a distance. He didn't feel any pain so he couldn't be the one making the noise, maybe someone was nearby who could help him, someone who could—

Then the bear bit down on his head.

For a brief flash of time, he could hear the screams blending with the coughing grunts of the bear, discordant and harsh, and then there was nothing.

Chapter Four

The next day, Angie got up at the crack of dawn and started work. The day before leaving on a guide trip was the most work-intensive, every time. Her dad had built three small guest cabins, just big enough for private sleeping and bath areas, and today was the day she had to clean the two cabins that would be used, put on fresh sheets, lay out fresh towels, etc. When her dad had been alive, and for the first year she'd been back, there had been enough money to hire a local woman to do that work, but since then Angie had been doing it all herself.

On top of getting the cabins ready, with Harlan coming to take pictures for the website, she did some major damage control in the main house, too. Living alone as she did, sometimes she'd let little things slide, and before she knew it there were a ton of little things that threatened to become an avalanche of junk.

Her clients were due in late that afternoon. They were renting a vehicle in Butte and driving in. Rather than go through the hassle of bringing their rifles through the airport, they'd shipped them in; the boxes had arrived four days ago. She had all the permits in order, they had their licenses, and all of that was good to go. Tonight she'd have to feed them, so she put a hearty stew in the slow cooker.

By the time all of that was done, it was early afternoon. She sat at the kitchen table, half-listening to the television as she finished packing the supplies they would need. She had a checklist that she printed out before every trip, and as she added each item she checked it off the list. Basic first-aid items were included, as well as canned or dried food, bear spray—the big canisters, with as high a concentration of pepper as state law allowed, and four for each person—powerful LED flashlights with new batteries in them, and other items. She didn't take safety issues lightly. She didn't hunt, she merely guided, but all the same her rifle was freshly cleaned, the scope sighted in, and she had plenty of ammo . . . just in case.

The sound of a vehicle outside made her stand and look out the kitchen window as Harlan was climbing out of his truck. She'd set up the coffeemaker ahead of time, so as she passed by on the way to the door she pushed the brew button to start the machine.

"Come on in," she called, holding the door open. "Coffee's making."

"Sounds good."

When her dad was still alive Harlan had been over many times, but this was his first visit since she'd moved back and taken over the place. He looked around the kitchen with interest, noting the changes she'd made, such as refinishing the cabinet doors and replacing the old hardware and repainting. The appliances were nothing fancy but they were all fairly new, thank goodness, because now she couldn't afford to replace them.

"It looks good," he said in approval. "I like the color." As a man he probably didn't give a rip about the color, but as a real estate agent he knew what would sell and what wouldn't.

Angie laughed. "Any color would be better than what was here before." She wasn't a decorating whiz, by any means, but the old discolored, peeling wallpaper had been an eyesore even before she'd moved away. By the time she'd moved back, the wallpaper had gone from merely unattractive to a real disaster. Removing it and painting the walls a deep taupe *had* to be an improvement.

"There is that." He removed his hat and coat, hanging them on the pegs by the door. "Been a while since I've been here; any other improvements you've made?"

"Some lighting fixtures, paint, general repair. Nothing major needed to be taken care of. Let me show you around."

The place wasn't anything fancy, but it was solidly built. Everything eventually needed new roofing and maintenance, but her dad had stayed on top of things—except for cosmetic stuff like the wallpaper—so she hadn't been hit with any big expenses. So far, knock on wood, the new cabinet pulls had been her single biggest outlay as far as the buildings went.

She had de-cluttered the place and repainted, and turned the master bedroom into a guest room. Somehow, when she'd moved back, taking over her dad's bedroom hadn't been in the cards. Her old room had been way more inviting, and being there felt natural. Sometimes she had married couples as clients, and if she liked them enough and was comfortable with them staying in the house with her, she'd offered the master bedroom instead of putting them in one of the tiny cabins, which realistically were better suited for one person, not two.

Harlan was complimentary on what she'd accomplished, but he didn't take any photos the way she'd expected. For that matter, he hadn't brought a camera at all, unless it was one of those tiny digitals that could hide in his pocket.

"Did you leave your camera in the truck?"

"I forgot it," he said, a guilty look crossing his face.

Angie was dismayed by the delay; she was leaving early in the morning and the planned hunt could go as long as a week, which meant it would be at least that long before Harlan could list the property. She had so little leeway that she felt a little panicked over the forgotten camera, but she still managed to smile at him and say, "That gives you an excuse to come out again."

"There is that." He followed her back to the kitchen, and made himself at home at the table while she poured coffee for both of them. She stirred two teaspoons of sugar into his, one into hers, and carefully delivered his cup into his hands before she took her own seat.

He nodded at all the supplies spread out across the kitchen table, barely leaving enough space for them to set their cups. "Looks like a long hunt."

"A week, though you know how it goes: If they bag their prey the first day, the hunt's essentially over."

"Trophy hunter?"

"Yeah. I've made the usual arrangements for the meat." That meant that the meat would go to a homeless shelter, or to a family that needed a helping hand with food. The law was that the meat couldn't be wasted.

"Who are your clients?"

"One's a repeat; his name's Chad Krugman. Nice enough guy, but not much of a hunter. The other one, Davis, is *his* client. I guess this is the roughing-it equivalent of a golf game."

Harlan gave her a somber look. "Be careful."

"Always." She knew exactly what he was talking about, and didn't pretend otherwise. In a perfect world a female guide wouldn't have to take precautions when taking out a party of male hunters, but the world wasn't perfect and she wasn't stupid. Not only was she always armed when she was out on a guide trip, she made certain people knew where she was, who she was with, and when she was coming back—and that her clients knew she'd left their names with someone else, which was probably the best safe-guard she had.

Nevertheless, she was on birth control. She kept things on a no-nonsense basis, never flirted, and slept lightly with her rifle at hand. There were some things she couldn't control, and if two men decided to gang up on her she might or might not to be able to handle the situation, but she was fairly certain she'd be able to handle someone acting alone. She made things as safe for herself as possible, and had to be content with that.

One thing she didn't have that she wished she did: Her dad had gotten a satellite phone that he'd taken on guide trips, for emergencies, and she'd kept it for the first couple of years, but last year she'd had to cut expenses, and the satellite phone was one of the first things to go. She'd felt safer, having the phone. Thank goodness she hadn't had any real emergencies in all the years she'd been guiding. Come to think of it, neither had her dad, but he'd liked having the phone.

He'd modernized in other ways as well, such as buying the four-wheelers, but for the most part he'd liked the whole bit of going out on horseback and giving his clients a real sense of adventure. She should have sold the horses the first year and kept the four-wheelers, but sentiment had gotten in the way of good sense, and she'd kept the money-eaters not only because her dad had liked them, but because one of the horses was a particular favorite of hers. Then last year she'd lost Jupiter to colic anyway, and another horse had broken its leg and had to be put down, which meant she'd had to buy two new horses, neither of which she liked nearly as much as the horses they'd replaced.

Life just kept on happening, damn it.

In keeping with the rule of letting someone know where she was, she pulled a piece of paper toward her, wrote out all the pertinent information, and pushed the sheet toward Harlan. "I'll check in with you when I get back. If I don't call by this date, send out the search party."

Harlan nodded as he folded the paper and stuck it in his pocket. He'd done watchdog duty before, for her dad. He sipped his coffee, looking around at nothing in particular, and Angie noticed that guilty expression on his face again. An idea struck her and she said, "Wait, I'll get my camera. It isn't as good as yours, probably, but it takes decent pictures. You can take the SD card with you; I have another one." That was something else she always took with her: a camera for photographing the victorious hunters, just in case they forgot to bring their own cameras.

"That's okay," Harlan said quickly, then turned red. "I need to tell you something."

Angie stared at him in puzzlement. He seemed both embarrassed and disturbed, which was weird. "You can't handle the listing?" She couldn't think of anything else that would account for his expression.

"Of course, that isn't it. No problem there. It's just, well, I don't need to take pictures because there's already been an offer."

"*Already?*" Angie sat back, her eyes wide. She didn't know if she should be elated or terrified, because she hadn't in her wildest dreams imagined the property would move so fast. This would save her a ton of money; on the other hand, she hadn't had time to get herself emotionally or physically ready to move out, so this was kind of panic-inducing. Harlan must have immediately started spreading the word in the community, or e-mailed someone who—

Then a horrible thought occurred to her. She herself had told one person, someone who would have a vested interest in getting rid of her as soon as possible.

"Who?" She tried to keep her tone neutral, tried not to betray anything, but the look Harlan shot her told her that she'd failed . . . maybe because she could feel her eyes squinting into slits and her jaw clenching. No way was a neutral tone going to offset the Look of Death.

"Dare Callahan."

Fury welled up inside her. She tried to tamp it down, tried to be reasonable. After all, she *needed* to sell, and the sooner the better. Callahan was actually doing her a favor, whether he knew it or not. Yeah, she wished anyone else except him would buy the place, but she had to get past that.

Harlan coughed. "I, uh, I happened to look out the window yesterday and saw you in the parking lot with him. I gather you aren't on the best of terms."

"That's putting it mildly," she muttered. "If it wasn't for him, I wouldn't have to sell." She sighed and rubbed her face, looked out the kitchen window to keep from looking at Harlan while she gathered herself, pulled it all back in. Okay. This made her so angry she could spit nails; she'd have to deal with it. She'd signed a contract with Harlan. If Callahan met her price, she was legally bound to honor that contract. That was what had Harlan so bothered; he knew she was caught, and he hated being the trap Callahan had used to catch her.

"He came straight up to my office after you left, then got back with me this morning after meeting with his banker, and made an offer."

She was so focused on containing her feelings that it took her a few seconds to actually make sense of what Harlan was saying. Her head whipped around. "An offer?" That was different from taking the deal, which was what he would have said if Callahan had met her price.

"Yeah." He turned his cup back and forth. "Would you be willing to take thirty thousand less?"

Angie erupted from her chair, unable to sit still with so much red-hot anger pouring through her. Going to the window, she clamped her hands on the edge of the sink and held on hard as she stared out, not seeing anything but using the time to get control of herself. The bastard! The low-down, miserable bastard! He knew how tough things were for her, had to have figured out she was close to bankruptcy and *had* to sell; he also knew how miserable the real estate market was right now, and how difficult it was to get financing. He pretty much had her over a barrel, and he was using that to get the property at a dirt cheap price. She and Harlan had priced it to give her a little maneuvering room for negotiation, but not thirty thousand dollars worth!

She didn't have to accept the offer. Because Callahan hadn't met her price, she was free to turn it down. But if she did, there was no guarantee she'd get another offer from someone else, and later on she might be so desperate she'd take even less money. Even worse: Did Harlan need the commission, even one based on the reduced price? Of course he did. How long had it been since he'd had a sale?

So she was damned if she did and damned if she didn't. Either way would cost her money. The more she delayed, the more of her money she'd lose in operating expenses—and if she took the deal right now, she'd lose it by taking the lower price.

She gritted her teeth, took a deep breath, and did the adult thing. "Make a counteroffer. Come down ten thousand." That would buy her some time while she did this guide trip, but wouldn't eat up so much time that she'd lose a lot to operations. And, who knew? He might come up ten thousand. Maybe he'd be willing to truly negotiate. Maybe he couldn't swing her asking price, or the bank hadn't been willing, and had low-balled her on his offer to give himself some wiggle room. Anything was possible. Not likely, because she couldn't make herself give him the benefit of the doubt, but possible.

Harlan blew out a big sigh of relief. "Atta girl. I was afraid you'd turn him down flat."

"If I could afford to, I would. But if I could afford to, I wouldn't be selling in the first place."

"I know." Now that he could relax some, he took a big gulp of coffee. "I'll see what he says. In the meantime, I'll set things up with a home inspector and an appraiser, okay?"

"Sure. Let me get you a key, in case you can get things rolling while I'm gone."

The extra key was in her bedroom. She took it from the bureau drawer and stood there a minute, clutching it in her hand while she did deep breathing exercises. She could do this. Even if

Dare Callahan made the only offer, even if she couldn't afford to turn him down, she could do this.

He had to know that if he stuck to his guns, she could make counteroffers until she was blue in the face, but eventually she'd have to take his offer. The bastard.

Angie was so furious that as soon as Harlan left, she made a beeline to the computer in the den and e-mailed her pals in Billings. *"Want to guess which asshole is trying to buy my place for thirty thou less than the asking price???"*

Not that they could do anything other than join in her outrage, and offer some outlandish but satisfying suggestions for revenge. That was the best thing about female friends: the instant, unquestioning support, regardless of common sense or practicality. They were all at work, of course, so she didn't expect to hear back from them right away—

As soon as she had the thought, her e-mail pinged, and she saw she had an answer from Lisa, who had worked with her in the hospital administrative office. She'd sent the e-mail to Lisa's home account, so this had to be a coincidence. She clicked on the e-mail to open it.

"Got a new BlackBerry! Can get e-mail all the time now. That rat bastard. Makes you think of harvesting some mountain oysters, doesn't it?"

She typed back: *"His would be poisonous."*

"Well, if you can't even eat his nuts, what good is he?"

A few exchanges later Lisa said she had to get back to work, but by then Angie's mood was much lighter. She'd done the adult thing and made a counteroffer. The ball was now in Callahan's court, and until Harlan got back to her, she was wasting her time stewing about the entire situation. She still had work to do, and she'd be better off focusing on that. She couldn't do a damn thing about Dare Callahan and what he did or didn't do, but she could definitely make certain she did her job as a guide. That had to count for something, didn't it?

She just wished . . . well, there was no point in wishing, because nothing could change the past. Yet she was always aware of a deep sadness whenever she thought of Dare Callahan, a sadness she kept carefully buried under a thick layer of anger, because there was no point in letting herself feel anything other than anger. Reality was what it was.

But still, for a giddy while, back when they'd first met, her stomach felt as if it had taken flight, her heart rate had soared, and despite all common sense she'd let herself get lost in anticipation. She could remember the exact moment when they'd been introduced—in the feed store, standing beside fifty-pound sacks of grain. She'd looked up into the strong face shadowed by the brim of his black hat, met those vivid blue eyes, and it felt as if the world had fallen away. She remembered the feel of his hard, warm hand wrapping around hers, the calluses on his palm, the steely strength held firmly in check so he didn't crush her fingers. "Miss Powell," he'd said briefly, his voice so hoarse she'd wondered if he had a cold or something. Then she'd noticed the scar on his throat, and knew that raspy tone was permanent.

"Call me Angie," she'd said, and he'd given a curt nod.

Then someone else had called his name and he'd turned away, and though she'd lingered a little longer than necessary in getting her supplies, feeling as obvious and awkward as a fourteen-year-old trying to get a boy's attention, she didn't think he'd so much as glanced in her direction again. She had a million things to do to get ready for the guide trip she had booked for the next day, and there she was, wasting time, hoping he'd say something else to her.

Finally she'd given herself a mental shake and checked out. The feed had been loaded in the back of her pickup, and as she climbed into the cab he'd come out of the feed store. Angie hadn't let herself pause; she'd cranked the engine and started to put the transmission in gear when he motioned for her to lower her window.

She pressed the button and the window slid down. Deliberately she kept her expression neutral, because she was a tad embarrassed at herself for dithering in the feed store the way she had. After her wedding fiasco, she'd made it a point to keep men at a distance, but a set of (very) broad shoulders and a pair of (very) blue eyes had all but blown her self-control to smithereens, whatever a smithereen was.

That blue gaze had pinned on her like a laser. "Have dinner with me tomorrow night," he said abruptly, no lead-in, no chit-chat, just a bald and blunt invitation.

Regret almost made her sick. Why tomorrow night? She was leaving early in the morning and wouldn't be back for a week. Why couldn't he have given her a decent lead time, at least a week? "I can't," she blurted, her refusal just as blunt as his invitation.

She didn't have time to explain. He gave a curt dip of his head, turned around, and walked to his truck before she could get another word out.

And that was that. When she'd returned from the guide trip, tired, with another million things to do before yet another group of clients came in, she'd nevertheless raced into the house to check her answering machine, to see if he'd called during her absence. There had been a couple of calls, but his hadn't been one of them. As days turned to weeks, and weeks to months, he still hadn't called. Disappointed, after a while she'd stopped expecting him to.

During that time, she noticed her business falling off, and because the community was so small she inevitably heard about the people who were hiring Dare Callahan as their guide, and several of the names were ones she recognized as people she'd previously guided. He was stealing her business! Okay, not stealing, because it wasn't as if he'd accessed her files and called those people; they'd have searched him out, not the other way around. Still, the end result was the same.

He had asked her out again, months after that first time, and by that time she was so angry she'd simply given him a clipped "No, thanks" and walked away. Go out with him? She'd rather stake him out over an anthill.

Yet no matter how hard she tried, she couldn't completely forget that moment of first meeting him, the sensation of being in free fall as every cell in her body seemed to be supercharged. She tried, but even though she kept her attention focused forward, on getting things done, she was always aware on some level of what might have been.

Nothing. That's what might have been: exactly nothing. And she had to remember that. Regrets were a dime a dozen.

Chapter Five

Harlan was pensive as he drove back along the narrow dirt road that snaked several miles from Angie's place toward a blacktop. A couple of different things bothered him. He liked Dare Callahan, loved Angie the way you loved a kid you'd known most of her life, and it made him uncomfortable that he was stuck in this situation between them.

His professional loyalty was to Angie; she was the one who had signed the contract with him, she was the one paying his commission. He'd present her counteroffer to Dare, no problem; in fact, he was relieved she'd made a counteroffer at all, instead of turning Dare down flat, which was what he'd been afraid she would do. He didn't butt in where it wasn't his business, but what he'd seen yesterday in the parking lot below his office had made it plain the two weren't on good terms. Watching them had been like watching two boxers in the ring, trash-talking before the swinging began.

He didn't know what their problem was and in this part of the country people minded their own business. He'd never heard anything about a disagreement between them, but sometimes people just disliked each other and that was all there was to it. Angie kept more to herself now, after that problem at her wedding, than she had before it all happened, and Dare wasn't a happy-go-lucky type, period. With the bristles they both toted around, it wasn't a surprise they'd evidently managed to stick each other; more surprising was that no one had noticed it before now.

Another thing that was bothering him, which was silly because it wasn't as if the situation was anything new, was Angie going off with two men she didn't know. Never mind that one was a repeat customer; he sounded like a wimp, and wimps could be dangerous because they tended to go along with whoever was stronger, and not take a stand in a bad situation.

Realistically, Harlan knew this situation was nothing unusual, that Angie had been running the business for three years now and routinely guided people, mostly men, whom she didn't know. But logic had nothing to do with a gut feeling, and his gut was suddenly uneasy. Maybe it was because this other situation had him feeling protective, but it was the same kind of gut feeling that would suddenly have him slowing down on a highway, without rhyme or reason, and five minutes later coming up on an accident, or a deer would leap across the road in front of him—things like that. His gut was uneasy now, and slowing down wouldn't fix a damn thing.

He periodically checked his cell phone for service; sometimes he'd hit a service pocket that he hadn't known was there, or the atmospherics would magically deliver service where five minutes before none had existed. Out here the coverage was sketchy, but in his experience people lived here for a reason, and one of them was the more relaxed pace of life. He didn't feel the need to be in constant contact with the world, and neither did anyone else. If he moved closer to Noah—hell, *when* he moved closer to Noah and the family, he might as well stop playing with the idea and commit—he'd have to adjust to the barrage of information. Of course, he could always be the old coot who never turned on his cell phone unless he wanted to make a call, then promptly turned it off again. That worked for him.

He finally got service right before he got back to his office, which was normal. No point then in wasting any of his minutes, so he used the office landline. The answering machine picked up, but he'd have been surprised if Dare had actually answered, anyway; it wasn't as if he spent his time in the house waiting for a call, and cell service was just as bad out at Dare's place as it was everywhere else in the area, so he didn't even bother trying that number. "Dare, it's Harlan. I gave Angie your offer, and she's made a counteroffer. Call me."

The return call came less than half an hour later. Dare's voice was as raw and rough as January, as usual, and brusque, also as usual. Dare was a good guy and Harlan liked him, but even his friends thought he was as hard as nails and as ornery as a bull. "What's the counteroffer?"

"Ten thousand less than her asking price. It's a fair number."

"It was a fair number two years ago, but property values have tanked. That's twenty thousand more than I offered. I'm not made of cash," he said irritably. "I don't know if I can get the bank to go any higher on how much it'll finance."

At least he hadn't said a flat-out no. "Give it some thought," Harlan urged. "Nothing has to be done right now. In fact, Angie's taking two guys out in the morning on a weeklong guide trip, so she'll be out of pocket anyway. I'll get with the bank, get an appraisal done, then we'll both have a better idea on the value of the property. I think she's in the ballpark, though. I'd have told her if I thought she was asking too much." And she needed to sell, but Harlan kept that thought to himself. Her financial problems were her business, and not his to broadcast.

"All right, I'll think about it," Dare growled.

"That's good. I'll get back with you when she's home again." Harlan's gut nudged him; maybe he should get Dare's opinion on the situation. Never mind that Dare and Angie weren't the best of friends, this was kind of a professional consultation. And if he worked this right, he might be able to wrangle something even more important out of the conversation. "Say, there's something that's bothering me, and I want your opinion."

Dare paused briefly; he wasn't someone who obligated himself without knowing the details. Harlan had no doubt that if they hadn't known each other Dare would have said "No" and hung up the phone. But they did know each other, so he pushed the advantage. "It's about Angie."

A low grunt sounded. "What about her?"

"This guide trip . . . I feel a tad uneasy about it. She's going off for a week with two men she doesn't know. Well, one guy is someone she's guided before, but she said he isn't an outdoorsman, so I get the feeling he's sucking up to a business associate. You ever heard of any women guides having trouble . . . you know, with men while they're out on a hunt?"

"Aren't that many women guides," Dare said after a minute. "The few I know, other than Angie, work with their husbands. I'm not saying there aren't more female guides working on their own, but I don't know about them."

"Do you think it's safe?"

"She'll be armed, right?"

"Of course."

"Then she's as safe as any other woman with a rifle in her hand. But she isn't as safe as I'd be." He paused. "You asked if I'd heard of any women having trouble on a hunt, and the answer is yes. I've heard about it, but I don't have any firsthand knowledge, so I can't swear what I heard was true. Common sense says it probably is, though, people being people and assholes being assholes."

Harlan blew out a breath. "That's what I thought. Damn it."

His tone dragging with reluctance, Dare asked, "Where's she going? Do you know the area?"

"Yeah. She gave me her location, and the name of the men

she'll be with." Harlan passed along that information. "She's supposed to call me when she gets back."

"What are they hunting?"

"Bear, going by the bear call I saw her packing."

Dare grunted. "And both of her clients are first-timers?" He
meant the first time hunting bear in particular, not hunting in
general, but he didn't have to explain himself to Harlan.

"I don't know about the client's client; he might be experienced." Harlan felt he had to be fair about that, considering all
the other bad thoughts he was having about these two men whom
he didn't know. He cleared his throat, bracing himself for a sharp
rejection as he moved to the main part of his objective. "Like I
said, I have an uneasy feeling about this; don't know why. Do you
know anyone who could check up on her while she's out there,
kind of? You know, so she won't know she's being checked up on?"

There was a moment of silence during which Harlan could all
too plainly imagine Dare holding the phone out and staring at it
in disbelief, then his ear was blasted with a shout so raspy it
sounded as if it had been fashioned out of sandpaper. "You want
me to check up on her? That's what you're asking, right? There
isn't some convenient 'anyone' who's going to be up in that area."

"Unless you're busy," said Harlan, totally without shame or
guilt; in fact, he felt a sense of triumph. If Dare had had a guide
trip himself, he'd have immediately said he was busy, but he
hadn't, which meant he wasn't. Harlan had taken a gamble.

"I don't have anyone coming in, but that doesn't mean I'm
not busy," Dare said, sounding thoroughly pissed.

"I know I'm asking a lot—"

"A helluva lot more than you know. In case you haven't noticed, Angie and I don't exactly get along. She won't appreciate
seeing me."

"I had noticed," Harlan admitted. "And if she sees you she
won't be happy. But I'd rather she be unhappy than raped or
dead."

"You really think something like that might happen?"

"Normally I don't even think about it. This time, though, I've just got a bad feeling in my gut."

"Shit," said Dare, but it wasn't a dismissal of Harlan's instincts. If anything, it was an acknowledgment from someone who had been in a lot of tense situations and tight places; cops and soldiers learned to pay attention to their guts, more so than the general population. Harlan didn't think he was psychic or anything like that, but he did think that people had an animalistic sixth sense that could warn them of impending danger, if they'd only listen to it. Maybe Angie had picked up some of the same sense of danger and would be extra cautious, which might be all that was needed, but maybe she was too preoccupied with her situation to notice some details.

"I'll think about it," Dare finally said grudgingly. "But if I do go up there and she shoots my ass, I'm holding you responsible."

Fuck this. Angie Powell wasn't his problem. She was a pain in his ass, but she wasn't his problem.

Dare made a habit—no, a religion—of not taking on other people's shit if he could find a way around it, and he was no goddamn babysitter. Harlan was just being an old woman, worrying about Angie because his gut told him something wasn't right. More than likely he just felt overprotective because she was his dead best friend's daughter, he'd watched her grow up, and all that other psychological crap, so he'd worked himself into a fit of guilt. He was discounting that Angie had chosen to be a guide, knowing damn well that taking men she didn't know out for days or even weeks at a time would be part of the deal. She was a smart, tough cookie; she'd have thought of all that, and taken precautions.

But Angie was going through a tough time, selling out and

moving, so probably Harlan was just feeling extra protective. That explained it as well as anything else.

Dare snorted as he went through to the kitchen and snagged a bottle of water out of the refrigerator. He could just imagine what would happen if he showed up at her campsite, *checking up on the little lady* like some Old West throwback. Angie Powell would kick his ass if he even hinted that she wasn't capable of taking care of herself. Well, she'd try.

In spite of his sour mood, a smile twitched at his mouth. She pissed him off with those drop-dead looks she gave him, she got on his last nerve without even trying, but the mental picture of her coming after him with both fists swinging lifted his mood. For one thing, he'd win any tussle with her. For a second thing, the tussling would be fun. For a few seconds he enjoyed the scenario, imagining that almost-skinny body wiggling against him, that world-class ass right there where he could get his hands on it—yeah, right before the part where she head-butted him and broke his nose, which was way more likely than the ass-grabbing part, though if he kept his mind on the fight and his hands where they were supposed to be, she'd never be able to get near his nose, or his balls, or any other vulnerable part. He'd have to decide ahead of time if getting his hands on her ass was worth a knee in the balls.

His dick twitched a *Hell, yeah!* Dare snorted again. Stupid fucker . . . literally.

Spend a week up in the high country trying to stay hidden and watch over Angie Powell at the same time? What, did Harlan think he lived in a vacuum and didn't have his own shit to take care of?

Some of that shit was in a pile on the kitchen table, waiting for him. God, he hated paperwork. He loved what he did, but he fucking *hated* the nit-picking shit that went with it, the stack of crumpled receipts that he swore to God multiplied during the night. Maybe he should hire someone to do the books for him. He was making enough money now—though if he bought Angie's place, that extra money would disappear. Things would be tight for a while, but if he could make all his plans work . . .

Damn it, if she got killed on this guide job, all of those plans would evaporate. The property would be tied up for however long it took the estate to be settled. He didn't know who her relatives were, if she had a will, anything about that side of her life. If he wanted that land, she needed to be alive.

Damn it.

He growled as he took his bottle of water to the table and sat down. He picked up his calendar and flipped through it. Yeah, everything there was duplicated on his computer, but he preferred to keep the names of clients and the dates of their scheduled hunts written down on paper. It was nice to have a computer backup, but he didn't quite trust that the info would always be there when he needed it. Power outages, computer viruses, the blue screen of death . . . yeah, paper and pen were better.

The calendar was a map of his success. At first glance, it was a mess of chicken scratching. Maybe his penmanship wasn't great, but he could decipher it and that was all that mattered. Notes were scrawled in the margins of the notebook-sized organizing calendar, plans and names were scratched out here and there, and in some places other names were added in. He didn't get many cancellations, but it happened. Sometimes there were other clients on standby, regulars waiting to take the place of the ones who'd backed out for one reason or another—regulars who would prefer to wait for him than to sign on with someone else. He was proud of that, that for some hunters it was Dare Callahan or no one.

The calendar told him exactly what he'd known it would: He didn't have anything scheduled for the next ten days. There was no one on standby, either; the end of the busy season was coming up fast. The last few months had been so busy, Dare wouldn't mind taking a short break. It wasn't like he didn't have other things to do. The camps could always use maintenance, and he was always behind on his paperwork, witness the mound of receipts right in front of him now. He wasn't exactly a nester, but he needed to take care of a pile of laundry before he ran out of clothes, and he needed to lay in some more firewood for winter, and stock up on supplies. He was careful not to let himself run low on anything, but it never hurt to be prepared to hunker down for a good long while during a Montana winter. For a few minutes Dare sat there, thinking of all the things he needed to get accomplished in the next ten days.

He tapped the end of his pen against the tabletop. Flipped through the calendar with no particular purpose. Took a sip of water. Ground his teeth.

He tossed the calendar to the table, sending a few receipts dancing and flying. One fell to the floor, but Dare ignored it. Damn Harlan to hell. Why couldn't he have kept his fucking gut instincts to himself? He'd planted a seed of worry that Dare couldn't shake.

No way in hell was he going to tail Angie and her clients like some kind of unwanted bodyguard . . . or stalker. If nothing else, that was a good way to get shot. Antsy tourists with itchy trigger fingers might easily mistake him for game, from a distance. And if he wore an orange vest, as he should this time of year, it would be damn tough to remain out of sight.

He didn't think Angie would shoot him on purpose—maybe—if she caught him tailing her, but he wasn't her favorite person, so she probably wouldn't shed a tear over his body, either. Once again he tried to convince himself that this was *not his business*, but a little voice in the back of his head whispered that since he'd made an offer on her place, he'd made it his business. Well, shit.

He drank some more water, then capped the bottle and pushed it aside. Water wasn't doing it for him right now, and he was out of beer—another item on his list of things to get. The coffeepot still held a couple of inches of cold coffee. He eyed the coffee, thinking it would probably taste like shit, but what the hell. Shoving away from the table, he grabbed his morning coffee cup from the dishwasher—why mess up another one—and filled it, then put it in the microwave and set the timer for two minutes.

While it heated, he scowled at the floor. Why was he even thinking what he was thinking? Angie had made it clear she thought it was his fault that she had to sell, and that she hated his guts because of it. She'd hate him even more now that he'd made the offer on her property, because she'd think he was taking advantage of her situation. The last thing she'd want was him tagging along on a job to make sure she was safe, even if he had the time or the inclination, which he didn't. Mostly. That last word sneaked into his brain and made his scowl deeper.

The microwave dinged. He opened the door and stuck his finger in the coffee to see if the brew was hot enough, then quickly jerked it out. Shit, yeah. He dumped in enough sugar to disguise the crappy taste, stirred, then leaned back against the counter and took a sip. Not bad. Not bad at all. Why couldn't he just enjoy a cup of coffee and the fact that business was good? For the most part, *life* was good. He didn't need to take on Angie's problems.

Why did he let her get under his skin this way? In all his thirty-seven years, he'd never met another woman as annoying as she was. She was stubborn as an old goat, and she'd made it abundantly clear that she wouldn't piss on him if he was on fire. No ass in the world, no matter how fine, was worth the kind of aggravation she'd caused him. Like it or not, though, she was definitely under his skin, lodged there like a tick.

What was wrong with him? In a matter of moments he'd mentally compared her to both an old goat and a tick, and yet here he was, still stewing over Harlan's words and, damn it all, still worrying about a woman who wouldn't give him the time of day.

If Harlan had expressed the same concerns about anyone else in town, Dare wouldn't have given them a second thought. Angie was an adult. She'd be armed. Surely she vetted her clients before taking them on. She knew the territory as well as . . . no, better than anyone else, except him. She had such a pissy attitude, he should be more concerned about her clients' safety than he was about hers.

Dare drank his coffee, savoring each sip. His rancor eased some, as he glanced at the pile of paperwork on the table. He had ten days off, ten days of freedom. His winter preparations would do, for now. There was maintenance to be done, but nothing pressing. The paperwork wasn't going anywhere. And forget tailing Angie Powell as if she was a helpless female in need of a fucking white knight.

He was going to go fishing, damn it. He was going up on the mountain on his own for some much needed peace and quiet, a little down time. And if that down time put him in Angie's vicinity, maybe even in her path, well, that was just a coincidence.

Yeah, right. He'd just keep telling himself that. And he'd damn sure tell Angie, if he was unlucky enough that she saw him.

Once he'd made up his mind, Dare packed with the speed and precision of a man who'd done the same thing a thousand times. In his backpack he arranged strips of jerky, power bars, a small first-aid kit, some cans of bear spray, bottles of water, aspirin—because he might run into Angie and she was sure to give him a headache—and an extra flannel shirt. His satellite phone, charged and ready, went into the pack. There were more supplies up at the camp, but he never headed in empty-handed.

The fishing gear was another matter. Dare hadn't been fishing on his own in months, so he took some time to inspect the fly rod, put on new line. Most of his clients came in to hunt, but he'd taken out the occasional fishing party. He never fished when he was with clients, though; if he intended to fish he preferred to go on his own, to enjoy the peace and quiet.

If his fishing clients knew what they were doing, he enjoyed the trips. If they were novices, he'd rather eat ground glass. They talked, they splashed, they tangled themselves in the line, caught themselves on the hooks. Teaching a beginner to fly-fish was a huge pain in the ass. He'd started referring callers to a fishing guide in the next county over, because business was good enough that he didn't have to fuck with it if he didn't want to.

Dare thought about packing waders, but given the cooling weather and dropping temps of the water he decided against it. He'd cast from the bank.

As he sorted through the flies, he wondered if Angie could fish, and imagined maybe sending the beginners her way. It was a perversely satisfying thought.

A few times in his career as a guide, clients had come in with their wives. One nightmarish job had included two teenage daughters. He'd rather be shot than do that again. But a woman . . . how many wives would be more comfortable with another female around? Angie probably wouldn't be as annoyed by the constant chatter of a young woman as he was. He'd barked at that one girl when she'd squealed because she saw a deer, and then she'd cried. The trip had gone downhill from there. It wasn't like having women around was the norm, but still . . . it was worth some thought. Why hadn't Angie attempted to specialize in couples, families? Why hadn't she used her gender to her advantage? Instead she'd tried to step into her father's shoes and continue on as he had, as if nothing had changed, when in fact everything had changed.

It wasn't the best time of year for fly-fishing. Weather and water conditions were changing, but the trout weren't in their winter lies just yet. He might have good luck in a slow current, maybe target some pre-spawn browns. A big pan of trout would taste a helluva lot better than a power bar and jerky.

And if he happened to coincidentally keep an eye on Angie at the same time, well, keeping her safe would make one part of him very happy. His brain knew better, but his dick hadn't given up hope. Not just yet, anyway. This trip might be just what he needed to convince his little brain that it had had a lucky escape.

Chapter Six

Chad Krugman waited in the terminal at the Butte airport as the SkyWest flight carrying Mitchell Davis taxied closer. There were only a few commercial flights a day coming in and out of Butte, most of the traffic was general aviation, but for all that the flight times were decent. Davis was an experienced hunter, so he wasn't expecting to be able to fly first class in a 747 right up to the hunting area. Out-of-the-way was pretty much the norm for good hunting.

Out-of-the-way was perfect for his plans. In fact, the more remote the area their guide, Angie Powell, took them to, the better. He'd made a point of asking her about the general area, keeping the tone of his e-mails casual, but there was nothing casual about his interest. Once he'd known where they were going to be hunting, at least within about ten square miles, he'd studied maps, downloaded images from Google Maps, and taped them together to give him a better idea of topographical features and possible landmarks. The images weren't as close up and detailed as he'd have liked, but they did give him a very good idea of the terrain and what he would have to do to execute his plan.

He'd known this day would be coming, had known it from the moment he'd begun skimming cash from the money-laundering service he provided for Mitchell Davis. No, even before that, because what he'd done had been carefully thought out, and all possibilities considered, before he'd ever taken that first step. With that in mind, he'd set a silent alarm on the accounts and computer files, an automatic notice if anyone tried to access certain files and information. That was his tripwire, and he was so good at what he did he'd even anticipated how long it would take Davis to become suspicious, and timed this trip accordingly.

Chad couldn't help feeling a little smug. As the time neared for the hunting trip he'd begun to wonder if he'd overestimated Davis, the vicious bastard, but then, *bang!*—just yesterday his silent tripwire had sent out the alarm. The precision of the timing made him almost giddy with triumph. Was he accurate, or what?

For the past year he'd been training for this, making preparations, studying and learning and getting the timing down just right. Maybe he was too careful in making certain nothing he did would signal Davis that he himself had been alerted, but he'd bypassed certain toys and tools that might, if Davis was enterprising enough to search his belongings, have made him wary because they weren't something Chad would ordinarily have possessed—at least, not as far as Davis and everyone else knew. That meant no sophisticated GPS, no satellite maps, no passport. His passport was safe in a post office box here in Butte, easy to retrieve when he needed it. He'd have bought an airline ticket in advance, but he wasn't certain exactly which day he'd need it, so that was something he'd have to do at the last minute. No big deal.

Chad enjoyed the disconnect between the way people perceived him and how he really was. No one, literally no one, had any idea what he was capable of, but then he'd spent almost his entire life carefully building his persona, crafting his mask, as if he'd known from childhood that one day his life would depend on it. He'd been blessed—or cursed, depending on how you looked at it—with ordinary features, and he'd worked hard to make himself even more ordinary. He kept himself in fairly good shape, something no one would ever guess to look at him, because he deliberately dressed in clothes that never quite fit properly, that made him look shorter and heavier, and as dweebish as possible. Who would ever be wary or suspicious of a slightly plump Woody Allen? No one. And so he'd gone about his life all but invisible, and all the while he'd been amassing a fortune right under their noses.

It was second nature to him now; he didn't even have to think about stuttering, or the slightly off-balance way he'd taught himself to walk, or the fumbling way he handled everything from a water glass to a cell phone. God, the CIA could take lessons from him in undercover guises.

Mitchell Davis approached the baggage claim area, pulling a rolling duffel behind him and carrying a computer bag in his other hand. Chad stumbled to his feet, dropping his cell phone and sending it skittering across the floor. Clumsily he lurched for it, and when he straightened his face was red from being bent over. He didn't let himself even glance at the computer bag, though it was a solid confirmation, if he'd needed one, that Davis was on his electronic trail. He felt a little bit of a thrill, because Mitchell Davis would have him killed without a second's hesitation if he could find what he was looking for, but at the same time Chad was contemptuous of Davis, not only for bringing the laptop but evidently not being aware enough of where they were going to realize that not only would there not be wifi everywhere, there wouldn't even be cellular service.

"Good flight?" he asked, automatically monitoring the amount of nervousness he let enter his tone. He judged it to be perfect.

Davis grunted. He was several inches taller, his hair going gray, his eyes cold and hard. "I hope you've already got the rental."

"It's waiting for us. I got a four-wheel-drive SUV, is that okay? I thought we'd need one for, um, the room in back and all that. But I can change if—"

"It's fine," Davis said curtly. "Let's go."

Davis was accustomed to people kissing his ass, but he wasn't usually that brusque. He'd want to be certain, though. Chad was too good at what he did for Davis to have him eliminated without solid proof. There were money launderers, and then there were true currency geniuses, and Chad was the latter. To some people, those more astute than others, that would have been a tip-off, so Chad had countered that signal with his degree in accounting and the implication that his talent with money was more along the lines of savant than savviness. That way his talent could be regarded as an oddity, an outlier, rather than an integral part of his overall intelligence. For this he thanked that Tom Cruise/Dustin Hoffman movie about the autistic savant, because that was the image that had been planted in people's minds.

Davis followed the signs to the rental parking area, with Chad trailing behind, pulling his own duffel. "It's the red one," he said, keeping the uncertainty and nervousness foremost in his tone. "Is that okay? Red's kind of— We can get another color, maybe something black, if you don't—"

"Who cares what fucking color it is?" Davis interrupted impatiently, and held out his hand. "Give me the keys."

"Keys? Oh. Oh, sure." Chad released his duffel and let it fall, rather than standing it upright, as he fumbled in his pocket for the keys to the rental. No way would his character's persona argue about who was driving, the way a more dominant man would, even though he'd been to the Powell place before and actually knew where he was going. He'd fudge on that, too, consulting maps and directing Davis to make at least one wrong turn. The very last thing he wanted was to have Davis the least bit on guard.

Perception. It was all about perception.

Angie couldn't remember what Chad Krugman looked like, but she did remember that he didn't ride very well, which meant it was a good thing they were trailering the horses most of the way. She'd made arrangements for a place to park her truck and trailer, and they'd ride the final eight, maybe ten miles. Unless Krugman had been practicing his horsemanship, he'd still have a sore ass, but there wasn't anything she could do about that other than offer her sympathy, and she'd have to do that silently, because in her experience most men got all bent out of shape if she so much as hinted that they couldn't do something as well as she could, even when it was glaringly obvious.

When he and his client drove up just before dark, she automatically looked at the man who got out of the driver's seat, but he wasn't familiar at all. She was a little surprised, because logically Krugman should have been driving—he'd been here before, therefore he was more familiar with the sometimes confusing twists of the dirt roads, which might or might not be marked. She then looked at the passenger, and even though she'd refreshed her memory by looking at his photograph, there was still a blank moment before she had a vague "oh, yeah, now I remember" kind of thing that underscored how unremarkable Chad Krugman was.

He was an inch or two taller than she, soft around the middle, with thinning dark hair and forgettable features. His clothes were kind of baggy, and just as forgettable. He wasn't ugly, he wasn't attractive, he was just nondescript. If his personality had been stronger none of that would have mattered, but he might as well have been born with "ineffectual" stamped on his forehead in glowing neon, except that would have been too memorable. Whatever he did for a living, Angie was fairly certain he'd never be a howling success at it. He'd muddle by, mostly by escaping notice, and that would pretty much define his life.

His client, Mitchell Davis, was almost Krugman's polar opposite. Angie smiled at both of them as she went down the steps to
greet them. Krugman smiled hesitantly in return, but Davis
merely gave her a dismissive look, as if he had more important
things to do than being polite.

"Ms. Powell, it's nice to see you again," said Krugman, and
when Angie held out her hand he hastened to grab it in a slightly
moist grip.

"You, too," Angie said easily. "And please call me Angie."

"Of course. And I'm Chad." He looked pleased, then that expression was chased away by an anxious one as he said, "Mr. Davis,
this is our guide, Angie Powell. Angie, Mitchell Davis."

Davis merely nodded his head while he looked around, his
sharp gaze taking in her less-than-new truck and the horse trailer
that had seen better days; his upper lip curled slightly. She kept
her face bland. Maybe her truck and equipment weren't brand
new, but they were in good shape and got the job done. "I'm glad
to meet you," she said, keeping her manners in place even if he
wasn't making any effort to do the same.

Davis was everything Krugman wasn't. He was taller, leaner, his
dark hair touched with gray at the temples. His features were hard
and chiseled, his eyes a clear gray. His movements were crisp, authoritative. His clothes fit him as if they'd been custom made for
him.

Angie disliked him on sight.

She could already tell this was going to be a long, long week.
With any luck, Davis would bag his bear almost immediately, and
neither of them would see any need to hang around for the rest of
the week doing nothing. If not, well, she'd keep her mouth shut
and a smile in place, and get through it as best as possible. Like
anyone who worked with the public, she'd had clients before
whom she disliked, and they'd gone home none the wiser. Davis
wouldn't be any different. Maybe.

"Let me show you to your cabins," she said after the men had gotten their duffels from the back of their rented SUV. Krugman knew the way, of course, but she led them down the path that led to a patch of ponderosa pines behind the house. The cabins were tucked among the trees, partially visible from the house but positioned so both she and her clients had a sense of privacy. She had already turned on the lamps inside, and turned up the heat. Each cabin also had a working fireplace, if someone wanted the ambiance of a real fire, but the shared heating unit was more efficient and less work. Most people didn't bother with a fire.

"I've put the boxes with your rifles inside your cabins," she said. "Chad, the first cabin is yours." She unlocked the door and gave him the key. "Mr. Davis, this one is yours."

"Yeah, great," he said as he took the key from her, his tone making it plain he wasn't impressed by the accommodations, either. She pushed her annoyance away. She *would* be polite to him.

"I'll leave you to unpack," she said to both of them. "If either of you brought your laptop and need to go online, Internet is available at the house. There's also a television room, if you want to watch anything tonight. Supper will be served at seven. It isn't anything fancy, just stew and biscuits. I'll see you then, or you can come in earlier to watch television or talk."

"Sounds wonderful," Chad said, smiling nervously. Davis's hard, cold eyes said he disagreed, but at least he kept his opinion to himself.

As she strode back to the house, Angie reminded herself that this wasn't about her, it was more about the dynamics between Chad and his client, and they weren't good. He was trying so hard to impress Mr. Davis, and Davis was making it plain that he thought the entire trip was second-rate at best.

The success of the trip would depend on whether or not the hunt was a good one. Though it was getting late in the year, not all the bears would have denned yet; the weather had been relatively mild, so some bears would still be active. She would find Mr. Davis a bear or bust a gut trying.

She half-expected Chad to come up to the house before the dinner hour, but to her surprise it was Mr. Davis who showed up. He carried a laptop case. "I need to check some reports," he said brusquely.

"Sure. Right in here," she said, showing him to the small den outfitted with a flat-screen television and satellite Internet; in the corner was a desk with a wifi modem. She gave him an index card with a string of numbers typed on it. "This is the wifi password."

"Thanks." He was already taking out his laptop, but at least he'd made a nod toward manners.

"You're welcome."

She left to give him some privacy, and finished setting the table. People didn't come on hunting trips expecting bone china and silver utensils, so she didn't even try to go that route. The plates and bowls she set out were sturdy earthenware, glazed a dark green with black rims, and she used a particularly heavy set of stainless steel. She did put out cloth napkins, made from a thick, heavy-duty, dark green cotton that didn't show stains.

The meal was a simple one, with the stew, fresh homemade biscuits, and chocolate cake. She knew all three were above average. Maybe she wasn't a great cook but she was a darn good one, and she enjoyed it when she had the time. When she'd lived in Billings, with access to a greater variety of ingredients, she'd liked experimenting with different dishes. Maybe someday she'd be able to try her hand at different stuff again, but right now all she could handle was the basic, hearty dishes. Part of this stew, for instance, had already been put in the freezer for next week, when she was back from this hunt. With nothing else on her books, and no anticipation of any further income for the next several months, she couldn't afford to throw away any food.

At ten to seven, Chad appeared in the door to the dining room. "Smells good," he said.

"Thank you." She gave him a smile, keeping it neutral, but a smile all the same. "Mr. Davis is in the den, on his laptop."

Chad made an awkward gesture. "I won't disturb him. Is there, ah, any way I can help?"

"Just by eating your fill," she replied. "Everything's under control." She checked the time. "The biscuits are ready to come out of the oven, so if you'll excuse me—"

"I'm sorry. Sure. I didn't mean—"

"You're my guest," she said, breaking in on his stammered apology. She tried another smile on him, hoping to settle him down. "It'll take just a minute to bring in the food. I hope you like chocolate cake!"

"I love it," he said, looking relieved at the change of subject.

Dinner conversation was going to be heavy-going, but at least she didn't have to be in there, she reflected as she took the biscuits out of the oven and placed them in a napkin-lined bread basket, which she placed on a tray along with the big tureen of stew. She carried the tray into the dining room and set everything on the table, then put the tray aside. "What would you like to drink? I have milk, hot tea, coffee, and beer. Water, too, of course."

"Ah, beer." He seemed a little self-conscious as he said it, though she couldn't think why.

"A beer for me, too," said Mr. Davis as he came into the dining room.

Angie returned to the kitchen, got two beers from the refrigerator, and poured them into glasses. As she set the glasses down in front of the men, Chad said, "Aren't you eating with us?" When he'd been here before she'd done exactly that, but the company had been more convivial. She didn't have any hard-and-fast rule about eating with clients, but neither did she believe in torturing herself if she could get out of it, so no way was she having a meal with these two tonight.

"I've already eaten," she said, which was a bald-faced lie, but so what? She'd get something to eat in the kitchen, either that or wait until she was cleaning up and have a bowl of stew then. She'd rather do without entirely than eat with them.

"Have you scouted out the area where we're going?" Davis asked as they sat down to eat.

She paused on her way out of the dining room. "I have, a few days ago when I took supplies up to the camp I've leased. There was fresh bear sign."

"But you didn't actually see a bear?"

"No, but I wasn't trying to. I didn't want to make contact with one beforehand." She'd been armed, of course, but she'd also been alone. Bears gave her the heebie-jeebies, even when she was with a hunting party, so she sure wasn't about to go looking for one when she was by herself. That was something she'd keep to herself, of course; knowing your guide was afraid wasn't something that would make a client feel confident.

"So you don't know if the bear is a decent size."

The tone of his voice made it plain he thought she'd already failed test number two of guiding, the first one being not having a shiny new dual-axle pickup like Dare Callahan's. Chad looked embarrassed and fumbled his spoon, making a clattering noise when he dropped it on his plate. For his sake, Angie kept her voice bland and didn't let any hint of irritation show through. "I do, going by how high the claw marks are on the trees. I estimate this particular bear is about seven feet long, which is big for a black bear."

"And how do you know it's a black bear?"

"By the fur that was snagged on some chokeberry bushes. It's always possible a brown bear is also in the territory and didn't snag any of its fur," she said, before he could make that argument, "but I *know* a black bear is in the vicinity." She kept a death grip on her patience, and her tone pleasantly neutral.

"What's your plan if this bear has gone to den in the time since you've been up there?"

Every sentence was like an interrogation with this man. Angie reached for a larger supply of patience. "If we don't find fresh scat the first day or two, we move farther afield. A bear's territory is usually two to ten miles. This time of year they aren't as active as they would have been earlier, but some are still moving around. The weather is still relatively mild, thank goodness. This time last year, we were already a foot deep in snow." Last winter had been horrendous, beginning early and hanging on weeks later than normal, taking a huge chunk out of time when she normally had at least some photographers wanting to go out, and that had been another nail in her financial coffin.

"If you don't mind me asking, Miss Powell, how long have you been guiding?"

"Most of my life. When I was a kid, I helped my dad, and as I got older I began taking out clients on my own." That was all true; she kept to herself that her teenage solo trips had been mostly photography, some bird hunting. She had gone with her dad on a lot of his hunts, though, so she wasn't a novice. He'd loved teaching her what he knew about reading sign, how to call game to the hunter's location, and how to shoot. What she'd learned had gone deep; when he'd died and she moved back home, she'd stepped into the life with barely a pause.

"These are great biscuits," Chad offered, making an obvious stab at changing the subject, and taking a big bite of biscuit to prove his statement. "Did your mother teach you how to cook?"

"No, I learned by trial and error, and there were a lot of errors along the way." She put humor in her tone, and completely by-passed the mention of her mother because it was irrelevant. Some people had great mothers; she wasn't one of them. She'd had a great dad, so fifty percent wasn't bad. Life was what it was, and she'd been luckier than some.

She tried to leave again, but Mitchell Davis asked a few more pointed questions as if he were trying to trip her up. Chad kept awkwardly trying to change the subject and eventually earned himself a cold, pointed stare from Davis, which was when he gave up and simply sat there in squirming misery, eating some but otherwise withdrawn. Through it all, Angie stood without fidgeting and answered Davis's questions as if they were nothing out of the norm, keeping her expression bland, not letting him get to her.

She finally escaped to the kitchen, where she consoled herself with a big fat slice of chocolate cake, the first one cut. When it was time to serve the cake, she made sure Mitchell Davis's slice was about two-thirds as thick as Chad's, and served both of them with a smile before bugging out to the kitchen again. When they'd had time enough to finish, she stepped out and suggested everyone get a good night's sleep, as they had to get an early start.

Chad immediately stood and began making a slightly incoherent good night, mixed with a thank you for the meal, but Davis interrupted with an abrupt, "I have some more work to do on the Internet before I turn in. You go on, Krugman."

Chad immediately left, of course. Angie smiled at Davis. "It'll take me about half an hour to clean up; I hope that'll be long enough." No way was she letting him stay in the house with her while she got ready for bed, and neither was she sitting up all hours with a long day—a long *week*—looming in front of her. Tonight would be the last good night's sleep she'd get until she was back in her own bed. She didn't think she had to worry about Davis being a repeat customer, so there was a limit to how much she'd tolerate from him.

He gave her one of his cold looks. "I need more time than that."

"I'm sorry, but that's all I can give you tonight. If you want to grab some time while I'm cooking breakfast in the morning, the door will be unlocked. I'll be up at four in the morning."

"This really is a second-class operation, isn't it?" His lip curled in that faint sneer she'd seen on his face when he first looked around.

"I'm a hunting guide. This is my home, not a hotel. Some places, you wouldn't have Internet available at all." She gave him a sudden, concerned look. "You *are* an experienced hunter, aren't you?" Her booking information indicated that he was, but after all the borderline-rude remarks he'd made, she couldn't resist making her own little jab at him. She'd be as polite as possible, but what was possible was steadily shrinking. No matter what, she wouldn't let him bully her.

"I've probably been on more hunts than you have," he snapped. "Regardless of that fairy tale about helping your father since you were a child."

"It wasn't a fairy tale, Mr. Davis. I'm sorry you don't believe me. If it'll give you more confidence, I'll be glad to phone someone in the area for you to talk to, to verify my credentials." She waited a moment, then picked up the tureen, which was still half-full of stew. "No? In that case, I have things to do."

She carried the tureen into the kitchen; when she came back to finish clearing the table, the dining room was empty. Swiftly she loaded the dirty dishes on the tray she'd left there earlier. She felt safer in the kitchen, where she could easily get to a bunch of big knives, if necessary. Okay, that was melodramatic. If she truly believed Davis might attack her, she wouldn't have let him stay in the house to use the Internet, and she wouldn't be going off on a hunt. He had a nasty personality, but she wasn't picking up any physically dangerous vibes from him. Not by so much as a glance had he indicated that he viewed her in a predatory way.

Of course, if she'd been a great judge of men, her wedding fiasco would never have happened, would it?

She finished as fast as possible, then sat down to rest for a minute while she watched the clock, waiting for the half-hour she'd given him to be up. Right on the minute, she got up, locked the kitchen door, then went through to the den, where he was tapping away on his laptop. "Time for lights out," she said, keeping her tone easy.

The glance he threw her was furious, but he shut down the laptop and shoved it back into its case. "Good night," she said as he went out the front door.

He didn't reply. Shrugging, she closed the door behind him

and locked it. There were some outside lights she'd turned on to light their way to the guest cabins, and she'd leave those on all night in case something happened during the night. People did get sick, after all, or take a fall. She'd leave her bedroom door open, as usual, so she could hear if anyone knocked on the door during the night.

If anyone fell and broke a leg during the night, she hoped it was Mitchell Davis. No, scratch that. She hoped he went home at the end of the week safe and sound and happy, because he was undoubtedly the kind of bastard who would sue if he had an accident.

Yes, it was going to be a long, long week.

Chapter Seven

Angie hit the ground running the next morning. As soon as she stepped outside, she breathed a sigh of relief—the weather had turned milder during the night. The warm temperatures were coming in ahead of some rain, but it still felt good. According to the long-range forecast, no really cold weather or snow was forecast for the next ten days, which was great.

By five o'clock she'd fed and watered the horses, hooked the trailer to the truck, had all their supplies and the horses loaded. Davis hadn't shown up to get in any of his oh-so-important Internet work, so she figured it hadn't been that important and he'd just been making an ass of himself, which, considering how close his default starting point was to asshood, hadn't been a difficult thing to do.

For breakfast she made a pan of biscuits, put steak slices in half of the biscuits and ham slices in the other half, wrapped them individually in foil, and filled several thermoses with coffee. Some packs of sugar, artificial sweetener, and powdered creamer completed her preparations. After making sure Chad and Davis were waiting at the truck, at five forty-five, she stepped out the front door and locked it.

As she approached the truck she saw that their duffel bags were on the ground; before she could ask about them, Davis unlocked their SUV and swung open the back hatch, and he and Chad loaded their duffels. "We, uh, we decided to follow you, then when the hunt is over we can leave straight for Butte," Chad explained, his tone of voice sheepish.

"That's logical," Angie said easily. "But if it's too late and you want to spend the night here before going home, you're certainly welcome. It's up to you."

She took a wrapped biscuit and a thermos of coffee for herself, and handed the rest over to Chad. "Breakfast, gentlemen. Let's get on the road." They got in their SUV, with Davis driving again, and Angie climbed into the cab of her truck. She wasn't unhappy with this change of plans. This gave her some peace and quiet, and space to think. She turned on the radio and punched the button for the CD player, and the soothing sound of her instrumental music filled the cab. Nice. This was much better than trying to make conversation. She poured herself some coffee and pulled out, accelerating smoothly so the horses wouldn't be jerked around.

The sun wouldn't rise for another hour and a half, so by the time it was daylight they'd be at their drive destination. They'd unload the horses, saddle up, and be on their way. She liked driving in the dark early hours, liked the sense of getting a jump on the day, and watching the darkness slowly fade away as more and more of the incredible landscape became visible. The music didn't intrude, just laid another layer of beauty under the early morning. Very briefly she thought about Dare and his hardball real estate tactics, but she refused to let herself start stewing about it. This time belonged to her clients, and she refused to shortchange them by not paying full attention to what she was doing, even if it was nothing more exacting than driving.

Right on time, she pulled in to Ray Lattimore's place; he didn't have a big spread, but he took in a little extra money by providing parking space for guided parties and hikers. Angie gladly paid him. Even if he'd charged twice what he did, it was worth it to not worry about her truck being broken into or her trailer stolen.

Ray came out to meet them, show her where to park. Davis and Chad stood to the side while Ray helped her unload the horses, which was nice of him because he certainly didn't have to, but he gave her two clients a discerning look and without a word made himself useful.

The four horses nervously crab-hopped around, knowing that the end of the ride meant exercise. She was using the biggest one, a sure-footed dark bay named Samson, as a packhorse. If he'd been a suitable mount she'd have put Chad on him simply because he was so sure-footed, but Samson had more bad habits than the Rolling Stones—all of them. Put together. He hated being ridden, he bucked and crabbed and shied, he tried to bite, he blew his belly out when you tried to saddle him, he'd try to brush his rider off against a bush, a tree, a building, anything that was handy. But he was okay with carrying a load, and he was strong enough that he could carry more than the average horse.

She'd never admit it to anyone, but she was a bit fond of the cantankerous bastard. He was what he was, he knew what he'd do and wouldn't do, and the two of them got along fine as long as neither she nor anyone else tried to ride him.

The other three horses, a light bay, a chestnut, and a roan, had their own foibles but at least they'd tolerate riders. The horse she'd chosen to ride, the roan, was more fractious than the other two, which was why she'd chosen him for herself. She'd had him the shortest length of time and hadn't yet learned all his tricks, but if he decided to bite or buck, better it was with her than with a client. The chestnut was the most docile, so she put Chad on him. The light bay fell somewhere between the chestnut and the roan in temperament.

"Supposed to rain tonight, tomorrow," Ray said to her as he closed the gate on the trailer and latched it. "Not good hunting weather."

"I know." The rain wasn't good for people, that is; the animals hunted and fed regardless of whether or not it was raining. "We'll get in some time today, though."

"Good luck. Hope I see you back here tomorrow."

She flashed him a smile. "That *would* be nice, but even if they get a bear today, I'd rather not ride back here in the rain." The weather report she'd seen called for thunderstorms, which would be unusual for this time of year—unusual but not unheard of. One of the worst rainstorms she could remember had happened in November, when she was in grade school. Rain was almost always welcome, though, regardless of the time of year.

She began saddling the horses, and again Ray helped her, because Chad was watching them with a completely befuddled look on his face and Davis was scowling as he punched numbers on his cell phone, as if he could force it to have service out here if he just hit the magic combination of buttons.

"Can that guy ride?" Ray asked under his breath, nodding toward Chad.

"He can manage. I'm putting him on the chestnut." She was in the process of saddling the chestnut as she spoke. She eyed Chad's legs, made the stirrups just a little longer than if she'd been saddling a horse for herself.

"That's rough country you're heading into. Hope he can stay in the saddle. What about the other guy?"

"He said he's experienced. I'm taking him at his word." There was nothing else she could do. Make Davis demonstrate his riding ability, maybe? Sure. She could really see that happening.

Next Samson was loaded down with their supplies. The big boy blew out a breath and turned his head to nudge her rather gently, considering his size. She lightly slapped his neck. "Are you anxious to get on the trail?" she asked him, and he blew again as if he understood her.

While she was saddling Samson, Davis and Chad had finally begun doing something, taking their rifles from their cases, loading them, and sliding them into the scabbards on the right of the saddles. She had sighted her own rifle in the day before, and hoped they had done the same before shipping the weapons; they would do some shooting to re-sight, but with luck they'd need only a couple of shots. She hated to use more ammunition than necessary.

Finally, she handed out the canisters of bear spray, two each, and the holsters to carry them in. "Keep these within easy reach, not in a pocket or your saddle bag," she said.

Chad looked at the canister. "Why bother with this when we have the rifles?"

Angie grinned. "Ever tried to take a leak while you're holding a rifle? All that zipping and unzipping? You'd need three hands."

He turned beet red. Davis actually laughed, the sound surprising her because she hadn't expected any sign of humor from him, even at someone else's expense. "If a bear got after you, you wouldn't have to worry about unzipping," he said to Chad.

"I don't imagine any of us would," Angie interjected. If the two men had been friends, the comment would have been funny, but it was obvious they weren't friends at all. Even worse, Davis seemed to be downright hostile toward Chad, which made this outing not only strange, but downright uncomfortable.

"The difference between hunting bear and hunting elk is that the elk won't try to drag you off and eat you," she continued. "Have either of you ever used bear spray before?"

"Of course," Davis said, sounding bored, but Chad turned the canister over in his hand and was reading the directions.

"I can't show you when we get to the camp," Angie said, "because the spray itself contains food scents that can lead a bear to you. Right here is as good a place as any." She showed him how to aim it. "Spray a cloud between you and the bear, and don't wait until it's actually charging or it may be through the cloud and on you before the spray settles low enough. Never, never spray if the wind is blowing toward you, because then you're blind and you still have a bear after you. And always have two cans on you, because one might not be enough."

Chad gave her a disbelieving look. "I thought bear were shy, and ran away unless you just stumble onto one."

"Don't you believe it," Ray said. "Bears are predators. Now, I wouldn't want to startle a grizzly, especially a sow with a cub, but if you ever look back and see a black bear trailing you, you'd better pray you have a rifle and that you're a good shot, because it's coming after you and two things are certain: It can run faster, and climb better, than you can. If you don't get it, it's going to get you."

That was pretty much bears in a nutshell, so Angie didn't add to it right then. When they reached the camp she'd institute the camp safety rules, but all of that was better done when they could see the actual layout of the camp.

They were wasting daylight, time in which they might actually do some hunting and, please God, bag a bear right away, so she said, "Let's ride."

Chapter Eight

Mitchell Davis dismounted, looked around the camp she'd leased, and surveyed the portable toilet set off to the side. He turned and looked at her, an incredulous expression in his cold eyes. "You've got to be kidding me," he said in a tone so sarcastic that Chad flinched and turned red yet again; on the ride up, he'd been the target over and over again of Davis's serrated tongue, which chewed up and shredded rather than destroyed with a fast, clean slice. Davis had something to say, none of it good, about how Chad rode, the brand of rifle he owned, the cheapness of his scope, even the newness of his boots.

During the ride Angie had thought several times that if she'd been Chad, she'd have dug in her heels, told Davis to kiss her ass, and gone back to the truck. Now, with that hostility turned on her, she bit her tongue and silently apologized to Chad, because he'd no doubt kept his silence for the same reason she was keeping hers: She needed the money. This was her payback for feeling superior, when she wasn't at all; she was in the same boat Chad was in, paddling for all she was worth.

"Maybe I'll take up meditation," she mused aloud, earning a covert chuckle from Chad that he quickly turned into a cough.

She didn't know what the big deal was about the camp. Exactly what had Davis been expecting? A lodge, maybe? She had no idea what Chad had told him, how he'd described the accommodations to Davis, but she'd been completely honest with Chad about the camp when she had leased it. It wasn't the best she'd ever been at, but neither was it the worst. At least they weren't sleeping on the ground, and she'd done that more times than she cared to remember.

The campsite was in a picturesque spot, on a fairly level section of the mountainside, surrounded by lodgepole pine and tamarack. Below, a crystal clear creek wound its way along the valley floor, bracketed by stands of spruce and black cottonwood. Taller peaks, white-capped with snow, loomed over and around them. Huge boulders and thick tangles of chokeberry bushes dotted the landscape. The presence of the creek and the chokeberry bushes upped their chances of finding bear, which was the reason for being here in the first place. She could have taken them to a place with more luxurious accommodations, but the odds of Davis shooting a bear went down.

There were six wooden platforms, but only three of them were set up with tents. Angie deeply appreciated the platforms; when the rain began, that meant water wouldn't be running through their tents. The tents were heavy-duty canvas, each with a sort of offset wing in front of the entrance, for extra privacy. She knew for a fact that silhouettes couldn't be seen through the canvas, which was a big plus for her. The tents weren't huge, about seven and a half feet by five feet, but that was plenty big enough for a cot and their belongings. They each had an inflatable mattress to go on the cot, and a sleeping bag. The portable toilet took care of calls of nature, and she'd brought enough wet wipes for them to stay reasonably clean and unstinky for a week—longer than that, if need be.

A lot of their food was prepackaged, but a food-prep area had been set up a couple of hundred yards away. There was a camp stove for making coffee, which was as much of a necessity as clothing, in her opinion. There were battery-operated LED lamps in the tents, flashlights, extra batteries. She had Swedish steel for making fires, and if by chance the weather turned bitterly cold, which it wasn't supposed to do, each tent was stocked with a small oil heater.

Best of all, the rough corral had a section with a roof over the feed troughs, so the horses had a bit of shelter. If the wind got up, she'd cut some pine branches to brace against the corral as a wind break. She believed in taking care of her horses, because their lives could well depend on the animals.

As far as she was concerned, this camp pretty much had everything except television and cell phone service. If Davis was as experienced as he'd said he was, wouldn't he have known what to expect, or at least had a general idea?

"Which tent is mine?" he demanded, his voice tight.

Without hesitation, Angie pointed to the one on the far left. She'd take the one farthest to the right; she wanted to put as much distance between them as possible. Granted, it wasn't much, because the tents were separated by only about ten feet, but every little bit counted.

Davis left his horse standing and disappeared into the tent.

She stared after him, her mouth falling open at the absolute boorishness of the man.

"I'm so sorry," Chad whispered, actually wringing his hands.

She shook herself, and squared her shoulders. "His manners aren't your fault," she said, reaching for the reins of the dark bay before he could take it into his head to wander off.

Chad helped her get the horses unsaddled and watered, and the supplies put away in her tent. She wouldn't have much room to move around, but that didn't matter; she wouldn't be in the tent much anyway, and this way everything was at hand, plus no prowling predator could get into their supply and destroy every-thing, at least not without alerting her. She not only kept her rifle at hand, but she also had a pistol, and she slept with it.

As she'd expected, Chad was moving a little gingerly, but he didn't complain. Soon enough they had all the chores done, though the work would have gone faster if Davis had stirred him-self to help. She noticed Chad kept darting little anxious glances at the tent, and finally he said hesitantly, "Should I . . . I mean, were you planning to do any hunting today?"

"It's wasted time if we don't at least scout around," she pointed out. "I know where I found bear sign before, and we need to see if there's any fresh sign." Taking a bear wasn't an easy proposition; Montana didn't allow hunters to put out bait for bears or use scent to pull them in. They had to *find* the bear, if possible call one in using a bear call, and their hunting time was limited from half an hour before sunrise to half an hour after sunset.

"I'll, uh, I'll call Mitchell," Chad said, squaring his shoulders, and went off to Davis's tent.

Angie got out her hunter orange vest and put it on, checked her two cans of bear spray to make certain she could get to them without having to move anything out of the way. She loaded her rifle, put an extra box of ammo in one of the vest pockets. She had her binoculars, her bear call, a bottle of water, and while she was waiting for Chad to come back out of Davis's tent she hastily ate a protein bar, chasing it with water. The biscuit she'd eaten for breakfast had long since worn off and she was starving.

Chad came back out of the tent, his face the dark red that had become so familiar on the ride into the mountains. Sweat glis-tened on his forehead. "He, um, he said when you found the bear he'd come along. Until then, he isn't interested."

Now was a very good time to begin meditating. Angie held her breath for a few seconds, then let it out slowly. Again. There, that was better. Maybe there really was something to this breathing stuff. She didn't think she had any huge anger issues—other than where Dare Callahan was concerned, then all bets were off—but she supposed she had her moments. Everyone had a breaking point, and she was well past hers where Davis was concerned.

Most of the time she loved her job. Almost all of her clients were perfectly nice people who enjoyed the outdoors, who loved a challenge, who simply liked to hunt. When they weren't hunting they were telling stories, talking, joking, laughing. They came up here to relax, to have a good time.

This week wasn't going to be like that. She'd never refunded a fee and walked away in her professional life, and she wouldn't this time either because she needed the money, but oh, boy, she wanted to. Whether or not she and Dare agreed on a deal they could both live with, she had bills to pay, so she'd stick.

It hit her that this might very well be her last job as a hunting guide—here, anyway. She didn't have anything else scheduled, and the odds were that come spring she'd be living in a new place, getting accustomed to a new job and new neighbors. Maybe she didn't have any choice, but damn it, she didn't want to go out like this, annoyed and stressed to the max.

But it looked as if that was what she was going to get. Maybe this was a sign that she was doing the right thing, selling out and moving on.

"He's an ass," she muttered, then realized she'd said that aloud and looked at Chad with an appalled expression. "Oh, God, I'm so sorry. I apologize. I should never have said that."

Chad mopped his shiny face, then gave her a shy smile. "Yeah, I know," he said, keeping his tone low. Then he gave a helpless shrug, as if to say, What can you do?

She should have known, should have expected it when Davis had left her to take care of all the horses, not even tending to the bay he'd been riding. He was a decent horseman, she'd give him that, which made it even more incomprehensible that he hadn't offered to take care of the animal that had hauled his ass up here. His personality would be vastly improved if he were more like the horse he'd ridden: silent, and gelded. Come to think of it, that would apply to a certain other man she could think of, though it totally pissed her off that she couldn't put him completely out of her mind.

"I don't know what's wrong," Chad said, darting an anxious look at the closed tent on the far end. "I know he likes to hunt, he talks about it all the time. I really enjoyed going out with you last time, and I thought, well, I had no idea he'd be . . ." He let his sentence trail off, evidently not wanting to call his client a bastard.

"Not your fault, Chad," Angie said honestly. She smiled at him, trying to ease his discomfort. "Maybe we'll get lucky and both of you will bag a bear tomorrow. I don't think anyone would mind if this trip ends early."

Chad shrugged. "If he gets a bear, I'll be happy to call the hunt done. I mean, I have my permit for a bear, but I'm really not much of a hunter. I just don't get into it."

That was kind of sad, that he forced himself to go on this kind of a trip with a man who seemed bent on making everyone around him miserable.

"Then why don't you take it easy the rest of the day," she said, thinking of his sore muscles, "while I see what I can find."

A relieved expression chased across his face before he blinked and said, "But isn't that dangerous, going out on your own?"

"Dangerous enough, but I'm armed, and I have the bear spray." She thought about saddling up the roan and riding it, but the idea was to not spook any nearby bear. Besides, she wasn't going that far, and the horses needed a rest. The trail was rough and mostly uphill, and the brush was thick where she needed to go. She felt her stomach draw up tight at the idea of going in alone, but she'd done it before when she scouted up here. All she wanted was to find some fresh bear scat, then she'd quietly and quickly retreat, and tomorrow they'd go hunting.

Breathe.

Dare thought about calling Harlan so Harlan could remind him again why this was such a good idea. What else was the satellite phone good for if he couldn't call an old friend who'd convinced him to act like a stupid idiot, so he could reinforce the idea?

Fishing. He wanted to *fish*. That was definitely a good idea. Angie wouldn't need any help from him, or accept it even if she did, but he could use some down time. Fishing was just the ticket.

Even though guiding hunters and fishermen was his job and he spent a lot of time in the mountains, he still loved it here. The solitude, the rough landscape, the smell of the mountain—they never got old. When he'd been a hell-raising teenager he'd spent a lot of time up here on his own, but now he was a damn adult, responsible, a small-business owner, and he'd been too damn busy to enjoy life. He'd make trips up this way to resupply, or take care of repairs, but coming alone to fish? No. There was always too much to do, and taking a little vacation of his own was so far down on his list that he didn't even know it was there. Maybe he was way past due for this kind of break.

The fact that Angie was also on the mountain with the men who gave Harlan the willies . . . that was a coincidence. Nothing more.

Yeah, right. After dismounting, Dare turned so he faced the direction of the camp Angie had leased for the week. He had a great sense of direction and he knew this mountain better than anyone, so he mentally placed the camp almost immediately. If not for the mountains, trees, and the distance, he'd be looking right at Angie and her hunting party. He'd been there a time or two himself, knew how far it was from his camp, which paths led to that camp. It wasn't the best, nor was it the worst. What it was, was acceptable.

Harlan had written down the names of the men Angie was

with, and he'd said he'd do a search on the computer to see if he
could find anything suspicious, then call Dare on the sat phone if
he did. Dare doubted anything would turn up, but Harlan would
feel better if he was doing something productive.

Angie's truck and trailer, and an unknown SUV, had already
been at Ray Lattimore's place when Dare had pulled in with his
own horse trailer. Ray, in his early seventies but as tough as old
jerky, had come out to talk a bit. "Angie Powell went up early this
morning," he said, nodding toward her truck. "Two clients with
her. One's useless, the other's an asshole."

Dare grunted. "That so?"

Ray had more of his opinions to share, and did so at length. By
the time he was finished, Dare was an hour later than he'd
planned on being, but what the hell, this was a *vacation*. He wasn't
punching a damn time clock.

Because this wasn't a guided hunt, he'd decided to use the trip
to do some training on a new horse he'd bought, a three-year-old
buckskin that showed promise of being a great trail horse. The
youngster was full of piss and vinegar and Dare had to stay on his
toes, ready for anything, but he enjoyed the challenge. When they
arrived at his camp safe and sound, overall he was pleased. He
wouldn't put a client on the horse just yet, though; the buckskin
needed a lot more experience and settling down. This was his first
time in the mountains, and some of the less-secure footing made
him nervous.

Dare unpacked and settled in with the ease and automatic
mindlessness of a man who'd done it a thousand times. There was
comfort in the routine, almost a sense of coming home. He saw to
the buckskin first, then unpacked his fishing gear and supplies for
the week. This was the first time he'd ever had this place to himself, and it felt odd to bring in one air mattress, one sleeping bag.
Normally the quarters felt cramped, but with just himself and one
horse, damned if everything didn't feel roomy. He should do this
more often.

This was his camp, not a lease, and Dare had designed and built it himself, with safety from predators his foremost consideration. The building was small and rough-looking, blending into the background so well it was almost invisible from any distance, but it was two stories tall and a hell of a lot sturdier than any tent—sturdier than most hunting cabins, come to that, and definitely what he considered a better design for bear country.

The bottom of the building was horse stalls, while the top was a sleeping platform, partitioned into small areas with curtains that could be pulled over the openings for privacy, but the platform itself was open to the stalls below, with a ladder that could be pulled up. The heat from the horses' bodies rose, effectively heating the sleeping platform so during cold weather it was almost comfortable. During hot weather, the small windows in the upper section could be opened. The clients on the sleeping platform were always safe from predators of any kind, and they had a clear shot into the lower level in case a bear actually tried to claw through the heavy double door below. From the higher position, Dare knew he could take out any predator before it got near the horses.

He'd never had a bear try to get to his horses, but in the mountains it paid to be prepared for anything and everything.

Dare was nothing if not prepared.

Tomorrow morning would be soon enough to head to the stream he had in mind for a little fly-fishing. The trail to that stream would take him close by Angie's camp, but so what? It was a free country. If she saw him, she'd just have to deal.

But it wouldn't hurt to let those two guys she was with know there was someone nearby, someone who knew Angie, and who was also armed. Dare didn't mind doing the menacing act, because for the most part it wasn't an act. He'd lived through too much, done too much; menacing came natural to him.

Chapter Nine

Angie eased forward, ears straining for any snuffling noises, any sounds of twigs being broken. She tried to keep the wind in her face, because bears stank to high heaven, and her nose might pick up something before her ears did. On the other hand, she kept constant watch behind her, because a bear's sense of smell was a jillion times sharper than hers and one could easily be downwind of her. Just the thought of turning around and seeing a bear behind her made her heart squeeze in terror.

Out here by herself, there was no hiding from or disguising the fact that she wasn't just uneasy about hunting bear, she was downright afraid of them. The only thing that gave her the confidence to be out here looking for bear scat was the rifle in her hand, loaded with heavy-duty ammunition. But a big bear could keep coming another forty, fifty feet or more after taking a fatal hit, and if the shot was off by a little the animal could do a tremendous amount of damage before going down.

When she'd come up here to scout out the territory, she'd been terrified every minute, even though she'd done everything she could to mitigate the danger. She'd made her clothes as scent-free as possible, but that was standard. The last thing she wanted was for a big blackie to catch her scent and either vanish from the area or, worse, think *dinner!* and start stalking her. The absolute worst thing that could happen would be that in the heavy brush she'd stumble too close to a sow grizzly and her cub, or cubs, and be on them before she knew it. If there was a more ferocious animal on earth than that, her imagination wouldn't stretch far enough to envision it. A female grizzly protecting her cubs was a buzz saw of destruction; even male grizzlies would give her a wide berth.

Damn Mitchell Davis. Why couldn't he want an elk, or a big-horn sheep, or a moose? Moose were dangerous, but she wasn't terrified of them. Bear . . . the very first nightmare she could remember having, when she was five or six years old, had featured a bear. She had no idea what had triggered the nightmare, but it had been so vivid, and in technicolor, that to this day she remembered almost every detail. She'd been running, and a black bear had been after her. Various people had tried to help and the bear had killed them all, and kept coming. She'd awakened, whimpering, before it reached her and she remembered lying curled up in bed, shaking in terror, with the cover pulled over her head until morning came.

Viewed in that light, becoming a hunting guide wasn't the smartest move she'd ever made. This was bear territory; every guide trip she made, even if it was a photography expedition, brought her into their backyard. She didn't have a phobia about bears, exactly, but she was definitely afraid, which she hoped meant she was less likely to have a close encounter of the bad kind because she was extra cautious.

Bears weren't the only big predators around; there were cougars, too. Strange that she wasn't as afraid of them as she was a bear, because she wouldn't want to come face-to-face with a cougar, either, but she supposed she was allowed her points of il-

logic. She waited for five minutes, listening hard and hearing
nothing more than very small rustles—no grunts, no coughs, no
sounds of branches being snapped or logs rolled out of the way—
before she ventured closer to the game trail she'd located.

There was the tree with the claw marks, the thicket of chokeberry bushes where the black fur had been snagged. She mentally
mapped out a grid and walked it, taking her time, carefully examining the ground as well as constantly checking her surroundings.
The silver ribbon of creek below helped her keep her bearings, so
she always knew exactly where she was in relation to the camp.
The ground sloped away to the right of her, punctuated by groups
of boulders, stands of trees. Something metallic caught her eye,
over by some of the rocks, but bear scat wasn't metallic; probably
someone had left some trash, which ticked her off. She'd pick it
up on her way back to the camp.

No scat. She moved upward another hundred yards, but
though she found some scat it wasn't as fresh as what she'd found
a few days before. Reversing directions, she began working down
toward the creek. Water was a lodestone. Eventually, every creature in the mountains needed water.

When she reached the steep drop-away where she'd seen the
glint of metal, she left the game trail and carefully worked her way
over to it. A careless step could mean a sprained ankle, or, God
forbid, a broken leg or a concussion, and she didn't trust either
Chad Krugman or Mitchell Davis to help her. She'd told Chad in
detail where she was going, but as inept as he was in the wilderness
she didn't have a lot of faith he could find her. Davis had still been
in his tent when she left, so he didn't have any idea where she'd
gone. If anything happened, she'd have to depend on herself;
there was no one else.

A camera. The metallic glint came from a microdigital camera. She leaned down and picked it up. It was scuffed up, dirty,
and probably wouldn't work after being left out in the open. She
examined it, saw that the switch had been left in the "on" position.

When she flicked the switch again, the little screen lit up. Out of curiosity she hit "playback" and scrolled through some shots of the scenery. There were a hundred fifty-three pictures, but after viewing a few of them she turned the camera off. She'd look at the rest later, though she doubted there'd be any way of telling who the camera belonged to. It must have fallen out of the photographer's pocket, who knows how many days ago.

She slipped the camera into the inside pocket of her jacket and zipped it shut, then resettled her orange vest. She looked around once more, and that was when she saw a shred of cloth, maybe ten yards away, close to a big cluster of boulders. It looked like part of a blanket, maybe. She checked all around her, saw nothing, so she eased in that direction.

Not a blanket. Part of a plaid shirt. The plaid was visible on a small portion of the fabric; the rest of it was black and stiff with blood.

She stopped in her tracks, hair lifting on the back of her neck. She didn't go any closer to pick up the fabric, just stood where she was and once more checked her surroundings, three-sixty. The mountainside was quiet.

She looked back at the ground surrounding the fragment of shirt. The ground was dark in patches, gouges in the earth showing dark and raw, mixed with the imprints of big pads, the short claws that said black bear, not grizzly. There were scuff marks, as if something had been dragged. She followed the drag marks with her gaze, saw what looked like a piece of raw meat, dark red, stringy.

She edged back, away from the scene, so she wouldn't disturb it, then farther down the trail a few yards before once again working her way across. The going was harder now, the slope much steeper; she had to brace herself with one hand, check each step to make sure it was solid before she put all of her weight on it. When she was even with the cluster of boulders, she looked up.

And gagged.

The man's remains—possibly a man, she couldn't be certain, because there was no face that she could see—had had dirt scratched over them. Bear did that with a half-eaten kill. The viscera had been eaten. Part of an arm lay nearby. And as if to leave proof of ownership, she could see where the bear had crapped.

Holy shit. Holy shit. Holy shit! Not the bear shit, but oh-my-god-get-me-out-of-here kind of shit.

She'd seen wildlife kills before. Nature wasn't neat; it was messy and brutal. But she'd never before found a half-eaten human, and her stomach heaved. She fought down the nausea, fought the abrupt sense of panic as she suddenly imagined the bear looming right behind her on the trail just like in her nightmare.

Swiftly she pulled her rifle from the scabbard on her back, jacked a round into the firing chamber. The reassuring mechanical sounds of metal parts moving were all she could hear. She did another three-sixty check. No bear, no cougar, or coyotes attempting to raid the bear's kill. Nothing. The "nothing" was almost as terrifying as "something," because she knew the bear was in the vicinity. They didn't willingly abandon their kills. It wasn't close enough to scent her, though, or she'd have already been fending off an attack.

But if it came back for its kill, and crossed her scent trail, would it track her? Black bears did that. They stalked people. Humans were just part of their food chain.

She returned to the trail, heading back for the camp as fast as she could safely go. She checked the time, calculating distances. This had to be reported immediately, the Montana Fish and Wildlife Department alerted that there was a man-eater in the vicinity. The body had to be recovered and identified. But it was already so late in the afternoon that she'd barely have time to make it back to the camp before dark; there was no way they could make it to Ray Lattimore's.

Even though Mitchell Davis hadn't seemed thrilled with anything about the hunt, she bet he'd make a stink about it being canceled. She'd have to either refund the money or give them an extension on this hunt, if they could stay longer.

Or they could stay at the camp while she rode back to Latti-more's. If she left at first light, she could be back tomorrow afternoon. She'd be able to travel faster if she was alone. Maybe she could convince them to do that.

The sun had already sunk below the mountain peaks when she got back to camp. Neither of the two men were in sight. "Davis!" she called. "Chad! We have a problem!"

Chad almost immediately popped out of his tent, and Davis emerged, his cold and dark expression in place, from his tent a few seconds later. "Did you find bear sign?"

"Yeah," she said grimly. "I also found a body. Looks like a bear killed him. We'll have to head back down the mountain in the morning to report it."

"A body?" Chad echoed faintly.

"Bullshit," said Davis. "It was probably a wild animal you saw, and you panicked."

"Last time I checked, wild animals don't wear plaid shirts, or carry digital cameras," she snapped. "We go tomorrow to report it. If you don't want to make the ride, I'll go by myself. It's up to you. We can either extend the hunt a day or reschedule."

He looked around, disgust in his expression. "I want a refund."

"Fine, you'll get a refund." It wasn't worth arguing about. Someone had died a gruesome death, and this asshole didn't like being inconvenienced. Sure, she needed the money, but she'd get by. Dare Callahan's offer was still out there.

To her surprise, Chad said, "I want to stay. Angie rides down and back tomorrow, it's just one day." He shoved his hands into his pockets. "There's no reason to leave."

"Don't be stupid," Davis growled. "The body will have to be retrieved, and that'll take at least one team. Then the Fish and

Wildlife Department will have people all over this mountain, hunting for this particular bear. Everything will be spooked. This close to the end of the season, there won't be any decent hunting until next year."

He was probably right, and she didn't care. "I'll refund your money," she said with finality in her tone. "We ride back down to-morrow. I'm leaving at first light, so be ready." Because as of this minute she no longer considered Davis a client, she narrowed her eyes at him and said, "And you can saddle your own damn horse."

Supper, what there was of it, was strained and silent. Angie kept her rifle close to hand, because the theory went that once a man-killer, always a man-killer. Couple that with a black bear's propensity for stalking, and she had more than enough reason to be alert. It seemed everyone was angry at everyone else, so they all retired to their respective tents as soon as they returned from the food-prep site.

She secured the zipper on the tent flap so it couldn't be opened from the outside, then sat on the cot for a while, so mentally exhausted she needed a minute to regroup. She couldn't get the gruesome image of the mauled body out of her head. Yeah, she had to deal with people like Mitchell Davis, her business had taken a nosedive, and she had to deal with Dare Callahan, but all of that was nothing when balanced against what had happened to that poor guy.

Sleep might be impossible, but at least she could rest. Eventually she went through her nightly camp routine, using the wet wipes for the camp equivalent of a bath. Sleeping in jeans could get uncomfortable, so she always brought a pair of sweatpants to sleep in. In the summer she'd pair that with a T-shirt, but this time of year the T-shirt was exchanged for a sweatshirt. Between the sweats and the sleeping bag, she was usually toasty warm without having to resort to the camp heater. After pulling on a pair of thick socks, she crawled into the sleeping bag. She checked to make sure all essentials were right there at hand. Rifle—check. Boots—check. Pistol—check. Flashlight—check. She was as safe as she could make herself.

She reached out to turn off the camp light, and took one of those deep meditation breaths, because the darkness inside the tent was absolute. Normally that didn't bother her, and from experience she knew that after a while her eyes would adjust and there would be a very, very faint lightening, but tonight she felt as if the darkness was alive, pressing down on her. She lay very still, listening to the night, forcing herself to breathe.

Maybe she dozed, maybe she didn't. She heard the first far-off rumble of thunder, and lifted her hand to look at the luminous face of her watch. Thirteen after midnight. Great. She'd been hoping the rain would hold off, given that she had to ride back to Lattimore's, but it looked as if the weather front was rolling in right on schedule. She could almost feel the air changing, gathering force and electrical energy. The wind began whipping through the trees, producing a sound that was almost like a low, mournful whistle.

At first she thought it was the wind she heard. She'd been restlessly trying to find a comfortable position within the confines of the sleeping bag, which normally felt roomy enough, but tonight seemed to be twisting around her legs. With a sigh she forced herself to stillness, because she had to get *some* sleep, even if it wasn't much.

The noise came again. Angie stopped breathing, every muscle in her freezing as she listened. Her heart rate doubled. *Bear?* Without thought she darted out her hand, touched her rifle, and just the feel of the smooth wood settled her heart rate down.

She cocked her head, listening.

No, not a bear. And not the wind, either. Voices. She definitely heard voices, too far away for the words to be distinct. There was a sharpness, a tone, that told her an argument was going on. For whatever reason, Davis and Chad were going at it, though it was probably more Davis berating Chad for the hunt being a total failure than anything like a real argument. But—

At this time of night? Really?

Exasperation surged, pushing out the fright. Part of her wanted to just leave them out there, let them slug it out or do whatever else their manly little hearts pleased, but if she could possibly get some sleep, even just ten minutes, she'd rather do that than listen to them argue.

Growling to herself, she pulled herself free of the sleeping bag. She didn't want to turn on the camp light, because it was too bright, so she grabbed the flannel shirt she'd pulled off and draped it over the flashlight before she turned it on. There—that was just about right. She had enough dim light to see what she was doing, but her senses weren't being assaulted by so much light that it would overwhelm what little chance she had of getting some sleep that night.

She stomped her feet into her boots, tied the laces. Then she dragged on her coat, because even though the weather was mild for November, it was still November, she was still in Montana, and the mountain air at night was cold. Swiftly she unzipped the tent flap, then debated for about two seconds on whether or not to get the rifle or the pistol. The pistol was more convenient. The rifle packed more power. She got the rifle.

For reasons she couldn't explain even to herself, she turned off the flashlight. She gripped it in her left hand, and the rifle in her right, and ducked out of the tent.

Standing there, both of the other tents were to her left, and so were the sounds of argument. She stood a moment, letting her eyes adjust to the darkness again, because even the dim light she'd allowed from the flashlight had been enough to destroy her night vision. When she could make out dim outlines again, she headed toward the voices.

Lightning glowed overhead, outlining a towering mountain of

clouds, and thunder rumbled. The storm blew its breath ahead of it, as if to clear its path, and the wind whipped her hair around her head. She passed Chad's tent; it was dark, but there was a light on in Davis's. The voices weren't coming from there, though, they were coming from the direction of the cook camp . . . not as far away as that, but in the trees.

A few fat raindrops splatted on her head, on the ground around her. Great. She could turn around and get her rain slicker, or she could try to break up the argument and get everyone back in their tents before the real rain got here. She chose to plow ahead, on the theory that the sooner she cooled things down, the better. If she delayed, the situation might escalate to actual fist-swinging.

Another flash of lightning, this time closer, thunder booming right on its heels. In the corral, the horses began moving around, neighing anxiously. Samson didn't normally act up during a storm, but she didn't know how the new horses would react; storms sounded different up in the mountains than in the valleys. This high up, they were closer to the heart of the storm; the lightning was brighter, the thunder boomed and echoed as if it was right on top of them. After she got the humans settled down, she'd see what she could do about settling down the horses.

She skirted Davis's tent, and through the trees saw a light. Yet another flash of lightning briefly illuminated the two men, but neither of them were paying any attention to either the weather or their surroundings. She stomped toward them.

"—steal from me!" she heard Davis say, his tone low and vicious.

"Hey!" she yelled, and turned on her flashlight so they could see her, though the lightning aided her with another white-hot blast. "Damn it, put this on hold until tomorrow!"

Davis turned toward her, his jaw set. "Fuck that—" he began, then the night was split by a sharp crack that cut off his words, and the crack itself was swallowed by a tremendous crash of lightning that split open the heavens and let all the pent-up water come pouring down on them in a solid sheet.

Davis staggered back, then fell. Her flashlight beam cut through the thick veil of rain, played over him, and she saw the awkward, boneless position of his body. He wasn't moving. His eyes were open, but he wasn't moving. In the next second she swung the flashlight back toward Chad just as he pointed a pistol at her. One of the horses gave a shrill, panicked scream; his hand jerked, and he fired.

Chapter Ten

Angie dived to her left, hitting the ground hard and rolling as she desperately thumbed the switch on the flashlight, then kept on rolling. She tried to tuck the rifle against her body but it caught on something and tore loose from her grip. She didn't stop rolling, just left the rifle there on the ground because if she stopped she was dead. More shots came, so fast the booming cracks were right on top of each other. The blasts of lightning would reveal her position, she had to get behind a tree, something—

Another white-hot flash, and the earth shuddered as the lightning bolt went to ground somewhere nearby. The thunder was deafening. In that ungodly light she saw Chad, pistol still in his hand, but he was turned in the direction of the tents and didn't see her on the ground off to his right side. The horses were raising hell in the corral; it sounded as if they were trying to tear it down. Chad moved forward, swinging a flashlight from side to side, trying to find her. With nowhere to go, unable to reach cover, Angie simply buried her face in the wet ground and stayed still, praying, hoping the heavy rain would obscure his sight enough.

The rain pounded on her with a force that felt like a thousand tiny hammers. The earth was churned into instant mud, rivulets of water becoming streams that gushed down the side of the mountain.

Mentally Angie grappled with what had just happened, trying to make the last thirty seconds fit into her conception of reality. This couldn't have happened. Chad had *not* shot Davis, had *not* shot at her. Why would he? What had happened, what had she missed?

Out of the corner of her eye she saw Chad move past her position, playing the flashlight beam on the tents as if he expected to find her crouched between them. She lifted her head a tiny fraction, just enough that she could see the gleam of the rifle lying in the rain, ten, maybe fifteen feet away, but it might as well be a hundred feet. If she hadn't dropped the rifle, she'd have him; he was three-quarters turned away from her. But she *had* dropped the weapon, and if she leaped for it, he'd hear her, and the footing was so sloppy now she wasn't certain she could make the distance without falling.

One of the horses, probably Samson, was now doing his damnedest to knock down the corral. Chad jerked in that direction, his back now completely toward her, and Angie gathered herself, getting up on her hands and knees, the toes of her boots digging into the mud—

—and another flash of lightning revealed the monster coming out of the trees, a huge black hulk padding forward with a swinging gait, head down, jaws popping with a hideous sound as if it were cracking bones. Chad turned around just in time to catch a glimpse of it, then she heard the choked shriek he gave as he hurled himself toward the horses.

All the blood rushed from her head. She heard a buzzing noise, and even though the lightning kept flashing her vision kind of washed out, as if she were looking at a photograph faded almost beyond perception. She thought she might fall face forward in the mud, helpless, but if she made any movement the bear might see her and charge, so she forced herself to freeze there like a runner in the blocks, waiting for the monster to hurl itself after Chad and seize him in its popping jaws.

Instead, it raised one massive paw and swiped at Davis's body. It shoved its snout against him, flipped him over. Davis's legs and arms flopped like a rag doll's. The bear circled him, bouncing up and down a little on its front paws. From behind the tents came the clatter of poles falling, a sound she'd heard so many times she knew exactly what it was. A rush of hoofs pounding on the ground, one of the horses with a dark form hunched on its back— Chad taking the horses, all of them, and running.

Leaving her alone there with the bear.

For a few seconds that felt like an eternity, she couldn't force her panic-numbed brain to function. Then, slowly, she began to analyze the situation. The bear was . . . what . . . twenty, maybe thirty yards away? A bear didn't have great eyesight. It had very good hearing and a stupendous sense of smell, but the rain and wind were coming at her from the bear's direction. It couldn't smell her. Its attention was on Davis's body. It couldn't see all that well anyway, and the rain further shielded her.

Every one of her instincts shrieked at her not to move, not to attract its attention, but she needed that rifle. To get it, she'd have to crawl fifteen feet closer to the bear, and pray it didn't see her. Slowly, so slowly, she lifted her right hand from the mud and moved it forward. Next was her left knee. Then her left hand, still clutching the flashlight. Right knee. Repeat the process. Slowly, slowly, forcing herself to drag in deep, controlled breaths through her mouth, then silently letting the air ease out of her, not putting any force behind it. If she didn't make any noise, maybe the bear wouldn't notice her.

Her hand touched the stock of the rifle. She froze for a moment, making certain the bear was still preoccupied. The almost constant flashes of lightning showed it in a kind of freeze-frame effect as it bit into Davis's stomach and slung him around with a toss of its powerful head, tearing flesh free and sending his body tumbling. Like a cat with a new toy, the huge bear pounced on the dead man, completely oblivious to the storm crashing around them.

The bear's back was to her. *Now.* Angie pulled the rifle toward her. The mud sucked at it, resisted her efforts to lift it. Feverishly, her hands shaking, she tried to wipe the mud away but reality slapped her in the face: She couldn't fire this rifle until it had been cleaned. The mechanism was too caked with mud.

She almost whimpered, almost collapsed in the mud in despair. Only the thought of the bear doing to her what it was now doing to Davis kept her from dissolving into an unending wail. Silent. She had to be silent.

Just as slowly, deliberately, as she had crawled forward, she now repeated the process in reverse, dragging the rifle with her. She didn't stop until there were trees between her and the bear, until the blasts of lightning no longer revealed the gruesome scene. Only then did she stand, clinging to a tree trunk and hauling herself up. Her chest heaved with silent sobs, sobs she didn't dare give voice to.

Think! she commanded herself. She had to think, or she would die. She couldn't panic. These next few minutes might well determine whether she lived or died, so she'd better make some damn good decisions.

She couldn't stay here. Even minus the bear, there was Chad. She'd seen him kill a man; he'd already tried to kill her. The bear might continue on its way, but Chad would come back. He'd have to.

That meant she had to leave. She had to walk off this mountain, in the night, in one of the worst storms she'd ever seen. She might get struck by lightning, but she'd rather that happen than let the bear get her. And that lily-livered little bastard Chad had taken all the horses, probably hoping the bear would save him the trouble of taking care of her. By the time the bear got through with Davis, would it be possible to tell he'd died from a gunshot wound, rather than being *eaten*? Would there even be an investigation, or would the situation be so self-evident that it would be written off as a bear attack, a second one at that. And if she were the third victim . . . the rogue bear would be shot, and a murderer would walk free.

She was damned if she'd let that happen.

She needed things from her tent. Her instinct said to run, and run like hell. Her brain said she needed food and water, she needed a way to keep warm, she needed a weapon that actually worked. All of those things were in her tent.

Staying in the trees as much as possible, feeling her way between flashes of lightning and trying to stand motionless whenever the sky lit up, she made her way to the tent. She was completely drenched, her sweatpants soaking up water like a sponge and hanging heavy on her, threatening to slide down her hips. Her hair was plastered against her head, and she could almost feel her body heat leaching away. By the time she ducked into the tent, she was shaking so hard there was no way she could have stood motionless, so it was a damn good thing bears didn't have great eyesight.

Okay, what did she need? Her saddle bag. She'd have to have dry clothes, and the saddlebag would keep them dry. Her slicker. Her clothes couldn't get any wetter, but the slicker would help keep her body heat in, and if she found a place to shelter it would keep the rain off her. The pistol. It might not stop a bear, but it would damn sure stop Chad Krugman, and it would make the bear take notice.

What next? Food. She grabbed some protein bars, shoved

them into the saddlebag. Ditto a bottle of water. One bottle wasn't much, but water was heavy, and she didn't want to weigh herself down. The flashlight.

She thought of quickly stripping off her soaked sweatpants and replacing them with jeans, but soaked jeans wouldn't be any better. She hurriedly put some clothes into the saddlebags, added some extra boxes of ammo because regardless of weight extra ammo was always a good thing, then buckled the straps. She pulled her slicker on over her wet coat, slid her muddy rifle into the scabbard and slung it over her shoulder.

Then she opened the tent flap, and eased into the night.

She still didn't run. She had to put distance between herself and the bear, between herself and Chad, and the best way to do that was carefully. She couldn't turn on the flashlight, so she placed each step with care.

She couldn't even stop to think. Both of the killers she fled fell into the "what the hell?" category, but she didn't have the luxury of analyzing why things had happened, she simply had to get the hell away from there. She had to focus on keeping her footing, on staying downwind of the bear, on not getting hit on the head by a falling tree limb or struck by lightning. She had enough to think about. She'd worry about "why" later.

Lattimore's place was a long way away, and once Chad discovered she wasn't here in the camp, he'd have to know exactly where she was heading. All she could do was keep moving, away from the carnage, away from what she'd seen. Caution was more important than speed . . . but, *damn*, she could use some more speed. The urge to run beckoned her, and still she resisted. She couldn't run for hours, and she sure as hell didn't need to try running in the dark, on slippery mud.

Dare Callahan's camp was closer than Lattimore's, a lot closer, but she didn't need shelter; she needed help. Besides, the camp would be locked up tight, and even if she could locate it in the dark she wouldn't be able to get in. Heading that way on the off chance that she could get in would cost her precious time, and gain her nothing in reaching help. She didn't have a moment to lose, because Chad would be coming after her.

If not for the rain, she could stop for a moment and listen for them—the bear and the man—but the thundering rain seemed to overwhelm any other sound. The rain didn't just splatter, it hammered. The wind whistled. The only good thing was that if she couldn't hear them, then they couldn't hear her. The weather hampered her, beat at her, but it was also protecting her by shielding her within its ferocious heart.

She aimed downhill. Where else could she go? She didn't try to stay on the trail, which followed the path of least resistance, because that was where Chad was likely to be. The going was rough and uneven, so slick she could barely stay upright. She clung to whatever she could get her hand around: bushes, hanging tree limbs, rocks.

The wind shifted. She felt the difference on her face. She stopped, mentally working out the bear's location. Rain or no rain, the bear would be able to catch her scent if she continued in this direction. On the other hand, if she changed directions she'd be moving away from Lattimore's place. For that matter, without being able to see the bear, she had no idea if it was still in the same location or if it had moved on—to the west, away from her, or paralleling her movements at a higher altitude, or coming in behind her.

No matter what, she needed to move. She stretched out her left foot, feeling for solid ground, only to find a slope of mud. She tried to catch herself, grabbing for a bush, but she was already in mid-step when her left foot slid out from under her. She tried to catch herself with her right foot, only to have it land in a hole she hadn't been able to see in the darkness. She lurched forward, completely off-balance. In the split second during which she realized she was going down, feeling helpless and stupid and afraid,

she put out her hands to break the fall but at least had enough
sense not to straight-arm herself. The last thing she needed right
now was to break an arm or a collarbone. She landed hard, jarring
every bone in her body, and for a stunned moment she lay there
on the muddy ground, silently taking inventory.

She was jolted in every bone, every muscle, but she was pretty
sure she was okay, except for her right foot. It was still in the hole,
the toe of her boot caught, her foot twisted. The pain screamed at
her, her ankle throbbing inside the boot.

She lay there with the rain beating down on her back and
head, with water running under her body. Her heart beat so hard
she could feel it, thudding against the wet ground. Defeat pressed
down on her. God, she was cold. She didn't want to move, didn't
want to know how bad it was, because if she'd broken that ankle
she was as good as dead. Maybe if she just stayed still for a moment
the throbbing would ease. She'd sprained her ankle before, and
the pain had been excruciating for a few minutes, only to ease and
then she'd been able to walk it off.

But she didn't have the luxury of lying there for more than a
few seconds. Angie pushed the saddlebags aside, unslung the rifle
scabbard from her shoulder and propped it on the saddlebag,
then, very cautiously, she sat up and used both hands to free her
twisted foot from the hole. She didn't pull her boot off. If she did,
she wouldn't be able to get it back on. She wouldn't be able to see
what was wrong, anyway, and wouldn't be able to do anything even
if she could. If she'd broken her ankle, the boot would help brace
it, so better to leave things as they were.

With cold fingers she probed at the ankle, trying to feel any
break. There didn't seem to be any one particular place that pro-
duced any extra agony when she touched it, but when she tried to
rotate her foot pain shot straight to her head and threatened to
make her pass out. "Okay, that wasn't a good idea," she muttered.
She didn't think it was broken. If it was, maybe it was just a hairline
fracture. More than likely it was a bad sprain. On a practical basis,

it didn't matter which it was. All that mattered was whether or not she could walk on that ankle.

Gritting her teeth, putting her weight on her left foot and steadying herself by clutching a sapling, Angie levered herself upward. She hugged the tree, hauling herself up slow and steady. Bark scrapped against the slicker, snagging and scraping. It was a balancing act, but she made it to an upright position. She reoriented herself, checked the wind, took a deep breath, then let go of the tree and took a hobbling step forward, willing herself to stand the pain, to walk. As soon as she put weight on her right foot that blinding pain shot through her ankle again and it gave out beneath her, sending her sprawling again. This time she wasn't fast enough to brace herself, and she landed facedown in the mud.

She wanted to cry. She wanted to beat the mud with her fist and howl. Talk about bad karma! What had she ever done to deserve this? Her business was gone, she had to sell her home, throw in Dare Callahan, that asshole Davis, Killer Krugman, and, oh yeah, a fucking *bear.* And now she'd either broken or sprained her ankle, when she had to get off this mountain as fast as possible before either Killer Krugman or that monster bear got her. Beyond any doubt, her life had gone to shit.

If she couldn't walk off the mountain, which was a tough enough prospect under the best of circumstances, what would happen? What was she supposed to do, just lie here and wait for Krugman or the bear to find her? She had her rifle, but she had to clean it, somehow, before it would be usable again. Still, she had the pistol. She could handle Krugman, as long as she saw him coming. But that bear . . . yeah, she was more terrified of that huge son of a bitch, any day of the week, than she was of Krugman.

That bear would find her here if she didn't move.

Son of a *bitch!*

Abruptly she was mad. No, not just mad, she was furious. No way in hell would she lie here feeling sorry for herself and wait to die. It didn't matter why she'd ended up in this position; if she gave up she was dead. Damn it, no one could accuse Angie Powell of lacking determination or sheer damn stubbornness. She'd get off this mountain if she had to *crawl.*

She sat up, slung the rifle scabbard on her back again, got her saddlebags. Mud had splattered into her mouth when she'd fallen the second time, so she spat it out. Then, on elbows and knees, she began crawling. She tried to keep her injured ankle from banging into anything because it hurt like a son of a bitch if she didn't, but she kept going even when pain made her grind her teeth together.

She made progress, slow and steady and miserable, but progress all the same. Then her right hand hit nothing but air, and she stopped just short of tumbling over an unseen sheer drop. Panting, she eased back. What was she supposed to do now? How wide was this drop? Was she on the edge of a precipice? She waited for a flash of lightning, and after a few seconds of darkness realized that the heart of the storm had moved on, because the lightning wasn't nearly as intense or frequent as it had been. Briefly she debated turning on the flashlight, just long enough to see what she was facing. Was the chance worth it? Right now, she was invisible; Chad had no idea where she was. But the flashlight might well pinpoint her position for him. On the other hand, she was stuck unless she could see what kind of obstacle was in front of her.

Before she had to make a decision, a flash of lightning very obligingly lit up the landscape for her. The drop in front of her was straight down—for a few feet. Three feet, max. Getting down without putting any weight on her right foot was going to be tough, but she wasn't going to let this little cut in the earth stop her.

She dropped her saddlebags, heard them plop in the mud below. Then she unslung the rifle scabbard and carefully let it slide down. Then she turned around, spinning on her belly in the mud, and slid over the edge, her good foot feeling for the ground, her hands digging into the mud to steady herself until she had solid earth beneath her. She stood there a moment, balanced precariously, and took a deep breath. Maybe she wasn't moving quickly, but she *was* moving in the right direction: down.

The mud beneath her feet shifted, and the world was yanked out from under her. Helpless, she simply fell. She slid and tumbled through the mud, grabbing at anything, everything, and finding only more slippery mud and the occasional rock. She tried to dig in her left heel, tried to jam her fingers into the earth, but she continued to slide and roll. There were rocks, and she tried to grab them, but they were there and gone so fast she couldn't manage. The edge of one of the rocks sliced her palm; her head slammed dangerously close to another.

And then she stopped, her momentum halted by mud. She lay there, panting, and once again took inventory. No, nothing was broken. She felt battered from head to foot, but everything other than her ankle seemed to be functioning. How far had she fallen? The slope hadn't been horribly steep, but it was steep enough. Her rifle and saddlebags—which held her flashlight, pistol, and protein bars—were up there.

She had a choice. She could crawl up, or she could crawl down. She could keep going, or she could retrieve her stuff.

Neither option seemed like a good one, but one was definitely worse than the other. She needed the saddlebags, needed her food and the pistol. She needed that rifle. She couldn't leave her weapons up there.

It had been tough enough moving down the mountain with a damaged ankle; moving up was torturous. Her progress was measured an inch at a time, and every muscle in her body screamed at her to stop. She'd gotten banged up in the fall, and now gravity was working against her instead of with her.

What had taken seconds to do—fall—took an excruciatingly long time to navigate in reverse. She didn't want to think about how long it took her to climb back up, so she didn't; she just climbed. Every minute was precious, but she didn't have any choice. She didn't just crawl; she dragged herself up, a cursed inch at a time. She used her left foot to find purchase and *push.* She grabbed rocks with her bloody hands to keep herself from sliding back down. She clawed her way up, her fingers digging deep into the mud. Mud crept beneath her slicker, through her sweatpants, into her boots. Cold rain continued to beat down on her. All Angie thought about was her goal: her rifle, her flashlight, her pistol. Food.

Do it or die.

Do it or die.

She did it.

A bush gave her something to grab on to; she clutched it, pulled herself up, and then she was there, at the small shelf that had fallen out from under her. She wanted to cheer, but she stayed quiet. Even when she'd been falling, she hadn't screamed. Her survival instincts had kept her quiet—aside from the occasional thud—and they kept her quiet now. She'd celebrate later, when she was off this mountain.

She could reach her gear. She dug her left foot deep into the mud, bracing herself so she wouldn't slide back down before she had a good grip on the saddlebags and rifle. They were both safe, just a couple of feet way from the divot in the slope. She felt a brief spurt of triumph as she grabbed the rifle and slung it over her shoulder, then the bags.

She might not have made a success of her career as a guide, but she had never been a quitter, and she wasn't quitting now. It was tempting to sit down and rest, but she didn't let herself, because she wasn't a quitter.

Instead, she held on to her gear, positioned herself, and started a controlled slide back down the hill—on her ass, this time, half sitting so she had more control. Yeah, a controlled fall. She held the rifle up, trying to keep it out of the mud as much as possible, though she wasn't certain how it could get any muddier than it already was.

Then she was at the bottom of the slope, and the only way forward was on her hands and knees again. Angie started crawling.

Do it or die.

Dare heard the thunder well before the rain arrived. It woke him from a sound sleep and he lay in his warm sleeping bag, listening as the storm got closer. What the hell was he doing out here? He couldn't fish in a thunderstorm. Wasn't the rain supposed to last a day or two? He might be stuck here in camp for a couple of days, with nothing to do except twiddle his thumbs and curse himself for being an idiot.

He never should've listened to Harlan. He should be at home, he should be in his own fucking bed, where the rain would sound soothing instead of threatening. But he wasn't; he was here, and if he had it to do all over again . . . damn it, he'd still be here.

He should be asleep. Generally, under the right circumstances, he liked storms. The room was completely dark, except for those moments when flashes of lightning showed at the very edges of the shuttered window, and when the rain began he expected the sound to soothe him right to sleep. He couldn't stop himself from thinking about Angie, though. Were the tents in the camp she'd leased sturdy enough to withstand the storm? He imagined they were, because it wasn't like they didn't get thunderstorms up this way now and then, and the campsite she'd leased was frequently used, but still . . . tents and storms weren't a great combination.

Then a sharp sound echoed through the mountains and Dare bolted upright. That wasn't lightning, that was a pistol shot. He'd heard small arms fire too often to be mistaken.

A second shot followed the first, then more, and even with the windows shuttered tight and the storm raging around him, he knew those shots had come from the direction of Angie's camp.

Damn it, what was going on out there? A rifle shot wouldn't have been so out of the ordinary, but a pistol . . . in a hunting camp, the only legitimate reason he could think of to use a pistol was if something unexpected happened, and you couldn't get to your rifle.

What could have happened at Angie's camp that was unexpected?

Some very ugly possibilities occurred to him.

He didn't think twice, but turned on a single light, a battery-operated lantern powerful enough to light the entire upper level, and began dragging on his clothes. When he was dressed he grabbed a slicker and his hat, the sat phone and his rifle. He grabbed a heavy-duty flashlight and switched it on before turning off the lantern. No more than two minutes after he'd heard the second pistol shot he was descending the ladder into the horse stalls below.

The horse snickered as Dare saddled up quickly and efficiently, slipped his rifle into the scabbard, and dropped his sat phone into a saddlebag. Before he stored the phone he gave a fleeting thought to calling someone in town, Harlan or the sheriff, but what would he say? *I heard a shot and it seemed to come from Angie's camp.* Fat lot of good that would do. It would cost him precious time he didn't have to waste, and no one was coming up here in the dark anyway. No, he was here, and this was on him.

He opened the big double doors and led the horse through them. It danced nervously as he closed and bolted the doors, but calmed a bit when he mounted up. Dare pulled the brim of his hat down low, pointed the flashlight toward a stand of trees and the narrow path there, and headed toward Angie's camp.

The rain was pouring down in windswept sheets, like solid walls smashing into them. The footing was so treacherous he couldn't go any faster than a walk. The flashes of lightning let him see, but they also made the young horse nervous. He held his mount steady with knees and reins, calmed him when a bolt struck about half a mile away and the whole earth shuddered. "Easy, guy," he crooned, letting the horse know by his tone and touch that everything was okay, there was nothing to be afraid of.

The going was slow, damn slow. The rain knocked visibility down to almost nothing, and he could feel the horse's agitation growing. Even with the flashlight, the unevenness of the trail was dangerous. He had to let the animal pick its way along at a pace that left him silently swearing, because he was damn certain he could cover the distance faster on foot.

Damn it, he should've ridden into Angie's camp while it was still light, shown himself and glared at her clients a time or two, even though it would've pissed her off big time. Maybe if those men had realized she wasn't as alone as they thought she was, there wouldn't have been all those pistol shots in the middle of the fucking night.

The silence that had followed the initial shots worried him as much as anything else. Who had been doing the shooting? Angie, or someone else. He didn't know if she had a pistol, but he damn sure knew she had a rifle. If something had warranted a couple of pistol shots, why hadn't there been a follow-up of rifle fire? There should have been return fire, and the fact that there hadn't been bothered him.

If there had been only one shot, he could've eased his mind with the idea that maybe the loser Lattimore had told him about had brought a pistol along on the hunt and had somehow mistakenly fired it. But that many shots in a short span of time . . . that was no mistake, no misfire. He tried to come up with some explanation that didn't put Angie Powell in a world of hurt, but nothing came to him.

And while he was closer to her here than he'd have been if he were at home, where just a few minutes ago he'd been thinking he should be, he wasn't nearly as close as he needed to be to help her.

If anything happened to Angie, Harlan was going to kill him.

And if anything happened to Angie . . . Dare wouldn't lift a finger to stop the old man.

Chapter Eleven

Chad Krugman's heart was pounding so hard he thought he'd vomit, and he couldn't take a deep breath. It was raining in a way he'd never seen it rain before, the drops hitting his face like tiny rocks being blasted at him. He had a flashlight but he couldn't see where he was going, even with the almost constant lightning, because the rain was so heavy. Finally, to save the batteries, he turned off the flashlight and stuck it inside his coat.

He had his hands full, anyway. Guiding three horses while riding one bareback—he'd chosen to mount the horse he'd ridden to camp, figuring it would be easier than getting used to a new one, but nothing about this was easy—keeping a constant sharp eye out for a goddamn bear and a woman with a rifle was tough, possibly the hardest thing he'd ever done. At least the horses had calmed down, now that they were away from the bear. At first he'd thought it was the storm that had spooked the horses, but since the storm continued but the bear was behind them, he figured it had to be the animal that had stirred them up.

He couldn't blame the horses. That damn bear had freaked him out, too.

He'd been prepared to kill, to do what had to be done in order to survive—that had never been in question. But he'd never expected to see anything like that monster of a bear tearing into Davis's body. God, that thing had been *big*. Chad didn't feel one minute's regret about killing Mitchell Davis, but to be torn apart that way, to be eaten . . . that was sickening. And horrifying. He wouldn't wish that on his worst enemy, and, yes, Mitchell Davis had been his worst enemy.

Shit, shit, *shit*! Things had gone all wrong. If Angie Powell hadn't found that body up the trail and insisted on going back to town in the morning to report it, he would've had a chance to kill Davis while they were out on the hunt, so his body would be more difficult to find. Angie's body, too. He'd always planned on killing her, too; there was no way around it. He did feel some regret over that, but not enough to influence his plans. By the time anyone thought to look for them, then mounted a search, and finally found their bodies up on the mountain, he would have been long gone.

His plan was to ride back to that rancher's place where they'd left the SUV—arriving after dark so he wouldn't be seen—then he'd turn the horse loose and simply drive away. He might even have left the horse about a mile up in the mountains and walked the rest of the way down. He'd been practicing his riding with this whole plan in mind, since right after he'd gone on that first hunting trip last year. When the rancher got up in the morning all he'd notice was that the SUV was gone, but Angie's truck and trailer would still be there, so he'd probably assume that one of the hunters had had enough and opted out, but Angie had stayed on with the other client—and the rancher would have no way of knowing which client had left. He probably wouldn't think another thing about it until Angie failed to show up a week later.

By that time, Chad would have been long gone—first into Canada, and from Canada to Mexico. Once in Mexico, he would simply have disappeared; he had the money to do it, and in certain parts of the world disappearing was a lot easier than it was on the North American continent. He'd collect his passport from the post office box in Butte, along with all of his account numbers and passwords. He wouldn't have any trouble at all, if he just had that week or so before their bodies were found.

Angie was the perfect guide for this particular trip: Her outfit wasn't top of the line; he'd noticed that she didn't have a satellite phone or a personal locator, both of which could be used to summon help fast. He got the idea that money was tight for her, which was great for him.

But all of that had been in the perfect world of his plan, and now his plan was all fucked up, he didn't know if he'd wounded Angie or not, he was riding through blinding rain leading three horses who didn't like the situation at all, and he didn't know where the hell he was. Worse, riding like this at night was a good way to end up with a broken neck; all it would take would be for his horse to stumble and they'd all go down, and he'd be at the bottom of a four-horse pile-up.

Slowly he reined in; when the horses had all come to a nervous stop, with the three horses he was leading milling around and jerking hard on the leads he held in his left hand, he forced himself to take several deep breaths and hold them until his lungs protested, pushing the panic away. The horses knew he was scared and that was making them harder to handle.

Sitting on horseback out in the open, with huge flashes of lightning popping all around, was pretty much stupid, but he had no idea where to go. Taking shelter under some trees would be even more stupid. If the rain would let up, the lightning might reveal a rock overhang or something, but as it was he could barely see ten feet in front of him.

Just as he was thinking that, the huge sheets of rain lessened—

not by a lot, but the next lightning flash revealed some rock formations ahead. With any luck, there would be some overhang that he could shelter under. He'd tie the horses to something and they could tough it out. It wasn't as if they didn't stand around in pastures all the time getting rained on, anyway.

With a goal in view and his panic lessened, he turned his reluctant horse's head toward the rocks and nudged him into moving forward. The other three horses didn't like being bunched together the way they were, they didn't like the weather, and they almost pulled him backward off the horse before reluctantly getting with the plan. Chad cursed and considered just turning them loose now, but he hadn't had time to think things through yet, and he didn't want to jump the gun on anything else. He might let them go, he might not. Right now he couldn't think of any reason why he'd need all four of them, but that didn't mean something wouldn't occur to him once he'd calmed down and had time to assess the situation.

He reached the rocks, examining them as best he could whenever the heavens flashed. At first he thought there was nothing, just a lot of really huge rocks that looked as if they'd been dumped there, but he kept working his way forward and eventually the lightning revealed a dark slash that, when he got closer, was indeed an overhang—tall, shallow, but even meager shelter was better than none.

He got out the flashlight and turned it on, sweeping the beam from one end of the overhang to the other, making certain nothing else had also sheltered beneath the rock. The powerful LED beam seemed weak in comparison to the massive show of light and noise Mother Nature had been throwing at him, but it did the job, reassuring him that the overhang was his alone.

Cautiously he dismounted, making certain he kept a tight hold on the leather leads as he walked the horses forward. They followed obediently enough, for a change. The area beneath the overhang wasn't clean and barren; it was dotted with bushes, littered with rocks and probably sheep shit and things like that. The bushes, at least, were a good thing, because they gave him something to tie the horses to. It was also a bad thing, because he didn't have enough hands to hold all four horses, the flashlight, and lead them from bush to bush until he had them all secured.

What if they all ran away when he dropped the reins?

Fuck 'em.

The answer let him breathe easier. He kept a grip on his mount's reins, and dropped the three other sets. He led his horse to a bush and quickly tied it off.

Wonder of wonders, the other three horses just stood there. Maybe they were tired. Maybe they were as glad as he was to be out of the constant bombardment of the rain. Maybe they were so used to humans taking care of them they didn't know what else to do. For whatever reason, they didn't run. Chad led each horse to a bush and secured it, then kicked some rocks and debris to the side to make himself a place to sit, and sank to the ground with his back braced against the rough rock.

This wasn't exactly a cozy spot; lightning still lit the world like a maniacal disco ball, thunder still boomed and rolled, making the earth shudder, and he was soaking wet and shivering with cold, but he was out of the rain and he no longer felt as exposed as a lightning rod. He could rest. He could gather his thoughts.

At first, all he did was sit there and breathe; panic was more exhausting than physical labor. He'd done all right at first, shooting Davis the way he'd planned even if the timing and location weren't exactly what he'd wanted, but then the damn storm had hit and he hadn't been able to find Angie, didn't know if he'd wounded her, killed her, or missed her entirely. She'd had that damn rifle in her hand, though, and he'd been drawn in a knot expecting to get shot at any second, then that freakin' *bear* had shown up and started snacking on Davis, and—

His breathing was getting too fast again, just remembering

those nightmarish moments. Chad deliberately slowed it down, forced the gruesome pictures away. He had to *think*.

Angie hadn't shot at him. That meant he'd hit her after all, that she was either dead or wounded, right? And if she was dead or wounded, the bear would likely have moved on to her as soon as it finished with Davis—unless she wasn't hurt very bad and was able to run, but if she wasn't hurt much then it followed that she'd have shot him *and* the bear. He hadn't heard any shots at all, which meant he likely didn't have to worry about Angie.

But he didn't know for certain, and he'd have to make sure. He'd taken the horses and run like hell. With all the noise of the storm, the drumming of the horses' feet, his own heartbeat pounding in his ears, plus the distance he'd put between himself and the camp, would he have heard a shot that came several minutes later, especially if it came during one of those deafening blasts of lightning? The answer was no. Angie could be hurt, but still able to kill the bear.

She was a huge loose end that he couldn't afford to leave dangling. He needed time, time to get away and time to disappear. That was all he asked. He felt very bitter that she was interfering with his plans. His life depended on things working out the way he wanted.

He wasn't worried about the cops, except that he needed to get to Mexico as fast as possible, before his name was put on the watch list. The cops were nothing. Davis's associates were the real danger. That's why he'd have to completely disappear, change his name, but that wasn't a bad thing. He didn't want the life he'd built as Chad Krugman to follow him; it had been a useful tool, and perversely gratifying that no one saw beneath the facade, which was simply more proof of his skill, but he was ready to start fresh. Chad Krugman had to cease to exist. He'd start new, with a name that didn't scream *dork*, but nothing over-the-top cool, either. Something quiet and masculine would get the job done.

Maybe he'd have some plastic surgery, too. In fact, that was a damn good idea: chin and cheekbone implants, a more assertive nose. He wouldn't need to be the invisible twerp any longer. And with his talent for handling money, the sky was the limit.

Never underestimate the accountant.

Davis had. Everyone had. They all did, even Angie Powell, and she'd been nicer to him than anyone else, which almost made him feel bad that he had to make certain she was dead, but what the hell, it wasn't as if she'd ever have given him the real time of day. She'd been nice to him because he was a client, not because she liked him.

He'd made a slight miscalculation with Davis, and that galled him. Even with everything he knew about the murderous bastard he'd *still* underestimated him. A man didn't rise to Davis's position without having at least some intelligence and a lot of cunning to go with the inherent ruthlessness; Chad should have been prepared for the possibility that events could actually happen faster than he'd estimated.

That was what Davis had been doing on the Internet at Angie's house, searching through all his accounts, comparing numbers— and he'd been smart enough, when Angie kicked him out of the house after dinner, to simply sit on the porch where he could still access her wifi, and continue his electronic poking.

A big question was whether or not Davis had alerted anyone else—namely the people *he* dealt with—or if he had wanted to handle the problem himself and never let them know. After all, he was the one who'd chosen Chad. He wouldn't want to make himself look bad. But if he'd already spotted the problem and taken care of it, then no harm no foul. Chad thought the odds were in his favor that Davis had kept the problem to himself, that first he'd wanted to verify the money was missing.

Oh, the core of Chad's plan—killing Davis—had still been executed, but the location and circumstances were off, and that bothered him. The storm had been a wild card. Angie finding that body had been a wild card. He couldn't have controlled or changed any of that, but he hadn't been prepared for such an upheaval of his plan, and as a result Angie was still unaccounted for. He'd have to do better.

In the end, though, he was gratified that his crafted persona had saved his life. Davis had so completely dismissed him as a threat that he'd been prepared to wait until the hunt was finished before taking care of business, probably because Angie's presence was a complicating factor he figured he could do without. Chad had felt no such limitation. Taken down to the bottom level, once Angie had made plain her intention to report the body she'd found, thereby throwing Chad's whole timeline off, he had to meet with Davis right away and kill him, and then take care of Angie.

Maybe Davis had believed in his own reputation, which had in the end been a fatal weakness. No one stole from Davis and walked away unscathed. Unscathed, hell; you didn't steal from Mitchell Davis and *survive*—unless you were smarter than he expected, unless you could catch him with his guard down. Davis hadn't expected Chad to be armed; he hadn't expected the accountant to be faster to commit murder than he himself was, which had been a serious, serious miscalculation.

Krugman one, Davis zero. Final score.

Now all Chad needed was to make sure Angie was taken care of, then get a five- or six-day head start. He'd be safe—he'd be someone else entirely—before anyone thought to look for the bumbling accountant.

He had to figure out how to make that happen. He had no doubt that he could, he just had to settle down and let his brain start working. He could still make this happen to his advantage. Wounded or not, Angie wouldn't be riding off the mountain, because he had all the horses. He'd like to think that taking the animals was enough to ensure his safety, but he knew it wasn't. No, he had to make sure she was dead before he made his escape. He needed that head start.

It was a shame, in a way. He liked her. Angie Powell was a nice person. She'd treated him well even when she'd thought he was a world-class schmuck. She hadn't flirted with him—women didn't flirt with men like him, unless they were desperate—or put on a fake smile and a false front; she'd been decent to him, which was more than he got from a lot of people. Unfortunately, nice people ran to the cops, which was why he couldn't let her live.

Too bad, but he wasn't going to let her interfere with years of planning. He had a fortune socked away, and he'd be damned if he'd let Angie Powell or anyone else get in his way now. He'd lived on the edge, dealing with murderers, torturers, drug dealers, the scum of the earth, to get that money, and he deserved to spend the rest of his life enjoying it.

So. What were his options? What were the possibilities? Best-case scenario, and worst-case scenario?

That last one was easy. The best-case scenario was if the bear had killed Angie. Not only would it mean there was no evidence linking her death to him, but that would also throw a lot of doubt on what had happened to Davis. Add that to the body Angie had found, and any investigation would focus so sharply on the bear that they might completely overlook whatever evidence remained showing Davis had been shot. He guessed it depended on how much of Davis the bear ate. If they hunted the bear down and killed it, would they analyze its digestive system? If the bear ate a bullet, how long would it take for it to crap it out?

For that matter, would the bullet still be in Davis anyway, or would it have gone straight through? Chad's pistol was a 9mm, but all he knew about it was how to use it; he hadn't studied damn ballistics. Point and shoot, and hit what you aim at. What more did he need to know?

Worst-case scenario was if Angie wasn't wounded, she'd gotten away from the bear, and she was heading back toward the rancher's place as fast as she could.

Chad listened to the god-awful storm roaring around him, and calculated the odds. No, she probably wouldn't try making that trip in the dark, in this weather. She had the rifle, so she probably wasn't worried all that much about the bear, and in fact, the bear might already be dead. Would she then stay at the camp?

No, because she wouldn't know where *he* was.

An edge of excitement curled in his stomach. If not for his pressing need to get out of the country, he liked the idea of pitting his wits against Angie's in a real man, or woman, hunt. She was way more savvy about these mountains and this kind of life, but a big plus for him was that she'd underestimated him the way everyone else did.

Back to the scenario: She'd hole up somewhere, then, when the weather improved, she'd head down the mountain. His advantage was that he knew where she was going.

But his disadvantage right now was that he didn't know where he was, exactly. He sat there and concentrated, forced himself to tune out the storm, the restless horses. He wasn't a great outdoorsman, but he did have a general sense of direction. He and Davis had been to the left of and behind the camp; the bear had come from that direction. When he'd fled the camp he'd raced to the right, away from the bear, which had taken him generally north. He needed to go back south, then east. He had no idea how long he'd ridden, driven by panic, but he figured he couldn't be more than a couple of miles from the camp.

He'd oriented himself with some visual landmarks when they'd arrived, so he was pretty sure he could find the campsite again if he needed to. Did he need to? Did he really need to make sure Angie was dead, or should he just get to Lattimore's as fast as he could and get out of the country? He was riding, she was on foot. He'd be at least a day ahead of her, right?

Was a day long enough?

Maybe, maybe not. He'd rather have that week he'd planned on.

Then suddenly a horrifying thought occurred to him, and he groaned aloud. *Fuck!* How could he have been so stupid? He'd lost his head, panicked, and now . . . double fuck! He had to go back to the camp, and this had nothing to do with Angie and tying up loose ends.

He didn't have the keys to the SUV.

Davis had had them. They might have been in his pocket, or they might be somewhere in his tent, but one way or another Chad had to get those keys or his whole plan evaporated beneath him and left him sitting in a big pile of shit.

He'd have to go back to the camp, pick a position from which to watch, and see if Angie was still there. If she was, he'd have to wait for his chance to pick her off, then he'd go after the keys. He only hoped they were with Davis's belongings in his tent, and not in his pockets . . . or in the belly of a black bear.

Chapter Twelve

Angie hugged the ground and dragged herself along, over rocks and bushes, through rivulets of water that had already turned into rushing streams as the runoff from the mountain storm threatened to turn into a flood. Going through that water required her to check her common sense way back somewhere along the trail, because only an idiot would try to crawl through fast-running flood water without being tethered, but all in all she figured flood water was the least of her problems. If she got swept down the mountain and drowned in three inches of mud and water, well, to her that was more acceptable than getting mauled to death by a bear, or letting that murderous twerp Chad Krugman get the best of her.

So she made up her mind that she wasn't going to drown. The only way to get through this was to focus on only the moment, not letting herself think about how far it was to Ray Lattimore's place, or how long it would take her to get there, or how cold she was, or how much her ankle hurt—none of that had any place in her head right now, because she had to concentrate on surviving.

She'd always loved the smell of rain, the freshness it brought, the promise of life, the renewal. She'd loved to listen to it beating on the roof, lulling her to sleep at night. Oh, she'd worked out in the rain many times and that wasn't any fun, but livestock had to be taken care of regardless of the weather, and doing so was simply part of life and she hadn't wasted any time or effort fretting about it.

This was different. She didn't know if she'd ever be able to enjoy the rain again.

She moved forward inch by painful inch, her ankle throbbing so much sometimes she simply froze in place, her teeth grinding together, as she fought through the waves of pain. Her hands were like clumsy chunks of ice, so cold from the water that she could barely feel them, but at least the cold would slow down any bleeding and the water would wash away the scent of her blood.

Survive.

She would. No matter what. She made that promise to herself. And she kept going.

One moment became another. Every muddy inch was a victory. Every breath she took could be counted as a win.

That son of a bitch Chad Krugman was *not* going to get the best of her.

Whenever lightning flashed she lifted her head and looked around, trying to keep track of her direction and progress, and keep a sharp eye out for any pitfalls and obstacles ahead, because without the lightning and not daring to turn on her flashlight, she was literally moving forward blind. She also looked for movement, of any kind in general, but specifically Krugman or the bear. So far all she'd seen were trees whipping wildly in the wind.

Lightning didn't operate on command, so there were times when she needed to see what was ahead of her and she simply had to stop and wait for the next flash before moving forward again.

Gradually it occurred to her how well-camouflaged she was. Unless she did something to give away her position, such as turn-

ing on her flashlight, Chad wasn't likely to see her. She was covered in mud from head to toe, crawling along so close to the
ground she'd effectively become a part of the landscape. The mud
and water should also disguise her scent, at least to some degree,
protecting her from the bear's sensitive sense of smell.

Terror could be sustained for only so long; it took too much
energy. After a while the body would push it away and concentrate
instead on the mundane, and that was what she was doing now,
her world narrowed to each inch she crawled, and how the inches
became feet, and the feet, yards. Eventually she would reach her
destination. All she had to do was *not quit.*

For a while her progress had been so slow she would have
been discouraged if she'd let herself think about it, so she hadn't.
Her biggest asset was her will to live. She'd get through this. She'd
survive the storm, the cold, the pain. Her injured ankle, whether
it was sprained or broken, wouldn't kill her in and of itself, but it
could sure as hell contribute to her death if either the bear or
Krugman crossed her trail. She'd never felt so vulnerable, and she
didn't like that feeling any more than she liked the physical pain.

She made an effort to become a part of the earth, to use the
mud and the darkness to make herself invisible.

After an unknown length of time—an hour, a lifetime—the
fierce heart of the storm moved on. The rain continued, but less
forcefully, abating from a physical bombardment to a mere downpour. Not feeling as if she was about to be fried by lightning at any
second was a plus, but the lack of lightning also meant she couldn't
pick out her points of navigation—*crawl to that bush, then that rock*—
and had to go purely by feel. Unfortunately, she couldn't feel
much in her hands at all. Her pace slowed from a literal crawl to ag-
onizingly slow.

Without the brilliant lightning that revealed everything in
stark black and white, obliterating everything else, the pinpoint of
light off to her left immediately caught her attention. She froze,
not moving a muscle, blending into the earth. *Krugman.* No one

else would be out in this storm, with a flashlight. He was searching for her.

A sense of unreality washed over her. She didn't know whether to be insulted or relieved that he obviously didn't view her as any sort of threat. He had no way of knowing she was hurt, no way of knowing that her rifle was so encrusted with mud it was useless, and still he was out there with a flashlight looking for her, giving away his own position.

The stupid asshole. She'd be damned if she'd let someone like him get the best of her.

He had a horse. She needed that horse, but unless the perfect moment presented itself she had little or no chance of somehow getting it. She had her pistol, but that was for short-range targets, which meant Chad would be just as close to her. She couldn't chase him down and she sure as hell wasn't going to try to bait him into coming after her, not with her mobility so severely limited, but if he stumbled on her she wouldn't hesitate to use the pistol.

Knowing she was pretty well camouflaged didn't make her feel as secure as she needed to feel; laboriously she crawled to a tree, then pulled herself to a sitting position with the trunk between her and the pinprick of light, and pulled the muddy saddlebags close. At least the flashlight let her know that wasn't the bear after her. The pistol would do against Krugman; she'd rather have the rifle, but the smaller weapon was sufficient for a man, while it would only annoy a bear, especially one as big as the one that had attacked the camp and eaten Davis.

Memories flashed, much like the lightning, only much more gruesome, and she shuddered. For a while she'd been able to focus on survival and push those images out of her mind, but now they were back, curdling in her stomach, bringing the black edge of fear closer and closer until it threatened to destroy her control.

Taking deep breaths, she pushed it all away again. She could *not* let panic take over, or she'd never make it through this alive.

Resting her head against the tree trunk, she watched the almost fragile beam of light move closer. She didn't pull the pistol from her saddlebag, not yet, because there was no point in getting it wet when she might not have to use it, but she put her hand inside the saddlebag and rested her icy palm on the handle grip, so she could have the weapon out in a split second if she needed it.

Now that she'd stopped moving, waves of exhaustion swept over her, leaving her trembling in every limb. Until she'd stopped to shelter behind the tree trunk, Angie hadn't realized how tired she really was—or maybe she'd realized but hadn't let herself feel it, because if she'd let it get too close she might never have been able to push through the pain and effort, and she'd have stopped trying. This went beyond merely being tired. This was bone-deep, dragging down every cell in her body. Abruptly she felt as if even breathing might be more than she could ask of herself. The wavering of the flashlight beam might be because she was so exhausted she literally couldn't even see straight.

And cold. God, she was so cold. Every stitch she had on was soaking wet, and though the weather was mild for November, that didn't mean summer temperatures, it merely meant there wasn't a foot of snow on the ground. It was warm enough to storm. But the rain and her wet clothing were stealing warmth from her body, obliterating her ability to generate heat, and now that she wasn't moving she knew that she was in a life-and-death situation, that she was already suffering from hypothermia and might not be able to manage on her own. She needed shelter more than she needed to keep crawling down the mountainside. She needed warmth, she needed to be dry, and she didn't see how she was going to accomplish either of those goals . . . unless she could manage to kill Chad Krugman and get his horse . . . *her* horse.

She summoned the strength to peer around the tree trunk. The beam of light was moving closer, coming straight at her, bobbing up and down. She couldn't tell by the movement if Krugman was walking or on horseback. If he continued on that course, straight at her, she'd know in a few minutes.

Her heartbeat picked up, began to pound, and her stomach twisted with nausea. She'd been around hunting all of her life. She was good with a rifle, acceptable with a pistol. She'd hunted her own food before. But she'd never thought she'd be in a situation where she would have to shoot a *person,* and yet here she was, her hand gripping a pistol while she waited to see if tonight was the night she crossed a line she'd never before even considered. She'd do whatever she had to in order to survive. If it came down to her or Krugman, if it was kill or be killed, she wouldn't hesitate.

She had always thought she would have serious doubts about taking a life, but in this situation . . . no. She had none.

She had the advantage here. She knew Krugman was coming; his flashlight gave him away, while she was all but invisible. Unless a flash of lightning at just the wrong moment gave her away, she could stay hidden here for a very long time while he searched all around her. She was reasonably safe from discovery until at least dawn. The problem was, she didn't think she could last that long. By dawn, hypothermia would long since have brought her down.

She waited. Her body felt both heavy and empty, weighed down yet floating. She couldn't take action, she could only react, and hope she had enough strength left for it to matter. After a long stretch of complete darkness, lightning lit the sky. Angie took a quick peek around the tree, toward Krugman, hoping she could tell exactly where he was. He wasn't a good enough rider to hold both the flashlight and the reins in one hand and his pistol in the other, especially if . . . A memory stirred, of those hellish moments after the bear entered the camp and Krugman had taken the horses and bolted. *He hadn't had time to saddle one of the horses.* He'd be bareback. There was no way he could control a horse and hold a flashlight with just one hand, and likewise no way he could hold both a pistol and a flashlight in one hand while holding the reins in the other.

Would he even try to ride, under those conditions? Or was he more likely to be on foot, flashlight in one hand, pistol in the other? She needed to know what was coming.

The flash of lightning was too brief, and she wasn't able to locate him. Instead of drawing back she stayed in position, eyes straining, until once more she saw the sweep of the flashlight beam. Then she waited, gaze locked on that beam as it came closer and closer. The next flash came several seconds later, exposing a figure on horseback, as starkly revealed as a photo negative. The flash of light was brief, and when it was over she was blinded—and would be until her eyes adjusted to the darkness again—but she'd seen enough. Though the angle and trees disguised the rider, the flashlight was in the hand of someone on horseback, in a saddle . . . and it wasn't one of the horses she'd taken to the camp less than twenty-four hours ago.

Someone else was out here in this storm. Good God, *why*? No one would be searching for her other than Krugman, unless there was a lot going on that she didn't know about, and someone was looking for Krugman. But doing so in this weather, at night, was so unreasonable she couldn't think of any scenario that would fit. Either that, or her exhausted brain couldn't grasp the obvious.

She had to allow for that, that she might possibly be so exhausted she couldn't think straight, which made her decision more difficult. If the rider somehow found her, and it was someone she didn't know . . . could she, should she, shoot? She didn't know. She needed help, but what if this was a bad guy? She didn't want to make a wrong decision, so she focused on making herself small, on disappearing into the earth, so whoever it was wouldn't find her and she wouldn't be forced to make that choice.

She sat very still, willing the rider to move on past her position. Maybe she faded out of consciousness, her tired body just checking out for a moment, because there was nothing other than blackness inside and out, then suddenly the rider was almost directly in front of her, just down the slope, and a flickering sheet of lightning lit up the landscape again, and all the blood drained out of her head.

She couldn't see the rider's face, but she didn't need to. She knew the way he sat a saddle, and, damn it, she knew that hat. What the hell was Dare Callahan doing out in the storm in the middle of the night?

Angie tried to force her sluggish brain into action. Whatever the reason, he didn't know about the bear, and he didn't know about Krugman. With that flashlight in his hand pinpointing his location, he was a sitting duck. Her heart knocked hard against her ribs, and a silent cry formed in her throat.

She didn't know how she did it. One second she was sitting on the ground against the tree, and the next she was crawling forward, muscles and ankle screaming. She kept trying to pull enough air into her lungs to call to him, tried to force some sound, any sound, past the constriction of her throat, but all that came out was a weak moan that wasn't even his name.

He was moving past her now. No. *No!*

Desperately she scraped her hand across the ground, found a rock. She threw it. Rather, she tried to throw it. She didn't have any strength left. The rock sort of rolled out of her hand and thumped to the ground just a few yards away.

She searched through the mud and darkness, found a stick, and beat it on the ground. The noise was lost in that made by the steady drumming of rain, the increasingly distant rumble of thunder.

She crawled, toward the light, toward Dare. Minutes before she'd had the bleak thought that she might not make it. She wouldn't give up, she would never just surrender, but the thought had been there, sapping her strength. Now he was here, and she wasn't alone. He was literally the light at the end of a long, dark tunnel, and he was moving away from her.

Desperately she scrabbled for another rock, couldn't find one. *"Dare."*

The word was a whisper, strangled in her throat.

He reined the horse around, sweeping the flashlight beam across the ground. The horse shifted nervously, not at all happy with its circumstance but obeying the strong hand holding the reins. Horse and rider changed direction.

Angie fought to orient herself, and abruptly realized he was headed straight for her camp. He must have been at his camp; maybe he'd heard the shots and come to see if anything was wrong, and was having difficulty locating her camp in the darkness and hellish weather. No matter what the reason, he was here, he had no idea what might be waiting at the camp.

No. He couldn't go there.

She screamed. The sound burst out of her. It was one word, his name. "Dare!" Her voice was nothing more than a croak; she was cold and hoarse and exhausted. But it was loud enough that he reined in the horse, the flashlight beam sweeping around, and she heard his gravelly voice call back.

"Angie? Where the fuck are you?"

Yeah, it was definitely him. If she'd been the crying type, she'd have burst into tears.

He kneed the horse forward, straight toward her. She raised a shaky arm in the air, and almost fell on her face in the mud. Oh my God, she was so happy and relieved to see him she might cry anyway. She couldn't believe it, couldn't believe he was actually there, couldn't believe she was actually *happy*—no, make that *ecstatic*—to see Dare Callahan. Wasn't that a kick in the pants?

His voice called out as he came closer. "Where are you? Talk to me, goddamnit. Say something."

"Here," she said, louder than before, trying to grab a tree branch and pull herself up, and failing miserably. She sat on her ass in the mud, instead, with rain running down her cheeks, and tried to smile. "I'm here."

Chapter Thirteen

Dare's gut was tight as he swept the flashlight beam back and forth, looking for movement that would pinpoint Angie's location for him, but visibility was low and the landscape around him was in constant motion anyway, with the wind whipping everything back and forth; one more motion wouldn't necessarily stand out. Angie's voice had been weak, so weak he couldn't locate her by sound alone; the rain almost drowned her out entirely. A roll of thunder said another line of storms was approaching; he needed to find her, and fast, so they could get under some kind of shelter.

He'd been pushing his luck with the lightning from the moment he'd left the camp; only a damn fool went horseback riding during a storm, so he guessed this made him a damn fool. Hell, he knew it did. Anyone with a lick of sense would have taken shelter, but instead he'd pushed on, fighting his horse the whole way. He figured that meant the horse had more sense than he did; instead of getting used to the weather and settling down the young buckskin had gotten more fractious by the minute. Controlling the horse was taking almost all of his attention, which meant he

couldn't concentrate on his search. Once more he swept the flashlight from side to side, trying to blink the stinging rain from his
eyes and cursing every drop that fell. Then a pale gleam close to
the ground caught his eye, and he snapped the light downward.
There was something small and muddy, an animal of some kind—
Then he took a closer look, and a kind of furious disbelief roared
through him.

No, not an animal: *Angie.* She was just sitting there sort of
hunched over, a strange, twisted expression on her face as if she
were trying to smile, for fuck's sake. Something was seriously
wrong, because no way in hell would she ever smile at him under
normal circumstances.

He reined in hard, an action the buckskin took exception to,
but the damn horse had taken exception to everything else from
the moment Dare had ridden him out into the storm, so why stop
now? Adrenaline flooded through him, throwing his body into automatic combat mode as he pulled his rifle from the scabbard and
swung down from the saddle. The horse was too skittish to take
him close to Angie, so Dare looped the reins over a low-hanging
tree branch and gave the big animal a quick pat on the neck to reassure him, then reached Angie with four long strides.

"Where are you hurt? What the hell happened?" he snapped
at her, going down on one knee beside her. He shone the flashlight over her, starting at her head and working down. He didn't
see any blood, but she was so covered with mud that he wouldn't
be able to spot anything short of arterial spurting. He noted the
bulging saddlebags beside her, and she was clutching a rifle so
caked with mud it looked more like a club than a firearm. If she'd
needed to shoot, she'd have been shit out of luck.

She was shaking from head to foot, unceasing quakes that
were hard enough to rattle her bones, but she grabbed the flashlight and switched it off. "We have to move." Her voice was thin
and hoarse, but forceful for all that. "The light . . . our position."

That one word, *position,* was enough to flip a switch in him, because it could only mean trouble. His heart began pumping hard, but his brain was icy cold and clear as he took an immediate three-sixty threat assessment, looking for whatever had Angie Powell crawling through the mud over a mile from her camp.

He didn't see anything except trees and rocks and mud, lashed by wind and rain, but his senses stayed on high alert. Just because he couldn't see trouble coming didn't mean it wasn't there. His nerves and instincts had been forged in combat; a life-time away from war wouldn't be enough to counteract those instincts. Until the day he died, a part of him would always be ready to react to a split second of warning, and that part immediately understood what she was saying. Someone else, possibly the same someone who had fired those shots tonight, was out there hunting her. He hoped like hell Angie was the one who'd done the shooting, but he figured she'd have hit whatever she was aiming at, so it seemed more likely she'd been the target rather than the shooter.

His spidey sense didn't pick up that crawly sensation of being watched, though, and his memory of the land told him that they were in such rugged folds of the mountains that, combined with the low visibility, someone would have to be close by to have any chance of seeing the light. Tracking someone in this weather would be impossible and she wasn't on the trail anyway, which wasn't even a real trail, just the path of least resistance. In the del-uge of rain he'd gone off it himself, which was why he'd doubled back. Thank God he had.

But first things first, and he didn't like that she hadn't an-swered him right away when he asked the first time. He also didn't like the way she was listing to the side, as if she was about to fall over. He clamped one arm around her, propped her against his raised knee. "Were you hit?"

She was dragging in deep, ragged breaths, the way people breathed when they'd pushed themselves to the limit. Her head wagged to one side. "No. My right ankle."

"Break or sprain?"

Another shuddering breath. "I don't know. Sprain, I hope."

Either way, she obviously couldn't walk, and he couldn't do anything for her until he got her back to the camp. He rapidly assessed the situation. There were several things that he needed to do, and they all needed to be done more or less simultaneously, but the obvious number one priority was getting her on the horse. He could find out what happened, tend to her ankle, and use the sat phone to call for help once he had her safe. The sat phone was virtually useless right now, anyway, because of the fucking weather.

"Okay, let's get you on the horse," he said gently, hooking the rifle's strap over his shoulder to free both his hands. He slid his left arm under her knees, his right arm around her back, centered his own balance, and pushed himself up with her cradled in his arms. He'd barely reached an upright stance when he abruptly felt tingles race over his scalp and skin, like hundreds of spiders, making every hair on his body stand up. "*Shit!*" he said, and even as the word was coming out of his mouth he threw himself down, spread-eagled on the soggy ground with Angie under him, as if he could somehow shield her from a lightning bolt.

The blast of light was deafening. Light should be just light, but this was sound, too, an explosion of sheer energy that was almost like being body-slammed. There was no space between light and noise, it came all at once as if a giant had stomped the earth. The ground shuddered beneath them, something he found vaguely comforting, because if he could feel that then they hadn't just been fried. His ears rang, his nose burned from the chlorine stench of ozone, and beyond all of that he could hear the horse screaming in panic.

"Shit! *Fuck!*" He launched himself off Angie, forcing his body to respond even though his head was still reverberating from the force of the nearby strike. The buckskin was rearing, its eyes rolling white in terror, fighting for all it was worth to jerk free. Dare scrabbled on feet and hands for the first couple of feet before he could catch his balance, and in those crucial two seconds the delay cost him, disaster struck, in the form of a tree branch. It wasn't even that large of a branch, but the whipping wind broke it free and it came sailing out of the night like a rock from a slingshot, and slapped across the animal's chest and neck.

The buckskin went wild. Before Dare could throw himself at its head and catch the bridle to pull it down, with a powerful wrench of its neck it pulled the reins free and ran. It didn't just run a few yards and stop, the way horses usually did; it bolted, terrified out of its wits, and in a few seconds was completely lost in the night.

"God*damn*it!" Dare bellowed. "You stupid fuck!" He didn't know if he meant himself or the horse, but *fuck,* now they were stuck on foot and the damn sat phone was in the saddlebag, so he couldn't even call for help when the weather cleared. The horse might stop a hundred yards away, but with the darkness and the weather he'd never be able to see it. He didn't think so, though; that horse was so scared it might not stop running until it couldn't run any farther. He hoped it didn't stumble and break its fool neck.

He stood there, breathing hard and fuming with frustration, so angry at himself for not tying the reins more securely that if he hadn't needed his hat he'd have thrown it on the ground and stomped on it. This was his fault. He'd *known* how nervous the buckskin was, and instead of just looping the reins around the tree branch he should have actually tied them. He'd been in such a damn hurry to get to Angie that he'd let himself get careless, and now they were in a fine mess, with her hurt and—

She hadn't made a sound.

A chill ran through him, a chill that had nothing to do with the cold rain or the storm or even the serious situation. Surely to God the lightning current couldn't have gone through the ground and hit her, without also hitting him. But he'd all but slammed her to the ground; there might have been a rock, she might have hit her head . . . Slowly, almost sick with dread at what he might see, he turned his head to look at her.

She was struggling to sit, rolling half on her side and using her hands to push herself upright. The hood of her slicker was down, her head unprotected; her dark hair was plastered against her skull and running with water, she'd been crawling over incredibly rough ground for God only knew how long, but she was moving, she was still in the game, still *trying*.

His stomach clenched. He'd let her down by letting the horse get away. With the horse, he'd have had her safe and dry in about an hour. Now he'd have to carry her out of here, and he had no idea how long it would take on foot to reach his camp. If he were humping a pack on fairly level ground he knew he could easily set a pace of four miles an hour, but carrying a person, in this kind of terrain? No way. He'd end up stepping off a cliff and killing both of them. With luck, they'd reach his camp by daylight, which was hours from now, hours before he could see to her ankle, hours before she could get warm and dry.

He went back to her side, back down on one knee, and helped her to a sitting position. "Are you all right?"

"I don't know." She looked around, a little dazed. "I feel . . . a little funny. Where did . . . it hit?" She was trembling and breathless, and her voice was weak, but there was no hint of hysteria in her tone, thank God. Maybe one day he'd tell her how deeply he appreciated that she'd held it together. Male or female, and he'd seen some guys lose it in combat, hysteria in a life-or-death situation just made the odds for survival get even longer.

"Far enough away that we aren't dead, and that's all that matters." Lightning was still popping, thunder still rolling in metallic echoes across the mountains. Just because they'd survived one lightning strike that was way too close for comfort didn't mean they'd survive the next one. They weren't out of danger yet, not by a long shot.

"The horse is gone." He said it baldly, a flat statement of fact. She nodded, a single bob of her head.

He waited for the angry blast of recrimination, because no way Angie Powell would let the opportunity pass to tell him what a stupid asshole he'd been. Instead she sat there, her trembling increasing until it wasn't trembling at all but body-shaking shudders that left her gasping for air, and finally she opened her mouth.

"Chad . . . Krugman . . . killed Davis." She sucked in more air. "Shot at . . . me. Took the horses." She stopped, and if possible her shaking intensified. He remained silent, surprised that she hadn't ripped into him, changing into something far more deadly. Even though he'd called himself all kinds of a fool for riding out in such a dangerous storm, he'd kept going because those pistol shots in the dead of night couldn't have meant anything good. There were ramifications he had to think about, but not right now. Right now, the most important thing was getting to shelter. He'd concentrate on that for the time being, and after they'd had a chance to get some rest would be the time to think about strategy and possibles.

She tried to say something else but the words just wouldn't form, whether because she was so cold and exhausted or for some other reason he didn't yet know. Maybe she was in too much pain. He put his arm around her, pulled her in tight against his chest and shoulders as if by physically bracing her he could pass some of his strength on to her. He'd done it on battlefields, and for whatever reason the human contact always seemed to help. Finally she gathered her strength and said, "Bear."

Bear? The word came out of nowhere. His head jerked around, his gaze sharply scanning and his right hand already lifting the rifle he held, but no four-legged threat was in sight. Visibility was so poor that didn't mean much, but for now he was going with what his eyes were telling him. He scowled down at her. "Whaddaya mean, *bear?*"

"It came . . . must have been circling the camp . . . horses going crazy. It got . . . Davis's body. Huge. Biggest bear I've seen . . . I was right there, on the ground—"

She stopped, but then there really was nothing else she needed to say. Dare clamped his jaw tight. Seeing a bear savage a body at close range, even knowing the man was already dead, would be enough to traumatize anyone. And she knew bears, knew the danger she'd be in if this one had scented her.

Fucking great. Not only was there a killer out there after her, but now he had to factor a man-eating bear into the equation. He had only one other question, the most important one: "Grizzly or black?"

"Black."

He grunted. That sure as hell put the worst twist on an already bad situation. Grizzlies were aggressive as all hell, like a buzz saw wearing stinky fur, but they normally attacked for a reason: intruding into their territory, getting too close to a kill, startling it, or the worst situation of all, getting between a female and her cubs. Black bears were different; they came after people without any of the triggers that would set off a grizzly. Bear lovers could protest all they wanted that bear attacks were almost always the human's fault, but most people who actually lived in bear country knew better, at least where black bears were concerned.

They needed to be moving. With a predatory black bear in the area, the sooner they got to his camp, the better.

"Let's get going," he said. "It's a long way to camp. How do you want to start out, on my back or over my shoulder?"

She shook her head. "You can't carry me. It's too far."

"Don't start being a pain in the ass," he snapped. Patience wasn't his strong suit—or his weak one, come to that. And the comment was fucking stupid, because when *hadn't* she been a pain in the ass? "If you could walk at all, you wouldn't have been crawling, and even if I help you, you can't hop several miles in this terrain. I'll repeat your two choices: on my back, or over my shoulder. Choose."

Another flash of lightning made her flinch. She wiped a shaking hand across her face, and he realized again how close she was to the end of her rope. "Which one is easiest for you?" she finally asked, and the ease with which she gave in told him more than words ever would how much this night had taken out of her.

"*Easy* isn't a factor. Never mind, I just made up your mind for you. We'll start out with you over my shoulder, so I can keep my right hand free to carry the rifle. I want to be able to shoot if I need to. After we put some more distance between us and your camp, we'll switch to piggyback and you can carry the rifle. Think you can stay awake to shoot if you have to?"

Her eyes were huge, dark hollows in her pale face. "Oh, yeah," she said grimly. "I'll stay awake."

Chapter Fourteen

Dare pulled her upright and clamped an arm around her waist to hold her steady as she ground her teeth and worked through the surge of pain caused by blood going to her foot. When he could feel her relax a little he eased his grip, but kept her weight leaning against him; the way she was shaking, her balance was precarious even if she hadn't been holding her right foot off the ground.

"Okay, here's the way we're going to do this." He took the saddlebags from her and settled them over his left shoulder, with one bag hanging over his back and the other over his chest. The strap of her mud-caked rifle was hooked over his right shoulder. His own rifle was in his right hand. "You're going over my left shoulder. Use your left arm to hook around my waist, and I'll be using my left arm to steady you. Between the two of us, you should be fairly secure. I know you're tired and cold and you want to rest, but what I need you to do is hold the flashlight in your right hand and shine it in front of me, so I can see where I'm going. Can you manage?"

He couldn't really tell in the darkness, broken by the surreal flashes of light, but he thought she gave a faint, grim smile. "Hold a flashlight? Yeah . . . I can do that."

It *had* been a dumb-ass question; a woman who had crawled down a mountain could definitely handle a flashlight. And at any other time she'd have pointed out to him what a dumb-ass question it was, but tonight she seemed to be passing up opportunities to chew his ass out. That almost worried him more than the situation they were in, because what if she had a head injury she hadn't told him about?

Well, hell. Only one way to find out, and that was to ask. "Have you banged your head on anything?"

"No."

And that was it. All he could surmise, then, was that she was holding everything back until after she was safe; after all, she wouldn't want to alienate her rescuer, not when her general opinion of him was so low she'd expect him to leave her there if she said what she was thinking.

"Let's get going, then. Here's the flashlight." As she took the light he bent down, put his shoulder into her midsection, wrapped his left arm around her thighs, and straightened, his movements fast and seamless. For a moment she was rigid, her arms braced on his back, then he felt her force herself to relax and let her torso lie against him. She hooked her left arm around his waist. If he hadn't been wearing a slicker she could have grabbed hold of his belt, but as it was she had to use muscle power to keep herself anchored.

Pointing the flashlight at the ground, she switched it on and angled it so the beam was shining in front of him. "Is this okay?"

"Tilt it down a little more."

Silently she obeyed, and the bright LED lights lit the ground at his feet. She braced the flashlight against his leg, and he began walking.

Hiking through mountainous terrain in a storm, in the dark,

carrying another person, and without having a hand free for balance had to rank right up there with combat in the potential for getting hurt. If he hadn't had the flashlight, he likely would have killed them both within the first half hour. Dare didn't let himself think about whether or not the task he'd set himself was hard, didn't let himself think about maybe finding an outcropping of rock and waiting out the storm. He and Angie had one big advantage, and that was that the guy who'd tried to kill her had no idea anyone else was nearby. He wouldn't know about Dare's camp, its location or even its existence. Dare wasn't about to give up that advantage by hanging around.

Moreover, the storm was wiping out all trace of Dare's tracks as soon as he made them. The farther he could get while it was still raining, the better.

Angie was on the skinny side, but the skinny was all muscle and she was heavier than she looked, plus she had at least ten, fifteen pounds packed into the saddlebags she'd been carrying. Still, he'd toted deer off this mountain that weighed more than she did, so he ignored the complications of weather, having to carry his rifle instead of slinging it by the strap on his shoulder, all the while trying not to jostle her ankle.

She was still too quiet, and that bothered him. He appreciated the lack of complaints, because dangling upside down over his shoulder couldn't be comfortable, but she was *too* quiet. He'd have thought she was unconscious except for the tension he could feel in her body, and the fact that the flashlight remained in her hand instead of dropping to the ground.

After half an hour he asked, "You hanging in there?"

Her chest heaved a little; he could feel the movement against his back. "Uh . . . yeah. Literally."

Had she laughed? He hadn't meant to make a joke, but he was glad the question had come off as one. If she could laugh, she was okay.

On the other hand, she might have been gasping for breath.

She had been trembling and shivering, but the involuntary movements had stopped and he wondered if she was sliding into hypothermia. He plowed on for a few minutes, but when he saw a decent-sized boulder with a slight hollow on one side, he decided to make use of it. Stopping every half hour for a brief rest probably wasn't a bad idea; it would keep him from making mistakes, and give him a chance to assess her condition.

"Let's stop here for a minute," he said, propping his rifle against the rock and gently easing her off his shoulder and down to the ground. He retrieved the rifle, then crowded into the small space with her and turned the flashlight so they had just a little bit of light. He wasn't worried about the batteries going dead; LED lights lasted for months of normal use, and the batteries were new. He even had spares at the camp, just in case, but there was more than enough juice to get them there. Even if there wasn't, Angie's flashlight was in her saddlebags, so they had backup.

He sighed. Just being partially out of the rain was a huge relief. His boots were waterproof, but from the knees down his jeans were sopping wet and water had leaked down the inside of his boots. His socks weren't completely soaked yet, but they soon would be.

His hands were cold, but not as cold as hers. He put his arm around her shoulders and tugged her in close, almost in his lap, then took her hands and folded them against his palms, tucking them against his neck. She made a small sound that could have been either a bitten-off protest or a hum of relief.

"You stopped shivering," he said. "Are you warmer?"

A slow shake of her head.

Damn it. There wasn't a lot he could do, no way in hell he could build a fire in this downpour even if he had a fire-starter kit on him, which he didn't. There was a small camp heater at the cabin, which didn't do him a hell of a lot of good right now.

Swiftly he unsnapped and unzipped his slicker, then did the same to hers. She didn't protest, and when he got it open he saw why she was so cold. She was wearing a coat beneath the slicker, but the coat was wet through, and had been leaching her body heat away.

"Shit, we have to get you out of this," he said, pushing the slicker down her arms.

She frowned, as if she couldn't understand what he was doing, but didn't protest. He didn't have a lot of room to maneuver, and he banged his elbow against the rock; he cursed nonstop as he finished peeling her out of the slicker and the heavy coat. When that chore was finished, he had to put the slicker back on her. Then he unzipped his coat, pulled her across his lap in a half-lying position, and tucked her inside his open coat. Every stitch she had on was wet, and he caught his breath as water soaked from her clothes into his, but he pulled her even closer and did his best to wrap his coat and slicker over her, then covered them both with her wet coat.

That was the best he could do. It wasn't the same as blankets and hot coffee and a fire, but maybe his body heat was enough to pull her back from the brink.

Her nose, buried against his neck, was as cold as a pup's. He turned off the flashlight and sat in the dark with her, holding her as close as he could get her without stripping them both down to skin.

Ten minutes later, when she started shivering again, he felt grimly triumphant. He was shivering a little himself, but he wasn't freezing, and when they started out again his physical effort would warm him up, as long as he didn't push so hard he started sweating.

He checked his wristwatch, gave her another ten minutes. He'd do this every half hour: stop for a brief rest, get her warmed up a little, change positions. After this time she shouldn't be as cold. The rest periods would keep him from getting stupid with fatigue, and changing positions would help keep both of them going.

"Time to saddle up," he said when the ten minutes were up. "Piggyback this time. You ready?"

Reluctantly she sat up, but she was able to zip and snap her own slicker, and he helped her back into the wet coat. This time the coat went on the outside where it provided a barrier to the weather but wasn't against her body. It wasn't an ideal solution, but it would do.

They pulled up the hoods of their slickers, and Dare moved away from the shelter of the boulder into the heavy rain. After helping Angie up so she was balanced on her left foot, he knelt so she could climb onto his back.

They could do this.

They had to.

A touch of gray lit the sky to the east when Dare finally saw the cabin ahead. The darkness had been gradually fading for the past fifteen minutes, just enough that he could make out some details without the aid of the flashlight. The ferocious lightning and thunder had moved on, but the heavy rain hadn't slacked off at all. The wind had blown rain against his face, down his neck, soaking into his clothes beneath the slicker. Angie had already been soaked. The oiled leather of the saddlebags had probably held up okay, but everything else, including his hat, was dripping; they might as well have swam here.

Angie was hanging over his shoulder again. They had changed position every time they stopped, but that was the position that seemed to be most comfortable for her, maybe because it required the least effort on her part.

The periodic stops had kept pulling her back from hypothermia, but each time she seemed to lose a little ground. Since the last stop she'd been just hanging there, limp and completely silent.

Two hours ago he'd decided they could relax their vigilance, at least as far as not needing to have the rifle instantly at the ready, and he'd been able to sling it on his shoulder and use both hands; he'd taken over carrying the flashlight, because Angie had begun drifting off and letting it drop. Each time she would startle awake and apologize, but the fact was she'd pushed herself almost as far as she could go.

He never would have thought it, but now he wished she'd light into him, giving him hell for everything he'd done wrong: for losing the horse, for not finding her sooner, for not making an appearance in her camp to let her clients know she wasn't alone. The last two points wouldn't be fair, but he didn't care about fair right now, he just wanted her awake and spitting fire. He wanted her complaining about everything he did. He didn't like it when she didn't talk.

Keep them talking. He'd done that with wounded men, but Angie had stopped answering him a half-mile back. She was traumatized, hypothermic, possibly in shock. He'd forgone the last rest period, because getting her to shelter was more important than resting for ten minutes.

With nothing to distract him, he'd begun wondering about things he didn't want to think about. The events she'd described were bad enough, but he couldn't help thinking there might be more to the story, something she hadn't told him. He and Harlan had talked about the dangers of a woman guiding two men, especially men like Davis and Krugman, the bastards.

Had she been raped? It didn't make sense, not with the scenario she'd described, but then again he couldn't be positive that her version of the incident had been a complete one. Was there something she hadn't told him?

He hadn't wanted to kill anyone for a long time, but at the moment he could cheerfully have put a bullet into Krugman.

All through the long trek he'd not only been watching for an armed man and a killer bear, he'd also been looking for his fucking horse. He'd hoped, for a while, that the buckskin would find its way back to him, or maybe to the cabin. Horses were herd animals; they didn't like being alone. But there hadn't been any sign of the animal, and though he could now see the building ahead, there still wasn't.

Damn it all to hell, he might never find that damn horse. If it didn't manage to find its way here—not likely, considering this was its first trip here, and it wasn't familiar with the area—they'd have to walk off the mountain. He would, anyway. If Angie's ankle was broken, she'd have to stay here while he fetched help. If the damn knuckle-brained horse hadn't taken off, he'd have been able to use the sat phone to call for help.

Instead he was up here with a murderer, a killer bear, an injured woman, and no easy way out. The way things had gone to hell, he was surprised they *hadn't* been struck by lightning; that was about the only thing that hadn't happened. Of course, a lightning strike would have wiped away all his worries about the other stuff.

Dare was good at focusing. After allowing himself a brief respite by silently cursing at everything, he pulled his frustration back in and stuffed it away, so he could concentrate on what had to be done. Taking care of Angie was number one. Get her inside, get her dry and warm, check out her ankle—and any other injuries she hadn't bothered to tell him about—and get her to eat. Survival always came down to basics. She needed medical attention, food, water, and sleep.

He couldn't provide a hospital or a restaurant, but he did keep the basics on hand. Once she was taken care of, he'd make a plan for what came next.

"We're almost there," he said, jostling her a little to make her stir. "Are you okay?"

When she finally responded, her voice was thin and slurred. "You keep asking me that."

"Yeah, well, you're too fucking quiet."

She mumbled something he didn't catch.

"What?" he barked.

She lifted her head. He couldn't see the motion, but he felt it, felt the shift of her weight. "I said, you curse too much." Her voice was still weak, and she shook like a leaf, but she'd found the strength to criticize him.

He felt a little more cheerful. Things were looking up.

Chapter Fifteen

Dare stepped into the lower level of his cabin, out of the rain at last. He stopped, shuddering with relief, as he shone the flashlight around the stalls on the bottom floor, looking for any sign of disturbance. Everything was quiet, just as he'd left it. Only when he was certain that nothing else was in there did he close the door and throw the heavy latch, as glad as he'd ever been that his design made this place a defendable fortress.

Exhaustion dragged at him. He made it a point to stay in shape, but he wasn't Superman. He hadn't gotten much sleep last night before the storm had jarred him awake and the pistol shots pulled him out into the dark rain. For the past several hours he'd been pushing himself hard, so hard all he could do was thank God the cabin hadn't been even a hundred yards farther, because he might have had trouble making that hundred yards.

He couldn't rest yet, though. The next step was to get Angie up the damn ladder. Everything he needed to take care of her was on the upper level, and that was the safest place to be, anyway.

He stared at the ladder, debating with himself whether he

should carry everything up in one trip, or leave the gear here and take Angie up unencumbered. The second way would make getting her up there easier, but then he had to think about the effort of making another trip.

When he thought about the possibility of dropping her, that made the choice obvious. Angie first, then the rest. He put the flashlight on a shelf, unslung both rifles and propped them against a stall. "I'm going to put you on your feet," he explained, gripping her waist with both hands to shift her weight. "Foot, rather. Can you stand?"

There was a pause while she processed what he was saying, then she said, "I don't know."

Not what he wanted to hear, but honest. He lifted her off his shoulder and carefully let her slide down his body, and once he had her upright, close to the ladder, he kept one arm around her until she had her balance. She grabbed the ladder, leaning into it, and put all her weight on her left foot.

The lower level was dark with shadows, but enough light came through the two windows above that he could see she was trembling from head to foot. The hard rain had washed away a lot of the mud that had been covering her when he'd found her, but she still looked like hell, her face paper white in the dimness, her dark eyes huge and glassy and rimmed with the bruised look of utter fatigue. She stood there swaying and shaking, watching him without even a flicker of curiosity in her eyes, waiting for whatever he told her to do next.

He slid the heavy saddlebags from his left shoulder and let them drop, then glanced up, considering the different ways he could get her up there, visualizing each one. Piggyback would be easiest on him, but he didn't think she had enough strength left to hang on, so that was a nonstarter. Putting her in front of him and basically pushing her up would require too much effort on her part, and right now she probably didn't have the strength to handle that anyway. Only one way was left. He removed his hat and tossed it to the floor beside her saddlebags. "Over my shoulder one more time."

She didn't comment. He took in a deep breath and gathered his own strength, then gripped her waist, tossed her into position, and went up the ladder. He took it slow and steady, because he sure as hell didn't want to drop her on her head. The upper floor was a long flight up—fourteen rungs, to be precise. He had to hold her with his left arm and use his right hand for climbing, at the same time keeping her angled away from the ladder so he wouldn't bang her ankle.

The last two rungs, and stepping from the ladder onto the ledge of the sleeping platform, were the trickiest parts. He had to shift his balance, and he was reaching down for support rather than gripping something at eye level. He'd gone up that ladder hundreds of times without giving it a single thought, but with Angie on his shoulder he thought about every move, made sure it was the right one, then cautiously executed it. He was too tired to take anything for granted, not even muscle memory.

When he was standing solidly on the sleeping platform, he eased her off his shoulder and held her steady; if he didn't hang on to her, she'd collapse to the floor. Her knees weren't steady, and it wasn't just the ankle, it was sheer exhaustion.

He guided her hand to one of the partition walls. "Hold on for just a minute. Can you do that?"

Silently she nodded.

As swiftly as possible he removed her sodden coat and let it drop to the floor, then unsnapped and unzipped her slicker and tossed it to the side, too. While he was at it, he removed his own slicker and coat. The air inside the cabin wasn't warm, but they had to get dry before they could get warm.

Stepping inside the sleeping partition where he'd set up his mattress and sleeping bag, he turned on the small propane camp heater he'd brought, and the LED lantern. The too-white light that lit the small space was eerily, uncomfortably similar to lightning, but minus the drama. For a brief second Angie looked a lit-tle spooked, then fatigue washed the expression away.

"Okay, let's get you more comfortable," he said as he threw the sleeping bag off the mattress so it wouldn't get wet. Going back to her, he didn't waste time helping her hop to the bed; he simply picked her up and carried her the short distance, going down on his knee to lay her down, then carefully easing her right foot down. She shuddered, then sighed and closed her eyes.

"Thanks," she said, slurring the single word.

"I'm going to get our stuff and bring it up here. I'll be right back."

This time she didn't answer. Dare was down the ladder and back up in less than a minute, bringing everything, even Angie's muddy rifle. After dumping it all on the floor, he pulled the lad-der up and laid it on the ledge, making the sleeping platform in-accessible to both man and beast.

Angie hadn't moved since he'd laid her on the mattress; it looked as if she'd fallen into a deep, instant sleep . . . one in which she was still shaking and shivering.

He hated to wake her up, but he didn't have any choice. "Come on, Sleeping Beauty, shake it off," he said as he pulled out the clothes and provisions he'd need. "We have to get you out of those wet clothes."

Things were definitely screwed up when he actually wanted to hear her say, "*In your dreams, buster. I'd rather die of hypothermia than let you see me naked.*"

But she didn't say that, or anything else. She was either asleep or unconscious.

Shit.

He went through the clothes he'd brought, which didn't take long. Everything he owned was way too big for her, but it would have to do for now. He hadn't gone through her saddlebags yet, but even if she had packed a change of clothes they'd likely be damp, at the very least, and who the hell wanted to sleep in jeans, anyway? He grabbed a flannel shirt, a pair of long johns that would be too big but would be warm and comfortable—and easy to get on her—and the first-aid kit. Then he got a pack of wet wipes and sat down on the floor next to the mattress. Food and water would be next, but he wanted her dry and warm first, and he wanted a look at that ankle. He hoped like hell it was just a bad sprain. Sprained they could handle; broken would be a huge pain in the ass to deal with.

"Sit up," he said, putting his hand on her shoulder and shaking her.

Clumsily she knocked his hand aside. "Lea' me alone," she mumbled.

"No can do. Come on, sit up. You're going to die if you don't get out of those wet clothes. You're already hypothermic. You won't get warm until you're dry. So sit up." He put brisk command in his voice, as if he were still in the military.

She opened her swollen eyes a little and, like a good little soldier, tried to struggle to a sitting position, only to fall back when her muscles refused to obey.

"I can't."

"Yes, you can. I'll help." He slipped a hand under her back and very gently eased her up, then grabbed the saddlebags and stuffed them behind her to help prop her upright. As pillows, they sucked, but they were all he had. "Just sit up long enough for me to get you cleaned up and in dry clothes. That's all you have to do. I'll handle the rest."

"'kay."

She clutched the side of the mattress, swaying, but she stayed upright, with her solemn dark gaze fixed on his face. "You can't look."

"Bullshit," he scoffed. "You think I'm going to get you naked and not look?" Maybe he should have promised, but he'd have been lying and they both would have known it. He was a man; of course he was going to look.

"You'll laugh. I don't have any boobs."

She was definitely on the verge of being completely out of it, or she'd never have said something like that. He bit the inside of his cheek to keep from laughing, because he figured if he did it would hurt her feelings. He needed her cooperation, not a battle. "That's okay. I have a little dick." And this time he lied without compunction.

He watched her brow knit in a frown as she processed that, laboriously forcing her tired and hypothermic brain to work through whatever barriers of modesty and insecurity she had.

Finally she gave a tiny nod, and allowed him to undress her.

He kept his mind out of the gutter, which was tough because that was never a long trip for him, but this time he resolutely refused to let his thoughts go there. She had put her trust in him, and by God he'd honor that. He'd keep his mind on the chore at hand, and the reason for it, and save the lusting for later.

Once she'd given her permission, she seemed to sink back into deep lethargy, not showing any reaction at all as he peeled off her wet clothes, not even when he reached around to unsnap her bra, which wasn't much of a bra as far as he could tell, really just an extra layer of cloth. The bra wasn't as soaked as the rest of her clothes, but mud and water had seeped beneath her slicker and shirt and it was damp in places. He tossed it onto the sodden heap with the rest of her clothes.

Dare couldn't say he'd never imagined Angie naked. He had. Several times. Maybe a hundred or so. But he'd never imagined that the first time he saw her naked would be in these circumstances, or that he'd try really hard to keep his gaze from lingering on her small round breasts and tight nipples. She was wrong; she had boobs, pretty ones that were small and high, and he guessed she wore a bra more because she thought she was supposed to than because she really needed one. He loved tight nipples, but not when they were tight from cold instead of what he was doing to them. He didn't like that her skin looked almost bloodless, that she could barely sit up, and knowing how helpless she was, how much in danger she was, gave him the strength to keep his mind on what needed to be done and not on what he'd love to be doing.

He checked her for wounds on her upper body, but beyond a variety of scrapes and bruises there wasn't anything to concern him, no cuts, no punctures. He wiped her down quickly with a wet wipe, starting with her face and moving downward, followed that with a rubdown with the one towel he'd brought along, then slipped her arms into the sleeves of the flannel shirt and buttoned it up.

Once that was done, he eased her down on the mattress and began working her boots off. Cowardly, he removed the left one first, figuring he needed to work up to the tough stuff. He could cut the boot off if he had to, but if her ankle was just sprained she'd need that boot. When he moved to the right foot, he completely unlaced the boot so he could make it as loose as possible, then very gently began easing it off. Angie immediately tensed and uttered a choked cry. "Sorry," he murmured, working his fingers inside the opening and bracing her ankle as best he could, but there was no way that boot was coming off without her foot and ankle flexing at least a little. She clenched her fists and jaw, her eyes closed tight, and endured.

Finally the boot and sock were off, and he could see the ankle. It was swollen and bluish, but there was no bone poking through the skin, no obvious unnatural position. He didn't have X-ray vision, so maybe it was sprained or maybe there was a simple fracture. At any rate, the best he could do was cool it, wrap it, and keep her off it for now.

First things first, though. The rest of her clothes had to come off. He hooked his fingers in the waistband of her soaked sweatpants and began working them down, dragging her underwear along, too. Again, she flinched when he had to get her foot free, but she didn't make a sound. Thank God his flannel shirt was so big on her it covered her down to the middle of her thighs, because he could carry his good intentions only so far. As it was, the glimpse he got of dark pubic hair was enough to make his heartbeat jump into second gear. God almighty. How much could he take?

As much as was necessary, that was how much.

Almost growling as he pulled a fresh wet wipe from the pack, he set about cleaning away any mud he saw, then briskly dried her with the towel and got his thermal long johns on her without causing her too much discomfort. She made a low, inarticulate sound of relief at finally having dry clothes on; he gave another involuntary growl, whether of regret or relief that she was covered, he couldn't have said. Finally he put one of his clean socks on her left foot, leaving the other one bare so he could tend to her ankle.

Okay, he was making progress. Next he towel-dried her hair, which had been partially protected by the hood of the slicker but, like everything else, had gotten soaked anyway. Then he moved on to her hands.

Her hands were a mess, swollen and bruised, her palms almost shredded with cuts. As gently as possible, not wanting to hurt her, he began cleaning them. There was a real danger of infection, because she'd been crawling through mud with open wounds on her hands. After the mud was cleaned away, he tore open an antiseptic pad from the first-aid kit and once again gently but thoroughly wiped the wounds, looking for bits of trash in the cuts. She didn't say a word, and flinched only once, when he raked a splinter from a cut on the pad of her thumb. Then he smeared antibiotic ointment over all the cuts, wrapped her palms with gauze, and taped the bandages in place.

The ankle was next. He sat on the mattress next to her and lifted her right leg onto his lap, with her foot positioned so he had unencumbered access to it. There wasn't much he could do: tear open an alcohol wipe and gently lay it across the swollen joint to cool it, then wrap an Ace bandage firmly around her foot and ankle.

Through it all Angie just lay there, too damn quiet, too damn still. He put his hand on her shoulder and shook her a little, until her eyes cracked open. "Are you okay?"

"Cold." Her eyes closed again. "Sleepy."

"You have to eat and drink something first, then we'll get you into the sleeping bag."

She nodded, but he could tell even that was an effort.

If he hadn't been up most of the night, and so tired himself he would like nothing better than lying down for a little while, maybe seven or eight hours, he'd have already thought to start heating water on the camp stove he always left up here, so they could each have a cup of hot instant coffee. If nothing else, hell, hot water with some sugar in it would do wonders. In fact, he didn't want any caffeine, he wanted to sleep, so the sugar water sounded like a damn good idea.

He got the propane camp stove out of the locked storage bin where he kept it, and turned it on. There was a camp percolator, too, for making an entire pot of coffee when he had a hunting party up here, but this time all he did was dump two bottles of water into the percolator and set it on the flame to heat, then opened some packets of sugar and dumped them in, too. Good enough.

While the water was heating, he got some food and shook her awake and made her sit up one more time. She heaved an aggrieved sigh, which he took to be a good sign.

"Feeling any better?"

"A little." Her voice was still thin with fatigue, she was still shivering, but shivering was a good sign.

"I'm heating some sugar water. It'll be ready in a few minutes." He sat down on the mattress beside her, put his arm around her for support and warmth. "Until then, be chewing on this." He had a couple of power bars, which he opened and tore bite-sized pieces from, feeding her and himself in turn until the bars were gone. They both needed the calories, so their tired bodies would have fuel to burn.

By the time the bars were finished, the sugar water was steaming. He turned off the camp stove, then divided the water into two camp cups, and took them both over to sit beside her again. "Can you hold this?" he asked, holding out a cup to her.

"I think so." She took the cup and gave a little moan of pleasure as the heat from the metal sank into her cold fingers. Her hands were shaking, but she managed to get the cup to her mouth and sip the hot liquid. Before he settled down himself, he got a couple of aspirin out and handed them to her. She took them without comment, but hell, she wasn't an idiot, she recognized aspirin. Then he settled down beside her and concentrated on drinking his own sugar water, feeling the warmth spread through him as he stretched his legs out and finally let himself relax a little.

"Thanks," she said after several minutes of silence and companionable sipping.

"You're welcome. Sorry it isn't coffee, but—"

"Not for the water." Her voice was a little stronger now that she'd eaten, and having something hot to drink was working its magic. "For getting me here. For everything."

Dare snorted. "What did you expect? That I'd leave you out there on your own?" Thank God she hadn't yet thought to ask what he'd been doing out at night in such godforsaken weather in the first place.

She looked down at the cup in her hands, concentrated on it. "No, but . . . you could tell me how stupid I was to get myself into this mess. You could toss me a wet wipe and make me take care of myself. You could . . ."

"I could be an ass," he growled.

"Yeah." The single word wasn't much more than a breath.

"You're not stupid. You didn't get yourself into a mess, you got caught up in someone else's shit, and you were trying damn hard to get yourself out of it. As far as cleaning you up and all that, if I'd thought you were capable of dressing yourself, I'd have let you do it. But you weren't, so I took care of it. That's it. No big deal." She didn't have any idea how hard it was for a man to undress and wipe down a woman he had no shot at getting into the sack, and he wasn't about to enlighten her.

"I think saving my life is a pretty big deal."

He rubbed his jaw. Put that way, his comment hadn't been the most graceful one in the world, but what the hell, he'd never known his way around a pretty phrase. He was blunt, his temper burned on a fairly short fuse, and he didn't have a lot of patience. Throw those three characteristics together, and they didn't produce a man who had a slick way with words. "I can still be an ass," he said gruffly. "This good stretch probably won't last long."

Unbelievably, a very faint smile twitched at the corners of her mouth. "Probably not," she agreed.

All right, this was more the Angie he knew, the one who could throw him straight into pure fury faster than anyone else he'd ever met. But he was so glad to see that crappy effort at a smile that he didn't let her punch any of his buttons. He was feeling relieved on several points: She was still at the end of her rope, but she was rallying. Her ankle might be cracked, but it wasn't a compound fracture, so taking care of it wasn't an emergency. They had shelter, they had food and water, they had warmth. Getting here had been hell, but they were going to be all right.

He downed the rest of his water and she did the same. "Let's both get some rest," he said as he took the cups and set them aside. There was some mud on the mattress—big surprise there—so he cleaned it away, then arranged the sleeping bag on top of it and helped Angie slide inside it. She gasped in pain when she

bumped her ankle, then settled down and pulled the edge of the
bag around her, almost covering her head.

"I'm so tired," she murmured.

"Then go to sleep. I'm going to get into some dry clothes, then
stretch out beside you and get some sleep, myself."

She made a noise in her throat, her eyes drifting shut.

He set about pulling off his own wet clothes. A couple of times
he glanced toward Angie to see if she was watching, but she was
making like a turtle with that sleeping bag, and all he could see
was the top of her head. In any other circumstance, his ego would
be bruised. Yeah, right.

He tried to come up with a plan for tomorrow—well, *today,*
since it was morning now, though the rain still drummed on the
roof and the day didn't look a whole lot brighter than it had when
they'd first arrived here—but he couldn't think straight. He was
warmer, he'd had something to eat, and now exhaustion was taking over.

He moved the propane camp heater closer to their feet, but
not so close that he could accidentally kick it, then turned off the
lantern and in the deep shadows stretched out on the mattress beside her. His feet hung off; it was a double-sized mattress, which
was damn small by his standards but it was what fit best inside the
sleeping stalls, and he usually slept on the diagonal just to give
himself a little more length. Sometimes he folded his dirty clothes
and placed them on the floor at the bottom of the mattress so
he'd have something to rest his feet on, but right now he was too
tired to get up and he didn't give a shit whether his feet hung off
or not.

He'd thought he would drop right off to sleep, but he didn't.
Even as tired as he was, he could still feel the burn of adrenaline
pumping through his system. The ordeal wasn't over. They were
safe, for now, and relatively comfortable, but this situation wasn't
over by a long shot. There was still a killer out there, and a bear
that would have to be hunted down and eliminated. The storm

was over, but heavy rain was still complicating everything. He wouldn't be walking anywhere until the weather cleared, however long that took.

"Dare." His name floated into the shadows, just a whisper, as if she thought he might be asleep and didn't want to wake him if he was.

"What?" he responded. God, if she had to piss, he was going to cry. The portable toilet was behind the cabin, and not only was the rain still pouring down, but he'd have to get her down the ladder, into the toilet, back up the ladder . . . it boggled the mind. Hell, he'd make her pee in a cup if that was the problem.

She didn't need anything like that, though. Instead she said, "I can't get warm. I'm so cold."

"Do you want some more sugar water to drink?" Everything in him protested at the idea of getting up, but he'd make the effort.

"No. I—" She broke off, was silent for a few moments, then she took a shuddering breath. "Would you get . . . would you get under the cover with me? You're so warm, and I'm so cold I hurt." She sighed, made a sound from deep in her throat that was a cross between a moan and a gasp, and then she said one more word:

"Please."

Chapter Sixteen

As little as ten hours ago, if anyone had even suggested to Angie that she'd ever, under any circumstances, ask Dare Callahan to get in a sleeping bag with her, she'd have thought about seeing if that person could be committed for his or her own safety, because obviously said person was nutty as a fruitcake. But just eight hours ago she'd been peacefully asleep in her own camp, and the night's hellish events hadn't yet begun.

A lot of water had gone under the bridge since then, literally as well as figuratively. There had been times when she hadn't been certain she'd live another minute, but her only option had been to keep pushing, keep trying. Even after Dare had found her the pain and miserable cold had seemed unending; the only difference was that she hadn't been alone. He'd been there, strong and never-faltering even though she'd known, in the part of her brain that wasn't preoccupied with the struggle to survive, that the cold and rain and relentless effort were all wearing him down, too.

She had been so terrified that she felt as if some part of her soul had been permanently altered, in a way she couldn't yet fully comprehend. She had been smashed down to a tiny portion of herself, all of her resources pulled inward and devoted to survival, and only now could she feel herself begin to unfold again, feel her mind and body trying to resettle into normalcy.

There was, as yet, a disorienting sense of unreality about the whole situation that allowed her to ask Dare to get under the cover with her and share his body warmth, and to be unsurprised when he didn't hesitate.

"Just lie there," he said, getting on his knees and unzipping the bag all the way around so it would lie flat. "You don't have to do a thing. I'll pull the bag from under you."

She gave a brief nod, held herself in silence as he moved her around, pulling the sleeping bag free as he went. Every movement jarred her ankle, even with the elastic bandage snugly supporting it. Dare hadn't said anything while he was wrapping it, and she hadn't asked, but now her brain was reengaging. When he gently cupped her right calf and lifted her leg, she said, "Is it broken?"

He gave her a quick glance, the expression in his blue eyes sharp despite his obvious fatigue. "I don't know. If it is, it's just a simple fracture or a hairline crack, nothing major."

Good news, bad news, though she'd heard all her life that a simple break in the bone would heal a lot faster than a severe sprain. If her ankle was better tomorrow, then she'd know it was nothing more than a sprain. There was nothing she could do to change the situation one way or the other.

He spread the sleeping bag out over her and the mattress; she moved restlessly, trying to adjust her foot so the weight of the down was pressing down on her toes, which made her ankle throb. Damn, this was going to be a pain in the ass, in more ways than one. "I hate being helpless," she grumbled, then wished she hadn't complained.

"Yeah, it sucks," he said bluntly, not bothering with a pep talk or even sympathy, which was okay with her. He'd carried her on his back for hours, so she figured she should at least deal with the pain and inconvenience of a hurt ankle. He then moved on to the business at hand. "Okay, let's figure out the best way to do this, considering your ankle. We can try the spoon position, with you on your left side."

That sounded reasonable; she shifted onto her left side, curled into the smallest ball possible, and gingerly placed her right foot on top of her left one. Dare slid under the sleeping bag with her, tucked himself firmly against her and draped his right arm over her waist. They had spent so many hours in constant physical contact that she had felt a little adrift when they weren't touching; now, feeling him all along her back, his thighs against her butt and legs, something deep inside her relaxed, as if a previously unrecognized need had been fed.

If only the cold would go away. Shivering, she pulled the sleeping bag almost to the top of her head again, hoping their shared body heat would soon begin to seep into her. If she had a hair dryer for her hair . . . but she didn't, and having a damp head was making it even more difficult to get warm. Being so exhausted that all she wanted to do was sleep, and not being able to go to sleep because she was so cold, was miserable.

He gave a weary sigh and she felt his arm get heavier. Evidently he wasn't having the same trouble going to sleep. Angie tried to hold herself still, so her shivering wouldn't disturb him. She must not have been successful, because after a minute he muttered, "Go ahead and let your teeth chatter; it'll warm you up faster."

So she did. She let the bone-rattling shudders shake her from head to toe; her teeth clattered together like castanets. Wave after wave swept through her; she'd relax, thinking they were over, only to be seized by another. Dare held her through the quakes, and gradually the time between them lengthened as her body generated heat and Dare's warmth began to create a snug haven under the down-filled sleeping bag. With the cold banished, heavy lassitude melted her bones and she felt herself sinking from consciousness.

Just before she went out, Dare's rough, sleepy voice rumbled grumpily, "I'll wake up with a hard-on, so don't give me any shit about it."

"That's okay," Angie mumbled. "It's too little for me to worry about." He'd said so, hadn't he? Then she nestled her face against the mattress and went to sleep as suddenly and deeply as if she'd been dropped over a cliff.

Chad Krugman huddled miserably under the rocky overhang, watching the gray sheets of rain and wondering if it was ever going to stop. During the night the lightning storm had moved on and he'd begun to hope the storm was over, then another wave of thunder and lightning had arrived and the second was even worse than the first. He'd had to spend his time going from horse to horse, settling the bastards down, until that storm, too, had rolled on down the mountains.

That had been the pattern all night long. The thunderstorms just kept coming, and the rain never stopped. Now daylight had arrived, but the day didn't seem a lot better than the night, other than the fact that he could at least see—but what he could see wasn't pretty. All that water rushing downward had turned rivulets into torrents, creeks into boiling rivers, and the mountainsides into expanses of mud that he was afraid were going to start sliding, taking trees and rocks and everything else in the path along with it.

He was cold. He guessed it was a good thing that he had the horses, but spending all night in close quarters with four of them wasn't a good thing. They pissed, they shit, they farted. Sometimes he'd felt as if the smell was burning the hair out of his nose, but whenever he tried to put some distance between himself and the animals, the cold drove him back to them. They stank, but they put off a lot of heat. Chad had a personal misery index that he kept informal track of, and this ranked pretty close to a ten. He liked to know who was causing him trouble, and how much, but he thought actually writing things like that down would edge too close to crazy, plus he never wrote down anything that might come back to bite him in the ass.

Together, Mitchell Davis and Angie Powell had caused him to have a miserable night, and he was feeling very resentful toward both of them, even though Davis was already dead. If he hadn't had the bright idea of sitting on Angie's front porch in the dark so he could access her wifi, he never would have been able to track down those financials, and Chad would have been able to kill both of them the way he'd planned. Neither of them would have known what was happening; Angie would be out of the equation and he wouldn't have to worry about where she was. He still would have had to deal with the rain, but he could have spent the night snug in his tent; he'd have had food and water, and these fucking stupid horses would be in their corral, instead of nearly choking him with their farts.

From the way rain was still pouring down, it didn't look as if the sun was going to come out anytime soon. That might be good, might be bad. The rain would make it impossible for Angie to walk off the mountain—if she was still alive, which he had to assume until he knew differently—but it also hampered his own progress. The mud was everywhere, footing was treacherous, and he might get hypothermia while riding back to the camp. To make things even worse, visibility was so poor even during daylight that he could ride within a hundred yards of the camp and not be able to see it, which wasn't a good thing when he wasn't completely certain where it was.

He didn't have a choice, though; he didn't have the luxury of waiting, not that there was any "luxury" involved in his present situation. He had to get the keys to the SUV and get out of the country before the cops could be notified and start looking for him. He couldn't wait for better weather, because every hour now was one that he couldn't afford to waste.

The horses were a problem. They needed food and water, but

after the night he'd spent he didn't much care about the damn horses. He had to keep the chestnut fed and watered because he planned to ride it out of here as soon as the weather cleared, but as far as the other three were concerned, all he cared was that Angie not be able to get one of them, assuming she was still alive and capable of riding, which, again, until he knew better, was the assumption he had to go with.

Water was easy; there was water everywhere. He just didn't want to leave the shelter of the overhang, because he didn't have a slicker and his coat was still damp from being in the rain last night. Finally he decided that, as he was going to get wet anyway while riding back to the camp, getting wet now wouldn't make that much of a difference. It wasn't as if he didn't have dry clothes back at the camp. He was a decent person; he couldn't let them go without water.

So one by one he led them out into the rain and found places for them to drink. There wasn't much for them to graze on, but if they showed any interest in cropping at anything he stood hunched against the rain and let them grab at what food they could get. He got soaked to the skin all over again, of course. By the time he climbed on a rock and maneuvered himself onto the chestnut's back, he was feeling positively virtuous.

The other three horses he left tied under their rocky shelter, hoping they'd stay where they were and not try to shake the reins loose and wander off. He needed to know exactly where the horses were, so he'd know whether or not Angie had found one of them and was riding for help. At least they weren't on any recognizable trail, and the nightlong pounding rain had washed away any tracks they'd left. He was fairly certain Angie couldn't find them, not without a stroke of luck that would border on the miraculous.

The chestnut didn't like the soggy, insecure footing; he had to constantly urge it forward. He hunched his shoulders against the miserable pounding rain; wherever he ended up after he escaped from this godforsaken wilderness, he was damn certain it would be someplace where the sun shone every day, and he'd know which direction was which. If the sun had been out he would have been fairly certain of his direction, but the cloud cover was so thick he couldn't pick out a bright spot, so he had to rely completely on his sense of direction, which was tough when none of the landmarks were familiar—if you could call rocks and trees and bushes "landmarks." The only directions he could reliably tell were uphill and downhill, but that helped. The mountain chain ran north/south, so uphill, generally speaking, was west, and downhill was east. He wanted to go south, so that meant he kept the upward slope on his right.

Beyond that, the best he could do was try to pick out something in a visual straight line, at the edge of visibility, and ride to it. From there he'd pick out another target, and ride to it. The problem with that means of navigation was that he knew he hadn't ridden in a straight line during his panicked flight in the dark. But should he be angling uphill, or down? Who the fuck knew? He didn't even know how far he'd ridden last night; all he could do was estimate.

God, if only he didn't need those keys! If it hadn't been for that damn bear, he wouldn't be in this predicament. He'd have hunted Angie down and finished the job, he'd have the keys, and he'd have gotten a good night's rest. Granted, the weather today would still be crappy, but he could afford to wait out the rain, if that little detail had been taken care of.

The bear would be long gone by now, of course, but he'd love to be able to put a bullet in its ass for all the trouble it had caused him.

He actually found the campsite by accident. He came to a place where it seemed as if the mountainside had washed out, and he nudged the horse uphill to see if he could get above the mudslide that had turned into a roaring torrent that had taken some trees down with it. About seventy yards up he reached the head of the mudslide and started across, but the chestnut suddenly shied and began backing up, ignoring Chad's command. After a minute of trying to force the horse to go forward, he said to hell with it, and instead turned the horse uphill; it was willing to go up, and eagerly picked its way over the soggy, uneven footing.

Chad ducked his head; the rain was hitting him in the face. He didn't even have a hat with him. If he'd ever been more physically miserable in his life, he couldn't remember when. At least he'd improved his riding skills enough in the past year that he could stay on the chestnut bareback, otherwise he'd have been walking in this shit.

Then he saw, to the left and a little farther uphill, a corner of something orange, and a burst of excitement flooded him with so much adrenaline that he felt nauseated. The camp tents were a dirty orange, he assumed for safety reasons, so no one would shoot in that direction. Looking around, he thought he recognized the terrain.

He'd almost missed it. If the horse hadn't balked, he'd have ridden right past the camp, unable to see it in the pouring rain. Maybe the horse knew where it was and associated the camp with food.

His heart began slamming against his rib cage. Angie might be in one of those tents right now, armed and waiting to see if he came back. She'd be dry and comfortable, while he'd been stuck under an overhang with four horses, smelling their shit all night long. Maybe he'd just walk behind the tents and shoot into all of them, just to cover his bases—that would flush her out.

Except he didn't have any ammunition other than what was in the clip, so he didn't want to waste any. There was more ammo in his tent, of course, but until he had his hands on it he had to be careful.

Slowly he dismounted, and sank into muck that came up to his ankles. It pulled at him, resisting every step; if his boots hadn't been so tightly laced, it might have pulled them right off his feet.

No wonder the horse had been so jittery. He tied the reins to a low-hanging tree branch, even patted the horse's neck and said a few soothing words, keeping his voice low.

Jesus. All he had was this pistol. If Angie was there, she had a high-powered rifle capable of picking him off right where he stood. She'd be limited only by the poor visibility.

Slowly he eased forward, pistol in his hand. A part of him wanted to turn around and run, but running wasn't an option, so instead of focusing on his fear, he focused on the hunt. His plan to take care of Davis had thrilled him, in a way. Everyone always underestimated him; no one would have thought him capable of the meticulous strategy, the acting, the satisfaction that had come as he'd pulled the trigger. Hunting Angie Powell was a thrill of another sort, because she wouldn't be caught by surprise the way Davis had been.

He wasn't thrilled enough to show himself too soon, to take a chance that she might shoot him before he got the chance to shoot her.

At the edge of the thick wood he stopped, surveying the camp. It didn't look like much, but it was well situated; he'd give it that. Because the tents were on low platforms, they were still dry and snug, so well anchored that the wind hadn't taken them down. The place looked empty, though. There was no hint of movement, no smell of coffee or anything cooking, but that didn't mean anything. Angie knew what she was doing; she wouldn't give away her location so easily.

There wasn't any sign of that freaky bear, either. Weren't bears infamous for trashing camps looking for food? The tents looked undisturbed. Of course, Angie had done a big song and dance about keeping the food so far away from the camp, in a basket strung between two trees, about fifteen feet high, so maybe she'd been right about doing that.

He stood there for a long time, watching, listening, though he doubted he could hear anything over the steady drumming of the rain. Nothing moved. There was no sound other than wind and rain. Was it possible he'd been lucky enough to have hit her with that one wild shot and she was already dead? He didn't care if she'd died from a bullet or the bear, so long as she was no longer a problem.

It was also possible that she was stalking him as he was stalking her. He thought of her watching him, slowly bringing her rifle up, sighting through the scope . . . being hunted wasn't exactly the same kind of rush being the hunter was. She might be behind him, to the left, to the right . . . in one of those tents, watching and waiting for him to reveal himself. His heart began beating even harder. He gripped the pistol more tightly. If she'd seen him, she'd have already shot . . . right? One thing was certain; he couldn't stand here until night came again, waiting for inspiration, or luck.

Slowly he crept around the campsite, his gaze on Angie's tent. For the first time in hours he forgot about his physical misery, forgot about being cold and wet and hungry. All his discomfort was washed away in a heady combination of excitement and fear. It was impossible to separate the two, to tell which was making him breathe faster, which was making his stomach dance.

Finally he stood just behind Angie's tent, listening. Silence. If she was inside, she wasn't moving a muscle. She could have fallen asleep. Maybe she was worn out from staying awake all night waiting for him, poor baby. How would she have liked being stuck under a rock overhang with four horses all night, soaking wet, trying to keep them calm, with only their body heat to keep him from freezing? An almost vicious sense of anticipation seized him; he wanted to make her suffer the way he'd suffered.

He figured he'd be most vulnerable while he was unzipping the tent's entrance. He'd be crouched, one hand occupied, and the sound might wake her— No, wait. He wasn't thinking clearly. The zip would be secured from the inside. If she was there, he wouldn't be able to unzip the entrance, but on the up side, he'd know for certain she was in there, because tents couldn't zip themselves.

That realization was elating. He might not be as good at this wilderness shit as she was, but he'd outsmart her. He'd outsmarted everyone his whole life, because they expected him to be some doofus nerd. Why should she be any different?

Gingerly, one slow step at a time, he worked his way around the tent, until he could see the entrance.

It wasn't zipped. The entrance flap hung open.

His heart almost failed him. Had she heard him coming, and left the tent before he got close enough to see the entire camp? Or was she in there anyway, just out of sight, the entrance open so she could see him and—

He had to calm down, go back to his earlier thought: If she had the opportunity to shoot, why hadn't she already done so? He was an accountant; he was a logical person, and he could do some deductive reasoning. If she'd been able to shoot, he'd already be dead. He wasn't dead, therefore she wasn't able to shoot.

Emboldened, despite the way his knees were shaking, he quickly stuck his head inside the tent. It was empty.

Okay. All right. She wasn't here. Was she clever enough to hide in *his* tent, figuring he wouldn't think to look for her there? No, she had to figure he'd go to his own tent for dry clothes and a slicker, which would make it the perfect interception point, right? If she was there, the best place for her to be, and the most dangerous place for him to go, was his own tent.

He straightened away from Angie's tent and took another look around the silent camp. Well, fuck it. He had to have dry clothes. He made his way over to his tent, his feet sinking more deeply into the mud; the ground had deteriorated more in this direction.

He did the same routine, standing and listening for what felt like forever, and hearing nothing from inside the tent. He summoned his nerve, then quickly looked inside his own tent. No Angie. It was just as he'd left it.

That left Davis's tent. God, he hoped and prayed the SUV keys were in Davis's tent, and that Angie wasn't. Or, if she was, that she was already dead, but why would she crawl into Davis's tent to die? *Because it was the closest to where he'd last seen her.*

A chill ran down his spine that had nothing to do with the cold or wet. Shit! Why hadn't he thought of that before?

Calm down, calm down. This didn't change anything. He still would have had to check the other tents, and he'd been very quiet and careful. The same scenario still held: If she was inside the tent, the entrance would be zipped.

Davis's tent entrance was open, the way the other two had been. Chad checked inside, just to be certain, then straightened and looked around. Where the hell was she, unless the bear had dragged her off? He wished he had some way of knowing for certain. She wasn't in any of the tents, therefore she was either dead or trying to walk down the mountain. If she was walking, she couldn't be making very good time, but the fact that it was possible that she was out there made it more urgent that he find those keys and get out of the country. He didn't know all the paths on this mountain, but he did know the direction in which she'd be going: down. And her destination was the same as his.

Which meant he didn't have any time to waste. He ducked into Davis's tent, wiped away the water that was streaming down his face, and began searching. Davis hadn't brought a lot with him; he had more clothes and gear in the back of the SUV, of course, but everything he'd brought to the camp was in his saddle-bags and one small duffel. Chad dumped out the contents of both, muttering under his breath and willing the set of keys to be there. Nothing. He went through everything again, more slowly this time, running his hand into every pocket of every garment, even looking under the inflatable mattress and inside the sleeping bag.

The keys weren't here.

He sat down on the mattress and took a deep breath. Damn it, he needed those keys! Surely to God Davis hadn't kept them in his pocket, when there was no use for them up here, but logically, that was the only other place to look. They had to be on his body, or what was left of it. Chad shuddered at the thought of searching a partially eaten carcass, then wondered if the damn bear would swallow keys and clothes, too, the way sharks did. God.

Screw this. He didn't have time to look for Davis's remains and paw through bloody crap. Angie's keys would do just fine; that wasn't what he'd planned, and that rancher, Lattimore, would be suspicious when Angie's truck disappeared, but that was a risk he'd have to take. He burst from the tent, for the first time in hours not even noticing the rain, and headed back toward Angie's tent.

He went through the same process, emptying the contents of her duffel onto the tent floor, kicking things over and out of his way, then looked around for her saddlebags. Abruptly it sank in on him that the saddlebags weren't here. He checked everywhere again, just to make sure. No saddlebags.

His heart began racing again, because the implication was obvious: She wasn't dead. She was out there, heading down the mountain, and she had an hours' long head start on him. She'd come here for supplies first; now that he took more notice of what was in the tent, he realized that her slicker and rifle were missing, too.

He had to make it down the mountain before she did. And no matter how nauseating, he had to find the keys to the SUV.

He left Angie's tent and hurried once more to his own tent, got his rifle. The bear was probably long gone, but it wouldn't hurt to have more firepower, just in case. Then he left the camp and cautiously headed toward the cook site, willing himself to move forward. He was furious with himself, because Angie was ahead of him, and she might screw up all his plans. Damn it, he should've made sure she was dead, instead of panicking the way he had, taking the horses and running like a scared little girl.

Sure, everything had gone wrong. He hadn't expected Angie to see him shoot Davis, hadn't expected the bear—who would have?—and he'd panicked. There was no excuse. He couldn't let that happen again, because look how things had spiraled out of control.

Steeling himself, he pushed through the trees. It wasn't much farther; they hadn't gone more than thirty or forty yards, had they? Yes, right there. They'd been standing right there. But Davis's body was gone. Chad moved closer, and stepped on something squishy. The smell of shit made him gag. He looked down, blinking as it took him a moment to realize his foot wasn't in a pile of crap, but instead was tangled in a length of shredded intestine. "Shit!" He leaped to the side, then completely lost it.

He couldn't control his reaction. He turned his head and violently vomited onto the ground, gagging on bile. He hadn't eaten anything in hours, so in short order he had the dry heaves. Jesus! The pieces of carnage scattered around were no longer recognizable as a man, much less as Mitchell Davis. The rain had washed a lot of the blood into the ground, but nothing could cleanse this scene, nothing could make it anything less than horrible.

When he could control his stomach, he wiped his streaming eyes, then his mouth. He took small steps forward, trying not to step on anything else that had once been part of Davis. Even in the rain, the stench was almost overpowering. He tried to breathe through his mouth instead of his nose, but then he could actually taste the stench. His stomach heaved again, and he went through another convulsive spasm, bent over from the waist, snot streaming from his nose. He found himself looking at a piece of a shirt beside what looked to be a part of a hand. Yeah, that was a finger—badly mauled, but still recognizable.

Then he found that, after the initial horror, his brain either began accepting what he was seeing, or shut down any reaction at all. When he could straighten up and breathe again, even though he was wheezing like a hundred-year-old geezer, somehow the carnage didn't seem quite as bad. Maybe one piece of body wasn't any worse than the next piece. Forget about Davis; he'd already been dead when the bear began gnawing on his body, so it hadn't made any difference to him.

Feeling calmer, Chad scanned the clearing until he saw a scrap of denim. He made his way to it, looking only at the fabric, not the scattered remnants of what had once been a man. When he got closer, he saw that the denim appeared to be a scrap of a lower pant leg. That was useless. There were other blue scraps scattered here and there, some too small, too shredded, to be what he was looking for. If the keys had fallen to the ground, in this muddy mess, he might never find them. Damn Davis; why hadn't he left the keys in the tent? Or let Chad drive?

There was nothing here. Despairing, he turned in a complete circle, looking beyond the clearing into the undergrowth of bushes, and finally something that, well, it wasn't blue, but it was— He went closer, pushed the bush aside, yelped when a thorn cut across his palm.

He swallowed hard, then dropped to his haunches and stared at what was left of the torn, bloodstained jeans. Some of Davis was still in them. Not much, but he started gagging again. He steeled himself, then reached out and stuck his hand inside the pocket that was closest to him, searching for the keys. Even the inside of the pocket felt squishy and sticky. He closed his eyes, tried to pretend that these were just another pair of jeans, just another pocket. His fingers dipped all the way to the bottom of the pocket. No keys.

Fuck! In a fit of rage, he stood and kicked the piece of carcass. Now what was he supposed to do?

Think, he commanded himself. Think! What would Davis have done with the keys?

Then he almost slapped himself on the forehead. He was an

idiot. Davis was right-handed, so of course the keys would be in the right pocket. He'd poked through the mess in the *left* pocket, not the right.

Using the toe of his boot, he kicked and prodded until the piece of carcass was rolled onto its other side. "One more time," he whispered as he shoved his hand into the pocket. This time he wasn't so squeamish; he had to have those keys. If the bear had eaten them, he didn't know what he'd do. Ride his horse into the next town, steal a car, run like hell . . . The odds that plan would work were slim to none, and he knew it.

His fingers brushed metal. He grabbed the keys, pulled them out, held them clutched in his fist. He almost burst into tears.

For a minute he just stood there, eyes closed, keys clutched in his hand. He was so elated and relieved he almost couldn't believe he'd actually found them, that something had gone right after such a fucking miserable night when everything else had gone wrong.

Okay. He was back from the brink of disaster. This would still work. Maybe Angie Powell was out there, but he had a horse and she didn't, and he had a plan and she didn't. He'd worked too hard for this to let one woman screw it up.

Maybe he'd run into her along the trail. Maybe he'd get another chance to kill her. He wouldn't look for her—that would take too much time and priority number one was making his escape. But if he did run across her, he wouldn't hesitate to shoot her. This time he'd make sure she was dead before he ran.

Holding the keys in his hands made all the difference. Things were back on track. He was in charge of his own fate again, and by God, nothing was going to get in his way.

Chapter Seventeen

The bear roused. After it had fed all it wanted, sated and tired, it had taken shelter from the storm under a giant deadfall that had partially blocked the wind and rain and slept through the rest of the night.

It had fed well the past few days. Early in the evening, before the storm, it had gone back to its previous kill to finish eating, and picked up the fresh scent trail of another human. He followed it to a place that was rich with odors, that of big animals mingled with more of the humans. Then the smell of fresh blood had all but exploded in his nose and he hadn't been able to wait, the prey was there, the meat still hot and fresh, the blood still flowing. This prey hadn't even run; catching it was much easier than before.

Now the bear had rested, and for now it was content to stay in its shelter, curled up and content. He heard some noises, but the weather and his own well-fed state gave him no incentive to investigate. There were a couple of interesting smells, but in his content, sleepy state they weren't strong enough, enticing enough, to pull him back out into the rain.

He had scratched some debris over the uneaten remains, and when his stomach was no longer full he would go back to his kill.

The scent would still be there.

Chapter Eighteen

Angie jerked awake from a deep sleep, sharp pain shooting through her ankle. She must have made a sound, because the big hand resting on her stomach gave her a comforting pat.

"Ankle bothering you?" The mutter, in Dare's gravelly voice, came from just behind her ear. He sounded as if he were barely awake.

"Just when I move it," she answered groggily. Her head was so filled with fog she could barely form the words. Her body was still heavy with fatigue, her muscles like noodles. She managed to crack her eyes open a slit; the small space was gloomy with dark gray shadows. She knew where she was, but she didn't know when she was. Was it twilight? Dawn? Had they slept around the clock?

"How long have we been asleep?" she asked on a sigh, her eyes already closing as she nestled deeper into the delicious warmth.

"Couple of hours."

"'Zat all?"

He grunted. There was an upheaval behind her and chilly air rushed under the sleeping bag, making her hunch her shoulders as he sat up. Frowning, she cranked her eyelids open just enough to see what he was doing as he sat up and turned off the small propane heater. Oh, okay. They were warm now, so they should save the fuel.

Her eyelids drifted shut again, closed out the dim light. It was still raining, hard, but now that she was dry and warm the effect was soporific. Dare lay down behind her again, sliding up close and tight, his heavy arm resuming its place draped over her waist. It was almost like sitting in his lap. She snuggled even closer against him, wiggling her butt to find the most comfortable spot, and went back to sleep.

She surfaced again with a sharp "Ouch!" when she banged her foot against his. Still not fully awake, she struggled to a sitting position and sat there, owlishly blinking her eyes, looking around but not really seeing their surroundings. With a groan, Dare rolled onto his back, letting his arm fall over his face to block out the light.

Angie closed her eyes and leaned against her upraised left knee. The pain in her ankle had already subsided, leaving her with no imperative to do anything except sit there, caught in a sticky web of inertia. She would have glared at the offending joint, but that took too much effort, so she just sat there, grumpy and half asleep. "You awake?" she whispered after a few seconds, when Dare hadn't moved again. If he wasn't she didn't want to disturb him, but if he was . . . well, she didn't know why she was asking.

"After you punched me? Yeah, I'm awake," he growled.

She thought about that, wondering if she should be indignant at being falsely accused, but again unable to muster the energy. "I didn't punch you." Maybe. She was pretty sure she hadn't. She turned her head, still resting it against her knee, and opened her eyes a little. "But I might have kicked you, because it hurt my ankle."

"You punched me."

Even as sleepy as she was, as punch-drunk, she was still capable of logic. "How? You were behind me. I can't punch backward."

"When you sat up." He moved his arm just enough for one half-opened eye to glower at her. "You punched me in the stomach."

They glared at each other, sleepy and irritable. She could feel herself weaving. Heaving a sigh, she closed her eyes again while she thought about what he'd said. "Not a punch," she finally insisted, having fumbled her way through her cloudy memories and making a decision. "That was my elbow, not my fist."

"My stomach appreciates the difference. Go back to sleep."

"What time is it now?"

He looked at his watch. "About half an hour after the last time you asked."

This wasn't good. If she woke up every time she moved her foot, she wasn't going to get much rest at all.

He heaved his own sigh. "Okay, let's try this." He flipped the sleeping bag to the side. "Lie down on your back."

"Hey!" She reached for the sleeping bag, protesting as the chilly air reached her.

"I'll cover us up again. Damn it, would you just lie down?" He didn't wait for compliance, just kind of sandwiched her in his arms and laid her back. Then he hooked his right arm under her knees, lifted her legs, and he shifted into the spoon position around her before draping her legs over his thighs. "How's that?"

It was actually very comfortable, at least for now. "Good," she muttered.

He stretched to reach the edge of the sleeping bag, and pulled it around them again, making sure the fabric wasn't tight around her feet. A deep sigh eased from his chest as he settled down, not an impatient sigh but one of relaxation; he curled his left arm under his head, and went back to sleep like a stone dropping into dark water.

The moment, the situation, etched itself on her brain. Carefully she turned her head just enough that was she able to see his face. This close to him, even in the dim light, she could see every thick, dark lash, the details of his strong facial bone structure, the small scar across the bridge of his nose. He wasn't a pretty man, by any means, but he was definitely a *man*. As angry as she'd been at him, as much as she'd resented the way he'd siphoned off so much of her business just by being *him*, she had also never been immune to him. If he was anywhere in the vicinity, she was acutely aware of his exact location, the rough, scratchy timbre of his voice; the powerful, restrained grace of his movements. It was as if her skin was a compass to his magnetic north, and she'd hated that weakness in herself.

Angie lay awake for a few minutes—a very few—listening to the rain and the heavy, rhythmic sound of Dare's breathing. She was in the one place she'd never thought she would be—in bed with him, in his arms—and it felt so natural she wasn't certain she really *was* awake.

She needed to think, but . . . later.

He woke her by gently lifting her legs off his. "What're you doing?" she muttered fretfully, because she'd managed to get some decent sleep in that position. She should be sleeping like a dead person, but instead they seemed to be destined for one to wake the other every little while.

"Gotta go." He sat up and scrubbed both hands over his face, his bristly growth of beard sounding like sandpaper on his rough palms.

"Go *where*? It's still pouring down." More asleep than awake, she gave him a look that managed to be both befuddled and grumpy.

"Not 'go where,' just go. As in, piss. How about you?"

Oh, God. Angie groaned. "I wish you hadn't mentioned it." But he had, and now she knew she wouldn't be able to go back to sleep until that problem had been taken care of. She turned her wrist to see what time it was, but was too groggy to focus her eyes. "I can't see my watch," she muttered, letting her arm fall back to the mattress. For all she knew, her watch wasn't working anyway, after being exposed to all that rain and mud. "What time is it?" As soon as she asked, she wondered what difference the time made.

"Almost noon."

Well, no wonder she needed to go. She pondered the situation for a moment longer, as dread and resignation grew. She struggled to sit up, braced herself on one arm as she tried to psych herself up to leave the warm cocoon of the sleeping bag. Hoping against hope, she said, "Please tell me this place has a flush toilet."

He snorted. Okay, that was answer enough.

"Portable toilet?" At least then she wouldn't be squatting behind a bush somewhere. She tried not to think of the effort involved, with a sprained ankle that wouldn't support her weight.

"Out back."

Whew! That still meant putting on boots, slicker, getting down the ladder, and going out in the rain, hopping on her one good foot, but it was worlds better than that bush she'd been thinking about.

"I can maybe find something for you to pee in," he said, but sounded doubtful. "Think you could hit a bottle?"

"I think I could hit a portable toilet," she growled. "What do you think I am, a precision pisser? Women don't practice things like that."

His mouth quirked, a movement that made the small scar in his cheek look even more like a dimple. She had the feeling that anyone else would have laughed out loud, but Dare didn't strike her as a man who laughed very much. She wondered if he ever had, if he'd been more open when he was growing up, and his transition to an ill-tempered, closed-in man had happened during his years in the military.

Hard on that thought came the realization that she herself

had done exactly that. When she was younger she'd laughed more, been more outgoing, then she'd let embarrassment and self-doubt shut her down for a while, make her pull back from people. Once those walls were up, though, staying behind them was easier than letting herself be exposed and vulnerable. Reaching out to her friends again had taken an effort, but she was so glad she'd done it. Was that what had happened to him? He'd gotten caught behind his own walls?

"In that case, how about a bucket?" he asked prosaically. "There's one I use for the horses."

The image that brought to mind made *her* want to laugh, but her own issues kept her reply solemn. "No, thank you. I'll manage."

"Ladies first, then. Let's get you down the ladder; I can wait."

She was tempted, but common sense raised its sluggish head. "You go ahead. I'm going to pull off these pants and put on my sweatpants again; no point in getting another pair of pants wet when mine already are."

He didn't argue with that logic, just collected her wet and dirty sweatpants and dropped them close by the mattress, where she could easily reach them. After stomping his feet into his boots and pulling on his slicker, he let down the ladder and disappeared from view.

A *bucket*?

Alone, Angie let a wan smile curl her lips. She might have taken him up on the proposition, if it hadn't been for the distasteful prospect of emptying said bucket. If she could have handled it herself, no problem, but she wasn't letting Dare Callahan handle a personal chore like that for her. Uh-uh.

On the other hand, he *had* seen her naked boobs—almost all of her, in fact. At any other time she'd have been mortified, not because she was so modest, but because she'd actually told him not to laugh at her boobs because they were little. Maybe when she felt more normal, when she wasn't still numb from the horror of what had happened last night, followed by the sheer struggle just to survive that had whittled her down to little more than willpower—or stubbornness—all of this would bother her more. Right now, it just didn't, even though normally she hated betraying any sign of vulnerability. Too much had happened for her to worry about whether or not her boobs were little, or that he'd laugh at her.

But he hadn't laughed, and somehow she didn't think he would. He wasn't what she'd expected. The damn man was nothing short of heroic, and that really bothered her, because it proved that once again her judgment had been faulty. How could she trust anyone, when she couldn't trust herself?

All of that was a subject for later, though, because already she could feel herself tiring, and she hadn't even made the trip to the toilet yet. Gathering her strength, she tugged his baggy long thermal underwear off and her cold, wet, dirty sweatpants on, shuddering as the clammy material clung to her legs. The sensation was awful, but she comforted herself with the thought that the situation was temporary. As soon as she got back from the toilet, she could change back into the unlovely but blessedly warm thermals.

Her ankle was a problem. More precisely, the elastic bandage wrapping it was the problem, because she couldn't get her boot on that foot. The bandage would get wet. The only thing to do was unwrap it, which she set about doing. She winced when she saw her ankle; it was an unsavory black and blue and green, swollen to twice its normal size, and removing the pressure of the bandage made the joint throb like blue blazes.

Nothing she could do about it, though, so she shoved the pain aside and pulled on her left boot. It was wet, too, inside and out, another item to go on her list of things to ignore. Next came her rain slicker, but it, at least, didn't make her shudder when she came into contact with it. She zipped and snapped, pulled the hood up, and was as ready as she could be, except for the fact that she was on the second-story sleeping platform and she needed to be at the bottom of that long ladder.

"A journey of a thousand miles," she muttered, and hopped to the ladder.

Actually getting on the ladder was the toughest part. She had to grasp it, sit down, locate a rung with her left foot, then lever herself up and around. Once she was properly situated, she was strong enough to hold herself on the ladder using just her upper body strength while she took another step down with her left foot. The process wasn't pretty, but it was effective.

It also took an enormous amount of effort when her body hadn't rebuilt its reserves. Every muscle in her body was trembling, and she was breathing like a bellows; just as she neared the bottom rung, she heard the scrape of a door opening.

"Fucking nipples on ice!"

The hoarse, muted roar would have made her fall off the ladder if it hadn't been for the telltale noise of the door. Holding tight to the ladder, she peered through the rungs at him, where he was almost completely hidden by the dark shadows at the back of the camp building. The expression made her blink. "I've never heard that one before," she commented faintly. "Innovative."

Rapidly he strode forward, his expression both disbelieving and furious as he gripped her waist and peeled her off the ladder. He stood her up for a brief second as he switched positions, bending down to hook his left arm under her knees and lift her off the floor, holding her tight against his wet slicker. "You could have broken your damn fool neck!"

"But I didn't," she pointed out with impeccable logic, even though she was still gasping for breath. "So I saved both time, and wear and tear on you." She hooked her left arm around his neck, and felt a *ker-THUNK* kind of thud in her chest as her heart reacted to how natural it felt to be held like this, to feel free to sling her arms around him.

If anything, he looked even more furious. "I can handle getting you up and down the ladder."

He was just standing there, instead of taking her outside, and her exertion in getting down the ladder had made the situation more dire. "I wasn't impugning your manhood," she said impatiently. "Just handle getting me out to the toilet. Pee now, chew out later."

Muttering more obscenities under his breath, he strode to the back door. It wasn't a regular door, but part of the wall itself that had been cut out and hinges installed, and was secured by sliding a two-by-eight into steel brackets. "Hold your hood in place," he growled. "The wind's still gusting."

She grabbed her hood and held it as he turned sideways and maneuvered her through the door. It was like walking under a waterfall. The rain felt like a solid sheet of water, hammering at them. The portable was placed against the back of the building, just a few steps away, but if she hadn't been wearing a slicker she'd have been drenched in a second. Ducking his head against the onslaught of water, Dare pulled open the toilet door and stood her up inside. "I'll wait here," he half-yelled, because the drumming of the rain on the plastic roof of the toilet sounded like, well, actual *drumming*.

She started to tell him not to be silly, to go back inside, but realized he wasn't going to budge no matter what she said, so the best thing she could do was not waste time. She took care of business as fast as possible, cleaned her hands with the gel hand sanitizer, then opened the door. He had her swooped up into his arms and back inside the cabin before she could get her bearings.

He put her down so he could secure the heavy door and peel out of his dripping slicker. Balancing on one foot, Angie removed her own slicker, and he hung them over a rail to drip dry. She drew in a breath that was rich with the smell of hay, horse, and feed, which reminded her of her own horses. "The bastard," she blurted. "He stole all four of my horses. I know he won't take care of them; he can barely ride."

"Then maybe he'll get thrown and break his neck," Dare said with a calm intent that told her he meant the comment literally.

"I hope so," she muttered, and she was being just as literal as he was.

"We'll get your horses back. Mine, too, if the nitwit didn't run himself to death," he said as he put his hands on her waist. "Alley oop." Without pausing, he tossed her onto his shoulder. She grunted as the impact drove out her breath, but didn't waste time complaining. Instead she grabbed him to steady herself as he began the upward climb; she was more than glad to let him carry her, because she was wiped out, almost back to square one. She was exhausted and cold, but at least she wasn't soaking wet.

He turned his back and gave her some privacy while she pulled off the sweatpants and worked his thermal underwear back up her legs and hips, though to be honest she was already so close to conking out she wouldn't have cared if he'd looked; it wasn't as if he hadn't put them on her the first time. Lying back on the mattress, she almost dozed off while he was rewrapping her ankle. Maybe she did actually go to sleep, because the next thing she knew he was sliding close against her and pulling the sleeping bag over them, enveloping them in a warm cocoon.

She snuggled back against him, oddly content. Feeling him so close to her was deeply comforting, something she desperately needed right now when she felt so off balance. Eventually everything would settle into place and she'd get a grip on things, but that time wasn't now. For now, being warm and having him there was enough.

There were so many important things to think about, but a thought, an idea, would rise to the surface of her consciousness and then drift away, her mind too tired to hold on to it. She could actually feel sleep coming, feel herself sinking closer and closer to that delicious edge of unconsciousness, until it enveloped her as surely as his arms were wrapped around her.

Chapter Nineteen

The next time she woke, Angie had the feeling that several hours had passed, that she had finally, at last, gotten enough sleep to make a difference to her exhausted body. Outwardly nothing had changed; it was still raining, the light was still dim and gray, and they were still nestled under the sleeping bag. Somehow she knew, though, that it was now late afternoon. Dare must have slept, too, because if he'd been awake again and moving around, he hadn't disturbed her, and she had to think he would have. She wasn't used to sleeping with anyone, which had contributed to her restlessness, and she thought the same could probably be said about him.

He was still asleep now, his body hard and warm against hers, totally relaxed. His arm was heavy around her, his breath hot against the back of her neck, his chest rising and falling in a slow, deep rhythm. Feeling him there like that made her want to turn into his arms, press her face against his chest, and just inhale the heated scent of his skin; for a moment, she was still just sleepy enough that she almost did it, almost took that step, then reality slapped her in the face and with a small jerk she stopped.

Which, of course, woke him up. He took a deep breath and slowly exhaled, his arm tightening around her in what she would almost call a hug, if they were on hugging terms. The ridiculousness of the situation made her smile. They'd faced a life-or-death situation together, they'd slept cuddled as close to each other as they could get, and they weren't on hugging terms? She knew one thing for certain: She would never, ever again view him as the enemy. She couldn't; he wasn't. He maybe never had been, but circumstance and her own lack of self-confidence had kept her from seeing him as he was. She didn't think he'd ever be an easy man to get to know, his grumpy state was likely permanent, but at the center of him was a solid streak of steely willpower that kept him going when lesser men would have given up.

"You okay?" he muttered, his rough voice guttural with sleep, but he didn't seem really interested in the answer because he nestled his cheek against the back of her head and relaxed again, as if he were going back to sleep. A moment later, though, she knew he wasn't, because the hard-on he'd warned her not to bitch about began pushing against her butt.

She thought about bitching anyway, just to jerk his chain, but sex was another one of those areas where she wasn't as confident as she'd like to be. In her experience, it was more trouble than it was worth: In exchange for suffering the uncertainty of exposing her emotions, as well as her less-than-perfect body and her less-than-perfect judgment, to a man who might or might not appreciate any of them, she would get to experience a climax brought about by a hand. Climax-by-penis was a fairy tale, as far as she was concerned, so why not just bypass the middle man, so to speak, and take care of her climaxes herself? The process was a lot neater, less complicated, and easy on the emotions.

Not that she was going to have sex with Dare Callahan. She didn't want to go there and she couldn't imagine why he would, either, except as an automatic kind of thing. She felt about as sexy as roadkill, and probably looked not much better. She couldn't even feel flattered by his hard-on, because it was just a reaction to waking up, and had nothing to do with her, personally. He'd have one even if she wasn't there.

So her options were that she could lie there and kind of enjoy feeling an erection poking at her even if she wasn't the cause of it, or she could sort of casually shift away as if she hadn't even noticed, pretend she was just waking up herself.

"Hey, don't mind me," he growled. "I'm just the guy with the hard-on poking at you, not somebody you really need to answer."

And just like that her good intentions fell away, because nobody else had ever been able to jerk her chain the way Dare Callahan did. "Oh, is *that* what that is?" she cooed. "I thought it was a tube of Chapstick."

He made a smothered kind of sound that might have been amusement, if he'd been the type of man who laughed. His big hand closed on her shoulder and he gently tugged her onto her back as he shifted to the side and propped himself on his elbow. Before she had an inkling what he might do, he gripped her hand and pressed it to the thick, hard ridge in his jeans. "Chapstick, my ass," he said. There was a faint curve to his mouth that said he really might have laughed.

Angie froze, her mind going blank with shock at what he'd done, at suddenly finding herself in such uncharted territory she had no idea which way to go, or how she'd even got there. She turned as red as any teenager and jerked her hand away, stammering, "Wh-what're you doing?" God, had he thought she was *flirting*? She didn't know how to flirt. She sucked at it, so she never tried.

"Correcting a misconception," he said, as if her question actually needed an answer. "Two, as a matter of fact."

If she hadn't been so at sea, she wouldn't have responded, wouldn't have let curiosity get the better of her. "Two?" she blurted, completely off balance and almost panicked by the light-ning speed with which the situation had altered.

"The first one, you can figure out on your own." He actually gave a real smile, one that crinkled the corners of those vivid blue eyes, and if she'd been standing her knees would have gotten wob-bly. Oh, thank God he didn't smile all that often, she thought fer-vently, because the effect was lethal. "The second one, I'll tell you about later."

"Why not now?" *Damn it!* What was wrong with her? Why didn't she just leave well enough alone, keep her mouth shut, and let the subject drop? Dare Callahan had just put her hand on his penis and she needed to stop thinking about him, divert him from thinking about it, and in general pretend it had never happened. She waved her hand as if to erase the words. "Never mind. It isn't important."

"That's a matter of opinion, but it can wait." He yawned and sat up, rotated his neck from side to side, stretched his arms over his head and rolled his shoulders, grimacing as ligaments popped. Getting her here had to have been a terrible effort for him, she thought guiltily. She had thanked him, but there was no way any words could repay him for what he'd done.

"Do you need to make another trip outside?" he asked as he twisted his neck from side to side, which made more popping noises.

"No, I'm good." She made a helpless gesture. "I'm sorry."

"For what?"

"For nearly crippling you. You sound like Rice Krispies when you move."

"Snap, crackle, pop? Hell, I sound like that every morning when I get up."

"I had to have made things worse."

"The mud was the hardest part. Carrying someone conscious isn't that tough. Dead weight's a bitch, though." He said it with the slightly absentminded manner of someone who was well acquainted with carrying dead weight, then rolled to his feet with a litheness that belied any sore muscles or stiffness. "I'm starving. You have any preferences for supper? We're okay for food. I always have some supplies up here, plus I brought more when I came up. We have jerky or power bars if easy's what you want, or I can heat some water and we'll have hot soup or stew—"

"Stew," she said, sitting up as the thought made her mouth water. She was starving, which wasn't surprising considering how many calories they had both burned during the night, without anything to eat in almost twenty-four hours except the sugar water he'd made for them, and a power bar each. "Anything I can do to help?"

"Tidy up what you can reach," he replied. "I kind of left the area in a mess this morning."

She was absurdly gratified that he didn't dismiss her offer. No, she wasn't very mobile and couldn't do much, but she could definitely crawl around the small space and pick up the dirty, soggy clothing that had been scattered helter-skelter. Their muddy boots had been left where they'd fallen, her mud-encrusted rifle and scabbard were propped in a corner, though Dare's rifle was within easy reach. The cups they'd used that morning were on the floor, as well as the power bar wrappers.

Dare was a military man; for him not to police his area told her more than words could on how exhausted he had been when he'd carried her up the ladder early that morning.

She tidied as much as she could, putting the trash in a plastic trash bag, folding their wet clothing into a neat pile so he could take them down and hang them over the stalls to dry. While she was doing that, Dare moved the camp stove into their small area, set it down, and lit it. She appreciated the notion behind not wasting any heat. She wasn't cold now, thank goodness, but the cabin was definitely chilly.

"This is an interesting design," she said, waving her hand to indicate the cabin. "You built it yourself?"

"I designed it. Hired someone else to build it. I was too busy to take care of it myself, plus I hate hammering shit together." He paused in the act of pouring bottled water into the percolator, and glanced up at her, blue eyes glittering. "Guess that wasn't the most diplomatic thing to say."

"Which part? The one that pointed out your business was booming while mine was withering away, or the interesting mental image of hammering shit?"

Her tone was wry. To her own surprise, she couldn't muster even a little anger at her career downturn. It had happened, she was in the process of dealing with it, and she'd make things work out in the end. On the other hand, she was definitely amused at his turn of phrase.

"The first part."

He didn't back away from trouble, she noted, just met it head on and dealt with it. For now, though, there was no trouble. She couldn't say there wouldn't be later, but as far as she was concerned last night he'd bought himself a lot of leeway. There was no way to tell where that leeway might run out, but she knew for certain it wasn't right here, right now.

"It's okay. Anyway, I like that you designed it so the horses are completely safe and enclosed."

He set the percolator on the flame. "I'd rather use four-wheelers; they're faster and aren't as much trouble, but a lot of clients prefer to do the whole roughing-in routine with horses so I had to take that into account. This way, either four-wheelers or horses can be secured below."

"Bear proof." Just saying the words made the bottom drop out of her stomach as a vivid memory flashed in her mind. Bile rose in her throat, almost choking her. She would never forget, never get those images out of her mind.

"Yeah." He gave her a sharp look that told her he'd noted her change of expression, or maybe there had been something in her voice that gave her away. "Exactly what happened last night? Start at the beginning."

Using her left foot, she levered herself back so she could lean against the wall and stretch her legs out in front of her. "I'm not sure where the beginning is. There was probably trouble between my two clients before they got here. There had to have been."

"They were arguing?"

"No, but they weren't friends, either. Their names are Chad Krugman and Mitchell Davis. I've guided Krugman before. He isn't much of an outdoorsman, but last year he came with a client of his and when he booked again this year I figured it was the same setup, that he was doing it for business reasons."

Dare dumped stew mix into two disposable bowls, then scooted back to sit propped against the wall beside her. His hard triceps was warm against her shoulder, his thigh rubbed against hers. "I get a lot of business associates, but usually they're on good terms."

Resolutely, she kept her mind on what she was saying, rather than on the big man who sat so close against her, once more sharing his body heat. "Mitchell Davis wasn't happy when they got to my place, and he wasn't happy with anything about me, the accommodations, food, the campsite, or anything else. I thought he was just one of those people who is born a bastard and dies a bastard, you know?"

"I've met my share," he said drily.

She sighed. "Yesterday, I left them in camp while I scouted for fresh bear sign at a location where I'd seen some before. I thought I saw some trash lying off to the side, but when I got over there it was a digital camera, and part of a plaid shirt." She drew a deep breath. "There were bear tracks, and a lot of blood, and scuff marks where something had been dragged."

"God." He leaned his head back against the wall and said in a long-suffering, incredulous tone, "Please tell me you didn't follow the trail to a bear's kill."

"I was already closer to it than I ever wanted to be," she said grimly. "As soon as I realized, I didn't go any closer but worked my way around so I had a better angle, to verify the kill was human."

He turned a disbelieving glare down at her, then heaved a sigh and shook his head. "I guess I would've done the same thing."

"I had my rifle, and bear spray. Trust me, I listened and checked around me, in all directions, every time I took a step. It was a man. I think it was a man," she added in a soft tone. "He'd been half-eaten, and the bear had scratched some dirt over him."

"It has to be the same bear that came into your camp. Shit."

"Yeah, what are the odds there would be two man-eaters in the same area?"

He shook his head. "I wouldn't bet the ranch. Has to be the same bear."

"I went back to the camp and told Krugman and Davis we could all either go back to Lattimore's the next morning—today—so I could notify the Fish and Wildlife Department, or they could stay and I'd go. Davis was predictably nasty, I offered to refund their money, and that was that. I went to my tent as soon as I could, partly just to get away from Davis. Krugman was nicer and I felt sorry for him because Davis was so hateful to him, which shows you what a terrible judge of character I am. I woke up around midnight, heard their voices, and I could tell they were arguing. I pulled on my boots and coat, got my rifle and flashlight, and went to break up the fight."

She paused, going back over the night's events, gathering her thoughts. "They were back toward the cook site; I wouldn't have heard them except I don't sleep soundly when I'm guiding, I'm always half-listening for trouble."

"Have you had a lot of trouble?" he asked, scowling. She could feel his heightened focus on her face, studying her expression, and she turned her head enough that she could meet his surprisingly fierce gaze.

"No, of course not, but I'm alert. I'm a woman; I have to think about things that a man doesn't," she pointed out. "I'd be stupid if I didn't. But it isn't just that. I'm . . . I'm kind of afraid of bears," she admitted sheepishly.

"I'm leery of them myself."

"It's more than leery." Why not just get it all out there? "I've had nightmares about bears, and finding that body seriously spooked me. No way was I going to do much more than catnap. Anyway, when I got closer I heard Davis say something to Krugman about stealing from him. I yelled at them to knock it off, Davis looked in my direction, and Krugman shot him."

Her tone went flat, her gaze going distant. "He had to have been planning it. Davis hadn't made any threatening moves toward him, at least not that I saw. Then he started shooting at me. I threw myself on the ground and started rolling away from him, but when I hit the ground I lost my grip on the rifle. I just kept rolling. The horses were going crazy, the storm was right on top of us. Krugman went past my location, so I put my face down and stayed still; I was so muddy already I figured that was my best protection. Then . . . then the bear came."

Dare waited in silence while she took a few deep breaths. "Krugman saw the bear, and took off. He took all four horses and ran."

"He probably hoped the bear would get you, too."

Angie couldn't let her thoughts go there. She'd spent enough time already living with that scenario, and it still made the bottom drop out of her stomach. "He didn't bother saddling his horse so I don't know how far he got, because he isn't that great on horseback. When I first saw you, I thought you were Krugman, but then the lightning showed that you were in a saddle, and I knew it wasn't him. If it hadn't been for that, I'd have stayed hidden."

"Close call."

That was an understatement, for damn certain. Angie closed her eyes and let her head tip sideways so it rested against his shoulder, just for a moment, somehow needing that brief contact to reassure herself. Then she straightened, swallowed, and continued her story.

"I needed the rifle, but where I'd dropped it was close to where the bear had Davis. He played with the body," she said starkly. "Tearing it apart. I crawled toward the bear, freezing every time the lightning flashed. I knew it probably wouldn't see me, didn't think it would hear me with all the noise the storm was making, but if the wind had shifted and it had scented me . . . I don't know if it would have left Davis's body and come after me. I thought, just get the rifle, and drop the bear. But when I finally reached the rifle, the mechanism was so filled with mud I knew I didn't dare try shooting it. I worked my way back, went to my tent and got some things, and set out on foot."

"When did you sprain your ankle?"

She made a face. "Within the first half hour."

"So you'd been crawling for hours." His tone was neutral, though she sensed some tension beneath the words.

She gave a short, grim laugh. "What else could I do? Give up? Not likely." She nodded at the percolator. "I think our water's about to boil. Let's have some stew."

Chapter Twenty

They ate their bowls of stew in companionable silence, sitting side by side on the mattress, backs against the wall. She had always considered the dry mixes, with hot water added to turn them into "stew" or "soup," to be edible, but nothing more. This stew, though, more than made up in comfort what it lacked in taste, and with salt, pepper, and a little pack of ketchup and some hot sauce added to the mix, the taste wasn't bad at all. The best part, though, was having something hot and filling in her stomach. She could almost have hummed in contentment.

Cleaning up after themselves consisted of putting the plastic bowls and spoons in the trash bag. What daylight there had been was rapidly fading, so Dare turned on the LED lantern. Angie looked uneasily at the windows. "What if Krugman sees the light?"

"Not likely. For one thing, there's no reason for him to come this way. He doesn't know the cabin's here, doesn't know I'm here, and has no way of knowing you're with me now. If he's smart, he's sitting out this rain in your camp, with his rifle in his hand in case that bear comes back."

His assessment was reassuring, because he was absolutely right. Chad couldn't look for something he didn't know existed. He might not be much of an outdoorsman, but he knew he wanted to go down the mountain, not cut sideways across it. Now that she'd had some sleep and some food, her brain was beginning to kick back in, and draw some conclusions. One of those conclusions was definitely unsettling. "I think Krugman may have been planning to kill me, too, from the very beginning."

"Could be," Dare replied, and she was gratified that he hadn't immediately dismissed the idea as the product of an overactive imagination. "You have to think he knew Davis was on to him, otherwise why take a pistol with him?"

"I did tell them not to leave their tents without their flashlights and rifles; Krugman could have thought a pistol would do." She thought about that for a split second, then shook her head. "No, even someone inexperienced would know a pistol wouldn't stop a bear, and I specifically said *rifle*."

"Why would he even have a pistol with him, unless he'd planned something like this? You can't conceal a rifle. By the way, did Davis have his rifle with him?"

"He *should* have." Angie thought back, dragged up the memory of the two men, starkly lit by lightning, how they'd been standing. Davis had had his left side to her; he'd been right-handed, so if he'd been carrying his rifle it would have been in his right hand. "If he was, I didn't see it, but he could easily have been carrying it in his right hand, pointed at the ground."

"So Krugman took the pistol with him. Maybe Davis knew he had it, maybe not. For argument's sake, say Davis didn't know, because if he had he'd have been more alert. By the way, what's Krugman's occupation?"

"Accountant."

Dare grunted. He stepped out of sight for a few minutes, and returned with a gun-cleaning kit in his hands. "He was probably siphoning some of Davis's funds, and Davis found out about it. But

Krugman was one step ahead of him, all the way. If he'd planned to kill Davis on this hunt, then, yeah, he'd probably planned all along to kill you, too, because you were the only witness."

"But other people knew he was here. Ray Lattimore, for one. Harlan knows. How could he think he'd get away with it?"

"Maybe he expected to be identified, but if he killed both you and Davis on the first or second day of the hunt, that would give him almost a week to get out of the country before anyone would even begin looking for you." Dare's sandpaper voice had gone harsh and cold; his words sent a shiver up her spine, but the strategy he'd laid out reverberated inside her because all the pieces fit together the way she'd been thinking they might. What had happened had been bad enough when she'd thought it was something Krugman had done on the spur of the moment, maybe out of temper or desperation or because Mitchell Davis had been a son of a bitch one time too many. To think that Krugman hadn't panicked, that he'd deliberately murdered Davis and just as deliberately tried to kill her, hit her hard in the gut.

"Looking at it that way, the bear might have saved my life by showing up when he did." She tried hard, but couldn't dredge up any thankfulness to the animal, not when she'd lain helplessly on the ground and watched it savage Davis's body, all the while knowing it would do the same to her if she didn't play her cards just right. "I wonder what Krugman's doing, though. *Is* he sitting out the rain, is he out looking for me, or is he trying to make it back to Lattimore's as fast as he can?"

Dare picked up his rifle and sat down near the lantern and began to methodically take the weapon apart. "If he's trying to get to Lattimore's, he'll find out really fast that runoff from a rain like this will put rivers where there weren't any before, and that only a fool would try to cross a fast-moving current like that."

Angie scowled, knowing what could happen. "If one of my horses gets hurt or killed—" She stopped, fuming impotently, because the likelihood she'd be able to get her hands on Krugman was nonexistent. He was effectively out of her reach, no matter what his actions. If he somehow made it to Lattimore's and made his escape, law enforcement would be after him, but unless he settled in a country with an extradition treaty with the United States, he was home free—and she'd bet he'd researched that angle. If he got himself killed trying to get out of the mountains, then he was dead anyway. Scowling, she looked up at Dare. "I know I won't be able to do a damn thing to him, and that really pisses me off."

He gave a rusty chuckle, a real, honest-to-God laugh, Callahan style, and that weird squeeze in her chest made the bottom drop out of her stomach as if she'd gone over the big drop in a roller coaster. She watched him for a few minutes, then looked at her own rifle. Normally she would have cleaned it the first chance she had, but when they'd reached the cabin she and Dare had both been at the end of their rope—so, realistically, this was the first chance she'd had.

"Could I borrow that cleaning kit when you're finished with it?" she asked.

He glanced at her rifle, then resumed his task. "I'll clean it for you."

Angie was a bit nonplussed; she didn't know how to take his offer. Obviously she knew how to take care of her firearms, so it wasn't that he doubted her ability. Just to make certain, she said cautiously, "I know how to do it."

He lifted his head and gave her a long, unreadable look. "I know," he finally said. "But it's so muddy I'll take it down to the stalls to knock the dirt off, so this area stays clean."

"Oh. Good thinking." But she still had the feeling there was something more behind the offer, something she wasn't seeing. She suppressed a frustrated sigh. More than likely she was simply second-guessing herself to death, as usual. He was taking care of a chore for her because she wasn't very mobile, that was all there was to it.

There didn't seem to be anything she could do, so she pulled the sleeping bag over her lap and watched him as he efficiently stripped, cleaned, oiled, and reassembled his rifle, every movement reminding her of the years he'd spent in the military. How much did she really know about him? Growing up in such a small community, of course she'd known him by sight, but he was five or six years older than she, so they'd never connected socially. When she was in grade school, he was in middle school. When she was in middle school, he was in high school, and by the time she got to high school he was in the military.

She didn't think they'd ever spoken until he'd returned to the area. They'd both been in the hardware store, someone had introduced them, and she'd gone home with her hand tingling from shaking hands with him and feeling the roughness and strength of his hand wrapped around hers. The second time they'd spoken, he'd asked her out, but she'd been rushing around getting ready for a guide trip and hadn't had time, so she'd declined, very regretfully. Months had passed before he'd asked her out again, and by then she'd been so angry she wouldn't have crossed the road with him.

But the people in the community seemed to like him well enough; she'd never heard anyone, other than herself, call him a son of a bitch. She knew he was grouchy, though she had no idea if he came by it naturally or if it was something caused by his experiences in a war; she also knew that a man who'd carried her on his back for miles, under terrible conditions, deserved to be cut some slack for being grouchy. What else? He cussed a lot—and he'd taken care of her without a hint of sarcasm, or a single snide word. He still put butterflies in her stomach. And he'd lied about having a little dick.

Well, hell. Some people got married knowing less about each other than that.

She quickly pushed that thought away. It wasn't the state of *being* married that gave her the willies, it was the act of *getting* married. She'd tried it, and made a complete hash out of the deal. If she could do it over . . . but there weren't any do-overs for some things.

When he was finished with his rifle, he took hers down to the stalls below, and she listened to him moving around. He'd turned on one of the flashlights; she could tell by the blue-white glow. Glancing at one of the windows, she saw that night had fallen, and the steady rain was still coming down. She'd always enjoyed rain before, but after this she didn't know if she'd ever feel the same way about it again. The rain was like the bear: If it hadn't been for the bear, Krugman would likely have killed her. If it hadn't been for the storm, the bear would likely have heard or seen her, and she doubted the outcome would have been a happy one for her. But the storm had also almost killed her, though, come to think of it, she'd rather die from hypothermia or drowning than from being eaten alive.

Don't think about it.

She concentrated on listening to Dare, and reminding herself that she was safe, they were both safe. They had shelter, food, water, heat, even a pretty damn comfortable bed. They weren't in any danger. There were things, urgent things, that they needed to do, but until the weather cleared everything would have to wait. The runoff from a storm could be deadly in the mountains, all that water gathering on its way down from the peaks, gaining in speed and volume, washing boulders and trees down the ravines with astonishing power. Even on horseback, the trip down-mountain would be dangerous, and walking out right now would be almost impossible, even for Dare.

When the weather cleared and the flash floods had subsided, if she still couldn't walk, Dare would have to leave her here while he trekked to Lattimore's place. She didn't worry about being alone here, but when she thought of everything that could go wrong for *him,* nausea knotted her stomach.

He climbed back up the ladder with her rifle slung over his shoulder. Most of the mud had been wiped from the weapon, but the mechanism would have to be carefully cleaned. He settled on the floor in his former position, by the lantern, and methodically began the process. She leaned her head against the wall and watched him through half-closed eyes, strangely soothed by the sureness of his movements, the almost fierce concentration he gave to the chore, the way he smoothed his lean, powerful hands over the wood and metal, feeling for any roughness, any grit.

He glanced up once, and a corner of his mouth kicked up. "You look half asleep."

She couldn't argue with his assessment. Instead she yawned. "It doesn't make sense to be sleepy after being awake for just an hour or so."

"We both burned a lot of energy last night. It'll take more than a few hours of sleep to get back to normal." Pouring gun oil on a cloth, he slowly rubbed it along the length of the barrel. "After I'm finished with this, I'm all for turning in again."

"Suits me. Do you have any disposable toothbrushes?"

"Sure. I also set the bucket—you know, the one you refused to pee in—outside to catch some rainwater to heat, if you want to wash off with water instead of wet wipes."

"Water," she said immediately. "But it doesn't have to be heated. I don't mind using cold water." The prospect of washing with water cheered her. Wipes were great on the trail, but as far as she was concerned they couldn't take the place of water. They left her with a slightly sticky feel that she thought might mostly be in her head, but if she had an alternative, she'd rather take a break from the wipes.

"There should be some hot water left in the percolator, so you won't be taking an icy bath. I imagine you're about ready for another trip outside?"

She was, and she'd been dreading it, because her ankle made the process such an effort. "Trip first, then I'll clean up." Half an hour later, the whole exhausting procedure was finished; Dare had divided the water and he was on the lower level washing off and brushing his teeth, while she did the same sitting on the mattress in the sleeping stall. After bringing her back up the ladder he'd pulled the heavy privacy curtain over the opening so she'd feel comfortable stripping off as much as she wanted, then he'd left her alone.

Add "gentleman" to the list of complimentary adjectives she had to apply to the damn man.

But she was undeniably grateful for the privacy; even though he'd stripped her clothes off that morning *and* cleaned her up, she'd been so exhausted and spent she'd been mostly out of it, so that didn't count. Now that she was thinking more clearly, she was well aware of the risks of letting herself get carried away by the physical closeness, the dependence, and tricking herself into reading more into their closeness than really existed. That would be so, so easy to do, and seeing the risk set off her protective internal alarms. She didn't know what she was doing when it came to man/woman situations, so the best way to keep from making a fool of herself again was to steer clear. Normally that wasn't difficult, but, well, Dare and those damn butterflies could lead her into temptation.

Forewarned was forearmed—if she could just keep that in mind.

She had stuffed some clean clothes into her saddlebags, but she'd been in a hurry, trying to keep from panicking, so she wasn't certain exactly what she'd packed. Pulling the bags toward her, she unloaded them. Protein bars, water, her pistol, ammo—from a survival standpoint, she'd grabbed the correct stuff. In the way of clothing she'd put in two pairs each of clean socks and underwear, a pair of jeans, and two flannel shirts. Not bad; if she'd been able to get her coat dry, she'd have been fairly well prepared for the weather.

But one thing she hadn't packed was a clean set of sweats to sleep in. She'd have to continue making do with Dare's thermal bottoms. She *could* give him back his flannel shirt and sleep in her own, but she didn't want to. Oh, God, she'd be in serious trouble if she didn't watch out.

After washing in the cool water and brushing her teeth with one of the disposable toothbrushes, which was essentially a piece of pink sponge glued to a lollipop stick with a minty-tasting something in the sponge to take the place of toothpaste, she pulled Dare's clothes back on, and put on one of her own thick socks. She was rewrapping her ankle when she heard Dare coming up the ladder.

"You finished?"

"Yes." The curtain was swept aside almost before the word was out of her mouth. She looked up at him with a little smile curving her mouth. "Thanks. I feel a lot better now, almost human."

For one second a hard, unreadable expression set his face, almost as if he was clenching his teeth, then it was gone so fast she wasn't sure she'd truly seen it or if it was a shadow thrown on his face by the stark light of the lantern. "Is something wrong?" She fought hard to keep her voice level. If something was going on, some disaster about to befall them, then she wanted to know about it, so she could meet the problem head-on. She liked to be prepared for any eventuality.

"No, why?"

"You just had a funny expression—funny strange, not funny ha-ha."

"Nothing's wrong."

"If there is, I want to know about it, so I won't be surprised."

"Nothing's wrong."

"I don't like surprises. I want to be prepared, so I can handle whatever it is."

This time she had no problem reading his expression, because exasperation was an easy one. "Nothing's. Wrong."

"Then why did you look as if you had a gas pain?"

His dark brows came down to a point over his nose. "You're a pain in the ass, you know that?"

"And you aren't?" she retorted. She felt more certain of her-self now that they were back on familiar ground: arguing. Not that they'd argued a lot—just once, in fact, the day she'd put her place up for sale—because after she'd seen how he was killing her busi-ness she'd actively avoided him, but in her imagination she'd had many, many aggressive conversations with him.

"Yeah, but you're taking the lead on this one."

Despite herself, she laughed.

Dare stared down at her for a split second, that strange expres-sion back on his face. Then he moved fast, bending down and seiz-ing her shoulders. Startled, she looked up at him and opened her mouth to either protest or blast him, and he kissed her.

Angie's mind went blank. All of her gray matter seemed to freeze, because abruptly it was producing nothing, not a thought, not a word. His taste filled her, the same minty taste of the tooth-brushes underlaid with *him,* Dare, man. Sensation flooded her, a hundred sensations that stood out crystal clear: the firmness of his lips, the scratchiness of the bristle on his face, the hard grip of his hands on her shoulders, the teasing stroke of his tongue against hers.

Somehow her fists knotted in the fabric of his shirt, holding on tight as if she might fall over if she didn't, though the way he was gripping her there was no danger of falling anywhere. Some-how her mouth was open under the pressure of his, and she was vaguely aware that she was kissing him in return, her tongue meet-ing his, her lips clinging.

Then heat came roaring in like a wildfire, scorching along her nerve endings. Everything about him got to her: the hot scent of his skin underlying that of the fresh rainwater he'd used to wash, his taste filling her mouth, the strength of the hands holding her, and, God, yes, the size of the erection he'd put her hand on. Everything she felt physically mingled with the emotional whiplash he'd given her in the past fifteen hours and exploded in-side her, hurling her straight into heaven or hell, maybe both, because she couldn't tell one from the other. But it all became want, curling deep in her belly, clenching between her legs, taking her as unaware as if she had no idea what sex was about.

But she did, and this was Dare, and when her brain sluggishly began working again she couldn't make sense of what was happening.

She pulled her head back with a jerk, staring up at him with huge dark eyes, blinking in bewilderment. "What are you *doing?*" she blurted.

And he smiled, that heart-thumping, stomach-knotting smile. "Shutting you up," he said. "Now let's get some damn sleep. I'm still bushed, so I hope you don't twitch around like a squirrel on hot coals the way you did before."

Chapter Twenty-one

Dare lay with Angie's ass cuddled tight against his aching dick, hoping, praying, she'd twitch like that squirrel on hot coals he'd compared her to, but she was sound asleep. Despite the way she'd stared at him in shock after he kissed her, once she lay down again and got settled, she'd dropped off to sleep like a baby, which told him exactly how much the night before had taken out of her. He was still pretty wiped himself, and could feel sleep coming on, but he wanted to enjoy the feel of her snuggled against him for a while before he let go.

In a very surprising way, he'd enjoyed spending time with her, just having her company while he cleaned their rifles. She didn't chatter, with one thought after another spilling out of her mouth, but if she had something to say she said it, no beating around the bush. She didn't complain, she didn't bitch, even though she'd had reason. Hell, he bitched his own head off occasionally, so he wouldn't have held it against her.

Another thing: She was the most low-maintenance woman he'd ever met. If she had any hint of vanity, he hadn't seen it. Not once had she even mentioned combing her hair; being clean and brushing her teeth seemed to be the extent of her upkeep. He wasn't certain she wore makeup, anyway; if she ever had, it had been subtle enough that he hadn't noticed it, not that he normally did anyway unless a woman went way overboard with the stuff. Maybe her thick, heavy dark hair was naturally sleek and she didn't have to do a lot to it, period. Maybe tomorrow she'd wake up fretting because she didn't have mascara and a blow-dryer, but he'd bet she didn't.

He had a head-fucking mixture of frustration, amusement, and tenderness going on because of her. The first two he could deal with: He was frustrated because he'd wanted to get in her pants from the minute he'd first seen her, which meant he was dealing with two years' worth of build-up, and he was amused because he had the upper hand now and she kind of knew it, and the way she was fighting back was as smart-ass as always, but she hadn't yet really figured things out so she was a little off track.

But . . . *tenderness?* What the fuck did he know about that? He just knew that those solemn dark eyes of hers got to him, and when she'd smiled at him, for the first time ever, her face kind of lit up and the adrenaline hit had been almost like going into combat. When she'd actually laughed, that had been it, he'd *had* to kiss her, and if she hadn't pulled away he'd still be kissing her plus doing a whole lot more.

He'd had his share of women, but one thing he'd noticed was that chemistry started with kissing. There had been women he'd been attracted to, women he'd slept with, whom he didn't like to kiss, and all the relationships went nowhere fast. It was as if their incompatibility went all the way to the molecular stage. There had been other women who he hadn't been all that attracted to, at first, until he kissed them, and their taste just did it for him.

Angie was a bull's-eye, in more ways than one. He was more powerfully attracted to her than he'd ever been to anyone else, and she tasted as if she'd been made for him. What had started out as something physical had rapidly turned into something he was almost afraid to look at, because, shit, what if he was falling in love with her, and she was being nice now because of the situation, but for her the bottom line would always be that he'd run her out of business and forced her to sell her home? That was a hard thing for anyone to get over. Yeah, he had a plan for that, but would she listen?

Maybe, maybe not. He didn't want to take that risk. Actions spoke louder than words, and this opportunity was too good to pass up.

By the time Chad had gotten the horse in the corral, the weak light, filtered through that hellish, unending rain, had faded completely away. He had to use his flashlight to maneuver the horse; thank God the animal seemed as glad to reach shelter as he was, because if it had given him any trouble right now he swore he'd shoot the bastard.

The day had been a big piece of shit from start to finish, nothing but wasted effort. He'd already been tired from the night before, but just the thought of getting down the mountain and driving away, *winning*, had kept him going. He might as well have saved himself the effort and gotten some rest instead. Now he was cold, wet, exhausted, and thoroughly miserable.

It should have been easy. All he'd had to do was ride down the mountain, and if he got to that rancher's place before dark, just hang out until dark, then get in the SUV and drive away. Piece of cake. In spite of the crappy weather, in spite of the fact that he knew Angie had escaped and was out there somewhere, as well as having a killer bear in the vicinity . . . it should've been easy.

It wasn't.

He knew he wasn't a great outdoorsman, but he was smart, and he was better prepared than anyone else knew. He'd practiced his riding for a year. He'd bought the pistol and practiced with it. He'd been as prepared as he'd logically expected he would need to be. This fucking weather, though—no way could he have expected the violence of the storm, the deluge of rain.

He hadn't expected any real problems on the trek down the mountains, unless by some evil twist of fate he'd encountered an armed and pissed Angie Powell. Once he'd found the campsite, he'd been certain he could get back to Lattimore's place. He knew which way was down; and he'd studied maps before heading out on this trip, because he knew he'd be making his way off the mountain alone. He and the horse were getting along well enough, so he had that going for him. But the intense rain had slowed him down, making the way so treacherous that every single step was a victory. He'd zigzagged around pitfalls that hadn't been there on the way up, and after a while he'd lost any real idea of where the trail might actually be.

Water rushed down the mountain in rivulets that turned to streams that turned to rivers. The ground beneath the horse's hooves was soft and uncertain, making the horse nervous and easily spooked. At one point the horse stumbled and Chad held his breath and prayed as the animal regained its balance. If his ride broke a leg he'd be forced to walk the rest of the way. He was sure he wouldn't get far on foot, not in this mess.

After a few hours of what felt like constant struggle, he was exhausted from the effort of staying on the horse and being hyperalert to every detail. Constant vigilance was as tiring as physical effort. At least now the horse had a saddle on it, so riding was easier. He'd put on dry clothes and his slicker before heading out, so at least he wasn't soaking wet, but the chill and dampness slowly began sinking through to the bone. At one point he had to dismount to lead the horse over a particularly treacherous spot; he'd slipped and fallen in the water, so then, damn it, he was wet as well. He hated this fucking rain. Once he was wet, he got colder and colder; his joints were screaming at him, and he shuddered uncontrollably. Every movement, no matter how small, took intense effort. He felt as if he'd aged twenty years in a matter of hours. He'd known he couldn't survive much more of this.

Finally he had to make a decision. If he couldn't make it to Lattimore's, or at least nearby, before dark, he was in real trouble. He'd dismounted in a sea of mud, grabbed a protein bar from his saddlebag, and stood there in the rain, miserable and pissed, his head down to protect his little bit of dry, tasteless food from the rain while he chewed and thought. He hadn't gotten very far, not nearly as far as he'd planned, and his options were to try to find some shelter now and wait it out, or go back to the campsite. Both options held the element of risk. The good news was if he couldn't make it off the mountain, neither could Angie. She was probably holed up in a cave somewhere, and the bitch probably knew how to find dry wood even in a downpour like this, and how to build a fire.

He didn't want to wait out the storm in a cave, or huddling under a rock overhang like the one he'd cowered beneath last night. What he really wanted was a nice hotel suite with room service and a whirlpool tub filled to the brim with hot water. He wanted clean sheets, a soft mattress, and a pile of warm blankets. He wanted a hot bowl of lobster bisque and a pot of even hotter coffee. Unfortunately, all that was going to have to wait.

Maybe he didn't have access to that hotel room and everything that would come with it just yet, but there were tents back at the camp, and a lot more comfort than out here on the mountainside. He hated to backtrack, but he wasn't sure how long he was going to have to wait before he could travel at a decent pace. There was food, shelter, and dry clothes at the camp. Yeah, the remains of Davis's carcass were there, too, but he figured the bear had eaten all it wanted and moved on. Didn't other animals move in really fast? Probably there was nothing left of Davis by now.

He shuddered. If he thought too much about what he'd seen he wouldn't be able to move forward or back, he'd be frozen in terror and then he'd literally die here, whether it was from the damn cold, or Angie, or some other complication just waiting to trip him up.

No, staying here wasn't an option. He hadn't come this far just to give up, no matter what the reason.

Reluctantly, he led the horse back the way they'd come, not willing to risk injuring his ride off this mountain on the uncertain terrain by getting back in the saddle for the trip up the river of mud he found himself in. He cursed under his breath, angry at being forced to turn back, but he didn't see that he had any other real choice. One thing about it, though: He was very much looking forward to getting out of this damned rain.

He was stuck until the weather cleared, and he might as well accept that. But so was Angie, so she wasn't gaining any more on him than she had the night before, when she was probably able to cover some ground because the flood conditions hadn't gotten quite as bad. She was on foot, though, so once he was able to start again, he'd quickly make up for his lost time.

No matter. His ultimate goal remained unchanged; it was just going to take longer to get there than he'd planned. A good strategist was flexible.

So he'd reversed his path down the mountain, and to his dismay found that already he had to make detours from the way he'd traveled just hours ago, because of the unending sea of water pouring from the heavens and rushing down the mountain. Anxiously he noticed the light begin to fade, so he said to hell with leading the horse and got back into the saddle, hoping to speed up his pace a little.

Finally, on the last gasp of daylight, he made it to the campsite.

He put the horse into the corral, resenting every minute he had to spend taking care of it before he could take care of himself, but he'd be in deep shit without the animal, so he forced himself to take the time. He even fed the bastard. Then he stumbled into his tent, turned on the lantern and the small camp heater, and began stripping off his wet clothes. Fuck, he was cold!

He'd never before thought of dry, clean clothes as a luxury, but as he quickly dried himself with a hand towel, Chad knew he'd never again take the simple things, like food, water, and shelter, for granted. This life wasn't for him, that was for certain.

He *wanted* to take the basics for granted. He wanted to forget what it felt like to be wet and cold, he wanted to put all of this behind him and never look back. He wanted to expect around-the-clock comfort again—and oh, what comforts he could afford with the money he'd stashed away! All he had to do was get out of here, which wasn't going to be today, tonight, and maybe not tomorrow.

He got dressed: dry underwear, jeans, a camo sweatshirt that felt like heaven on his chilled body, thick socks. Unfortunately, he didn't have an extra pair of boots, so he left his wet boots sitting to the side, close to the camp heater. Maybe they'd dry out before he had to put them back on.

Once he felt fairly decent again, with warm, dry clothing on, he heaved a deep sigh and just sat for a minute, listening to the rain fall hard on the tent. Then he ate another protein bar and drank a bottle of water. He really, really wanted something hot to eat, but that wasn't possible just yet. So he drank the water and tried not to think about coffee. He chewed on the bar and tried not to notice how shitty it tasted, how the texture was more like sticky sawdust than real food. Still, with every second that passed, his body eased, welcoming the warmth and dryness.

He'd never felt so alone. Except for the horse in the corral, he hadn't seen anyone or anything out in this mess, not even a bird. Everyone—man, woman, and beast—was holed up in some kind of shelter, waiting out the big rain.

But animals still had to eat, didn't they, whether it rained or not? Maybe that meant they'd come out at night. He thought of bears and cougars prowling around outside his tent and nervously he got his rifle and put it within easy reach. God, he was so tired. He couldn't stay awake another miserable night. He had to get some sleep tonight, or he'd be unable to function tomorrow even if the sun came out and the land miraculously dried up.

But he was afraid to sleep, afraid he'd conk out so completely that a bear would be in the tent chewing on him before he woke. He sat on the mattress, and kind of zoned out, thoughts flitting through his brain but not really stopping for him to examine them.

He wondered if the three horses he'd left tied up under the overhang had managed to shake free or if they were still there, waiting for him to return.

He wondered if the bear had come back to finish eating what was left of Mitchell Davis while he'd been trying, and failing, to make his escape.

He wondered if it was possible that Angie had succeeded where he'd failed, if she'd made it off the mountain today, or at least covered some significant ground. She might've found the horses, though that was a long shot.

Maybe she knew a shortcut; maybe she was tougher than he'd thought. She might be at Lattimore's. Unlikely, but he needed to have a plan for every contingency . . .

He almost laughed at that one. How could he possibly have planned for a killer bear and the storm of the century?

He had to keep going, though; he was much more afraid of Davis's associates than he was of the cops. He sure as hell didn't want to be arrested, but he'd rather take on a bear and the law together than, well, he knew what Davis's thugs had done to people who crossed him, and he knew that Davis himself had had to answer to someone even higher up the food chain, someone who was likely even more brutal. He had to disappear, and that was that. Even in prison, he wouldn't be safe.

His best bet for getting out of the country was still his original plan. He couldn't take the chance of heading in a different direction and trying to rent or steal a vehicle somewhere else. Hell, this was Montana. He might end up in some godforsaken part of the state where days passed without a vehicle being seen . . . kind of like the part where he was now.

He'd stick to what he thought would work best. He needed the SUV; it was rented in his name, so if he got stopped by some traffic cop for not using his turn signal or some other stupid-ass shit, there wouldn't be any problem. Besides, he'd waded through shit, literally, and stuck his hand in some disgusting things to get the keys out of Davis's pocket. He wasn't going to back down now.

If by some chance Angie had made it there before him, and she had men waiting for him, well, it wasn't like this was a city, or even a town, so how many of them could there be? He had a rifle and a pistol, and he wasn't afraid to use either of them. Once he made it off the mountain, he'd be smart and cautious and scout out the situation before he showed himself. If someone else was there, waiting for him, he'd look scared. He'd look helpless. After years of practice, he was good at that. He'd beg for mercy, maybe he'd even cry, tell them it was all a mistake and Davis had been about to kill him, it was self-defense, and he hadn't really shot at Angie at all, he'd seen the bear and panicked . . . yeah, that was good. And he was good enough that he could make even Angie doubt herself. And then, when they thought he wasn't a threat, he'd kill them all. He didn't have a problem with that. And if anyone thought he would, tough shit for them.

He could feel himself drifting. He was so tired, he knew he was punch drunk. He had to get some sleep, or die.

He leaned back and closed his eyes. Fifteen minutes, that was all he needed, just fifteen minutes to recharge his batteries. Not sleep, not really, he couldn't afford to be entirely out of it, but if he could just close his eyes. . . .

Chapter Twenty-two

As dreams went, this one sucked. Angie was awake just enough to know that she was dreaming, but was unable to pull herself out of it. No good could come of any dream that wouldn't let go, that kept pulling her down—

She was facedown in the mud. She was suffocating. Mud was in her eyes, up her nose, and every time she tried to take a breath she choked on the vile stuff. She struggled to breathe, to see, but everything was dark. She didn't know where she was or how she was going to get out of this. Panic pounded through her like drumbeats, she had to get out, get out, get out. . . . She fought, clawing, to move forward, to lift her head out of the stinking muck, but no matter how hard she tried she didn't gain any ground, couldn't fight free. Cold mud threatened to swallow her whole, to suck her down into the earth.

Being caught like this made her so angry. She wasn't afraid of drowning; there were worse things than being stuck in the mud, and if she couldn't get out of here those worse things would be there any minute. A murderer and a bear were coming for her. She couldn't see them, couldn't hear them, but she knew they were close. Behind her. Ahead of her. All around. They were coming for her.

And then the mud changed. What had been dark, smelly muck changed to something sweet and white. Straining every muscle in her neck, Angie was able to lift her head. Right in front of her was a yellow rose made of cake icing. Breathing hard, she licked her lips, tasted the white stuff that covered her from head to toe. Not mud: icing. Icing from her wedding cake was in her eyes and her nose and her mouth, between her fingers, between her toes. But why was she barefoot? Where were her boots?

She shuddered. The icing was worse than the mud, because it was wrong, it shouldn't be there. She tried to shake it away, but the stuff clung, coating her. Cold chills rippled down her spine. Moving in this sea of icing was more difficult than it had been to move in the mud.

She was trapped.

And behind her, an animal growled.

Angie wrenched herself out of the dream and into a sitting position, gasping for breath, and of course banging her damn ankle in the process. A sharp cry escaped before she could stop it, as if her sudden movements alone weren't enough to wake the man with whom she was sleeping.

Sleeping with Dare Callahan. Now, there were four words she'd never thought she'd string together in a sentence, in any context.

"What's wrong?" he growled, the sound slow and soothing, unlike the growl in her dream. She needed the calm he offered, she needed the solid warmth of his body close beside her, anchoring her in reality. What a stupid, disturbing dream!

"Just a bad dream." She tried to shake it off, to forget the images. Gingerly she rubbed at her ankle, trying to soothe the ache.

"What was it about?" He sat up, turned on the lantern.

After almost total darkness, the white light made her squint. Angie eased herself back down. "Nothing much." She didn't need to analyze the dream to know what it meant, or why she'd had it. She also didn't want to explain why she'd had a nightmare about wedding cake. That was so stupid. The mud, the bear, Chad . . . that would all make sense to him. Wedding cake? Not so much.

He was quiet for a few seconds, then said, "Maybe it'll help to talk about it."

She glanced at him, and—*Oh, holy shit!* He wasn't wearing a shirt. She could have sworn he'd been wearing one when they'd lain down, but . . . not now. Some time during the night he must have gotten too warm, and she'd been too out of it to wake up when he'd taken it off. She gaped at him, at the way the light gleamed on the powerful curve of his shoulders, the sinewy, vein-laced muscles in his arms. A dark patch of hair decorated the middle of his chest, spread lightly over his pecs. There was a scar on his right shoulder that ran in a jagged line about three inches long, but it was an old scar, smoothed by time to nothing more than a silver line. It was, nevertheless, a silent reminder that the man next to her was a warrior, a man who had seen battle and been shaped by it. He'd been wounded, he'd faced death, he'd maybe, probably, caused death. He'd know and understand strategy, and he'd go into any situation determined to win.

More rattled than seeing a half-naked man warranted, Angie squirmed, then casually tossed an arm over her eyes so she wouldn't have to look at him, but not because he was too hard on the eyes. Too much the opposite, in fact, so much so that seeing him like that interfered with her thought processes.

"After everything that's happened, I have enough nightmare fodder to last me a lifetime, including sleeping with you." She tried to sound insulting, but it didn't work. Being so close to all that muscle had obviously fried her brain, because she couldn't stop a teasing smile from quirking her lips. *Teasing?* Oh, God, was she actually trying to flirt with him? She needed to slap herself completely awake, and back to sanity, because otherwise she was just going to make a total fool of herself.

He laughed. Dare *laughed.* Despite the danger of seeing all that skin, Angie peeked out from under her arm, just enough to see that it was a genuine, natural laugh, the real deal. It was rusty and rough and sounded as if he had a hair ball caught in his throat, but it was a laugh, and she got that melty sensation in her chest again. She'd wanted to make him angry so he'd stop asking questions, but instead she'd undermined herself by smiling and he hadn't taken her seriously.

When he stopped laughing, he propped on his elbow and looked down at her, leaning over her a little, and abruptly her heart stopped melting and began thumping hard inside her chest. Probably it was the light making his expression look like something it wasn't, but right there, right then, she thought he was looking at her as if he wanted to eat her up.

Tension made her mouth go dry. She wasn't the most experienced woman on the planet, but she instinctively knew that expression even if no man had ever before turned it on her. It was a completely male, sexual, predatory, hungry look that both lured her closer and at the same time made her want to run. This kind of sexy look was a trap, because it would make any woman melt from its toe-tingling, butterfly-inducing intensity.

She knew better than to fall for that; Dare wanted sex, but even though he'd saved her life and she owed him big time, she didn't think she could handle going where he apparently thought this was going. She didn't think he was thinking about her owing him; he was a man, so more than likely he wasn't thinking about anything other than just sex. But if she had sex with him while *she* was thinking about owing him, then that put her in the category of prostitute, using her body to pay a debt. Then there was the big letdown that sex always was, the buildup that led to a fizzle. No matter how she looked at it, having sex was a bad idea.

"Don't even think about it," she warned.

His eyebrows went up, and he made a derisive sound in his throat. "You're about two years too late," he returned.

Two years? Startled, she gaped at him. "What?"

"We'll talk about it tomorrow. Tell me about your dream."

Dream? What dream? Completely distracted, she shook her head, then belatedly realized that her dream might be a good way to distract him, because there was nothing admirable about her wedding.

"Fine." She dropped her arm and glared at him, squarely meeting his gaze and ignoring the rugged attractiveness of his stubbled face. His expression didn't change; he didn't try to hide who he was and what he wanted. "I dreamed about mud and bears and wedding cake icing."

His eyebrows did that quirking thing again. "Icing?" He blinked, and she could tell he was trying to connect a wedding cake to the bear.

"I was drowning in it. Mud at first, then it turned to icing." She scowled at him. "You know I got married a few years back, right?" They lived in a small community. Everyone pretty much knew everything about everybody else, at least the pertinent information, though some details were less well known than others. Her dad had been at her wedding, of course, and had comforted and supported her afterward, but he'd never said what he'd told Harlan or anyone else once he got home, and she'd never asked.

"I heard you were supposed to, but something happened." A cautious note entered his rough voice, as if he thought she'd been ditched at the altar, or something like that.

"I had it annulled."

Surprise flickered in his eyes. "Annulled, huh?" An annulment wasn't like a divorce; you could pretty much get a divorce for anything. Even something as simple as liking different colors could be the basis for incompatibility, but an annulment had very specific legal requirements.

"A divorce would have been easier," she admitted grimly. "Even my lawyer advised me to just get a divorce, and he was right. But I was so . . . I just wanted it to be erased, as if it had never been, and there was no reasoning with me."

He snorted. "*You,* unreasonable? Fancy that." But there was no nastiness in his tone, just dry amusement.

He touched a fingertip to her cheekbone. Surprised, Angie put her hand up, and to her consternation discovered the damp track of a tear. Furiously she wiped it away. Crying over this, even getting just a little teary, would be so stupid. "Don't pay any attention to that," she ordered brusquely. "It's nothing, and I'm not crying."

"If you say so."

"I do. And if I did, it would be because I'm so angry at myself, and embarrassed. I was an idiot."

"What happened?"

"Nothing earth-shattering. That's what makes it so embarrassing."

He waited in silence while Angie sorted through all the anger and hurt feelings and sheer irrationality she still felt whenever she thought about the subject. Finally she fixed her gaze on the ceiling and firmed her lips.

"I've never been much of a girlie-girl," she confessed. "I never knew how. You know—the makeup, the fussing with hair, all that stuff. It wasn't like Dad could teach me any of that, and really, when I was a teenager, I wasn't all that interested anyway. Even though I did more of it when I lived in Billings, I wasn't—I'm still not—certain if I was doing it right and looked okay. But for my wedding I wanted to be pretty, I wanted my hair and makeup to be perfect."

Exposing her uncertainty made her cheeks turn hot. She knew she wasn't a beauty queen, but she wasn't unattractive, either. Normally she didn't give her looks any thought at all, beyond brushing her hair and using moisturizer with sunscreen. Admitting all of that to a man—to Dare Callahan, specifically—was still uncomfortable.

"How come your mom wasn't around to teach you stuff like that?" he asked bluntly. "I don't think I ever heard anyone say, not even Evelyn French, and that woman can talk the ears off a donkey."

Despite her embarrassment, Angie had to grin. Anyone who ever set foot in the hardware store learned exactly how much Evelyn liked to talk. "Then she must never have got up enough nerve to ask Dad about it, otherwise she'd have told it. It's no big deal. I don't remember my mother. She left Dad and me before I was two. She had some sleaze she was cheating on him with, and I guess she liked the sleaze more than she liked being with us. So she left."

His eyes narrowed. "That sucks."

"It could have," she agreed. "I can't say I haven't wondered what it would have been like if she'd stayed. But at the same time, Dad was great. He never talked bad about her, and when I asked he told me what had happened, and left it at that." She paused. "I went through his papers, after he died, and found their divorce decree. She gave him full custody, signed me away, and I guess never looked back, because she never tried to see me or contact me in any way. I've returned the favor."

"Pissed you off, huh?" His full attention was on her face, as if he wanted to catch every nuance of her expression. What? Did he think she was all messed up because her mother had abandoned her?

She started to deny it, then stopped herself. "In a way. I don't feel traumatized, because I don't remember her at all, but I think Dad must have been more torn up about it than he ever let on to me. That pisses me off, on his behalf. And, looking back, I wonder if he never dated much because he was so focused on taking care of me. It can't be easy for a man, for anyone, to suddenly be left with the sole care of an infant."

"I'd sure as hell panic," he observed.

"Bull," she scoffed. She had no doubt he'd handle it. He wasn't someone who panicked, he was a man who got the job done, regardless of what the job was. "Anyway. She was a quitter, and I guess you can say it affected me in that I won't let myself be a quitter. I don't want to be like her."

"You aren't," he said after a brief pause, his rough voice quiet. "You're not a quitter."

For some reason, hearing him say that made her throat feel thick, as if she was about to get teary. Horrified at the thought, she cleared her throat. "That's enough of that. Do you want to hear about my wedding, or not?" she asked, scowling.

"Yeah, I do. We kind of got sidetracked."

"You mean you did. I was telling you what happened when you went off on a tangent."

"I was curious. So shoot me. Back to your makeup and hairdo for the wedding."

She gave him a warning squint and considered refusing to say anything else, but what the hell, she'd already gotten this far, she might as well finish.

"I hired someone to do my hair and makeup, because I knew I couldn't manage it. Getting ready took *hours*. But when she was finished, I looked good. I looked even better than I'd hoped, and I was so happy. I thought he'd be—"

"He, who?" Dare interrupted. "Does the asshole have a name?"

"Todd," she said, then stopped, struck by the fact that Dare had automatically assumed the man she'd married was an asshole. "Todd Vincent. He wasn't . . . I mean, he kind of was, but I completely overreacted."

"Overreacted to what?"

She sighed and resumed her inspection of the ceiling. "He pushed cake in my face. Not a small piece, either, but a huge chunk that was covered in thick icing. It went up my nose, it was in my eyes . . . and he laughed when he did it." *Everyone* had laughed, but she didn't feel it was necessary to elaborate on that detail.

"The bastard," Dare said blandly.

He was going to make light of it, like everyone else had. He was going to tell her that she'd definitely overreacted. The bad part was that she knew she'd been unreasonable, and as a result she'd broken up with and ended her marriage to someone who was essentially a good man, someone she'd loved—all because of her wounded ego. But Dare didn't say anything else, and after a minute she continued.

"We'd discussed it beforehand. I don't like the cake-in-the-face thing anyway, I don't think it's funny, and I especially didn't want my hair and makeup to be ruined. I asked one thing of him on our wedding day, which was don't smack me in the face with wedding cake. He agreed. He *promised*. Was that too much to ask?" Angie heard her voice rising and didn't even attempt to rein in her indignation. "Apparently it was, because instead of sticking with the agreement he shoved that piece of cake in my face and ground it in, and I started crying and yelling at him, and then I ran out. He followed and tried to apologize, but I wouldn't listen. Dad tried to comfort me, but I asked him to just please get me out of there, so he did. The next day I filed for an annulment.

"Todd tried to talk me out of it. He apologized over and over. All of my friends tried to tell me to settle down, that he didn't mean anything by it, but I wouldn't listen, and pushed my lawyer to get the annulment done in record time." She took a deep breath. "And then I realized what a fool I'd made of myself over something so minor. I'd hurt a good man, humiliated him and myself, thrown away my marriage—"

"Bullshit," said Dare.

Taken aback, Angie stared at him. "What?"

"He broke his word."

"Yes, but—"

"That isn't minor. And you didn't love him."

"I did," she said, but surprised herself with the uncertainty in her tone that even she could hear.

Dare snorted. "No you didn't. If you'd loved him you'd have explained away his bad judgment, wiped the cake off your face, and gone on with the party. If he'd loved you, he wouldn't have broken the agreement in the first place. All in all you're better off that it ended then, because from where I sit it seems pretty clear that it would've ended eventually no matter how hard you tried to make it work. You deserve better."

"I could have handled it so much better—"

He gave an impatient shake of his head. "You weren't wrong. You did what you knew was right, so forget it and move on."

"Thank you, Dr. Phil," she said sharply, but without anger, because she was too startled by his assessment. Even more startling was that he didn't think she'd gone off the deep end when, hell, even *she* thought she had. And he'd said that Todd had poor judgment. She was so taken aback that she couldn't even think about it right now; she'd save that for later. Much later.

A wry smile turned up one corner of his mouth. "I do have my talents. So, what else?"

"What *else*?" Wasn't that enough? She'd just told him the most embarrassing episode of her life and he wanted more?

"The dream, sweetheart. What else happened in the dream." He made a rough sound, deep in his throat. "I've heard all about your wedding that I care to, and cake wasn't all you dreamed about. You mentioned mud and the bear."

Reorienting herself took a minute. She had to mentally pull herself away from her wedding and back to the hellish scene when the storm broke. "Yeah, cake, and mud, and that freakin' bear."

"Where was I?"

"Nowhere in *my* dream," she retorted. Not this time, anyway.

"Too bad."

"There's nothing much to tell. Like I said before, I was drowning in the mud, and then it turned into icing. I was caught in it, couldn't get free, and the bear was coming . . . enough said about that."

He heaved himself up, stretched out a long arm to snag two bottles of water from the floor. Twisting one open, he handed it to her, then opened the other for himself. Angie pushed herself to a sitting position and drank. She hadn't thought about being thirsty, but the water was unbelievably good. Maybe she'd put too much salt and hot sauce in her bowl of stew.

"What time is it?"

He glanced at his watch. "Close to midnight. We've slept about five hours."

She hoped they weren't caught up on sleep, because there were some long hours between now and daylight, and she didn't want to lie awake all that time in the dark with a half-naked Dare right beside her. Sleep was better, less risky.

Tilting her head, she listened to the rain. It didn't seem to be quite as heavy as before, but it was still steady, and until it stopped and the flash floods had subsided, she and Dare would inevitably be having more of these too-intimate conversations. There was something about being enclosed in this small space, safe and dry, that freed her tongue. On the other hand, she couldn't really regret any of the personal things she'd told him.

He couldn't know what it meant to her that he understood what she'd done—and she would never, ever tell him.

She capped the bottle of water and set it aside, then to her surprise was overtaken by a huge, jaw-popping yawn. She covered it with her hand, then blinked at him. "Sorry. You'd think I'd have caught up on my sleep by now."

"Takes a lot to make up for something like what you went through. I could use another few hours myself." He capped his own bottle, then reached down to turn off the lantern. Plunged into total darkness, Angie stretched out again and snuggled under the sleeping bag. A warm, muscled arm circled her waist, tugged her back until she nestled snugly against a very hard chest. He nuzzled her hair aside, lightly kissed the back of her neck, and murmured "Sweet dreams" in a voice that already sounded a little drowsy to her.

Her eyes popped open, straining wide against the darkness. After kissing her like that, he expected her to go to sleep? She could still feel the slightly moist heat of his breath, the barely there pressure of his firm mouth, as intensely as if he'd branded her instead of kissing her.

Abruptly her breasts were aching, and she caught herself pressing her thighs together to contain and relieve the tightening she could feel deep inside. No. Oh, no. She wasn't going there. No matter how he kissed her she wasn't going to let her own body sabotage her resolve.

She tried to find some anger she could use to bolster herself, but there simply wasn't any. Instead, she had to admit that sleeping beside him was sweeter and more seductive than anything she'd ever done.

She was in deep, deep trouble.

Chapter Twenty-three

It was still raining. Angie pondered that awful fact for a moment, then pushed it away, because there was nothing she could do about it. She sat up, yawned, pushed her hair out of her eyes, and said to Dare, "If you don't have coffee, I may have to kill you."

He opened one vivid blue eye, surveyed her in silence for a moment, then muttered, "Hell, I believe you."

"So?"

"So I guess I'll get up and make you some coffee."

"Good deal." She'd been pretty sure he would have coffee; he had a percolator, didn't he? But there had been the chance he'd kept the percolator up here only for his clients, and that he was some kind of unnatural creature who drank only water.

He stretched his long body, his arms banging against the partition wall and the sleeping bag sliding to the side. She had to swallow a sudden rush of moisture in her mouth; he looked both disreputable and delicious, with a beard that was about forty-eight hours past being a five o'clock shadow, and sleep-mussed dark hair. Angie deliberately looked away from the play of muscle, instead focusing on the more mundane, such as the tiresome need to take care of physical matters.

Maybe she could put some weight on her ankle today, which would make the trip outside so much easier. She eased her right foot from under the sleeping bag and surveyed it. Her toes still looked a little swollen, but not much. Very carefully she wiggled them, just to see if she could. That felt okay, so she wiggled them some more. "If my ankle was broken, would wiggling my toes hurt?"

"I don't know. I've broken my arm, three ribs, a collarbone, my nose, and cracked my kneecap, but I've never broken an ankle."

She turned to look at him, frowning. "Are you accident prone?"

"I prefer to think of it as adventurous. I broke my nose when I was eight, trying to jump my bicycle over a ramp."

"It doesn't look as if it's been broken." And it didn't. The bridge was perfectly straight.

"Kids heal better than adults. The ribs were broken when a horse kicked me when I was fourteen. The cracked kneecap was a football game. The broken arm and collarbone were a training accident."

"What happened?"

"It was a climb. The guy above me lost his grip and fell, and took me and another guy with him."

He could have been killed. If he'd hit his head, or his spine . . . Angie had to turn her head before he could read the sudden horror in her expression. She felt sick at the possibility, even though it was in the past, much as she felt sick whenever she saw the scar on his throat and realized how easily that piece of shrapnel could have killed him if it had hit his carotid artery. He'd been so close to death so many times, a matter of inches, a split second of time—

She loved him. Or at least *could* love him. She pressed a hand to her stomach, fighting to control the same nauseating sensation she got on a Ferris wheel, which she didn't enjoy at all. Her own history had taught her that having feelings for someone didn't automatically turn everything into wine and roses. There was some sexual attraction going on, Dare had made that plain, but odds were sexual attraction was all that was going on.

"You okay? You look a little green," he commented as he stuffed his feet into his boots.

"Headache," she automatically replied, which was true enough because she hadn't had coffee, or any other caffeine source, in two days. "I need that coffee." She hoped he wouldn't mention that she'd been pressing her hand to her stomach, not her head, because she didn't want to get drawn into a personal conversation. Her instinct was to pull back, to protect herself. Maybe someone more self-confident in relationships would react differently, but she wasn't that person, never had been. She was confident in her career, in commonsense stuff, but as far as she could see emotions had nothing to do with common sense.

"Yes, ma'am, I'm putting the water on to heat right now," he drawled, though he was obviously still lacing his boots.

"I can see that." She decided to make herself useful, so she lit the heater, and checked the water level in the percolator. There were a couple of inches left. "How many cups will you drink?"

"Two or three."

"Same here. Pass me three bottles of water, and it can be heating while we go downstairs."

He did better than that; he not only pulled three bottles of water from the case of water sitting on the floor, he rooted around and pulled out a bag of ground coffee. There was even a scoop inside the half-empty bag. She opened the bag and took a deep breath; just breathing in the aroma of the coffee was a pleasure. She was a by-the-numbers kind of coffeemaker, so she began doing math in her head, mumbling to herself as she did so. "Three bottles at sixteen-point-nine ounces . . . fifty point seven . . . add six . . . divide by five . . . eleven something . . . divide by two—"

"What the *hell* are you doing?" he asked incredulously, staring at her with a kind of horrified, I-don't-believe-it expression.

"Figuring out how many scoops of coffee to use." Wasn't it obvious? She frowned at him. She'd specifically mentioned the bottles, so what else would she have been doing?

"Multiplying and dividing?"

"Well, how do you do it?" She crossed her arms, both feeling and sounding defensive.

"I put in the water, and I dump in how much coffee I think I'll need."

"How does it taste?"

He blew out a breath. "Sometimes it tastes pretty good," he said cautiously.

"I get better results than 'sometimes' with my method."

"But you need a fu— a damn calculator to figure it out!"

"Oh, really?" Ostentatiously, she looked around. "I don't believe I see one, and I was doing just fine." She couldn't believe it. He'd just caught himself before he said *fucking,* and substituted *damn.* When was the last time he'd bothered to moderate his language? Huh. She was beginning to have a little fun.

"So what's this magic formula?" he demanded after a few seconds, when she simply sat there looking at him, her head cocked a little as if she were waiting.

"Figure out how many ounces of water you have and divide by five—"

"Why?"

"Because, for reasons unknown to mankind, coffeemakers figure a cup of coffee is five ounces, rather than eight."

"Bullshit."

"No, it's true. Haven't you ever measured water into a coffeemaker and noticed it doesn't match?"

"I don't pay attention to shit like that. But this isn't a cof-feemaker. It's a percolator."

"But the scoops seem to be based on how much coffee you need for five ounces, so it doesn't matter. Then the type of grind makes a difference—"

"I don't want to hear it. You're making this way too compli-cated."

"I make good coffee." She was beginning to feel a little indig-nant on behalf of her coffeemaking skills.

"So you say. I haven't seen any proof yet. Finish with this math-ematical thing." He was glaring at her as if she'd told him there was no Santa Claus.

"If the grind is coarse, then you need to use a little bit more; if it's fine, a little less. This looks like a medium grind, but the scoop looks big, so I'm estimating two cups for each scoop of coffee. Therefore, after I divide the ounces of water by five, I divide that answer by two, and that gives me how many scoops of coffee I need."

Still looking like a thundercloud, he pointed at the percolator. "All right, get the coffee going. This had better be good."

"Or what?" she taunted. "You'll strip me of my coffee privi-leges, and risk death by dismemberment?"

"Just make the damn coffee!"

"Do you like it strong, weak, or medium?"

His jaw clenched. "Go for medium."

"All right." As she measured the coffee into the basket in the percolator, she couldn't help prodding the beast just a little. "Do your clients like your coffee?"

His jaw got even tighter. "One of them usually takes over mak-ing it, after the first day," he finally admitted.

"*My* clients like my coffee," she said smugly. She added an-other half-scoop, because she figured he'd like it a little stronger than she did, and a half-scoop seemed like a nice compromise. Turning on the camp stove, she set the percolator on the fire. By the time they finished their trips to the outside, the coffee should be ready.

With that in mind, she gingerly flexed her foot; the ache wasn't too bad. "I think I can put some weight on my foot today, if you'll help me up."

"And I think you're rushing things," he said, but he got to his feet and held both his hands out to her. She gripped them, and he effortlessly pulled her upright, releasing her hands to put both arms around her and support her weight.

That wasn't exactly what she'd had in mind . . . and he still didn't have a shirt on. She tried to ignore being cradled against that naked chest, and the strong arms that were wrapped around her, concentrating instead on gaining her balance as she stood on her left foot. Cautiously she put her right foot on the ground, held her breath, and transferred a little of her weight to her injured ankle. It hurt. It ached. But it wasn't the shooting agony it had been when she'd first hurt it, and it didn't buckle under the stress.

"Let me see if I can take a step."

His deep voice rumbled against her temple. "I've got you. Go ahead."

And he did have her. She couldn't have put all her weight on her feet even if she'd wanted to. She eased more pressure onto her foot and took one short, hobbling step. "Ouch. Wow." She took a deep breath of relief. "It's definitely better than it was, so I guess that means it's a sprain and not a break."

"That's enough. If you try to do too much, you'll make it worse. C'mon, let's go down and get this over with."

"Getting it over with" meant, of course, that she once again made the trip down the ladder while draped over his shoulder, as that was the fastest method. But it also meant that he had to put on his shirt, so all in all she considered that a good trade-off. She didn't know how much longer she could have borne looking at all that muscle.

Instead she was looking at something else.

"Staring at your butt is getting old," she mumbled, clinging like a limpet so she didn't fall down an entire story and land on her head.

"Aw now, be nice," he admonished as he easily moved down the ladder with no more effort than if she'd been a child. "I wouldn't say that about *your* butt."

"You haven't spent hours staring at my butt, or you might be singing a different song."

Having reached the bottom, he patted her on the butt in question, then boosted her off his shoulder and stood her upright, holding her close to him and looking down so that they were practically nose to nose. "You'd be wrong about that; I've stared at your ass every time I got the chance."

Thump thump! Her heartbeat went into drum-pounding mode again. What was she supposed to say to that? Was he just flirting because he wanted sex, saying whatever he thought would work, or was he serious? Wide-eyed, feeling as if she were a deer in the headlights, she stared into that intent blue gaze and tried to decide if she should blow it off as a joke or if he was serious. How could he possibly be serious?

With all the animosity that had been between them, and the fact that he was buying her out and she'd be leaving soon to set up her business in a less-competitive area, he *had* to be thinking about nothing more than having sex. Men could do that, compartmentalize things so that their emotions were in one storage area, their sex drives in another, and never the twain shall meet. She didn't want anything to happen here that could foul up her thinking when they got out of this situation and things were back to normal.

He was waiting for her reaction, and from his alert, narrow-eyed expression she got the idea he was halfway expecting her to take a swing at him. Her arms wanted to move, all right, but for some reason they wanted to fling themselves around his neck; she couldn't have that, no body parts moving independently of her will, so she firmed her lips and said, "Then stop it. No more looking at my butt."

He made a derisive sound. "Make me. I happen to think your ass is one of the seven wonders, so no way am I going to deprive myself of the view."

She began shaking her head in denial, waving her hands back and forth in front of him as if she could erase his words, backing a couple of awkward, hobbling steps away from him as she did. "No, no, no. Not going there. Just get all of that out of your head, because it isn't going to happen."

"Don't be so sure of that," he warned, the corners of his eyes crinkling as if he wanted to smile at her protests.

There had to be something she could say to make him back up, and suddenly she knew just what it was. "I'm very grateful to you," she said, throwing the words at him like a weapon. "I'll agree to selling my place to you without any problem. You don't have to use sex to get your way."

He straightened as if he'd been kicked by a mule, his dark brows snapping together over his nose and his eyes narrowing even more, blue fire sparking. "Damn it, don't try to make this about any fucking piece of property!"

"What else am I supposed to think?" she asked with what she thought was a very reasonable tone. "All of a sudden you're acting as if I'm God's gift to men, when we both know better. Either you're looking for easy sex, or you think you can use sex to get your way. Neither of those look like a good deal to me."

Tight-lipped, he grabbed her slicker off the post and tossed it to her. "Let's get this over with," he snapped.

As she pulled on the slicker she wondered if she'd done a smart thing, pissing off the man who would be carrying her up a tall ladder, but she couldn't have let him continue saying suggestive things that completely threw her off balance. What if he was only teasing and she'd taken him seriously? She'd have humiliated herself beyond recovery. She had kind of gotten over the embarrassment of how she'd acted at her wedding—kind of; she still felt uncomfortable at the very thought of seeing people who had been there that day, and she'd come up with every excuse in the book for not keeping in touch with the friends she'd had in Billings for that very reason. But taking Dare seriously, and then discovering he'd just been joking about finding her attractive, would be more than she could bear.

He carried her outside and she shut herself in the plastic cubicle, hurrying so he could take his turn. By the time they were back inside and had shed their wet slickers, she could hear the coffee perking. Without a word he took her back up the ladder, and Angie promised herself right then that, no matter how long it took or how much it hurt, she'd negotiate the way on her own the next time, even if she had to hop on one foot. There were things to hold on to for balance.

He all but dumped her onto the mattress as he rasped, "How do you like your coffee?"

She thought about snapping that she'd fix her own coffee, but reined in her temper. If she let herself get pulled into a red-hot back-and-forth with him, God only knew what she'd end up saying, and they'd end up doing. Her goal was to keep everything under control. "One sugar. Thank you." She sounded so prim she wanted to slap herself.

He prepared their cups of coffee, putting one packet of sugar into hers and a whole lot more than that into his. She started to comment, but deemed silence more prudent. She wouldn't even ask him if the coffee tasted good to him, because that would be like prodding an ill-tempered tiger. Taking the cup when he held it out to her, she scooted back against the wall, stretched her legs out, and sipped.

Despite everything, the hot coffee felt and tasted like heaven. She took another couple of sips, then leaned her head back against the wall, closed her eyes, and felt her headache begin to disappear as if it were going down a drain. Maybe it wasn't really going away that fast, but her head definitely felt better.

She felt him settle into place beside her, heard him sip. Grudgingly he muttered, "It's good."

"Thank you."

My, weren't they polite?

Okay, the best way to go on was to just . . . go on. Something occurred to her and she asked, "By the way, you've never said . . . why were you here? Were you doing some scouting for a late hunting party you have coming in?"

"No, I came up to do some fishing, and to get away from paperwork. You were a few hours ahead of me."

She opened her eyes and turned her head, still resting against the wall, to look at him. "Lucky coincidence, for me. If you hadn't been, who knows if I'd still be alive right now. What were you doing out in the storm, anyway, at that hour?"

"Looking for your camp." Wrapping his hands around the warm cup, he drank some more, then adjusted his shoulders to a more comfortable position. "The storm woke me up, and then I heard the shots. I knew they were pistol shots, and I couldn't think of any good reason why you or anyone else would be shooting a pistol at that time of night. If a bear or cougar had come into your camp and was attacking, you'd have used your rifle. The pistol shots meant people trouble," he said flatly.

"Yeah," she agreed, and sighed. "They did."

"So I saddled up that crab-hopping young son of a bitch and set out in the worst storm I've seen up here since I was a kid. I'd lost the trail and was doubling back when I heard you. You know the rest."

"But how did you know where my camp was? I mean, you might be able to tell the general direction the shots came from, but—"

"Harlan told me which camp."

"*Harlan?*"

"He was worried."

Angie digested that in silence. Harlan's concern was probably because she was a woman and her two clients were men, something she couldn't completely discount because she was always careful, herself, in that regard.

"So he knew you were coming up here and—" She stopped, confused. And, what? Keep an eye on her? This cabin was several miles from her campsite, so if it hadn't been for those shots in the middle of the night, there was no way Dare could have known that anything was going wrong at her camp. If Chad had waited until the next day, and shot Davis and her with the rifle, there was nothing that would have alarmed Dare because rifle shots were to be expected during a hunt.

He drank some more coffee, his eyelids lowered as if he were thinking. Then he said, "No, not exactly."

"Not exactly?"

"I wasn't coming up here. Harlan was worried and asked me to keep an eye on you, just in case. I decided to do some fishing while I was here."

She almost dropped her cup, she was so flabbergasted. She stared at him, trying to sort through all the implications that were rushing through her brain. "So you . . . I . . ."

"Yeah. It wasn't coincidence I was up here."

He'd come up here, taken what could have been an entire week out of his time, to do a favor for Harlan? She could see him doing Harlan any number of favors, but considering the hostility in her own relationship with Dare, she couldn't think of why he'd do that particular one.

"I can't tell you how happy I am that you're here," she said, "but for the life of me I can't imagine why you agreed to do that."

"I've told you," he returned, eyeing her over the rim of the cup. "I've been watching your ass for two years now. By the way, this really is some damn fine coffee."

Chapter Twenty-four

Alarm bells once again began ringing in the back of her head. Her reaction was instantaneous. "Oh, no," she warned. "I told you, I'm not going there."

"Yeah? Why not?"

From his tone of voice he might as well have been asking her why she didn't want pizza for supper. That definitely punched her buttons, making her feel as if he were looking for nothing more than a sexual tissue, to be used and discarded. She scowled at him. "I have a better question: *Why?* I'm not into recreational sex, period, and it isn't as if we're dating."

He cocked one knee up and rested his forearm on it, coffee cup in hand, giving her a long, considering look. "We could have been. Damn it, I asked you out twice. So now let me ask you a question: Are you attracted to me, or not? I've made it as plain as I can that I'm attracted to you, so now tell me straight out how you feel."

Angie felt her face getting hot. She could lie—that is, if she hadn't kissed him back the way she had, hanging on to him and meeting him tongue to tongue. He was asking a loaded question, one to which he already knew the answer. "That isn't the point," she muttered, shifting uncomfortably.

"That's exactly the damn point. The least you can do is be as up-front with me as I've been with you." He didn't take his gaze from her face, studying every minute change of her expression. Such intense scrutiny made her feel emotionally naked, but then she'd given him that power by telling him all about her wedding, how much she doubted herself because of her own actions. He could figure out now what made her tick, how to get to her, and that was by making himself appear as vulnerable as she felt. The problem with that was she doubted this man had ever felt vulnerable in his entire life, even when shrapnel had sliced his throat. Some people just had that innate self-confidence that spilled over into every facet of their lives. She wasn't one of them. Her self-confidence seemed to be confined to very specific areas, and didn't bleed over into the others.

"It isn't that I don't find you attractive," she snapped, resenting being cornered this way.

"Then why did you turn me down, *twice?*"

He sounded really grumpy about that; surprised out of her resentment, Angie blinked at him. She couldn't believe it mattered so much to him. Not that he sounded hurt or uncertain; he just sounded grumpy. "The first time, I wanted to go," she blurted.

"But you didn't."

"I *couldn't.* I was taking a hunting party out the next day, and I was running flat out getting everything ready and stocking up on supplies because I'd just gotten back from another hunt. I said I couldn't, and you stomped off," she charged, indignation growing. "You didn't give me a chance to tell you why. What was I supposed to do, yell it at your back?"

"Maybe. Guys don't know what the hell to do." He scowled at her. "If we're persistent, we're stalkers. If we don't push, then we aren't interested enough. You tell me what else I could have done. I *did* ask you out again."

"That was different," she grumbled. "It was months later. By that time, you'd already siphoned off so much of my business that I saw red every time I heard your name."

He shoved his hand through his hair. "Look, I can't do anything about that. I didn't deliberately hurt your business, but I didn't turn down anyone who contacted me. What would you have wanted me to do? What would you have done?"

That was a million-dollar question, because there was no easy, cut-and-dried answer. He hadn't done anything illegal, or even unethical. He had as much right to make a living as she did. He hadn't undercut her prices; if anything, he charged more for his services than she did for hers. She'd lost business simply because he was there, and was who he was, with different experiences and strengths that some of her clients had wanted more than they'd wanted hers.

It still pissed her off.

"I'm not saying you should have done anything," she forced herself to admit. "Things are what they are. Regardless of whether or not we're attracted to each other, the reality is that I'm going to be moving away and I'm really not interested in a temporary fling."

He drank some more coffee, eyeing her above the rim of the cup. "Flings can be a lot of fun."

Angie snorted. It wasn't the most elegant sound but it expressed exactly how she felt. Goaded, she said, "Yeah, right. For a man, maybe."

His head snapped back a little. He lowered the cup, his eyebrows peaking in surprise as he studied her. "You don't like sex?"

"I didn't say that. It's okay."

Shit! Why had she said that? She knew better. She might as well have waved a red flag in front of a bull, and as soon as the words were out of her mouth she wished like hell she could have taken them back. Men seemed to take it as a personal affront if a woman didn't think sex was the greatest thing since sliced bread, then of course they wanted to show her how wrong she was, that—

He set the coffee down with a thunk that made the contents slosh dangerously close to the rim. "If it's just 'okay,' then obviously you haven't been with anyone who knew his ass from a hole in the ground."

And . . . *bingo!* It took a great effort, but Angie didn't roll her eyes. Not completely, anyway. She did cast them upward, as if asking for divine aid. Her common sense began shouting at her to just let it drop, to change the subject or even fake choking to death, but sex had been a source of dissatisfaction for her from the beginning, and she was tired of faking anything, even choking.

"Look," she said impatiently, "it feels okay, but I don't see what the great song and dance is about it. A man gets his rocks off doing it. A woman gets her rocks off by hand—or mouth, if the guy's feeling generous. I prefer to cut out the middleman, so to speak. No fuss, no muss. It's a lot less effort, and the payoff is guaranteed."

He looked like a thundercloud, all dark intent rolling toward her as he leaned down so close their noses were almost bumping, just as he'd done during their argument in the parking lot. "I repeat: You haven't been with anyone who knows what he's doing."

She suspected a lot of people would have found him intimidating—she once had, but not now. Too much water, literally, had gone under that bridge. She just lowered her own brows and met him glare for glare. Her common sense escalated from shouting to all but howling *Abort! Abort!* and still she couldn't stop her mouth. "I suppose you think you have the magic dick that can make everything wonderful, right?"

"You bet your sweet ass," he said flatly. "It isn't rocket science. What you know about making coffee, I know about fucking."

She fell over laughing. Literally. Howls of laughter burst from her throat and he grabbed her coffee cup, rescuing it as she toppled onto her side, clutching her middle. "You . . . you mean you get the total volume and d-divide—" It was so ridiculous she couldn't continue.

Very deliberately he set both cups of coffee on the floor, then rolled over on top of her. She stopped laughing, the sound abruptly cut off when his heavy weight, all that heat and hardness, bore down on her. If she'd been immune to him, his action would have made her angry, but she wasn't; she never had been. Neither was she afraid of him, at least not physically. She had no intention of trusting him with her emotions, but her body, her physical safety? Oh, yeah, without hesitation.

"Not quite that way," he said in his rough, hoarse voice, the tone going so low she could almost feel the vibration against her skin. His gaze roamed over her face, settled on her mouth. "Let's make a deal."

"This isn't a game show. I don't play around with sex." She felt really strange having a conversation with him while he was on top of her, but though she rested her hands on his sides she didn't put any pressure on him, didn't try to push him off. Considering everything she'd just said about sex, feeling him lying heavy and warm on top of her was a guilty pleasure, one she had no intention of letting him know she felt. What made her pleasure even more guilty was the fact that he had an erection. She wanted to spread her legs, let him nestle it against her, but wouldn't that be using him the way she didn't want him to use her? Or was it just part of sex, the taking and giving of pleasure? At the moment she was too distracted to decide.

"Good, because I'm not playing, either." He settled more heavily onto her, moving his legs in a subtle, or maybe not so subtle, adjustment that widened her thighs just a little, letting his erection push further between her legs, nudging hard against her clitoris. "My deal is this: If I can make you come while we're fucking, no hands or mouths allowed—though I gotta say, to me the important part is coming, not how you get there—then we have our fling for as long as you're here. Who knows? In this economy, that could be months. I don't know if my bank would okay a loan for the amount you're asking."

She drew her head back as far as she was able, which wasn't very far considering she was lying on her back, and stared at him in disbelief. "You're using the economy and a bank loan to try to talk me into having sex with you?" She was actually talking, carrying on a conversation, and she had no idea how because almost all of her attention was focused on the pressure he was putting between her legs. Her heart was literally pounding away; he *had* to feel it against him, because her rib cage was rattling from the force of the beats.

"You've ignored or rejected everything else."

"Dare, we've had one kiss! *One!* What gives you the idea that I'm anywhere near taking a risk like that, even if I were the risk-taking type, which I'm not?"

"That one kiss," he replied, and kissed her again, but this time the kiss was light and soft, cajoling instead of demanding, tender instead of intense. Angie tried to hold herself distant from it, to not respond—for about two whole seconds. Then the utter sweetness of the kiss, the temptation of it, completely swamped her willpower.

She felt the same way she did when she really, really wanted chocolate ice cream but told herself no, then opened the freezer door and there it was, right in front of her, and she grabbed the carton out and in three seconds flat was eating the ice cream as if it were a gazelle and she a starving lioness. Like that. She wanted him like that. The fierceness of the way she felt took her by surprise, because she'd never really lusted after anyone before. She'd had teenage crushes, and she'd *thought*, would have sworn, that she'd loved Todd, but she'd never before felt this ache to touch and be touched.

Then he was releasing her and sitting up, and she stared at him in bewilderment, trying to get her pounding heart under control, trying not to reach her arms out for him. She literally *ached* between her legs, and deep inside, an ache that made all her inner muscles clench, made her nipples feel pinched.

"I'm not going to push," he said. "Not too hard, anyway. You can trust me in that, at least."

"Of course I trust you," she immediately replied, then felt troubled by her own answer, not only because it was the truth, but because he had so closely mirrored what she'd been thinking just a moment before.

"In some ways, yeah, but that isn't what this is about, is it?"

He was far too astute for her comfort, but then she'd opened herself up to him more than she ever had to anyone else. She'd told him the most embarrassing stuff about herself, and anyone with half a brain could read between the lines to find all the things and places where she had the most doubt, where she was the least confident. "Do you want to know what I think this is about? I think it's about you being horny, and nothing more complicated than that. You're horny, and I'm conveniently here—for now. Regardless of anything else, I'm leaving in the not-too-distant future. We don't have a future, and I'm not interested in temporary."

"You don't have to leave," he snapped back.

"To make a living, yeah, I do."

"Ah, hell. I wasn't going to throw this at you so soon, but—"

Suspicion made the bottom drop out of her stomach, and she sat bolt upright, her gaze narrowed. "Throw what at me?"

Clearly annoyed at her tone, he said, "Nothing horrible. Shit, you'd think I'd just suggested robbing a bank. It's something for you to think about, is all."

Still wary, she said, "Okay, let's hear it."

"Let's get something to eat, first, and have another cup of coffee."

He was stalling. The realization worried her, because Dare was about as blunt as a person could be and not get locked up. But it wasn't as if they weren't going to be there all day, with plenty of time to talk. While she wasn't really hungry, another cup of coffee would be welcome.

His stockpile of food from the locker included instant oat-

meal, breakfast cereal bars, trail mix, jerky, and the instant soup
and stew mixes, as well as a few individually wrapped muffins. She
chose cinnamon-flavored oatmeal, then brooded over the bowl
while she ate, wondering what he had up his sleeve. He'd said she
didn't have to leave, but she had to make a living, and it wasn't as
if their little community in the back of beyond was seething with
job opportunities.

"Before we talk, I want to get some clothes on," she said when
she was finished with her oatmeal. She cradled the warm cup of
coffee in her hands, relishing the comfort of hot food in her stomach and coffee to drink even if she did have other things on her
mind. One thing she did know: Even though she knew it was completely psychological, she'd feel better if she was fully dressed
when they had this serious discussion. Sitting around wearing his
thermal underwear bottoms and one of his flannel shirts was comfortable, but she didn't feel capable of handling a lot. She also
wanted to brush her teeth again. For some reason, good grooming felt essential.

He shrugged; maybe he was glad of more time to marshal his
argument, whatever it was. After collecting their trash and drinking his third cup of coffee, he stepped outside the sleep area and
drew the privacy curtain closed. "While you're changing, I'll rinse
the mud out of your other clothes and hang them up to dry. You
might need them when we start walking out of here."

"Okay. Thanks."

She listened to him go down the ladder, heard the sounds
from below as he donned his slicker, then the sound of the door
opening and closing. Hurriedly she stripped, she used a couple of
wet wipes to freshen up, and brushed her teeth. She'd love to
brush her hair, but a hairbrush was one thing she hadn't stuffed
into her saddlebags, so she settled for briskly massaging her scalp
with her fingertips, then raking her fingers through her hair.

Dare came back in, presumably with the bucket he'd set out
again to catch more rainwater. With the sound of rain on the roof,

she could barely hear the sloshing of water as he rinsed out her sweats.

Putting on underwear and her own shirt felt fantastic. Her bra was nowhere in sight, but what the heck, she didn't really need one anyway. She didn't have enough to jiggle; mostly her bra was to keep the imprint of her nipples from showing through. Working her jeans on was a chore. She couldn't flex her right foot enough to point her toes and work her foot through the opening of the pant leg, so she carefully bunched the fabric and worked it up and over her swollen ankle.

When she fastened her jeans, she realized they felt loose in the waist. She'd lost some weight, probably when her body was burning calories like crazy trying to stave off hypothermia, not to mention the effort she'd been putting out. Dare would have lost weight, too, from carrying her for miles, and from his own body fighting to stay warm.

That horrible night seemed unreal now, as if she were thinking about a movie she'd seen instead of something that had actually happened to her. The contrast between then and now, when she was tucked inside this snug little cabin, her world narrowed down to this mattress on the floor in a partitioned area maybe two feet wider than the mattress itself, to just herself and Dare, was so great her mind seemed to have let go of "then" so it could completely hold on to "now." Her subconscious had dealt with it by dreaming about it, and now that she was awake the reality seemed even further removed.

When she had nothing else to do, she unwrapped the elastic bandage around her ankle. Some of the swelling was definitely gone. Another day of sitting on her butt should make a big difference in the ankle's condition. If she could get her boot on, and if the weather cooperated, with the aid of a walking stick she might be able to walk out of here. The weather was the big thing. Even after the rain stopped, it would take a while for the flash floods to stop. Until then, they weren't going anywhere.

She pulled a clean sock on her left foot, and tried working one onto her right foot, but her ankle was still too swollen for the sock to be comfortable, so she put the sock aside and rewrapped her ankle. Her toes got cold unless she kept her foot covered by the sleeping bag; she'd either have to sit on the mattress all day or deal with cold toes.

Down below, the door opened and closed again. Dare would be setting the bucket out again, to catch more water.

Even though he wasn't spending a lot of time out in the rain, the air was chilly and the water was cold, so he might appreciate another cup of coffee when he came up again. Angie checked the coffeepot: enough in there for another two cups, at least, but it might be tasting bitter by now. She freshened it up by adding a little water, then put the pot on the camp stove and turned on the flame.

When she heard him reenter below, she pulled back the privacy curtain and called down, "I reheated the coffee, if you want a cup."

"Sounds good. I'll be up in a minute, after I get these clothes wrung out and hung up to dry."

She gave him a minute, then dumped enough sugar into the cup to choke a horse, estimating that was how much he'd used before, and poured the hot coffee on top of it to dissolve it. She'd just poured herself a cup when his dark head appeared at the top of the ladder. Her heartbeat gave its normal jump and the butterflies fluttered in her stomach. "I've already sugared it," she said as she handed his cup to him, ignoring both her heart and the butterflies.

"Thanks." He took a long swallow. "Damn, that's good. You can make the coffee from now on."

"I'd planned on it," she said drily. "How's it looking out there?" The only view she'd had was a brief look at some trees while Dare carried her to the portable toilet, as the cabin was built in a protected spot with limited straight-line visibility.

"The only way I'd try to go anywhere in that mess would be if it were a matter of life and death. It's bad. On the good side, it isn't raining as hard now. If the weather service was anywhere close to accurate, it should start tapering off late this afternoon."

"The amount of rain was kind of underestimated."

"Tell me about it." He sat down on the mattress and pulled off his boots, wiping them down with a remnant of towel before setting them aside. Then he picked up his coffee cup and scooted back to lean against the wall. She would have liked to face him, but she couldn't fold her legs under her without hurting her ankle, so she shifted into position beside him, her legs stretched out alongside his, but with maybe ten inches separating them.

"I was going to get Harlan to lay this out for you," he muttered.

"That bad, huh?"

"I actually think it would work for both of us. I want to expand the business, be able to bring in more clients, a wider variety, but I'm spread so thin I can't handle it on my own."

Angie's lips thinned. He was spread so thin because he had most of her former clients. "Not scoring points here, Callahan," she warned.

"I'm not trying to score points, Powell, I'm trying to offer you a fu— a . . . damn it, I can't talk if I can't cuss. I was in the army too long. I'm fucking offering you a deal, got it?"

Warily she eyed him. "Not yet."

"I want to hire you," he said impatiently. "With your place I'll have more room for clients to stay, but I'm still just one person, so having more room won't do me any good unless it's one big party. It doesn't make sense to expand my space but not my capability, right? I need someone else who can take out the additional hunting parties, someone I trust, who knows the area. You won't have to leave, or even move, because I'll need someone to look after the place."

"Hire me." Her tone was blank. She was so astonished she didn't know whether to be flattered or insulted, upset or happy.

She'd lose her home, but she wouldn't lose it. She'd lose her business, but she'd still be doing what she loved. She wouldn't be autonomous, but that wasn't all it was cracked up to be anyway, because she was autonomous only as far as the constraints of responsibility would allow.

"I also need someone to take over the paperwork."

"Ah, now we get to the *real* reason." She said it with light sarcasm, but the truth was, now that her shock was fading she was a little grateful and a lot touched by the offer. After she had time to really think things over, she might be a lot grateful, but right now she was still trying to absorb the possibility of not being her own boss. She'd worked for others before, for longer than she'd had her own business, so it wasn't as if she couldn't do it. But she *liked* having her own business, *liked* doing the planning and preparation, liked answering to no one other than herself.

Right away she could see both pros and cons. One big pro was that she'd have the money from selling her place, money that she could invest for her future. She'd be out from under a mortgage—that would become Dare's headache. The most immediate con would be giving up control of her working life. She liked doing things her way.

But if she took the job, she'd be *home*. And she'd be near Dare . . . but he'd be her boss. And that was a very, very big con. If he thought he'd get something going with her and employ her at the same time . . . no. Wasn't going to happen. The bottom dropped out of her stomach in dismay.

She struggled to get her thoughts in better order. Why would that bother her, unless she'd already subconsciously decided to sleep with him?

Oh, God. He'd taken an already complicated situation and made it worse.

Chapter Twenty-five

"I have to think about it," she finally said.

"Why? You either want to stay, or you don't."

Wasn't that just like a man? Damn the torpedoes, full steam ahead. The situation was simple to him: He was offering her a deal, and she either liked it or didn't. But she saw the torpedoes, and she didn't want to blow herself out of the water. What she wanted . . . she didn't know exactly what she wanted, because she hadn't thought about all the nuances and possibilities yet.

She couldn't just say, *Because I won't sleep with my boss* because she was still at sea regarding their possible relationship, period. Everything except her brain seemed to be pulling her toward him, but until her brain got onboard with the idea, she wasn't making that move. How could she make a definite decision about something that wasn't definite? It didn't make sense to decide to try having a relationship with him, both emotional and physical, and at the same time decide on a business deal that, if she refused it, would take her away from him, but if she took the deal it would make it impossible to have a relationship . . . she was confusing herself trying to think about it. The two couldn't mix, but neither could they be separated.

"Well?" he demanded. "Do you want to stay?"

"Don't rush me, okay? It isn't as if you know for certain you'll be able to get a bank loan, and"—she waved her hand around, indicating the cabin—"there's nothing we can do right now, anyway. We're stuck here, so there's no rush."

"But if you decide, then we could start working out details."

"I don't want to start working out details, I want to take my time so I don't make any mistakes!" she said impatiently. "God, what rank did you have in the army, chief nagger?"

"The army doesn't have chiefs. That's the navy." But his mouth quirked in a little smile, and he settled his shoulders more comfortably against the wall. "And I was an E-seven."

"Which translates into English as . . . ?"

"Sergeant first class."

She didn't know anything about military rank, beyond the basic enlisted and officer ranks. "Am I impressed?" she asked warily.

He gave his stifled, sand-papery laugh. "Not really. A sergeant is like an office manager who makes the vice president look good, but catches all the shit when things go wrong. The only difference is, in the army there are weapons and explosives and other interesting shit to help make up for the paperwork. My main job was training lieutenants."

She had the feeling he was understating what he'd done, otherwise he wouldn't have those shrapnel wounds. "You have to train an officer?"

"Like any other newbie in any other job. They come in, they're young, they don't have any experience, haven't seen combat, and they make stupid decisions. The smart ones listen to the sergeants. If we're lucky, the stupid-ass ones decide they don't really want a career in the military and get out, before they either end up dead or cause a lot of other people to die."

Angie had gone her entire life without thinking about life in the military, but abruptly she found herself trying to imagine what it was like. She wanted to know what he'd done, how he'd filled his days, the friends he'd made. She wanted to know how he'd been hurt, but didn't want to ask. The sharp turnabout in their relationship wasn't even thirty-six hours old yet. Granted, a lot had been packed into those hours, but some things, such as personal questions, still took time.

"Did you like it? Being in the army, I mean."

"I had a lot of fun. Good times, bad times." He tilted his head back, his eyes half-closed as he revisited memories. "There are guys I served with who'll be my friends until the day I die. But I never meant to make a fucking career of it. When I enlisted, I thought ten years max. I'd get a college degree, see something of the world." He gave his rough, stifled chuckle. "I did that, all right. But after my last encounter with sharp metallic objects, I reassessed my position. I'd already been in five years longer than I'd planned. So I got out."

He'd brought the subject up, so Angie felt perfectly justified in pursuing it. "Is that when you got the wound on your throat?"

"Yeah. For the first couple of weeks I couldn't talk, but that was because of swelling. The docs had told me I'd be okay, so I didn't sweat it. It was frustrating as hell, though. After I got my voice back, it was hoarse, but shit, if that's the worst thing that ever happens to me in my life, I'm one lucky son of a bitch."

She rolled her head sideways to smile at him. "I bet it was a real strain on your nervous system, not being able to swear."

"Damn near drove me nucking futs." He looked completely raffish and so masculine he made her hurt inside, with that black stubble on his face and those wicked blue eyes glinting at her, his mouth curled in a smirk.

She burst out laughing. She'd thought he was so dour and grumpy, but he was proving to have a side to him that really appealed to her own sense of humor. He considered her for a moment, then looped his arm around her neck and pulled her in, his mouth closing over hers, stopping the laughter.

Angie couldn't help it. She kissed him back. Kissing was like anything else; after you've done it once, doing it again became easier. She put her hand on his bristly jaw and let herself savor the taste of him, the pressure of those firm lips, the undeniable surge of excitement when he made a low, rough sound in the back of his throat and abruptly deepened the kiss, changing the angle of his head so that she found herself giving way, sinking back. His arms cradled her, supported her, then his heavy weight settled in place on top of her and all she could do was cradle him in turn, her arms and legs opening to accept and hold him.

The weight of a man on her . . . she had enjoyed that, missed it. She slid her hand up the back of his neck, her fingers sliding into his hair as she clasped the back of his skull. Still, she felt compelled to free her lips long enough to warn, "Just because I'm kissing you doesn't mean I'm going to have sex with you."

He lifted his head a little. Blue eyes glinted down at her, heavy-lidded with sexual intent. "Yet," he replied, and she let the word stand unchallenged.

He gripped her hip, his fingers tightening, then relaxing and gently massaging before sliding up her side, under her shirt. Almost before she knew it his big warm hand was closing over her breast, his palm rough against the exquisite sensitivity of her nipple. She felt a moment of anxiety because her boobs were so small, but then his eyelids lowered even more and he made that rough humming sound again, the one she was coming to associate with pure pleasure, and with one swift motion he jerked her shirt up and dipped his head to her breasts.

There was a dizzying split-second of combined surprise and anticipation, then his mouth, hot and wet, closed over her nipple. His tongue swirled around the nub, lightly, gently, making it harden and extend. Pleasure spread through her, pleasure that made her abdominal muscles contract, made her skin feel electri-

fied. With his lips and tongue and teeth he played with her, moving his attention to the other nipple while his fingers gently
kneaded. Then he pressed her nipple against the roof of his
mouth and sucked hard; she clutched at him, bucking under the
lash of excitement and desire. He bore down on her, controlling
her with his weight; she could feel his tongue rhythmically working the extended bud, the suction of his mouth pulling at her and
sparking an echo of the same sensation between her legs, deep inside her.

He lifted his head, the expression in his eyes fierce, hot, his
mouth set in a sensually ruthless line. "More?" he asked hoarsely.

Instantly she realized what he was doing. Making love was like
a snowball rolling downhill, gaining speed and momentum and
inevitability. If he hadn't stopped right now, this very minute,
likely they wouldn't. He could have continued, seducing her with
pleasure, and made love to her without a single word of protest
from her, which embarrassed her considering how firmly she'd
told him she wasn't going to have sex. But he wasn't going to allow
her to get cold feet afterward and claim he'd rushed her, not
given her time to think. He was forcing her to be with him every
step of the way. She didn't know whether to be pissed that he
thought she might be such a coward as that, or grateful that he
was giving her this chance to slow things down.

Both.

She took a deep breath, only a little comforted that his own
breathing was harder and faster than usual. "No, I think this is as
far as we should go," she said. "Thank you. Asshole."

He levered himself to the side but remained propped on his
elbow, leaning over her. His expression took on a slight smugness.
"Feeling a little tempted, huh?" he asked, lightly tracing her lips
with one fingertip.

Denying it would only make her a liar. "Enjoying kissing you
doesn't make the issues go away."

"Exactly what issues are we talking about? Everything looks

pretty cut and dried to me. You either like me or you don't—on
the evidence, I'd say you do—and you either want to stay here or
you don't."

"You'd be my boss," she pointed out.

"I don't think that would stop you from telling me off if you
thought I needed it." His tone was wry. Then his gaze sharpened.
"Are you saying you think I'd use that to pressure you into sleeping with me?"

"No, I'm thinking more what it would say about me if I slept
with the boss." She scowled up at him. "And that would mean I'd
decided to sleep with you, which I haven't, so you can see. why I
need to think this out."

He fell over onto his back and stared at the ceiling. "God save
me from a woman's way of thinking. What the hell kind of logic is
that? One has nothing to do with the other."

"Maybe not to you, but let's face it, you're plankton, and I'm a
higher life form. Details matter to me."

His lips quirked and, without turning his head, he cut his gaze
to her. Sounding a tad disgruntled, he said, "Plankton?"

"Maybe algae."

"How about a fucking amoeba?"

"Amoebas don't fuck, they just divide."

"Hummph." He made a growly noise and lay there looking annoyed. "That would be me, then, because evidently I don't fuck,
either."

Angie turned onto her side facing him, smiling. Lying here
like this with him was way, way too intimate, but in a completely
unexpected way just talking with him was even more enticing. He
was funny and sexy, grumpy and profane, and she didn't think
she'd ever get bored listening to him. "Not right now, anyway. So,
ruling out getting naked, what are we going to do all day? Did you
bring any books with you? Cards? You weren't planning to sit up
here for a week with nothing to entertain yourself, I hope?"

"I have books *and* cards, and my iPod. You just said I was algae.

What makes you think you're going to get your hands on either one?"

"Your sense of fair play."

"You're way fucking off-base there. I play to win."

"Wouldn't that be 'fay wucking'?"

"Never heard of her."

He made her beg for the books, but he wasn't serious so she didn't mind. Then he pulled the books from his saddlebags and she could have hit him, because if she'd known what they were beforehand she definitely wouldn't have begged. One was an extremely dry and technical book on custom-loading your own shells, and the other was a geological study of the earth's tectonic plates. She gave him an appalled look. "Couldn't you at least have some popular fiction?"

"I do, but it's at home. I figure the only way I'll read this shit is if I don't have anything else to read, so this was the perfect time."

She laughed and put the books aside, picked up the deck of cards. "What do you want to play? Blackjack, Texas Hold 'em, rummy?"

"Not rummy. That's a sissy-ass game."

"Ah ha. That means you're afraid I'll kick your ass at rummy, so you don't want to play it."

He narrowed his eyes at her. "You think?" He moved so he was sitting cross-legged on the mattress, facing her. "Game on, Powell."

She should have remembered his years in the military. He played rummy as ruthlessly as if it were war, but she was pretty good herself, if she did say so, and once she realized how good he was she buckled down, concentrated, and won two out of four. He wanted to go for a tie-breaker, of course, but she refused. "What good is that? If you beat me, you'll crow about it, and that would lower my opinion of you. If I win, you'll pout, and that'll lower my opinion of you. Trust me, you won't come out looking good no matter what happens."

He chuckled as he shuffled and dealt. "You hate losing, don't you?"

"Like poison."

"Good to know. So when we fight, I should let you win at least half the time?"

"*Let* me win?" she posed delicately, her tone light but her eyebrows drawing to a point over her nose.

"You'll never know, will you?" He gave her that smug smirk and began dealing out the cards. "Texas Hold 'em. What's the bet?"

"Bet? We're playing for funsies."

He stopped dealing. "I don't play for fucking funsies. Cards are serious."

"You just played rummy for fun."

"No, I played rummy to prove to you I could beat you at it."

"Is everything a contest to you?"

"I'm a man. Even pissing is a contest."

The easy bantering continued over several games of Texas Hold 'em—he was definitely better at that game than she was—then they moved on to blackjack. They got tired of playing cards after a while, and with a sigh of resignation she picked up the book on loading her own ammunition and began reading; at least that was some information she might one day be able to use, while she was certain she'd never be able to influence tectonic plates one way or the other. Dare didn't fuss about her choice, just picked up the other book, moved the lantern so they both had sufficient light, and settled back with his legs stretched out.

The day was slow and lazy. There was chilly gray rain outside, companionship and laughter and an underlying sexual attraction inside. After reading a while she got drowsy, so she stretched out and took a nap, feeling relaxed and safe. When she woke, they each had soup and a protein bar for lunch.

He went down the ladder without explanation and out into the rain, then came back up the ladder carefully holding the bucket, which was three-quarters full of water.

"If you can get your foot in this bucket, it may be too late, but the cold water might help the swelling a little and soreness in your ankle."

Angie unwrapped her ankle, folded up the hem of her jeans, and eased her foot into the water. She hissed as she lowered her foot into the bucket; the water wasn't icy, but it was close. Because the bucket narrowed at the bottom she couldn't just set her foot into it, but by carefully bending her toes she managed to get the water over her ankle. "How did you collect this much water so fast?" The rain had slacked off enough that no way was it coming down hard enough to fill this bucket this much.

"I set the bucket so it caught what's coming off the roof. I did that thinking about getting water for washing up tonight, but then it occurred to me you could be soaking that ankle. There'll be time enough to catch more fresh water for later." While she soaked her ankle, he settled down again with the evidently fascinating subject of plate tectonics.

She propped her chin on her knee, watching the way he furrowed his brow as he read, liking that he sometimes turned the book sideways to look at charts and maps. She wouldn't have figured him for a reader, but then what had she really known about him? She'd resented him so much, been so angry, that she hadn't let herself see him as anything other than a thorn in her side.

Oh, she'd known from the beginning—those damn butterflies were a dead giveaway—that on a sexual basis she was deeply affected by him, which was why she'd given him such a wide berth. But she hadn't known that he could make her laugh. She hadn't known that just being with him would give her this sense of comfort, of lightness, as if things that had weighed her down were no longer quite as heavy.

Did she love him? She didn't trust the suddenness of her emotional flip-flop—if it was indeed a flip-flop, considering the presence of the butterflies. Still, she couldn't make a decision like that based on roughly thirty-six hours of close acquaintance, no matter how momentous those thirty-six hours had been, or that she'd spent about half that time sleeping in his arms. Survival had forged lifelong bonds between them, so she understood exactly what he meant about having friends in the army who would be his friends until the day he died. She felt the same about him, now.

"Why're you looking at me that way?" he asked absently, proving that no matter how absorbed he seemed to be in something, he was still aware of his surroundings.

"Thinking."

"Reached any decisions yet?"

"Not yet."

"I could shave," he offered.

"Wouldn't matter."

"Good, because I'd have to use my knife. I didn't bring a razor on this trip."

And there it was again, the smile that wasn't just on her face, but in her heart.

Chapter Twenty-six

Late that afternoon, the rain slackened to a drizzle, then after a few minutes died completely away. After hearing the sound for so long, the sudden silence was almost as jarring as the storm had been. Dare lifted his head, listening, then said, "I might as well bring the bucket in, because that's all the water we'll be collecting."

Angie breathed a sigh of relief. She hadn't let it get to her, but the rain had been oppressive, and she was glad it was over. The temperature might drop now, as it usually did this time of year after a front moved through, but she had ample clothing to stay warm. Unless a surprise snowstorm set in, they would soon be able to travel.

They would have to be very cautious, because the rush of water down the mountain would make for some treacherous going, but the flash floods would rapidly disappear. The creeks and rivers would stay swollen for days, but between the two of them, she and Dare probably knew every place where it would be possible to ford them.

"If we have to, we can go due south until we hit Badger Road," he said, startling her because their thoughts once again had been so closely aligned. "You know where I'm talking about, don't you?"

"I think so. It's a dirt road, right?"

"That's it. Definitely the long way around. I hope we don't have to go that far out of the way."

The big question, though, was if her ankle would hold up for that long of a walk, or any walk at all. She wouldn't know until tomorrow. The cold water soak had helped; the joint wasn't as sore, and she could flex her foot a little. Whether or not she could get a sock on, and her boot, was something she wouldn't know until the time came.

The state police needed to be notified about Chad Krugman as soon as possible, plus there was the matter of the bear, but— "If I can't get my boot on tomorrow, or walk enough to get by, I don't want you trying to walk out of here by yourself." She said it fast, before she could talk herself out of it. "The ground is too unstable for you to try it alone; if you got hurt, or—"

"Don't worry, there's no way in hell I'd leave you behind. If you can't walk, then we'll stay here another fu— day." He gave her a hooded look, and that slight smile curved his lips. "You're worried about me."

She felt her face getting hot, which was ridiculous when she considered everything that had already happened between them, but physical stuff was one thing and emotions were something else entirely. Well, she'd known when she opened her mouth exactly what his reaction would be, and she'd said it anyway. She couldn't even deny it. The best she could do at this point was cross her arms and say, "So?"

He shook his head, still smiling.

She wasn't fooling him, and she certainly wasn't fooling herself. She couldn't bear the thought of him setting out by himself, even though logic said that he was wilderness-savvy, smart, well-armed, in excellent condition, and all sorts of other things that should have reassured her but didn't. She simply didn't want him to take the risk of setting out alone, on foot.

On the other hand, they both knew she would be perfectly fine waiting here; there was food and water, she could keep warm, she was armed. She knew what it said about her that she wanted to stay with him, but it also said a lot about his self-confidence that he was certain he could keep her safe, even though taking her along was the more risky course for her. That was fine with her, so long as she got what she wanted.

Taking the last trip outside that night was definitely easier without having to don a slicker first. When Dare carried her outside, she looked up and actually saw stars peeking through the scudding clouds. The wind was picking up, though, signaling an approaching cold front. They might wake up to below-freezing temperatures, but the clearing sky meant there wouldn't be any snow. Yay!

He carried her back in and they began getting ready for sleep: heating the water a little and washing off—she on the upper level, Dare down below—brushing teeth, changing out of her jeans into the much more comfortable thermal bottoms.

As she got comfortable on the mattress and spread out the sleeping bag, she was swamped by a sudden sadness. They would be leaving soon, and she didn't want to go. These two days had, weirdly, been . . . somehow enriching, and she was reluctant to leave. The enforced closeness with Dare had turned her world upside down. She wasn't certain yet if that was good, but she definitely knew it had been enjoyable.

They had been safe, here in Dare's cabin. The improving weather meant they would soon be leaving that safety, either tomorrow or the next day for certain, and the real world loomed. Abruptly she felt the danger of what they didn't know, such as what Chad Krugman had done, or where he was. The bear was still out there, too, but she thought they were far enough from its territory that they were fairly safe. Chad, however, had proven himself to be surprisingly dangerous. Had he tried to get off the mountain that first night, or had he found shelter somewhere and waited out the storm? There was a possibility he'd even gone back to the campsite and finished off the bear—a slim possibility, because she hadn't heard another shot, and he would have had to retrieve his rifle from his tent first. The shot could have coincided with a blast of thunder and lightning that covered the sound, but that was asking a lot of coincidence.

She wouldn't bet her life on coincidence. He could have done the same thing they'd done, wait out the storm, and start out tomorrow now that better weather was here. He was on horseback, unless he'd somehow managed to lose her horse, so he'd make better time than they would. Would he come this far south, or try to follow the same general path she'd used taking the hunting party up into the mountains? If he did that, he'd run into a lot of difficulty. She knew that land, knew the creeks he'd have to cross, creeks that had been ankle-deep on the horses when they'd gone up, but would now be raging torrents. If he were smart, he wouldn't try to ford those creeks, but Chad wasn't experienced and he might not have any idea how powerful those currents could be.

There was no way she could predict what he might do. They wouldn't know, until they reached Lattimore's, if Chad had made it down ahead of them; all they could do in any case was notify the state police and let them handle it.

And what then? She went back to her house, and Dare went to his?

"Are you finished?" he called, pulling her from her moody thoughts.

"Yes, come on up."

He was up the ladder in seconds, pulling the privacy curtain closed behind him, to help keep in the heat as the temperature fell during the night. His tall, broad-shouldered frame made the small space seem even smaller. He unbuttoned his flannel shirt and pulled it off, then shucked his T-shirt off over his head and tossed it aside, too. The lantern light gleamed on the skin of his shoulders, and she found herself having to swallow. The damn man was making her drool.

"Don't you get cold without a shirt?"

Blue eyes gleamed. "With you snuggling that world-class ass of yours up to me? Not likely."

She was absurdly pleased that he thought her ass was world class. She'd never thought about it much one way or the other, unlike her lack of boobs, which was right out in front for her, and everyone else, to notice. Todd had never said anything about liking her butt. He'd made the usual statements men knew they were supposed to make about small boobs—anything over a mouthful was a waste, et cetera—but he hadn't been very convincing, especially when she'd see him checking out women who had bigger busts. Todd hadn't been the cheating type, she'd never suspected him of that, but still it had hurt that her body hadn't been visually appealing to him.

She stared at Dare as the truth dawned. "My God. You're an ass man."

He snorted. "No shit. What gave me away? The three thousand comments I've made about your ass, maybe?"

"Men usually like boobs, that's all. I'm surprised."

"I like boobs. Yours are pretty, but your ass is a work of art." He sat down on the mattress and began unlacing his boots, set them aside. He turned off the heater and the lantern and in the darkness lay down beside her, curling his heat and strength around her like before. Once again she felt his mouth on the back of her neck, then his arm tightened around her waist and he tucked her in tight against him.

"Good night," he murmured, his rough voice low.

She put her hand on top of his, replied "Good night," and closed her eyes, but she didn't think she would be sleeping any time soon, not with her thoughts churning the way they were.

He didn't go immediately to sleep, either. He was relaxed, but he wasn't asleep. She could feel him waiting for her to make a decision she hadn't, until now, realized was so immediate. He wasn't forcing the timing in any way, if she wanted to go to sleep he would, too, without a word.

But tomorrow, if she could get her boot on, they'd be leaving here. Circumstances would be different. The world would intrude again.

Did she really need to decide, or just trust the decision that had already been made?

Temptation beckoned, a lorelei that was as much emotional as physical. She was at least halfway in love with him, and she shouldn't take this final step unless she was willing to commit herself to what loving him could mean. Everything wouldn't suddenly become all sweetness and rose. petals. A relationship with him would inevitably include some rocky portions, because he wasn't and never would be an easy man, but neither was she a smiling Stepford, so she couldn't expect him to be what she herself wasn't. The legal issues could be worked out, whether or not their relationship was temporary or permanent. All she had to do was take that step.

Was it a matter of trusting him, or of trusting herself? More than anything, she had to trust herself, trust that she had chosen the right man this time. Todd hadn't done anything heinous; Dare was right about that. If she'd truly loved Todd, she might have kicked him in the shin, but in the end she would have forgiven him for not understanding, for not being as perceptive as he could have been. If he'd truly loved her, he'd have kept his word. What they'd had together had been Love Lite. Whether or not it would have grown into more was something she'd never know.

Because, now, there was Dare—Dare, who had come searching for her in the middle of a horrendous storm, who had carried her for miles on his back, then continued taking care of her, in ways that hadn't even occurred to her. Dare had done something that even her friends hadn't done: He'd taken her side. He trusted her judgment even when she herself didn't.

Angie opened her eyes and lay staring into the darkness, which wasn't as absolute as it had been, with starlight now filtering through the windows. Things were changing, time was moving on; she sensed that she needed to reach out and grasp life now, or lose this opportunity perhaps forever.

She could hold herself apart, not take a chance, but it seemed to her that *not* taking the risk, *not* trusting both Dare and herself, would be a far greater mistake than taking the chance and perhaps striking out again. It might not work out; if it didn't, she would still have had the experience of loving him. If, in the end, he didn't love her enough to want more, well, that would be his mistake, not hers.

Before she lost her nerve, she shifted in the darkness, turning over and putting her arm around his neck, and pressed her mouth to his.

No words were needed, not when they had touch, and need, and desire. He slipped his hand around the back of her neck, his long fingers sliding under her hair and clasping her skull as he took control of the kiss, angling his head and deepening the pressure. The warmth and taste of him filled her, easing a hunger that needed to be fed.

In the darkness there didn't seem to be any hurry. They kissed and touched, exploring, and Angie lost herself in the tactile magic of it. His hands were on her, sliding over every curve, and her hands were on him. The differences of his body from hers both shook and thrilled her to the core: the heavy muscularity of his shoulders, the hardness of his chest and abdomen, the spinal groove down his back and the thick pads of muscle that laced each side. One at a time, they shed their garments. Her shirt went first and then she was lying with her bare breasts nestled against him, the sensation making her move and slide so she could feel more of the electrifying friction of skin against skin. Her nipples ached and throbbed from just that, then he added the abrasion of his rough hands, the hard pull of his mouth.

He unsnapped, unzipped his fly, and pushed both jeans and underwear down and off, kicked them aside. Angie eagerly reached for him, found his penis already iron hard and heftier than she'd expected, even though she'd already known he'd been lying about having a little dick. Reaching down, she cupped his heavy testicles while with her other hand she began a slow stroke that wrung a groan from deep in his chest.

He stopped her almost immediately. "Uh uh, that's not the way we do this."

Because his voice was guttural with pleasure, she smiled against his chest. "It isn't? Are you sure?"

"Next time, maybe. Not this time."

"Why not?" Was that sultry voice actually *hers*? She found one of his nipples, dipped her head to give it a slow lick. "I think you like it."

"Fucking love it, and that's why not this time. My fuse is too short." With a lithe movement he flipped her to her back and pinned her hands above her head while he licked and sucked and slowly fanned the heat that was growing inside her.

She liked sex. She liked the way it felt, liked the anticipation, the closeness, the pleasure. The fact that she'd never had a climax from intercourse itself annoyed her, because she felt as if she were missing out on something that was probably fantastic, going by the way her friends had talked. After she'd broken up with Todd, she hadn't wanted another relationship, especially not one just for sex, and gradually her need for sex had kind of gone away, and that had bothered her, too. Had all the romance in her, both emotional and sexual, just withered away?

The more Dare touched her, the more emphatic the answer to that question became. *No.*

Then he tugged the thermal bottoms down and off, and they were lying together naked, kissing as if the slightest distance between them was intolerable. She loved kissing him, loved everything about it, the taste, the way his lips felt, the hot smell of his skin. He kissed his way down to her breasts, where his beard stubble scraped across her sensitive nipples and startled a cry from her, not in pain, but in a sharp, exquisite pleasure that took her by surprise.

His hand dipped between her legs, his thumb finding her clitoris and lightly stroking, circling, until she felt as if it had engorged beyond bearing, needing more, feeling empty and wanting him to fill her. Her legs were open, her back arched, everything in her straining and desperate for release.

"I want to see you when you come," he growled, lifting away from her and stretching out a long arm to turn on the lantern.

Angie instinctively flinched from the light; she made an aborted movement to reach for the sleeping bag, but then Dare was there, covering her with his body, settling between her legs and reaching down between their bodies to guide the thick head of his penis gently to her opening.

He didn't enter her, not right away. Instead he slowly, gently rocked, putting just enough pressure behind the movement so that he dipped into her a little, then out, then back in. She caught her breath, her fingers digging into his shoulders, but even though she was holding on for dear life she couldn't stop her body from writhing beneath him, searching for more, for the completion promised by his penetration.

"More?" The single word was hoarse; his face was set in the hard, strained lines of a man who was holding himself under ruthless control.

She couldn't answer; even that one word was beyond her. Instead she hooked her left leg around his waist and lifted herself, blindly taking more of him in. The physical shock of the intrusion was uncomfortable, verging on pain, but she didn't care. The feel of him sliding deep was exquisite and shattering, and she felt tears gathering in her eyes.

He was breathing so hard that every exhalation seemed to rasp from deep in his chest. His gaze burned down at her like blue fire, the color deeper and more intense than she'd ever seen it. "Now," he said, sliding a muscular arm under her hips and lifting. He grabbed something, maybe his jeans, maybe part of the sleeping bag, bunched it up, and slid it under her to keep her hips tilted. Then he braced himself over her on his elbows and began thrusting, slow and steady, keeping the penetration fairly shallow at first and then going deep and hard. The gasp had barely died in her throat when he dragged himself back and began anew that slow, steady rhythm. Hard and deep. Slow and steady. Over and over again, alternating his rhythm until she was all but climbing him, the pleasure built to such a pitch that it verged on torment. She heard the raw sounds tearing from her own throat, but it didn't matter, nothing mattered, except the shattering release that still hovered just out of reach.

She needed him, needed him, needed release from this pleasure that was so acute it felt like torment, unbearable, as if she would come apart under the tension—and then she broke, a savage cry exploding from deep inside her, sensation pulsing, her entire body feeling as if every muscle in her clamped down on the thick penis moving back and forth inside her. And he broke, too, abruptly driving his body hard into hers, over and over again, groaning, his teeth grinding together until the shuddering, throbbing pleasure released its hold on him and dropped him down onto her where he lay, heavy and boneless, almost crushing her.

Neither of them moved for a long time. The chilly air felt wonderful on her overheated skin. Her bones had turned to water, her muscles to mush, her brain to utter blankness. Breathing was the best she could manage. She dozed, if falling off a cliff into unconsciousness could be called dozing, and woke when he groaned against her neck and muttered something she couldn't understand.

She licked her lips, took a few deep breaths, and mustered the energy to say, "What?"

He did his own deep breathing, gathered himself, managed to heave his weight up onto his elbows. He wobbled a little, but the expression in his heavy-lidded eyes was fiercely satisfied. "I said, 'This is serious.' Us." He cupped her face in his rough palms, kissed her mouth. "I love you. I have from the first. I think you love me, too, if you'll stop doubting yourself and just go with your gut."

Angie opened her mouth to deny it, panic already blooming, but at the last minute she caught herself. She had to stop being such a coward; if Dare could hang himself out emotionally like that, she could at least have the courage and honor to tell him the truth. "I think so, too," she finally managed to say, her heartbeat double-timing at the risk she was taking, but as soon as the words were out of her mouth she felt a massive sense of relief, a lightening inside, as if she'd dropped a burden she hadn't even realized she was carrying.

"What did you say?" He tilted his head at her. "I didn't hear you."

Of course he heard her, unless he'd gone deaf in the past five seconds. She put her hands over his and raised her gaze to his. "Yes, you did. I thought: How could I possibly love anyone in such a short length of time? The same goes for you, too."

"Two years? That isn't such a short length of time?"

"You can't love someone you don't know," she chided.

"I knew you were the one. Drove me bunny-boiling nuts every time you looked at me like I was a pile of horse shit you'd stepped in. This thing with buying your place was one last effort to work things out between us, because that was the only way I could think of to keep you here."

She was silent, thinking that she very likely wouldn't have listened to the deal he'd offered; she would have taken the money and left, started over somewhere else, probably near Missoula. If circumstances hadn't intervened and given them this time together, she would have missed this. Suddenly she identified the feeling she had inside, that sense of lightening; it was happiness.

He kissed her, his mouth tender. This big, rough man had been nothing but tender with her from the moment he'd found her crawling down the mountainside in a torrential rain. He'd laid himself on the line for her, in more ways than one. Angie could have lain there with his softening penis nestled inside her for the rest of the night, loving that link, the mingling of their bodies, but with a sigh of repletion he gently disengaged their bodies and sat up. There were practical matters to attend to, but once they'd cleaned up Dare turned out the lantern and once more they snuggled close together under the sleeping bag. This time, however, they were both naked, and Angie's head was nestled on his shoulder, her hand resting on his chest.

She smiled in the darkness. "It *is* a magic dick," she teased, hoping she could get a laugh out of him.

"No magic involved. It's just angles and self-control, honey, angles and self-control. But you can think I have a magic dick as long as you want to."

Chapter Twenty-seven

The morning dawned bright and cold. Angie woke to sunshine filtering around the edges of the curtain, feeling warm and relaxed, her bones like butter. They had slept, woke to make love again, then slept some more. Sometime during the night she had turned on her side and he had curled around her the way they'd slept before, as if he could cocoon her in warmth and safety. Despite being naked, despite the colder temperatures, she'd either been completely comfortable or so relaxed and tired from truly wonderful sex that she'd slept like a baby anyway.

In the strange way that Dare was so attuned to her, she could feel him wake up, even though she hadn't moved a muscle to disturb him. His breathing changed, and the subtle tension of awareness changed the way his arm felt, draped around her. This time, though, his hand cupped her breast, instead of resting on her stomach. His thumb moved, lightly flicking over her nipple and sending sparks of sensation cascading down her nerve endings.

"I like waking up with you," he rasped sleepily, his morning voice rough and strained, as if he had a case of laryngitis. His morning erection prodded at her, and he tightened his arm. "Want to satisfy one of my fantasies?"

"No, I want to pee and have a cup of coffee." She turned her head to give him a narrow-eyed gimlet look. "Your fantasy can wait."

He surveyed her don't-mess-with-me face. "You're not a morning person, are you?" The question was obviously rhetorical. "If peeing and coffee always take precedence over sex, I won't ever get to satisfy that particular fantasy."

"If it involves sex before we do anything else, no." But she found herself smiling, because the way he'd phrased his complaint made it plain he was expecting to wake up beside her for . . . *always?* That was the word he'd used: always.

"Always" was kind of a definite thing, but she didn't let herself dwell on it. They were together, in a way she'd never imagined was even remotely likely, and that was enough for now. When they were back in the real world and this situation had been dealt with, that would be the time to start thinking about what might be in the future.

She had more immediate things on her plate, one of which was the fact that she was stark naked, and regardless of what they'd done during the night or that he'd made love to her with the lantern on, she still felt awkward about getting out from under the protection of the sleeping bag and getting dressed in front of him.

She was mulling over the different ways she might handle this when he simply tossed the sleeping bag aside and got up. She yelped, grabbed the edge of the sleeping bag and pulled it up to her shoulders, but not entirely from modesty. The temperature had dropped a lot during the night; when the cold air hit her bare skin, she began to think about getting dressed completely under the cover. "Aren't you cold?"

"It's chilly," he agreed as he stepped into a pair of underwear, then grabbed his jeans and pulled them on. When he had a T-shirt on and a flannel shirt over that, he stopped to turn on the heater.

"Just get your clothes on as fast as possible, and get it over with, so you can get the coffee started. The faster you move, the sooner we'll have coffee."

"Where's my shirt?" She looked around for the flannel shirt she'd been wearing the night before, and found it stuffed halfway under the privacy curtain. Quickly she pulled it on, and only then did she emerge from beneath the sleeping bag to finish dressing. He opened three bottles of water and poured them into the percolator, then Angie quickly measured the coffee into the basket. With coffee brewing and water heating for more hot oatmeal, he carried her down the ladder, because that was faster than waiting to see if she could get a sock and boot on her right foot, and outside.

There was a heavy frost coating everything, sparkling like diamonds in the sunlight, and ice edged every hollow and dip in the ground where water remained. Her breath fogged in front of her face, even when she was inside the portable toilet, which made it imperative that she be as fast as possible. Her bare foot was freezing. But the sky was clear, not a cloud anywhere, so the temperatures would probably be moderate; the last weather report she'd listened to seemed so long ago, she couldn't remember if the cold front coming in behind the thunderstorms was supposed to be really cold or more moderate. By himself, Dare could probably push on all the way back to Lattimore's, but her ankle would force them to a slower pace and they might have to find shelter for the night. They'd need heat, food, water, the sleeping bag . . . Long accustomed to making supply lists, her brain automatically settled into preparation mode.

After they were finished and Dare had lugged her back up the ladder, for what she hoped was the last time, Angie sat on the mattress and unwrapped her ankle. The coffee hadn't finished perking, damn it; while she waited for that was as good a time as any to see where they stood for the day.

Critically she examined her foot. The bruising was still there, beginning to morph into green and yellow shades, but most of the swelling was gone. Her toes were normal. While there was still some puffiness on the outside of her ankle, she thought she'd be able to get a sock on, at least. Whether or not she'd be able to flex her foot enough to get her boot on was the big question.

Silently she picked up the thick sock and began working it onto her foot. It went up and over her ankle without a problem. Step number one, accomplished.

Dare sat down across from her and gently lifted her foot onto his lap, then picked up the elastic bandage. "You'll need this for extra support, but I'll wrap it so it isn't as thick around your ankle." He swiftly rolled the bandage up, then began wrapping it around her foot and ankle, unrolling as he went. Once it was secured, he stretched out to snag her boot, and silently offered it to her.

Carefully she worked the boot on, wiggling it back and forth instead of moving her foot; when it wouldn't go any further without flexing her foot, she set her jaw, moved the joint as little as necessary, and her foot slid the rest of the way into the boot.

"Success!" she said, and heaved a sigh of relief. "For part of it, anyway." She was pretty sure she could walk, even though she'd definitely need a thick, sturdy stick for support. The next question was if she could walk well enough to try trekking down a mountain, complicated by slippery footing.

"You want to try walking now, or have some coffee?"

"Coffee," she said fervently.

"So even walking can wait until after you've had coffee?"

"Damn straight, cowboy, and don't you forget it."

After she'd been fortified by two cups of coffee and a bowl of hot oatmeal, she felt jazzed and ready to go. "Okay, let's see how it goes."

He got to his feet and held his hands down to her. Without hesitation, Angie placed her hands in his and he effortlessly pulled her to her feet. She balanced on her left foot until she was fully upright, then shifted her weight until she was centered on both feet. He released her hands, and she took a step, then another. Her ankle ached, and she limped, but she could walk much better than yesterday's hobble. She took a few more steps and felt the joint loosening even more. "It feels better than I thought it would," she commented.

"Hiking is going to make it hurt, you know that."

"I know. But the alternative is waiting another day, and I don't want to do that." There was nothing they could have done before, but now that the weather had cleared, and she could walk, if they delayed any longer and Chad escaped because of that, she'd feel guilty. She didn't want Dare to go on by himself and he didn't want to leave her here, so she would walk. As long as her ankle would bear her weight, she'd keep going.

With the decision made, there was no point in delay, so they set about getting ready. Dare stowed the lantern and camp stove in the storage bin, secured their trash to be taken care of on a return trip, packed away his dried food supplies. "You'll need a walking stick," he said, taking a small hatchet from the storage bin. "I'll take care of that while you pack what we'll need in case we have to spend the night on the trail."

While he was gone, Angie completely emptied her saddlebags, then looked over their supplies and set about packing the necessities: food and water, fire steel for making a fire, trash bags they could use as tarps if needed, the sleeping bag, which she folded and rolled as tightly as possible, and tied with the attached cords.

She opened the new box of shells she'd grabbed from her tent the night of the storm and reloaded her rifle, then put the rest of the shells in the saddlebags. Her heavy coat was dry, thank goodness; with that and her sweats, she should have enough clothes to stay warm even if they did have to stop for the night. They would also have a fire, the sleeping bag, and each other for warmth—they'd be okay, not comfortable, but okay.

Dare came back up the ladder, carrying a limb that was about five feet long and two inches thick. He'd trimmed off all the smaller branches to even the limb, except for one he'd left sticking out an inch or so, as a natural stop for her hand. "See how this fits you," he said. She took the limb and walked up and down with it, using it for support; it was sturdy without being too heavy, and he'd cut the length with a good eye for her height. Satisfied, he dug some black electrician's tape out of the storage bin and wrapped it around the limb where her hand fit, so the bark wouldn't abrade the skin from her palm and fingers.

Out of curiosity, she said, "Why do you have electrician's tape here, when there's no electricity?"

"Because the shit sticks to everything—and you never know when you'll need it. I've made a splint for a broken leg using tree limbs and electrician's tape, I've repaired radiator hoses, fuel lines—you name it. It isn't perfect, but it'll usually get me by." While he was talking, he was expertly loading his own rifle. "We don't know what's happened to Krugman or where he is. He could be ahead of us, if he didn't drown trying to cross one of the rivers, but you never know. Someone inexperienced would probably head straight down, though. We aren't likely to run into him, but we'll keep an eye out, anyway. You have everything?"

"Except for what's downstairs."

He didn't start naming off items, double-checking to make sure she'd packed them, simply nodded and swung the heavy saddlebags over his own shoulder before heading down. He trusted her to know what she was doing, she realized, a lump forming in her throat. Of course, *she* knew that she knew what she was doing, but it meant something that Dare took her expertise for granted.

She pulled on her coat, dropped the walking stick and sleeping bag down to him, then slung the rifle over her shoulder and went down the ladder under her own steam, which felt damn good. Her ankle was stiff, and she was careful about how she placed her foot, securing her balance and keeping a firm hold on the ladder rung just in case, but she made it down without incident. They finished loading up: her sweats, their slickers, then they left the cabin that had been their sanctuary for the past two days and stepped out into the cold, clear morning.

Chad poked his head out of his tent, blinking at the bright sunshine. Yesterday the damn rain had finally let up, but it was too late in the day to start out, so he'd had to spend another night in this godforsaken tent. If he'd had to spend much longer listening to the rain pounding against the heavy canvas, he'd have gone fucking crazy. Some people actually liked hunting and camping, but they were idiots. The only reason he'd done it last year was because one of his clients had made such a big deal about going on a hunt, so Chad had thought he'd impress the stupid bastard and earn some brownie points, but he'd hated every minute of it.

On the other hand, he'd been smart enough to see the potential for ridding himself of a problem, and he'd been prepared. Davis had been a little quicker on the scent than he'd expected, which annoyed him, but still, if it hadn't been for elements beyond his control, namely Angie finding that body on the mountain and deciding she had to notify the backwater cops right away, everything would have gone just the way he'd planned.

After pushing himself so hard that first day, trying and failing to get down the mountain, Chad had stopped trying to deny himself much-needed sleep. No bear had come lumbering through the camp, Angie was nowhere around—he'd been terrified, and for nothing. That was a lot of energy wasted. So he'd slept when he was tired, ate when he was hungry, drank when he was thirsty. He'd been almost bored to death, but that was all.

He was warm, dry, and fed—not *well* fed, but not starving, either. The crap he'd been eating was sustenance, but that was about all he could say for it. He'd thought a time or two about the food tied high at the cook site, out of reach of bears and other animals, but he figured if the bear was still anywhere around it would be there, closer to what was left of Davis, so that had been enough to dissuade him from trying to get the food supply. Not only that, he didn't want to wade through what was left of Davis; once was enough.

He'd left the tent only when he had to, to see to the horse. He wasn't a great animal lover, but he needed that horse to be in good enough shape for him to ride it down the mountain. If anything happened to the horse he'd either have to walk out or try to make it back to where he'd left the other three horses, and hope they'd still be there. Just taking care of the horse that was here seemed like the easiest course of action.

He walked around outside the tent, testing the footing. Frost covered everything, making the footing even more slippery. Damn, it was cold! He wasn't wild about slogging through the mud, but he had no choice. The day would probably get warmer, and the longer he waited the more the flash floods would recede, if he could afford to wait it out. But he couldn't. He had to assume that Angie was alive and that she was also setting out now that the rain had stopped. The one thing he couldn't do was let her get down the mountain ahead of him.

Chad closed his eyes and mentally pulled up the map he'd studied for hours in preparation for this trip. If he'd known about the difficulties he'd encounter he would've packed the damn map, as well as a handheld GPS, but he hadn't wanted to pack anything that Davis could possibly see that would have made him suspicious, so he'd taken the chance. That particular decision hadn't paid off.

He had an excellent memory, though, and a sharp eye for detail: two more qualities most people didn't expect him to have, which suited him just fine. It had come in handy to have some hidden talents, to be constantly underestimated.

He pictured the path he'd planned to take, the path he'd *tried* to take, and then he let the image in his mind expand, moving east and west, north and south. He needed to move in a direction that would take him away from the creeks that had swollen to an impassible level, and from there find his way down. It would be a longer trek, but considering that the way shouldn't be impeded by rushing water he'd likely save himself some time.

He needed to go south, he figured. From what he remembered, the land became a little less rugged the farther south he went, but if he went too far he'd overshoot Lattimore's place and have to double back, which would cost him precious time. He'd go a few miles and then try to cut east, down the mountain. If that didn't work, he'd go a little farther south and try again.

Going off plan, again, did bring up the potential for unknown obstacles. The thing about unknown stuff was that he couldn't anticipate problems beforehand and already have the solution figured out. What was the most likely problem he'd run into? That was probably Angie, because they were heading to the same place; therefore it was at least feasible that at some point he'd overtake her. He had to be prepared for that.

What else might stand between him and his way out? There could be people stranded at other camps, guides and hunters who'd been trapped by the weather. It wasn't like this mountain was a mecca for vacationers, but he couldn't discount the possibility. There were other guides in the area, he knew from his research, and then there were hunters who might rent a camp and go out without a guide.

But they wouldn't know what had happened; they wouldn't be keeping an eye out for him, unless somehow Angie had stumbled across another hunting party when she'd made her escape. If that had happened, he had to assume that anyone he came across would know about him, and they'd have to be eliminated. They wouldn't expect him to just start shooting, which would give him the upper hand, something he'd need if he had to take out an entire party of hunters. If his surprise tactic didn't work, then he'd rather go out in a blaze of glory than give up after all he'd been through to get here. He sure as hell wasn't going to lie down and surrender.

He hoped with everything he had that Angie Powell was dead. The odds of that were at least fifty-fifty. There was so much that could have taken care of her: hypothermia, that fucking bear, falling off a cliff, getting washed away by the flood waters. He didn't care how she went, he just wanted her out of the picture.

He prayed that she was dead, but was prepared for her to be alive.

No matter what, he couldn't let himself get caught. He wouldn't last a week in jail. Even if he did survive—which was un-likely because Davis's bosses had people everywhere, even in prison—the confinement and the class of criminal he'd be forced to deal with would kill him, one way or another. He knew how he looked, like a total pushover, knew how prison tough guys would assess him. He'd rather be dead.

That thought spurred him on. He checked his weapons—rifle and pistol—stuffed a couple more power bars into his pockets where they'd be easily accessible, and put on his boots, lacing and tying them tight. He got his heavy coat, his gloves, his slicker, and some water. He thought about taking his duffel, considered the pros and cons. He might be able to use the supplies he'd then be able to take along, but anything more than that would also weigh him down. Not only that, leaving the duffel here might lead searchers to think he was still in the vicinity. He had to commit to this, because there was no coming back. Time was running out for him.

With his new route in mind, he walked to the corral. The ground was soaked, muddy, so his steps were cautious. The horse was moving around restlessly, its eyes rolling a little. He stopped, his hair standing on end as he remembered how the horses had acted when the bear was prowling around the camp. Holding his rifle at the ready, he looked all around, but didn't see or hear anything. After a few minutes he shrugged and set the rifle aside. Maybe the damn horse was just tired of standing around.

He saddled the chestnut, talking softly to it to settle it down. He was a little excited himself, now that the end of the ordeal was right in front of him. A few hours—maybe longer, depending on what conditions he ran into and how much he'd have to detour— and he'd be free.

He'd come too far, done too much, to consider anything less.

He mounted and turned the chestnut's head toward the south. A light wind was blowing, the sun was bright. The chestnut didn't make great time, but the footing was already a little more firm than it had been two days before, and after a few minutes the horse settled down. Chad's spirit rose. Just being able to *do* something was a relief.

Half an hour later, the bear cut across his scent trail.

Chapter Twenty-eight

"How're you doing?" Dare asked, an hour into the trek. They hadn't talked much, because both of them had to pay close attention to their footing. The ground was mushy, with a thin layer of ice on top; a misstep like the one she'd made the night of the storm could cause a real emergency.

"I'm okay. The boot's helping a lot." The snug lacing and the elastic bandage provided much-needed support, helping stabilize her ankle.

"Are you hurting?"

"It's kind of a dull ache, that's all. I'm good."

Dare kept the pace slow, his eagle eye measuring her progress and the amount of effort she was making. Angie just walked, not making any effort to camouflage her limp; if she had, he'd have known and that would have concerned him more. She was deeply appreciative of the walking stick, which gave her support over the uneven footing and took a lion's share of strain off her ankle. Tomorrow her arm and shoulder might be sore from the effort, but big deal.

In an ideal situation, she would be sitting on a sofa or recliner with a pillow under her foot and an ice pack on the joint, but "ideal" was dreamland, and reality was that she had to walk. If they'd been moving across flat ground she wouldn't have had much of a problem, but they weren't. Downhill, uphill—the angles put a lot of stress on her ankle. Dare tried to mitigate that by moving at a diagonal as much as possible, but the hard reality was that they had to go down.

The mountains weren't completely tree-covered; there were thick stands of trees, but there were also meadows, rock formations, outcrops, and steep drops. The meadows looked as if they would be the easiest to navigate, but they were so rocky that every step was uneven and her pace slowed to a crawl. They reached one section where there simply was no secure place for her to step. Dare held up his hand. "Wait right there." He laid his rifle and the saddlebags aside, then returned to grasp her waist. Without noticeable effort he lifted her and swung her over the treacherous part to more solid footing.

She didn't analyze the moment, she simply put her arms around his neck and kissed him. His size and strength made her feel more feminine than she'd ever felt before in her life, but that paled in comparison to the way he made her feel . . . treasured. Without hesitation he wrapped his arms around her and pulled her in tight, hungrily taking her mouth, kissing her as deeply and thoroughly as if they had all day, as if his plans included pulling off their clothes right there and pushing inside her. Even if that was what he wanted, she didn't know that she'd object. Her body knew him now, knew his taste and touch and scent, the weight and heft of him, the sounds he made when he came, and she responded to him on what felt like a molecular level, a calling of like to like.

But then he lifted his head and his narrowed blue eyes glinted down at her. "Not that I'm complaining, but what was that for?"

She had to swallow, hard, but she said honestly, "For treating me as if I matter."

He lifted her off the ground, holding her so their gazes were almost level. His voice went even more gravelly than usual. "You matter to me; you matter a hell of a lot."

"You matter a hell of a lot to me, too," she said, and kissed him again, reveling in the moment.

After a minute he pulled his head back, sucking air, his hands kneading her butt cheeks as he worked her back and forth against his erection. "We either stop now, or you're going to be feeling the wind on your bare ass."

"If my ass gets bare, yours does, too," she teased, then rested her face against his and sighed. "But I suppose we'd better keep going. I'm sorry I'm so slow; at this rate, we won't make it to Lattimore's before dark."

"If we don't, we don't," he replied, unperturbed.

Being the cause of their slow pace bothered her, though. At a brisk pace, a person could walk a mile roughly every fifteen minutes; she had no doubt Dare could handle that speed without breaking a sweat if the terrain hadn't been so rough. She estimated they were moving no faster than a quarter of a mile every fifteen minutes, probably less than that, so not counting any stops to rest or eat they were traveling at less than one mile an hour. What would have been about a four- or five-hour trek for Dare, traveling alone, would take them eight to ten hours because of her, and that wasn't taking into account any rest stops. There would be places where she could increase her speed, but in the end that wouldn't be enough to make much difference, especially if they had to take any detours that cost them a lot of time and distance.

They set out again. Determined not to hold him back any more than necessary, Angie did the same thing she'd done when she'd first injured her ankle and was crawling down the mountain: She put the time and distance out of her mind, and concentrated on simply moving. She concentrated on the rhythm of step, walking stick, step; she'd read somewhere that when you were using a

single crutch or a cane you held it on your strong side, but that
didn't make sense to her, so she held the walking stick in her right
hand and used her upper body strength to take pressure off her
ankle. Whether or not her system was as stable as holding the
walking stick in her left hand, she couldn't say, but her object was
to keep her ankle from swelling up more than necessary.

Step, walking stick, step. She didn't let herself flag, didn't fal-
ter. Step, walking stick, step. She kept moving.

If he could have, Dare would have carried her. Did she have any
idea how she looked, with her dark eyes so focused and intent, yet
at the same time the expression in them was so faraway he
doubted she'd hear him if he spoke? She wasn't going to stop, she
wasn't going to give up.

This was how she'd come down the mountain during the
storm, with everything else pushed to the side except what she
needed to do; at least this time she was walking instead of crawling. She soldiered on, regardless, with the kind of resolve that the
most hardened soldier would be proud to have.

His heart pounded hard, just watching her. There were mil-
lions of sweet, regular women in the world he could have fallen in
love with, but he'd chosen her, a woman with grit in her gut and
steel in her spine. When they fought—and they *would* fight—she
wouldn't back down an inch if she thought she was right. There
might be some hard living in the days and years ahead of him.
Hell yeah! He could hardly wait.

Not that he'd even breathed the word "marriage" yet, because
he didn't want to spook her until she was a little more settled with
the idea of them being a couple. She was still brooding over the
idea of him being her boss, which told him it hadn't even occurred to her that the situation might be the other way around,
that she was thinking about a semiprofessional relationship instead of a one hundred percent personal relationship in which

she'd definitely have the upper hand, because, hell, she was a woman.

What was it with her? Weren't women supposed to be the ones so focused on relationships and shit like that? She'd made one mistake, she'd had the balls to make sure that one mistake didn't go one inch further, but then she'd beat herself up for not caving and pretending everything was all right, and staying with someone who she knew didn't love her the way he should. Dare had the feeling Angie didn't do anything halfway; from the very final and definite step she'd taken to get rid of the man who'd disappointed her, she was willing to go the distance—and beyond—to make her point.

He had to be crazy to be so crazy about her, but there it was, and damn if he wasn't happy about it . . . now. Three days ago, he'd thought he needed his head examined, but even as bad as the night of the storm had been, since then he'd recognized what an opportunity God, or fate, had handed him. He'd made the best of it, too. Last night had been damn good. They fit together, physically, temperamentally, even their personalities. They made each other laugh. Even as solemn as she could be sometimes, he'd seen her eyes light up, seen her face relax and her lips curve and damn if she didn't have some fuckable lips—

He wrenched his thoughts from that direction, because hiking with a hard-on could get damn uncomfortable.

After they'd been walking for two hours, he called a halt to let her rest, and for them both to drink some water. They hadn't started out until close to nine o'clock, so he figured there was no way they'd reach Lattimore's before dark, but they'd be okay. They were experienced in the outdoors, and they were prepared.

Angie sat on a rock while she sipped from a water bottle, her gaze sweeping over the rugged valleys opening up before them. Dare sat beside her and studied the same vista. Down below, the flood-swollen creek curved away to the left, but some distance ahead it swept back to the right, and somewhere, somehow, they

would have to cross it. He could hear the creek even from this distance, a dull, distant roar as the rushing water tumbled over the
rocky creek bed.

He pictured the topography, planning their route. He didn't
want to go all the way down to the creek, because there were rock
formations that covered acres, and Angie couldn't handle crossing them. In some places, going around them would be even
more hazardous than crossing the rocks, so their best bet was to
stay high enough to bypass the creek bank entirely. There was one
place where they might—*might*—be able to cross the creek, and
he'd check it out when they reached the area, but his plan right
now was to go far enough south to pick up the road. That would
take longer, but ultimately be a lot safer.

What the hell. He didn't mind spending another night with
Angie before they got back to the real world.

Progress was slow. Chad thought he could head east, but a swollen
stream kept forcing him farther and farther to the south, till finally he was going in the right direction: down the mountain instead of cutting across it . . . at least for now. Time after time, just
when he thought he was making some real progress, he ran into
something that forced him off his chosen direction. He had to
backtrack and go around obstacles so often he kind of lost track of
how far he'd traveled, and that worried the hell out of him. What
if he didn't make it to Lattimore's today? As cold as the weather
was, he'd freeze his ass off tonight if he had to sleep out in the
open.

Common sense told him he hadn't traveled that far out of the
way, that it was his impatience making every delay feel like hours
when in reality it hadn't been that long. The horse wasn't making
great time, but it was still faster than if he'd been on foot. Angie
had mentioned that the camp had been almost ten miles away
from Lattimore's ranch, which wasn't a great distance, so with any

luck, he'd be on the road in a couple of hours, four at the most—
hooray and hallelujah. His stomach growled, but he didn't want
another protein bar; he wasn't that hungry yet. When this was over
with, he hoped to hell he never had to see another protein bar in
his whole life. After he crossed into Canada there'd be time to
stop for a good, hot meal before he caught the next flight out to
Mexico.

He could almost see it, could almost taste the freedom. Another name, more money than he knew what to do with . . . and
he was so close . . .

He guided the horse along the tree line of a meadow, studying
the land falling away below him, trying to figure out exactly where
he was and where he needed to go, when something far down the
meadow caught his eye.

He'd grown so accustomed to seeing nothing before him but
mud and trees and blessed blue sky, it took him a moment to focus
on and identify the movement down and to his right.

People. Two of them—a man and a woman. They were still a
good distance away, and unless they turned around and really
searched for movement, they wouldn't see him, because he was
still under cover of the trees. They were in a large clearing at the
moment, unprotected by the trees that shielded Chad.

He didn't have binoculars with him, but he did have the scope
on his rifle. Moving carefully, he lifted the rifle to his shoulder and
peered through the scope; at first he didn't see anything because
the field of vision was so narrow and he had to "acquire the target," as the man he'd gone to for lessons had called it. Using small
movements, he swept the scope back and forth until he found
them, then adjusted the focus. Davis had made fun of his scope
when he saw it, because it wasn't one of the fancy brand names,
but who was laughing now? Chad hadn't seen any point in spending a thousand dollars for a scope he didn't intend to use other
than for show. He was pleased now that the scope worked just fine.

The man below was a big son of a bitch, but Chad didn't recognize him. He identified Angie right away, though: the dark hair, her height, her shape—not that he could see her shape, because she was wearing that heavy coat, but he knew the coat. She hobbled along, with occasional help from the big guy. She'd been hurt after all, somehow, but not badly enough to stop her. He couldn't begin to imagine how she'd met up with someone else who was also on foot; what were the fucking odds of that?

They both carried rifles slung over their shoulders, and they were on the path Chad needed to take in order to get off this damn mountain. He wasn't going to waste a minute trying to go around them. Damn it, they were *in his way.*

Chad dismounted, said a couple of soft words to the horse, and looped the reins loosely over a branch. Rifle in hand, he sighted in on the couple below, but he couldn't hold the weapon rock steady and at that distance even a tiny waver meant he'd miss his target.

No, shooting from this far away was too risky. He couldn't be certain he'd hit his target, and he didn't want to give them any warning. Rapidly he formulated a plan. Kill the man first, before they suspected that they weren't alone. Not that Angie wasn't a good shot, but she wasn't very mobile, and he could outmaneuver her if by chance he couldn't take her down, too, before she could react.

He'd practiced with both the pistol and the rifle, and he was a good marksman, but shooting downhill was a bitch at the best of times and his targets were moving—slowly, but moving. He had to get closer, but getting closer meant leaving the cover of the trees and exposing himself to view if they should happen to look behind them, not to mention return fire. And if he didn't manage to get both of them, there *would* be return fire; he had to plan on it, choose his position accordingly.

The long downward sweep of the meadow was heavily dotted with rock—slabs of rock, boulders big and small, some barely jutting out of the earth and others sitting there like huge lumps.

There was a lot of cover to be had, if he could get to it without being noticed.

He took notice of the wind. It had been swirling all day, coming first from one direction and then another, but now it was blowing straight into his face. Marksmanship was mathematics, taking every little factor such as wind and drop and bullet velocity into account. He'd focused more on the pistol, knowing that was how he'd take down Davis, but he knew the basics of distance shooting. This didn't qualify for true distance shooting, because they were no more than a hundred and fifty yards away at the most, but considering what was at stake he didn't want to risk a shot that might miss.

They were moving at a snail's pace, which was to his advantage, but he couldn't delay too long or they'd reach the tree line below and he'd lose them. With the wind blowing sound away from them, they weren't likely to hear him. Chad moved to his left, putting one of those big boulders between him and his targets, and headed for the boulder at a half-run, crouched low.

He was getting excited. It looked as if he'd get his hunt, after all. This was the wild, and in the wild survival of the fittest was the rule nature and man—and woman—lived by.

Ninety yards behind him, the bear was padding closer and closer to his prey, the scent now blowing strong in his nostrils.

Chapter Twenty-nine

Chad had worked his way to within fifty yards of his targets, which was as close as he dared go without running a huge risk that Angie or the big guy might see or hear him. Besides, they were getting into some rocks that would provide them with cover, and beyond the rocks was the edge of the meadow. If he let them get to the trees, he'd have a harder time getting off a good shot: too many shadows, too many tree trunks. He lifted the rifle to his shoulder, sighted it on the middle of the guy's back, allowed for the curve of the hill, the distance, and the light wind. He'd never met the man with Angie, had no animosity toward the soon-to-be-dead guy, but he was in the way and that was reason enough to take him out.

Killing was easy, as Chad had discovered when he'd shot Davis. One well-placed bullet and a life could be snuffed out for good; alive one moment, dead the next. One moment a problem, the next . . . no problem at all. He wouldn't say that he got off on it, but he'd been surprised at how easy it was, how completely regret-free he felt afterward. He did what had to be done, that was all.

He took careful aim, took in a breath, let it out halfway as he'd been taught, and pulled the trigger. The man with Angie jerked, and as he fell he pushed Angie away from him. She took one off-balance, stumbling step, and fell. Before Chad could reacquire her in his scope, she scrambled behind one of those damn rocks.

"Dare!"

Angie was screaming his name almost before she hit the ground. The rifle shot had come from so close behind them that she'd heard the reverberating blast almost simultaneously with the deep *"Uhhh!"* sound Dare had made, then he'd shoved her away from him even as he was falling to the side. Instinctively she half-rolled, half-crawled to one of the rocks and crouched there, already getting her feet under her to launch herself across the opening to where Dare was sprawled.

But then he dragged himself to a sitting position and barked, "Stay there!"

Blood was pouring down his face, but his voice was as strong as ever; Angie froze in place, relief and adrenaline searing through her system and throwing all of her senses into hyperalertness. Dare was hurt, but he was mobile, he was conscious. He was also losing a lot of blood, so she had to do something, and fast.

She didn't have to wonder what had happened; she knew. Somehow Chad had come up behind them. In a flash she knew it wasn't even that much of a coincidence, because the flooded creeks would have forced him in the same direction they'd been traveling.

"Where are you hit?" she called frantically, because Dare was wiping blood from his eyes and it was streaming down, effectively blinding him, as fast as he wiped, but surely to God if he'd been shot in the head he wouldn't be—

"Shoulder," he grunted, his tone tight against the pain.

Shoulder?

Didn't matter. She had to get to him. Ducking low, she darted her head to the side to look around the rock, to see if she could locate Chad's position. Another shot boomed, chipping off some rock above her head; Chad had been anticipating that she'd take a look, because she'd have to, but he'd expected her to stick her head up over the top of the rock instead of peeking around the side.

"Fuck!" Dare exploded. "Don't do that again." He struggled onto his knees, reached for his rifle, then let loose a long, inventive string of curses as he wiped his sleeve across his eyes.

Angie shrugged the sleeping bag roll off her shoulder, pulled her rifle into position, and slapped the bolt down. "Damn it, Dare, you can't see! Stay where you are." She kept her voice low but forceful, the words punching through the air. "What's wrong with your head?"

"It's just a cut. I hit a fucking rock."

But it was a cut that was bleeding profusely, directly above his right eye. Now that he was on his knees she could see the dark stain on the back of his coat, just below his right shoulder. He couldn't shoot, at least not effectively. He could hold the rifle with his left hand and pull the trigger, but if he hit anything it would be pure luck because he couldn't see to aim.

She knew where Chad was, about fifty yards away and uphill, slightly to the right. He had shot twice, so he had one more shot before he'd have to reload. If she could bait him into shooting, then she could set up her own shot while he was reloading, wait for him to stick his head up—

Behind him, the horse suddenly began whinnying in a shrill, unmistakably panicked sound. Chad whirled around, his back to the rock. What the hell? The chestnut was rearing, shaking its head, pulling hard on the simple loop Chad had used to tether it. Fuck!

If the stupid horse bolted, how was he going to get off this stupid fucking mountain?

Then, with a convulsive jerk, the chestnut pulled its reins free and thundered down the mountain toward him.

Chad froze for a split second, all of his options flashing in front of his eyes and none of them good. If he didn't catch the horse he was screwed. If he left the cover of the rock Angie would probably shoot him, and he was screwed. Either way, he was screwed.

But maybe she wouldn't be expecting him to try for the horse. He had no time to weigh the odds, no time to do anything except act. Chad lunged from the protection of the boulder, desperately trying to catch the horse's reins as it thundered by, but it swerved to avoid him and he missed.

Convulsively, expecting the white-hot pain of a bullet to tear through him at any second, he threw himself back toward the boulder. God, he couldn't believe it, he was still in one piece. Screwed, stranded, but in one piece. He grabbed his rifle, and as he did a dark blur of movement in the tree line caught his attention.

A massive black bear padded out of the trees straight toward him, its head low and swinging.

The horse was in the way. She couldn't believe it when Chad jumped for the panicked animal, but as she brought her rifle up to her shoulder the chestnut swerved, coming toward her, and she couldn't make the shot. Swearing under her breath, using words that would make Dare proud, she ducked back down. The chestnut swerved again, thundered past Dare's position on the far side of him, heading toward the tree line below them.

Another shot came from above, but there was no hot zinging sound, no chips of rock flying, no dirt kicking up. She didn't stop to wonder why the shot went so wild, she just knew that was the third one and now he'd have to reload, so she rolled to a kneeling position and braced her rifle barrel against the side of the boulder, leaning forward and putting her eye to the scope.

A scream clogged in Chad's throat. Hastily he jerked the rifle up, fired, but the bear was moving and maybe he hit it, maybe he didn't, but it kept coming. Swiftly he worked the bolt, ejecting the spent cartridge, slammed it home again, pulled the trigger, but as soon as he heard the click he knew the firing pin had hit an empty chamber.

Almost sobbing in terror, he fumbled in his coat pocket for the box of ammunition, dropped it, bent to scrabble on the ground for it. The bear kept coming, he could see its eyes now, feral, piggish. He tried to fit a cartridge into the chamber, fumbled, dropped it, too. Close, close, God, the fucking monster was so close and he couldn't make his fingers work; he fumbled another cartridge from the box but couldn't get the stupid fucker to go into the chamber—

It began popping its massive jaws, and from a distance of about twenty yards, it charged.

He did scream now, his voice rising high and sharp as he threw down the rifle and ran.

For just a second, maybe two, he had a wild hope that Angie would shoot the bear, that even after everything he'd done instinct would kick in and she'd just shoot the damn thing. He'd have a chance and that's all he wanted, just a chance, he'd adjust his plans, maybe—

Then an avalanche of fur and muscle, teeth and claws, hit him and slammed him face-first into the ground. Claws raked like fire across his side and back, pain exploded through his entire body as the bear sank its canines into his shoulder and slung him through the air.

He landed with an impact that almost paralyzed him. He

heard his voice sobbing, knew his nose was running with snot, but everything was kind of distant and blurry except for the sheer terror that somehow spurred him to roll over, fingers digging into the muddy ground as he tried to get to his feet.

There was a deep, growling roar that almost deafened him, and a stench that burned his lungs, his nose. A thousand barbs shredded his legs, caught, began dragging him backward.

"No, no, no." It was the only word he could manage to say, over and over as he was pulled across the muddy ground.

He dug his fingers into the mud as if his grip on the earth might save him. On some level he realized that the monster bear had already killed him. The pain of claws tearing into his legs brought back the vivid memory of what had happened to Davis.

But Davis had already been dead. He wasn't.

He felt himself being lifted again. Without warning the ground he'd been clinging to was gone and he hung there for a moment, helpless, caught in the monster's jaws and shaken like a child's toy. He tried to scream again but couldn't. He had no breath, no strength. He couldn't even say "No" anymore; instead he could hear pitiful, weak, mewling sounds that caught in his throat.

The bear slung its head and tossed him again. He screamed, flying through the air for what seemed like forever, screamed his frustration and rage and terror, his knowledge that this was the end and it was going to be horrible. He even screamed for help, though without hope, because there was no coming back from this. He bounced off the boulder. Bones broke—he felt them shatter, and he was left lying there, a limp body with no internal structure for support. Blood filled his mouth. The bear lunged, and Chad prayed for instant death.

His prayer wasn't answered.

He wanted to pass out. He wanted to be unaware when he died. There was a moment, as his vision began to fade, when Chad was almost certain the bear was playing with him, purposely prolonging his suffering, making sure that he felt as much pain as was possible in his last minutes of life.

The bear bit into his stomach, slung its head, ripped his insides out. Detached, his brain shutting down, he was still capable of a distant surprise at the pointed accuracy of his last thought: "*Survival of the fittest.*"

Angie had just acquired Chad in her scope when he screamed; a split second later, he disappeared in a blur of motion. She jerked the rifle from her shoulder and stared in frozen horror at the nightmare taking place in front of her.

It was happening again, just as it had happened the night of the storm, the hellish images bombarding her brain and savaging it, swamping her with blind panic. She thought she screamed, but her throat wouldn't work and the scream stayed inside, tearing its way through her heart and stomach and mind. She could hear Dare—she thought she could hear him, but she wasn't certain, she couldn't make out any words because something in her mind had simply disconnected.

The bear tore Chad Krugman apart. Time slowed to the speed of molasses and the attack seemed to last forever, though deep inside she knew only seconds had passed, seconds that were all such a powerful predator needed to kill its prey.

Then—*God!*—the bear tossed Chad's remains aside and began coming down the hill toward them.

The horse. The bear smelled the horse, and maybe Dare's blood, though how it could smell more fresh blood when its snout was covered with gore, she didn't know. She didn't know how she could think at all. She didn't know how she could move.

But she did. Every movement felt as if she were caught in the mud she'd dreamed about, the stupid idiotic cake icing, but she lifted the rifle to her shoulder, looked through the scope, acquired her target, which was looming larger and larger as it padded down the slope. This was a bad angle, almost straight on; the perfect shot was heart and lungs but its head was down, swinging back and forth. She couldn't wait for a perfect shot. She inhaled, let part of her breath out, and pulled the trigger.

Nothing happened. The firing pin snapped, but nothing happened. Shit! What had she done wrong? Hadn't she completely locked the bolt home? Swiftly she worked the bolt, ejecting a cartridge, slammed the bolt home. The bear was closer, making a deep grunting, barking sound in its chest, forty yards away, getting ready to charge.

She pulled the trigger.

Nothing.

She heard herself swearing, heard Dare saying something and some instinct had her moving from behind the boulder, drawing the bear's attention to herself, God, anything to keep him away from Dare—

"Angie!"

She heard the roar, jerked her head a little to the side just in time to see Dare's blood-drenched face as he grabbed up his own rifle with his left arm and tossed it to her. The weapon seemed to sail in slow motion through the air toward her, sunlight glinting on the barrel, the glass lens of the powerful scope.

The bear was at thirty yards.

She caught the rifle, jerked it to her shoulder, took a split second to settle the crosshairs on the bear's head, and fired. Before the powerful explosive crack of the shot had faded she ejected the spent cartridge, slammed the bolt home again.

The bullet caught the monster in the shoulder. It roared, spinning around, then abruptly charged straight toward her.

Angie fired again, hit him again. "Come on, you son of a bitch," she screamed, answering it roar for roar because by God she wasn't going to run, she wasn't going to let it get to Dare. She worked the bolt one last time. This was it. If this last shot didn't take him down, they were both dead. A wounded bear could do massive damage. She wanted to panic, maybe she had already panicked and just didn't realize it yet, but she didn't have the luxury of time to do anything other than place her last shot straight into his brain.

The massive animal kept moving, sheer momentum keeping it going, then its front legs buckled and it skidded to a halt not ten feet away.

She stood there staring at it, the unbearable stench almost making her gag, but her feet were rooted to the ground and she couldn't make herself move.

Dare struggled to his feet and staggered toward her, swiping at the blood that had turned his entire face into a red mask. "Angie." His rough voice was as gentle as it would ever be, could ever be. "Nice shooting, sweetheart." Very carefully he took his rifle from her, propped it against the rock, then eased his left arm around her.

Her knees buckled, but he was there, his powerful body providing support. Her head swam, and she clutched his coat, afraid she might pass out. She couldn't faint; she refused to faint. But now that it was over, she could panic. She deserved a little panic. Her vision swam a little, her heart pounded. The temperature was still cold, but her palms were sweating. She'd almost lost Dare. That was all she could think. He'd been bleeding and the bear had been going straight for him, and she'd almost lost him. She'd just found him, and that damn bear— No, she couldn't even complete the thought, not after watching what it had done to Chad.

She tried to say something, but couldn't. Dare wrapped both of his arms around her, even the arm that was bloody, and pulled her in close and tight, and she sighed. She cried, but just a little, because she wasn't a crier. Taking a page from his book, she cussed a blue streak, and felt better for it. She tried to stop shaking, but couldn't. Finally she simply allowed herself to tremble. She'd earned it, damn it.

When she could think, she said, "Damn it, Dare, you're bleeding all over me. If you bleed to death I'll never forgive you."

He said, "Yeah, I love you, too."

There were things to do, things she had to do. Afterward she couldn't be certain exactly when she forced herself from the shelter of his arms, but she did. She made him sit down. She wiped at the blood on his face until she could see the gash above his right eye; it would definitely need stitches. When she questioned him, he admitted that he had a little bit of double vision, so he'd probably given himself a mild concussion when his head hit the rock. She helped him take off his coat and both shirts, so she could examine that wound. It was actually bleeding less than the cut on his head, but it was an ugly wound, purplish and jagged, tearing through the pad of flesh just under his arm. She washed it with some of their drinking water, then tore his T-shirt into strips and tied a thick pad over the wound, then did the same for the cut over his eye.

When she was finished, he said, "If we don't move away from that stinking fucker, I'm going to choke."

The smell was overwhelming, but she'd ignored it by focusing instead on taking care of Dare. Now that he'd mentioned it, though, she suddenly found herself gagging, and they moved farther downhill as fast as they could.

Her mind hummed with details, unable to settle on anything. Her rifle hadn't fired, and she couldn't figure out why. Dare had cleaned it, reassembled it. The firing pin had worked; she'd heard it.

She'd never handled his rifle before. She hadn't known at what distance he'd sighted in his scope, she hadn't thought about it, she'd simply aimed and fired.

The bear had spooked the horse, of course. That was why—

The horse.

"Hey," she said, "we have a ride."

"If you can catch it."

She gave him a withering look, trying to act normal even though it was an effort. Her insides felt like gelatin. "Of course I can catch it. It's my horse."

"Then you do that, while I figure out why your rifle wouldn't fire."

He needed to be sitting still, conserving both strength and blood, but she didn't waste time arguing with him because she knew it wouldn't do any good. They needed to know why her rifle hadn't fired; Chad was dead and the bear was dead, but that didn't mean there would be no more danger crossing their path. They had his rifle, sure, but what if something happened to it? The wilderness wasn't forgiving; for safety's sake, they should have a backup.

She couldn't let herself think too much about either Chad or the bear, at least not now. Maybe later, when the carnage wasn't right there, both physically and mentally. Instead she focused on what needed doing right now, which was catching the chestnut. It hadn't completely bolted, the way Dare's horse had done. She could catch a glimpse of it below them in the tree line, but the animal was moving nervously. The wind was blowing toward her so it was carrying the scent of the bear away from the horse, which should make it possible for her to calm it down. It knew her scent, her voice; other than that, horses were herd animals that didn't like being alone. On the other hand, Dare's blood was on her, and when she got close the chestnut might not like that. She'd told Dare she could catch her horse, but she had to admit to herself that, with her bad ankle and the other factors, it might not happen.

Getting her walking stick, she carefully picked her way down the sloping meadow and into the trees, talking calmly the whole time, using the same words she often used when she was feeding or grooming them. The chestnut shifted around, pawed the ground with one hoof, but it didn't shy away as she got closer.

Still, instinct made her stop in her tracks, sensing that if she moved any farther she might frighten it into running again. With her bum ankle she didn't want to pursue the chestnut even one foot more than necessary. She even backed up a couple of steps, let the horse eye her, let it shake its head as it considered the situation by whatever horsey standards it used.

Several minutes ticked by. She remained in place, still calmly talking. The chestnut took a couple of steps toward her, then stopped to nose a bush, looking for something to graze. Angie took a step forward and the chestnut abruptly raised its head. She stopped again, and crooned to it. The horse stood and watched her, but didn't come any closer.

Slowly, keeping her movements measured, Angie lowered herself to the ground, sitting as comfortably as she could without bending her ankle.

After a few minutes of watching her, the chestnut blew out air that sounded like a big human sigh, and began ambling toward her. When it was close enough it dropped its head down and snuffled her hair, then along her shoulder. She held her breath, waiting to see if the smell of blood spooked it, but it continued to check her out. "Good boy," Angie said softly, reaching up to grip the trailing reins. "*Good* boy."

She led the horse out of the tree line and started up the slope with him, but Dare motioned for her to stay where she was and not bring him any closer, where the smells might spook the chestnut again. Dare shouldered all their supplies and both rifles, despite the wound in his shoulder, and made his way down to them.

"Bad ammunition," he reported tersely. "The whole box. I tried some shells in my rifle, and not one of them would fire. I've reloaded both rifles with my shells."

Bad ammo. It happened. It had never happened to her before, but her dad had gotten a bad batch once. If Dare hadn't been there, if he'd been wounded so badly he hadn't been able to toss his rifle to her . . . but he had. There was no point in thinking about what might have happened.

What mattered was that they were alive, they were together, and they were going home.

Chapter Thirty

Of course they argued about who would ride and who would walk. Dare had been shot, and she was hobbled by a bum ankle. Dare wasn't a lightweight and the chestnut wasn't a big horse like Samson, so riding double wasn't a really good option. In the end, he won the argument because even though he was woozy, he was still faster on his feet than she was. He ate two protein bars, drank two bottles of water, and pronounced himself good to go. She pronounced him too thick-headed to be anything other than half-Neanderthal, with maybe a little troglodyte thrown into the genetic mixture, then she'd completely humiliated herself by getting teary again and telling him that she loved him.

He just looked smug and said, "Yeah, I know."

They made it to Ray Lattimore's place in the nick of time, just as twilight was giving way to complete darkness. Not much got by Ray—he kept an eagle eye out, not just on his own property but on that of the people who parked their equipment there—and the porch lights came on before they were halfway up the driveway to his house. Ray came outside, flashlight in his hand. "Who's there?"

"Dare Callahan and Angie Powell," Dare called back.

"What the—?" The powerful flashlight beam went over them. They had to look the worse for wear after everything that had happened. After continued applied pressure had stopped Dare's head wound from bleeding she'd wiped away as much of the blood as she could, but he still looked as if he'd escaped from a slaughterhouse. She wasn't wounded, but she figured she looked like some wild woman who'd never seen electric lights before. "What the hell happened to you two?" Ray asked, coming down off the porch and heading toward them as fast as he could move, which was still pretty fast even at his age.

"Short story, one of Angie's clients murdered the other, then a bear got him, and Angie got the bear," Dare replied in his growly voice, condensing the events into fewer than twenty words. She stared at him, her mouth open.

"Not to mention Dare's been *shot*!" she snapped. "But he's too butt-stubborn to ride."

"Angie sprained her ankle. We made better time with her riding instead of walking," Dare returned, and damn if Ray didn't nod his head in agreement. Dare clasped his hands around her waist and bodily lifted her off the horse, even though there was no reason why she couldn't dismount on her own. He was taking care of her, and her throat clogged up. She might never get used to this feeling of being treasured, but damn if it didn't get to her.

"You two come on in, let's get you taken care of," Ray said. "I'll start making calls. You ran into a man-eater, huh? Gonna be a lot of questions about that."

Ray's wife, Janetta, came out on the porch just in time to hear what Ray said, and caught her breath when she saw them. "Angie! Dare! Oh, my lord," she said, rushing down the steps. "A bear did this?"

"No, the bear didn't get us," Angie replied. "I sprained my ankle, is all, but Dare got shot." She slanted him a gimlet look. "The stubborn ass needs taking care of," she added with grim triumph, because Janetta's reputation for commando nursing was known all over the area. If you didn't want a poultice, splint, stitches, or any number of other remedies applied to you, then it was best not to let her know about any ailment.

Dare shot her a quick look that promised retribution, then Janetta was on him, and he was swept up on the tide of orders she issued. Angie smiled in satisfaction. She'd come in for her own share of Janetta-style attention, eventually, but a sprained ankle was boring compared to a gunshot wound.

Things happened fast after that. Ray made his calls, and soon his place was swarming with law enforcement and wildlife management types, as well as medics. The medics didn't have a lot to do, because by then Janetta had done a lot of cleaning and bandaging. Angie and Dare were both transported to Butte for medical attention. Her ankle was X-rayed, just to make sure she didn't have a simple fracture, but Dare not only had to be stitched up; he was put on an IV round of heavy antibiotics, which meant he had to stay overnight, which massively pissed him off.

There was a mountain of absolutely necessary reports that had to be filed, and an endless supply of questions that had to be answered. Angie and Dare were kept separated, questioned separately, but though it was annoying she wasn't alarmed, because when the authorities got up to the three kill sites they'd find exactly what they were told they'd find.

Word spread fast. The next day Dare was released from the hospital, without so much as even a low fever. A small group of friends gathered at Lattimore's and went with the authorities up into the mountains to search for their missing horses. The group returned that afternoon with her three, which had been found fairly quickly—they'd pulled their reins free but remained together, which wasn't all that surprising.

Angie almost burst into tears when she saw them; she had to get over this sudden inclination to let things make her teary-eyed, but the truth was it would take time for her emotions to settle down. Samson nudged her, hard enough to almost knock her off her feet, as if he was admonishing her for not taking better care of them, and she briefly laid her head against his muscled neck. They were in pretty good shape—hungry, some scratches, but no damage other than that. Some of the tension drained away from her, now that she had them back and they were okay.

Dare's buckskin wasn't found for three more days, miles to the north. When the animal was finally trailered back to Dare's barn, he called the horse every name in the book and then some, all the while gently patting its neck and calming down the nervous animal.

"My horses are evidently smarter than yours," Angie told him, just to take a jab, because she'd been taking it easy on him—after all, he'd been shot—and enough was enough.

"He's not much more than a baby," Dare had countered. "Give him a couple more years, and he'll be a damn good trail horse. I'm a patient man. I can wait."

That about said it all, though she'd have described it more as stubborn than patient. He simply didn't give up.

After about a week, they'd settled down to serious discussions. Somehow, by then, there hadn't seemed any doubt in either of their minds that they'd be getting married, so much so that he never actually asked. They simply started talking about property and making wedding plans, and that was it.

They got married late in the spring, after the heavy winter snow had finally melted and the flowers were blooming. Angie would've been happy with a judge and a few friends, but Dare had insisted, in his words, "If we're going to fucking do this, we're doing it fucking right." She hadn't argued with him.

So here they were, in church on a bright Saturday afternoon. There were flowers and candles, well-dressed friends and neighbors who had gathered for the day. Her old friends from Billings had even made the two-hundred-plus-mile drive to be there, and she wasn't even embarrassed that they'd witnessed her first fiasco of a wedding. That was then, and this was, well, this was Dare. They had even celebrated with her—by e-mail, and completely without sarcasm—when she announced that she'd fallen in love with the man she'd previously referred to only as The Asshole. Only true friends would do that.

Dare hadn't bought her property; she felt guilty about Harlan not getting the sales commission, but he didn't seem to mind. Her property remained in her name, because taking out a new mortgage on it would just add more to their debt load, which didn't make sense. With their guide businesses combined, financially they were in good shape; they could have afforded a bigger wedding, but that wasn't anything either of them wanted.

She wore a white gown. It was nothing fancy, just a simple sheath dress. Her shoes were awesome. Normally she didn't get all excited about shoes, but this was her wedding day and she wanted to be able to show her kids—there was a shocker, Dare wanted kids, and when she thought about it she wanted them, too, with a ferocity that surprised even herself—her sparkly and beautiful shoes, especially if one of those kids was a daughter. She wore her hair down, sleek and heavy, the way Dare liked it, and carried a bouquet of spring flowers. Harlan was going to give her away.

Dare had gotten more and more testy as their wedding date got closer, because the one thing she hadn't done was move in with him, no matter how he argued and growled. Their little community was too small, the values too traditional. They seldom spent a night apart, either at his place or hers, but she insisted on keeping a separate household until they got married.

And that day was here, finally.

Angie held on to Harlan's arm, her heartbeat hammering as her gaze roamed up and down the aisle of the small church. People had already turned to look at her, but the music hadn't yet begun for her to begin the long walk. At the altar, the preacher

waited along with Dare. There was no best man, no bridal atten-
dants, just Dare and her. There were familiar faces turned toward
her, but all she could see was her soon-to-be husband—in a suit.
Damn, he looked good, tall and hard and tough. *He* was the reason her heart was hammering, and those damn butterflies were
swarming in her stomach.

Angie looked up at Harlan, broke into a grin, and abruptly
forgot about bridal dignity; exuberantly she threw her arms
around his neck and squeezed. "Thank you," she whispered.

"Again?" Harlan huffed, obviously a little embarrassed even
though he gave her an encompassing hug in return, rocking her
back and forth. "You've thanked me probably once a week for the
past six months."

"Then you should be used to it by now." Just because, she
kissed him on the cheek, too. If he hadn't sent Dare into the
mountains to keep an eye on her, she might not be alive today.
And just as important . . . she wouldn't have found what she'd
found with Dare: both love and a partner in all ways. And he'd
been right under her stubborn nose the entire time; if it hadn't
been for Harlan, who knows what might have happened? Anything was possible, but she doubted she'd be as happy as she was
at this moment.

"I thought you might be mad at me for, you know, worrying
that you couldn't handle things on your own," Harlan confessed,
as if he hadn't already told her the same thing every time she
thanked him.

"Some things aren't supposed to be handled alone." She resumed her dignified stance, with her head held high and her
smile in place, her gaze locked on Dare. "You saved my life as
surely as he did, and I won't forget that. Not ever."

Harlan pressed his lips together, lifted his chin. "Don't you
make me cry, young lady. This is an important duty, filling in for
your father, and I won't do it blubbering like an old man."

The music changed, swelled. Wedding guests rose to their feet and turned to watch her. There were wide smiles all along the aisle. The time had come, and Angie took her first step toward Dare.

It was all she could do not to run down the aisle into his arms.

Afterward, the reception was held in the church's fellowship hall. It wasn't big, but then neither was the community. The fellowship hall was roomy enough to accommodate damn near everyone in town, as well as the handful of out-of-town guests. Nothing and no one could turn it into a fancy place, but Dare didn't care about fancy and neither did Angie. With flowers and candles and a big-ass cake, the fellowship hall sufficed.

Dare grinned like a jackass every time he looked at the ring on his finger, or the matching one on her hand. They were married. Six months ago he couldn't get her to even go on a date with him, or look at him without pure fire shooting out of her dark eyes, and now here they were: married.

From now on she was going to do *all* the paperwork. And that wasn't anywhere near the best benefit he was getting out of this deal.

There was music, food, and dancing. Dare wasn't much of a dancer, but he could pull off a slow dance with his new wife. He'd made arrangements with a neighbor to look after their horses while he took her on a Caribbean cruise, where he planned to do nothing except eat and have the occasional adult beverage, lie around, and have sex. He still had some fantasies that hadn't been fulfilled. Wasn't that what honeymoons were for?

When the time came to cut the cake, he wondered if Angie was having flashbacks. She damn well better not be. On their wedding day she shouldn't be thinking about any other man but him.

And she didn't seem to be; her face was glowing, her eyes sparkling, as they stood at the table where the big-ass cake—four tiers tall, with cream and white roses all along the sides and a traditional bride and groom on top—sat. Dare looked down at her and she looked up at him, her face both relaxed and radiant. There were no shadows at all in her expression, no hesitation or doubt or even what looked like a distant memory showing. That other wedding didn't exist for her, not now.

All the guests had gathered around to watch, and he wondered for a split second if any of them had been at Angie's other wedding and had witnessed her embarrassment. Yeah, sure, her friends from Billings had, but they didn't seem to be thinking about that, either.

This was the only wedding that mattered.

She hadn't asked him not to shove cake in her face, but she hadn't had to. He knew what she wanted. More important, he knew what she didn't want. Even though she hadn't wasted her time hiring someone else to fix her hair and do her makeup— thank goodness because she looked damn good just as she was— he knew better.

He wasn't a complete idiot.

They cut the cake together, his hand over hers. Then he dipped his finger into the fancy icing and lifted it to her lips, offering it to her. She smiled, her expression luminous, as she took the tip of his finger into her mouth and quickly licked the icing off, with her tongue dancing around his fingertip and her lips applying gentle suction.

His eyes almost rolled back in his head. Fuck. Shit. Yeah, she could still do that to him, blow the top of his head off with pleasure. His entire body twitched with anticipation; he enjoyed the anticipation, but he'd rather save the twitching for when they were alone.

Then she broke off a very small piece of the slice of cake they'd carved together, and popped it into his mouth. It was all very neat, very dignified. Dare made a rough sound in his throat. Angie Callahan could feed him any time.

Angie Callahan. Damn, that sounded good.

He leaned down and whispered in her ear. "You look good enough to eat. Later."

"Back at you," she said smiling, and damn if he didn't start twitching again.

About the Author

LINDA HOWARD is the award-winning author of many *New York Times* bestsellers, including *Veil of Night, Ice, Burn, Death Angel, Up Close and Dangerous,* and *Drop Dead Gorgeous.* She also writes a paranormal romance series with Linda Jones. They have recently published *Blood Born.* She lives in Alabama with her husband and a golden retriever.

About the Type

This book was set in Baskerville, a typeface that was designed by John Baskerville, an amateur printer and typefounder, and cut for him by John Handy in 1750. The type became popular again when The Lanston Monotype Corporation of London revived the classic Roman face in 1923. The Mergenthaler Linotype Company in England and the United States cut a version of Baskerville in 1931, making it one of the most widely used typefaces today.